IT'S ABOUT TIME

IT'S ABOUT TIME

GREG ANTON

RARE BIRD
LOS ANGELES, CALIF.

RARE BIRD

THIS IS A GENUINE RARE BIRD BOOK

Rare Bird Books
6044 North Figueroa Street
Los Angeles, California 90042
rarebirdbooks.com

FIRST HARDCOVER EDITION

For more information, address:
Rare Bird Books Subsidiary Rights Department
6044 North Figueroa Street
Los Angeles, California 90042

Cover artwork by Stanley Mouse

Set in Adobe Garamond
Printed in the United States

10 9 8 7 6 5 4 3 2 1

Library of Congress Cataloging-in-Publication Data available upon request

That sound that sounds like
Polar bears crossing Arctic ice pans
A herd of musk ox in full flight
Male walruses diving to the bottom of the sea
Fumaroles smoking on the slopes of Mt. Katmai
Wild turkey walking through the deep, soft forest
Beavers chewing trees in an Appalachian marsh
An oyster fungus growing on an aspen trunk
A mule deer wandering a montane of the Sierra Nevada
Prairie dogs kissing
Witchgrass tumbling
A river meandering
Manatees munching seaweed at Cape Sable
Coatimundis moving in packs across the face of Arkansas
The cutting edge of life

—Donald Barthelme describing the sound of a trombone solo.

"There music business is a cruel and shallow money trench, a long plastic hallway where thieves and pimps run free and good men die like dogs. There's also a negative side."

—Hunter S. Thompson

CHAPTER 1

Ray Bell looked out from the stage at a colorful sea of swirling six-foot foam wands. A living, breathing, amoeba-like organism, the audience moving like lava, a slow-motion tsunami of slag descending from the bleachers, inundating the reserved seats, swallowing the stage.

Ray spun around and faced his band: a humped-backed bass player under a dangerously-leaning tower of black speaker cabinets; two guitar players in grotesque horse-head masks with brown, stained buckteeth; and a drummer in a full-body horse costume pounding his tom-toms with flailing hooves. When Ray turned back to the audience, a sound wave of white noise came crashing over him. He pressed the side of his face against his shoulder, thrust his arm straight up, and punched through the foamy surface, pumping his fist, whipping the crowd into a frenzy. With the energy approaching critical mass, he reached for the microphone on its stand and wrapped his hand around a red-hot branding iron, searing his palm, filling the stage with smoke and the stench of burning flesh. Recoiling in pain, he flung down the mic, ran off stage-right, and was inundated by a seething mass of fans violating his space, screaming in his ears, pulling out clumps of his hair. In the roiling collage of faces, one face stood out: his nemesis, Woody, strumming an acoustic guitar and watching the onslaught of fans with a sardonic smile.

Trying not to fall and be trampled, deflecting incursions with his forearms, Ray pushed forward until he felt the smooth aluminum bar of the backstage door. He burst into the chilled night air, inhaling gulps of thick fog, and dove headfirst into his waiting black Mercedes, the engine running and revved. The car propelled itself across the city, gliding like a hovercraft above the pavement. He pressed the throttle into the floor, through the floor, doing a 120 MPH onto the Golden Gate Bridge, the thin red speedometer needle spinning in circles like a compass gone crazy. He slammed on the brakes in the center of the bridge, skidded sideways to a stop, left the car door wide open, ran across four lanes of traffic, and stood at the railing, panting, gazing out at the white-line horizon of the moonlit ocean.

The horde of fans following from the concert began pummeling him, tearing off his shirt, stabbing him with autograph pens. And there was Woody with his hot blue eyes, leading the charge, waving his arm like a windmill across his guitar strings, long curly hair co-mingling with the steel-wound suspension cables of the bridge.

The muscles of Ray's legs bulged like thick ropes, straining under the weight of the frenzied fans hanging on his neck. Trying to maintain his grip on the wet railing, he leaned over and peered into the dark velvety water. He reached down, straining every fiber in his body, extending his hand farther than he thought possible, until he felt the ice-cold water with his fingertips. He looked out to the horizon, summoned the power of the Pacific Ocean and propelled himself over the railing in a perfect swan dive, arched back, pointed toes, wrinkled white bottoms of his bare feet reflecting the silvery moonlight. Chin tucked into his chest, hurtling down at superman speed, the blast of air forced his eyelids open until he had no eyelids, nostrils flared like two black quarters, cheeks distended into a hideous clown expression. His knuckles smashed against the rock-hard surface of the water, cracking it open into a gaping maw, a bottomless smoking fissure exposing the black satin sheets of his bed.

Ray bolted up, heart pounding, molars grinding. He wiped the sweat from his forehead. When he exhaled, it came out as a groan.

Maria stood with her back to him in front of his full-length mirror, putting on her makeup. "You were making these distressed-sounding noises. I was going to wake you up, but I thought I should let you sleep." She spoke with the thin affected speech of a woman applying her lipstick.

Ray put his hands flat on the sheets and looked out his bedroom picture window at the Golden Gate Bridge a half-mile away. He scanned the empty railing, then the surface of the water, half expecting to see a ripple.

"You okay, Ray?"

He sat up on the pile of pillows on his four-poster bed, pulled the blankets down to his waist, and reached for his cigarettes. "I was having this crazy dream. I've been having them every night." He examined his palm. "I was performing at a concert, and the microphone was so hot it burned my hand." He took a chrome Zippo lighter from the side table and lit a cigarette.

"Sounds symbolic," Maria said. "Maybe it's time to play a concert instead of dreaming about one."

"I've never been so glad to be awake. I could actually smell my hand burning." He turned his hand over and examined it. "I've never smelled something in a dream before." He leaned back, took a long drag, and blew a thin stream of smoke at the ceiling. "Woody's blue eyes," he said as if he was talking to himself.

"Woody's blue eyes?"

"In my dream." He took another slow drag. "I've heard people with blue eyes can tolerate more pain." His head deep in the divot of a down pillow, he brought his gaze down to Maria unrolling dark nylon stockings up her creamy white thighs. "I can't tell which I enjoy more, watching you get undressed or watching you get dressed."

"Now it's sounding like a *wet* dream." She bent over and reached for the black slip bunched up under her skirt. "A slip's purpose in life has always been questionable." She drew back her shoulders and smoothed down her skirt, flexing her knees in a way she seemed to enjoy. "I guess you could say that about a lot of things."

"Seems like you're always dressed up, even when you're not working."

"You only see me when I know you're going to see me." Dabbing the corner of her mouth with her little finger, she acknowledged his reflection in the mirror. "I've been researching the copyright law. We should file that suit, get our share of royalties for 'Stephanie.' The way Pearlman got us to sign that release was straight-up coercion. We'll get that thrown out, then any jury listening to the song would hear what you added. Your vocal melody made it a hit."

"Another fucking lawsuit? What about that rehearsal tape...that stuff I said about Woody being the one that wrote it?"

"You added your melody *after* that, when you recorded it." Their eyes met in the mirror. "We'll deal with the tape. There's ways to get around things, explain them away. Politicians do it all the time. Repeat anything three times; the third time it becomes reality. We'll just keep focusing on what you added to the song." She retrieved her fake leopard-skin makeup purse from the top of a cardboard box, exchanged the lipstick for a small round brush, and began highlighting her cheeks. "And there are a couple of other things we could focus on with a lawsuit."

"Like what?"

"Like Stephanie's breasts."

"What?"

"You remember them, don't you?"

"Me and every other guy in North Beach with ten bucks. So what?"

She dabbed her face. "If this case goes to trial, you think Woody wants people hearing about what went on at that strip club with you and his wife?"

"All that really happened was—"

"I'm not actually interested in what went on between you and her. But a federal courtroom would be packed with music-industry reporters hungry for the backstory." She ran her hands up the front of her thin blouse and cupped her breasts. "I can picture the headlines: *Jury finds Ray Bell inserted his melody into 'Stephanie.'* "

Ray smoked, staring at the ceiling.

She applied jerky upstrokes of mascara to her eyelashes. "Thinking about those breasts?"

"I'm thinking that'd be pretty harsh for Woody and his wife and kid."

"That's the whole point. If we play our cards right, there won't be a trial that nobody wants." She nodded at her open briefcase on top of a cardboard box. "I've already drafted a complaint."

Ray noticed a glint of light reflecting off the pearl handle of a pistol sticking out from under a legal pad. "Is that a gun? Since when do you carry a gun?"

"Since I was at the police academy before I decided to go to law school. My school was in a bad part of town for night classes. I got used to carrying it."

"You have it when we've been together? Next to the bed when we're having sex?"

"I carry it when I feel like carrying it, it's not your concern." She slammed shut the briefcase. "We should just file that lawsuit. I know your finances are tenuous right now."

"Tenuous?" Ray gestured around the room. "I'm living out of fucking cardboard boxes. I get a new loan, I start unpacking boxes, then I get another notice from the bank. They're about to repossess this house."

"Getting any percentage of our song royalties would help."

"*Our* royalties?"

She jerked her head around to look at him. "That's right, *our* royalties. We have a contract, in case you don't remember."

He knew not to press it. "I'd just rather sing songs than have a lawyer do my talking." He reached across the bed toward her. "How come you never stay overnight?"

She wrapped her thick black hair into a bun and stabbed in a red hairpin that matched her lipstick. "I feel that maintaining a professional distance is important for both of us."

"Professional distance? That's rich." He looked her up and down. "There wasn't much professional distance between us a half hour ago."

She turned her back to him. "A mirror is such a simple device, it's amazing how much information it produces. I'll bet there was a major change in human behavior when mirrors were invented."

'She's probably never looked in a mirror she didn't fall in love with,' he thought and took another drag. "What about releasing that live version of 'Stephanie' from the Greek Theater, like we talked about?"

She turned and faced him. "That's the master plan. Secure our share of writer's royalties, release the live version, combine it with a world tour."

"It'd be nice to get my reputation back." He held his hand in the shape of a pistol, his index finger against his temple, and pulled the trigger. "People can't even listen to that song without wondering who wrote it." He rolled over to the ashtray exposing his broad back covered with dark curly hair twisted into patterns of Rorschach ringlets from tossing during his dream. "I'll cook you breakfast if you ever decide to stick around."

"You know how busy I've been, trying to get my law practice going." She neatly arranged her things into her makeup bag. "It feels like the only time I have to myself anymore is when we're having sex."

Ray scrunched up his face as if from a foul smell. "You're saying…what?"

Maria continued on in her officious lawyer-like tone. "The type of settlement we'd get is usually sealed by the court. It won't do much for your reputation, but it'll help your bank account. Revenue from that song is worth hundreds of thousands. What percentage did your melody add to make it a hit? Do the math." She sealed her cosmetic bag with a loud zip. "I need to get going."

Ray extended his open hand. "Kiss goodbye?"

She gave him a tight smile. "You saw all the work I just did on my lipstick. We'll talk tomorrow."

When she picked up her briefcase, an artist's pad that had been propped against a cardboard box fell onto the floor. The top page was a black and white charcoal drawing of a singer holding a microphone at the front of a stage, the building collapsing down around him. The stage was strewn with piles of debris, frayed electrical wires, and billowing clouds of dust. Splintered wooden beams marked with violent black slashes were about to crush the singer.

"You drew that?"

His eyes locked on the drawing as if he was seeing it for the first time.

"All that confusion of wires and boards," she said, "it's like you drew it with your left hand."

Ray stared at it wide-eyed.

"Ray? You okay?"

"Those dreams…they're always the same. I'm afraid to sleep. They're fucking destroying me."

CHAPTER 2

Sitting on his living room couch, an acoustic guitar in his lap, Woody strummed an elegant, classical-sounding musical progression and concluded with a jarring diminished chord. "Whaddya think of that last chord? Too harsh?"

Lily sat at the other end of the couch, staring into the middle distance, gnawing on an apple.

"The dissonance is intentional," Woody said, "but maybe I played it a little loud. *Fortissimo*?" He played the progression again, softening the last chord. "Better?"

Lily stared straight ahead without expression.

"In a perfect world, time actually stands still going into a chorus. It's like you can stare at a clock all day and never see the hour hand move. I know what you're thinking: so get to the chorus. I'm aware of the moral obligation—it's like returning a library book. But first I create a bit of instability, then the release, and *then* the chorus, home to comfort and security, like life…know what I'm saying?"

She ignored him.

He played a couple of chords from a song he knew she liked and sang the two Robert Hunter lines. *"Certain as solace after the pain. Certain as sunshine after the rain."* He dropped his hand on the couch toward her and raised his eyebrows. "Emancipation of the dissonance?"

She acted as if he hadn't spoken.

Woody played his new song again, taking what he thought might be the troublesome note out of the last chord. "Some notes are lonely. I can relate. I'm actually feeling kinda lonely down here at this end of the couch."

She inspected her apple for a new place to bite.

"You're awfully hard to please today." He tried a variety of voicings, reassembled the chord progression, and ended with a suspended chord. "That makes the last chord more palatable, but it still has a little hair on it. The ending's better now, no?"

Lily brought the half-eaten apple down to her lap and began rolling it around with the tips of her fingers like she was about to let it fall on the floor.

"You don't have to act like that. It's not like the chords are unrelated. They're distant cousins. I just don't want it sounding too syrupy." He replayed the suspended chord. "Maybe it's me. Maybe I just thrive on suspense." He went back to strumming. "You know how certain places in the house always collect dust? Songs have places in them like that."

No acknowledgement.

"Songs ideas are like seeds—you plant them and let 'em grow. They grow on their own volition and actually spin in the ground to get their roots facing the right direction. And they do it without hands or feet." He made a fist with two fingers pointing up and flipped his hand over. "What's this all about anyway? Symmetry, right? The planet is half men and half women. It's why you have to straighten a crooked picture. Symmetry, it's built-in everywhere with everything. I mean, c'mon, Mozart composing at age five? Where did that come from, out of thin air?"

Still no response.

He strummed a chord, deadened his strings, and decided to wait her out.

She looked down the length of the couch with a kind of demonic grin and hurled her apple at him—a decent throw that bounced off his shoulder.

With an exaggerated frown, Woody put his head down, dug his pick into his strings, and played his song loud and fast, jerking his shoulders up and down with the neck of his guitar. He ended with an expansive windmill motion of his right arm, a resounding major chord, and a big smile. "Happy now?"

Lily turned her back to him, let herself off the couch feet-first, and crawled toward the kitchen, her cloth diaper about to fall off. Woody felt a twinge of joy watching her chubby little legs churning across the carpet to the kitchen to find her mother. "I'll never be happier than my most unhappy child," he thought, "and if that means a lifetime of major chords"...he played another one..."things could be worse."

—

After trying everything he could think of, Woody's chord progression just wasn't working. He propped his guitar against an armchair across the room, grabbed a notebook and headed back to the couch to try a new approach. Looking at the neck of his guitar, he visualized the fingering of the chords and heard the tonal clusters in his mind. Subtleties created by adding or taking away a note seemed more pure without the distraction of actual sound. Playing the verses in his mind, he was determined to resist the pressure to get to the chorus. He'd heard it a thousand times from other songwriters: "You get thirty seconds before you lose the listener, something has to happen, get to the orgasm." He looked at a few phrases he'd written in his notebook. Trying to connect the words to melody felt like forcing a rough square peg into a smooth round hole. The words he'd hurriedly scribbled the night before in a flood of emotion had unfolded like some kind of poetic haiku or iambic pentameter. Now they sounded like drivel. He slapped his notebook closed and saw what he'd written on the cover: *Write for people smarter than you.*

Across the room, it felt as if his guitar was trying to tell him something. It often divulged notes he couldn't find on his own. Like so many musicians he knew, he had trouble verbalizing his feelings, but his instrument could speak volumes.

His eyes travelled down the mahogany neck to the distinctive "bear-claw" markings on the body of the thirty-five-year-old Martin. In guitar lore, it was made from a spruce tree a bear had sharpened its claws on. It glowed with a yellow patina from years of hayrides and hoedowns, but he'd chosen it for its pure sound. It'd become his most honest friend, and together they were navigating the urgency to come up with new songs. He flipped his guitar pick into the air in a long arching curve that ricocheted off the strings. He smiled. Artists made paintings by throwing paint at a canvas, why not make music throwing things at a guitar?

Woody slunk back deeper into the couch. He knew the only way his music could be marketable was if it was recorded, frozen in time. Before recording technology, there was live music at every campfire or front porch. Songs lasted all night with commensurate breaks to swig beer, take a leak, or rest a musician's hand. Sleep didn't enter the equation. Now, with the advent of records, songs were imprisoned, sentenced to a life of five minutes, sounding the same every time they got played. Songs had morphed into identical round McDonald's hamburgers.

Woody kicked off his sneakers, dug a joint out of an ashtray, lit up, and scanned the room. The new house's living room alone was twice the size of his last crummy apartment in San Francisco. If he could just get out of his head, he might be able to appreciate the redwood-beamed ceilings, picture windows overlooking the ocean, and Steinway grand piano. No more carrying a seventy-pound guitar amp up three flights of stairs and listening to neighbors fight through thin walls. No more going to the laundromat. He hated the fluorescent-lit sounds, smells, and culture of laundromats. Just the idea of being there made him sad. Now he had his own washing machine and enjoyed the rhythm of his clothes flapping in the breeze on the clothesline he, Stephanie, and Lily had tied to their backyard trees.

All this newfound luxury had come from one song, "Stephanie." The muscles in his stomach tightened at the thought of how close he'd come to losing the song, losing Stephanie, losing everything. He glanced down at his two-inch scar—a squiggly white worm across the back of his right hand—and tried making a fist. It still felt tight over a year after he'd been mugged on the street and the cleated heel of an engineer boot ground his hand into the pavement. Having his right hand out of commission had initiated his slide into hard drugs. He wrapped his left hand around his right wrist and flexed his fingers. He remembered one night, one of his lowest times in that bottomless funk. Ray Bell had stolen his song. He was broke, homeless, convinced he'd never be able to play guitar again. Worse, Stephanie had left him.

That night, under a streetlight on a dirty sidewalk in the Haight, he'd had a dinner of packets of mayonnaise and mustard spread on stale bread. Opening the little packets with his injured hand was almost impossible. He'd get one started with his teeth, a bead of mayo would spurt out, lubricate his fingers, and the packet became a slippery nemesis. After limited success at allaying his hunger, he gave up, wiped his greasy hands on his pants, and lay down on his bed of newspapers on the gritty sidewalk. After a cold, miserable hour of sleep, he'd rolled over and opened his eyes to an article six inches from his face in the Leisure Living section of the San Francisco Chronicle—*Dogs Allowed To Sleep Indoors Live Longer.*

Woody shook his head. *I'm sitting on this fat leather couch in this comfy living room, tripping out on some kind of existential songwriting angst. I got my song back from Ray, Stephanie's here, life's good. Is pain a criterion for songwriting? Music, a panacea for pain?* He retrieved the guitar, took another hit of pot, and went back to his song. It sounded different. The pot turned him into more of a spectator, observing his own creative process. The verse transformed itself into a pleasing pattern, expanding internally, never going to a chorus. *What is a chorus, anyway? Song science terminology? Like studying geography compared to watching a river flow?* He sang one of his favorite choruses, something he'd heard a busker play during those days living on the street. "You find a chorus when you figure out how it goes, find a clitoris when you bump it with your nose, but it takes a thesaurus for pros to write prose." He ended with an odd-sounding tri-tone and smiled. He'd heard that tri-tones were once outlawed by the church, so dissonant they were considered Satan's music. And at the other end of the spectrum, some regular combinations of notes played at unpredictable times actually sounded funny? He'd seen it happen a thousand times: a room full of musicians, somebody plays an unexpected chord, and everyone laughs—the audio essence of humor.

Woody decided to give his hands a break and was warming down with slow scales when an aromatic bouquet wafted in from the kitchen. He cocked his head, trying to discern if his wife was cooking something or changing the baby's diaper. Just then Stephanie appeared in the doorway holding their twelve-month-old daughter. Shirtless, in a white cloth diaper, Lily wriggled out of Stephanie's arms and crawled a beeline across the carpet toward Woody. Using the bottom guitar strings as a handhold, she pulled herself onto his lap.

Accommodating both Lily and the guitar was impossible. He put the guitar down, lifted her over his head, and she shrieked with glee, flapping her wings.

"Dinner's almost ready." Stephanie leaned against the doorway smiling, arms folded under a veil of curly red hair. "Ready for your recording session tomorrow?" Her hair was the same shoulder length as Woody's—hers a striking copper-tone red, his strawberry blonde, Lily's full head of Shirley Temple curls a blend of the two. The three of them had pale white skin and freckles, a color-coordinated family.

Woody rubbed the top of Lily's head. "This whole ambition thing is wearing me down."

"Jeff got you the record deal you wanted, now the record company's getting antsy. Careful what you ask for."

"I just want to play music, not be some validation junky with glitzy songs." He gave a little wave. "Hey everybody, look how clever I am." He shrugged. "The attention this all brings is actually the downside."

"Be patient, relax, just let the music appear. The words and music always rise the way the sun always rises. Just write music you like to listen to, write whatever kind of music you want, but we can't live forever on royalties from one song."

He looked down at Lily. "You don't blame a child for not being an adult. My songs mature at their own natural pace. It just feels funky laying this trip on them, putting pressure on them to make money."

"The pressure's on *us*." She gestured around the room. "This could all become an illusion. We don't want to raise Lily in a place like your old moldy apartment with junkies sleeping on the sidewalk. Or have her walking to school in *my* old neighborhood, where I almost got raped." When she saw the deep lines appear on his forehead, she softened her tone. "Your music is beautiful; just relax and let it happen."

He hit the side of his head with the heel of his hand. "My songs are banging around in there, trying to escape. They're digging tunnels under the walls, peeking out from manhole covers."

Imitating him, Lily slapped her head with her hand. Stephanie slapped her own forehead, and the three of them shared a communal laugh. "I found a box of your poems when we moved," she said, "maybe there's some ideas you could use. There's one delightful poem called 'A Good Song Makes You Feel Less Alone.'"

As if sensing the inception of a boring conversation, Lily dropped herself off Woody's lap and crawled back toward the kitchen.

Woody picked up his guitar and strummed a chord. "Feelings," he sang, "can't have a thought without feeling a feeling. The moon's made of cheese, the earth's made of...one...big...feeling."

She smiled. "See, you just wrote a song." She wrapped a strand of curls around her finger. "I love how you pull poetic phrases out of thin air."

"I have plenty of ideas, they're just not talking to each other. Songwriting is one percent inspiration, ninety percent perspiration."

"Maybe just get out of the way, let your songs live a life of their own."

Woody nodded at his guitar. "I feel responsible for them, like raising kids. Like, say a song has a boring section that goes nowhere for a minute. Then the song goes on a record and a thousand people listen to it. That's a thousand wasted minutes. If it's a hit, that's a million wasted minutes of human evolution." He shrugged. "Writing a song's like trying to get a fish to evolve into a mammal with legs and lungs in five minutes. Things happen when they happen."

She raised her arm and looked at her freckled bare wrist. "Any idea when that might be?"

"Look," he pointed at his own bare wrist, "it's still now."

She walked over and ran her finger across his strings. He gently took her hand, picked up his ballpoint pen, and drew little circles around a pattern of freckles on her wrist, connecting them with crooked arrows like a Salvador Dali melting clock.

She checked her new watch. "I'm late for an appointment with Lily in the kitchen."

—

Woody re-strummed the open chord Stephanie had sounded, transitioned back to his song, once again felt a pressing need to get somewhere…maybe a chorus or a bridge? Then he realized that this time it was his bladder talking. He walked to the bathroom playing his guitar, singing an exercise of progressive accents he'd heard his drummer sing:

> ***How*** can I be so dumb?
> How ***can*** I be so dumb?
> How can ***I*** be so dumb?
> How can I ***be*** so dumb?
> How can I be ***so*** dumb?
> How can I be so ***dumb***?

As he played, he thought about what Stephanie had said about patience and his songwriting. She wasn't a musician, but she had a kind of objective wisdom that he knew exceeded his own understanding of the creative process. He felt a hot tingle up the nape of his neck, grateful for having her in his life.

CHAPTER 3

The curly hair sticking out of Woody's baseball cap was dripping wet from the Marin County fog as he drove with the top down on his 1964 Corvette Stingray. Negotiating the tight turns on the road from his home on Mount Tamalpais, he peered through the thick haze, switched on his wipers, and wondered if two cups of coffee was enough to clear his foggy brain for a potentially stressful recording session. On the next fifteen mph curve, his wide Corvette tires crushed the menthol-packed eucalyptus tree nuts littering the road and a flood of minty fumes shot into his sinuses, sending a signal to his brain. Minutes later, his car, as if of its own volition, took a left turn into the town of Mill Valley instead of onto the freeway toward the studio.

Navigating narrow neighborhood streets, Woody parked a half-block from his destination and walked down a dirt path between two houses through a familiar floppy wooden gate to a bungalow in the back.

Whitey answered the door in his year-round flip-flops, shorts, Ray-Bans, and Hawaiian shirt. "Woody!" His wide grin exposed a sterling-silver incisor with a tiny diamond in its center. "Come right in, step right up. How's that polished wooden veneer of yours holding up with that band of crepuscular musicians slip-slidin' around on it?"

Woody stepped into the small room. "I can't tell if my band is supposed to be a democracy, a dictatorship, or some kinda free-for-all. Sometimes it smells like a democracy, but you know what they say: a camel is a horse designed by a committee." He stuck his arms straight out to his sides and took two small steps into the room like he was walking a tightrope. "I'm just tryin' to maintain my balance while everything's going on around me. What's happenin' with you Whitey? I need a bindle, just a half-g for a little afternoon boost. I'm running late." Woody dropped his arms, gazing around the crowded room at the paraphernalia overflowing from every surface.

"Your timing's impeccable, brother. My main man just dropped off some of the finest Peruvian flake I've had the pleasure of imbibing. Care to sample a taste?"

"Maybe a taste for the ride. I really gotta split."

Whitey's eyes sparkled with anticipation. He gestured to the chair on the other side of a low square table, twirled the ends of his pale-yellow Yosemite Sam moustache, and produced a blue-glass dinner plate with a pile of sparkling-white crystalline powder deep enough to bury a ping-pong ball. A delicately designed black widow spider was tattooed on the translucent skin on the back of his right hand, each slender finger a spikey-haired spider leg. He impaled the pile of fluffy powder with the extra-long fingernail of his little finger and efficiently dispatched a scoop into each nostril. Then he took a single-edge razor blade, chopped up two thick lines to the side of the mound, and handed the plate to Woody with a stub of a red plastic straw.

Woody leaned in, snorted up the lines, dabbed the residue, and rubbed it on his gums. "Nice." Woody sniffled and wiped his nose. "Better make it a g."

Whitey performed his precision work with a silver spoon and triple-beam scale while Woody took a hundred-dollar bill out of his wallet and looked for a place to set it on the crowded table. "How's things been going, Whitey?"

"Don't get so personal."

Woody looked to see if he was joking. Whitey was sucking on his teeth and focused on his triple-beam scale, incrementally nudging a lead weight across the worn horizontal bar. "If you have to know...from outward appearances, it might look like I'm doing fine, but deep down in my right shoe, my sock is slipping off."

The knee-high table between them looked like a cross between a jeweler's workbench, a voodoo altar, and a garage sale. It was three-deep in crystals, pistols, and pipes, with a few gold wedding rings and Rolex watches that Woody pictured being slipped off a customer's wrist to prod an extra spoonful out of Whitey.

Whitey adjusted weights on the scale to accommodate Woody's new request, neatly arranged tiny spoons of varying sizes on a small hand towel, and folded and re-folded an origami-quality white paper bindle. "Anything I can do to help?" Woody asked.

Without breaking stride, Whitey nodded at a rusty, dented metal sign from a Harley shop that was nailed to his wall:

MECHANICS LABOR:
$25/hr.
$30/hr. if you watch.
$40/hr. if you help.

A miniature muffled voice came from the direction of a small Hawaiian doll on the table in a hula skirt holding a ukulele. Woody pointed at her. "She trying to tell us something?"

Whitey reached across the table and lifted a silk pillow off a transistor radio next to the doll that was tuned to a chattering AM talk show, the sound fifty-percent static. "Keeping current with the news. Jimmy Carter pardoned the draft-dodgers on his second day in office. Forgiving stuff that happened in the past feels good." He put the pillow back on the radio. "The key to happiness is having a poor memory."

With a Svengali sleight-of-hand, Whitey exchanged the paper bindle of coke for Woody's hundred-dollar bill. "A thing of God exchanged for a thing of man." He efficiently folded the bill in half, in half again, and tucked it into his shirt pocket. "Poke some snot?"

"What?"

"Smoke some pot?" Whitey gave his signature wink, holding a dropped eyelid for an extra half-second and, seemingly out of nowhere, produced a palm-full of nugget-size marijuana buds and held them under Woody's nose. "Care for some choice hooch? Purple-passion mind expansion?"

"Smells great, but not today. I've got a session with scatter-brain musicians that require mind contraction, not expansion. And I don't think this session's gonna be purple."

"A taste for the road?" With another slight-of-hand, Whitey produced a thick, perfectly rolled joint. Woody wondered if he'd had it up his sleeve. "You know how to decide which end of a joint to light?"

Woody raised his eyebrows.

"Determine which end would work best in your mouth, then light the other end." He lit up, took a hit, and handed it to Woody.

The joint had an unusually efficient draw. Woody got a much bigger hit than he'd expected, exhaled a dense cloud of white smoke, and went into a deep hacking cough. "Thanks, Whitey." He stood up, coughing into his fist. "I really gotta split."

"Keep an even keel, brother—that purp can be trippy." Whitey winked. "If I don't see you in the future, I'll see you in the pasture."

—

The Record Plant recording studio in Sausalito was tucked away at the end of a private road past a community of houseboats on a shallow inlet of the San Francisco Bay. The stationary boats were every shape, size, and color, adorned with peace signs, pirate flags, and flowerpots, some half-submerged in mud at cockeyed angles.

Parking his Corvette in front of the studio with the top down, Woody gave the security guard a thumbs-up. Inside, he made his way through the fun-house maze of hallways lined with framed photos of rock stars and rock stars' guitars. His hand on the heavy insulated door to Studio A, he impulsively turned back down the hallway, ducked into the bathroom, locked the door, reached up behind the light fixture above the sink, and retrieved a small mirror and single-edged razor blade from last night's recording session.

Chopping up two lines from Whitey's bindle, he thought about what song to start with. Was there time for a jam to loosen up, or did he have to plunge right into the quagmire of everyone's opinions about musical arrangements? He glanced around for a clock. The entire studio complex was intentionally void of them, but he knew his time to get his record done was ticking like a dynamite clock. When he got his recording budget it was made abundantly clear that without timely, tangible results, it'd be his first and maybe his last contract. He was further behind schedule than he cared to think about, and it was all on him to come up with the goods. He rolled up a ten-dollar bill, snorted the lines, and felt the residue run down the back of his throat. If he lost his recording budget, he'd be back living in the city playing shitty clubs. He pictured Lily walking to school in Stephanie's old neighborhood, where she got attacked on her way to work at the strip club. What an environment for Lily in her little dress and backpack. He considered the bindle in his hand. One more line? No, it was time to get to work. He checked his nose in the mirror and headed to Studio A.

—

Woody's band had been working in the windowless studio for almost four weeks. Littered with beer bottles, bongs, pizza boxes, and half-bottles of Jack Daniels, it looked like scree from a group of teenagers on their first camping trip. Guitars and electric basses leaned everywhere, saxophones rested in stands with a mandala of snare drums flat on the floor around the drum set.

Woody acknowledged everyone with a quick nod, walked across the room, chose a red Fender Stratocaster, and began tuning up. Facing his amp, he started a chord progression, adjusted the settings, started again, and repeated the process a half-dozen times before dialing in a tone he liked.

One by one, the other guys wandered over to their instruments. The keyboard player sat at his L-shaped piano-organ station and flicked on the switches of his Hammond B-3. Two Bakelite trumpets spun in a Leslie speaker cabinet creating a Doppler effect that mimicked the sound of a train horn approaching and receding in the distance. The top of the organ, spotted with water rings from a thousand drinks, now had a Bible on it.

In a white T-shirt with the sleeves rolled up, arms covered with tattoos, Billy the drummer pried open a beer bottle with his cigarette lighter and gestured a toast to his girlfriend, Twig, sitting nearby. She glanced around, put her hand beside her on her chair, and covertly raised four fingers.

Billy looked at her quizzically.

She raised four fingers again, indicating how many beers he'd had.

His beer and a drumstick in the same hand, Billy hit his paper-thin crash cymbal, splashing beer on his tom-toms.

"I've been thinking," the keyboard player said from across the room, "maybe the way to be the most productive and at the same time the most righteous with God and each other would be to do whatever drugs or alcohol anybody wants to do *after* the recording session." He shrugged. "No judgment intended, just saying."

"The God I *don't* believe in is a different God than the one you believe in," Woody said, and started playing a soft, chunky rhythm.

Four beats later the bass player went into a funky groove, slapping the edge of his calloused thumb on the heavy-wound strings.

Jupiter, the tenor saxophone player, a big black man with huge meaty hands and silver rings on every finger, adjusted the cane reed on his mouthpiece, licked it twice like an ice cream cone, and blew a long ascending phrase, climbing progressively higher to a piercing squeal, instilling a sense of urgency in the room.

The drummer glanced at Twig and broke into a slamming kick-snare pattern that matched the bass line.

The keyboard player brought his hands down across three octaves of an authoritative ten-note chord, creating a foundation that allowed everyone to go harmonically wherever they wanted to go.

When Woody heard the piano chord, he launched into a circular, repeating arpeggio, lassoing in aberrant frayed ends of the sound, fitting together parts of the musical puzzle that moments before seemed to be from different puzzles. Everyone adjusted their parts, playing musical tag until they settled into a tight, percolating rhythm under Woody's melody, cleansing the room of negativity, creating smiles where there had been none.

Ten minutes later, the band humming like a finely tuned engine hitting on all cylinders, the door to the studio opened a few inches as if opening on its own. At first no one had a sight line over the amps to see it was Lily. She crawled across the polished wooden floor, through the thick sound, up onto Woody's knees, and reached for his guitar strings. Woody did his best to play without the bottom E and B strings she had a grip on, finally gave up and stopped playing. So did everyone else.

All eyes were on the open door, wondering why Lily was there on her own. Woody picked her up, went out to the lounge, and found Stephanie talking with Jeff Pearlman, his music attorney.

Woody handed Lily to Stephanie and kissed her on the cheek before turning to the lawyer. "Hi, Jeff."

"How're things going in there?" Jeff Pearlman was in his mid-forties in pleated khaki pants, a polo shirt, a boyish mop of light-brown hair, and creased dimples when he smiled. Confident, relaxed, he exuded a disarming charisma that his peers in the music industry knew he wouldn't hesitate to use with a judge or jury. "Anything close enough to record?"

"How close is close?"

Pearlman stood up. "The Warner Brothers guys are coming up from Burbank next week. We need some songs on tape. Let's hear what you've got."

Stephanie stood up holding Lily. "We just stopped by to say hi. We need to get home. She's tired, she needs to be changed...we've both had a long day." She kissed Woody. "Careful driving up the mountain, it's getting foggy."

—

When Woody and Pearlman walked into the studio, Malcolm the keyboard player was standing in front of the drum set with his Bible under his arm, talking to the drummer in a constrained monotone. Twig stood by the hi-hat, chewing on her knuckle, nodding in agreement with what Malcolm was saying. The drummer sat with a beer in his hand, shoulders hunched, staring down at his snare drum.

"Billy," Twig said, "try listening to what Malcolm's saying without getting all defensive."

Malcolm nodded. "Twig's right. You don't have to agree with everything I'm saying. Maybe just hear it. Praying may not always work, but it never hurts."

"Hear *what,* mate?" Billy said in his cockney British accent. "I'm a bloody musician. I'm always bloody listenin'. Exactly what is it you want me to 'ear?"

"Billy," Twig planted her hands on her hips, "maybe you'll hear *this.* I'm quitting drinking. You can do what you do, but it's affecting your playing and everybody knows it. I'm going to Malcolm's ministry this week. You can come with me if you want, but I'm going."

Billy's eyes widened. He took a long drink from his beer bottle and wiped his mouth on his sleeve. "What ya sayin' then?"

She glanced at Malcolm, then back at Billy. "I'm saying don't squat with your spurs on, dude. You're bringing this on yourself!"

"Bringing on *what*?"

Woody picked up his guitar while Pearlman leaned against the wall just inside the door, arms folded across his chest. "You guys feel like playing something?"

"Billy's sloshed again," Malcolm said. "Looks like we're gonna have a lava lamp for a metronome."

“What the hell ya talkin’ about!” Billy stood up so fast he hit a cymbal with his shoulder and knocked the stand onto the floor. “Why don’t ya’ go sit at your goddamn piano and get outta me’ space and worry about yer own bloody playin’!” He bent forward over his tom-toms, inches from Malcolm’s face. “And while yer at it, mate, why don’t you convert your *own* bloody girlfriend or boyfriend or whatever yer buggering!” He took a quick swig of beer and spat it on the floor next to Malcolm.

Malcolm wiped his Bible off on his sleeve, looked at Twig, and stalked out the door past Pearlman.

Twig glared at Billy. “You’re drunk!” She started toward the door.

“Where the hell ya’ goin’ then?” Billy stepped around his floor tom, almost knocking it over, and grabbed Twig’s arm. “You don’t have to bloody believe in God to get help from him. You talk to God, people think you’re praying; God talks to you, people think you’re schizophrenic. Where the hell you think yer goin’?”

Twig yanked her arm away. “I’m outta here, dude! The sushi bar is closed! Go suck on a drumstick!”

“Goddamnit!” Billy drained his beer, slammed it down on the table next to three empties and, tripping over the cymbal stand on the floor, headed after her past Pearlman who was up against the wall trying to stay out of traffic. No one acknowledged him but they were well aware of his presence; Jeff Pearlman had made the recording session possible.

The bass player carefully set his bass in its stand. “Seems like a good time for a break.” He took his cigarettes off the top of his amp and walked out.

Jupiter unhooked his saxophone from the strap around his neck and took a few long strides toward the door. Woody took notice, as he often did, of how far back Jupiter leaned when he walked, his long legs so far out in front of him that his upper body seemed to defy gravity.

Woody and Pearlman were now the only ones left in the room. Their eyes met, then Pearlman looked down at the front of Woody’s shirt and smiled. Woody looked down at himself, shook his head, and they both chuckled. There was a big wet spot where he’d been holding Lily. He took a cassette tape out of a guitar case and handed it to Pearlman. “Some song sketches we did last night. We just let the tape roll. Verses and choruses are lashed together with bungee cords, but you'll get the idea. Each piece of music has a beginning, middle, and end, but not necessarily in that order."

Pearlman took the tape and pointed it at Woody. "This record was supposed to be already done. If you're not careful, you could blow this whole deal and end up back—"

"I know!" Woody stopped and took a breath. "Sorry. Everything's been so…I get it. I really get it." He perused his selection of guitars and chose one to take home until he came back the next day. "I was up all last night working on a song. I'm totally beat. I'm going to hit the head and take off. Let me know what you think of that tape." He headed for the door.

"Woody?"

Woody raised his hand in a little wave back over his head and kept walking.

"Woody?"

He stopped, looked back, and raised his eyebrows.

Pearlman folded his arms. "There's something I've been meaning to talk to you about."

Woody set down the butt end of his hard-shell guitar case and rested his forearms on top.

"Are you using drugs?"

Woody dropped his weight onto the case. "It's not a simple yes or no question."

"Taking a hit of pot for a little creativity never hurt anybody. But I've seen some of the most talented musicians get taken out of the game behind coke."

Woody stared at the floor for a long moment then straightened himself up. He started talking softly and got progressively louder. "Everything I do—everything—is in service of my music. It's not a luxury, it's a necessity like food. My family and my music. For me, that's all there is." He grabbed the handle and swung his guitar case parallel to the ground. "I work full time for this cruel, mean, boss who's constantly criticizing me: it's my mind. I won't quit for anything until I finish this record and get it perfect…nothing!" As he turned and started walking away, he looked back at Pearlman. "They had to cut off slaves' hands to get them to stop playing their drums."

CHAPTER 4

Stephanie got out of bed at 8:00 the next morning and walked into the kitchen holding Lily. Woody was sitting at the counter, a cup of coffee in front of him, his acoustic guitar in his lap, just about to dip into a white paper bindle of coke with the tip of a butter knife. He gave her a sheepish smile, did a quick snort, folded the bindle into his shirt pocket, strummed a chord, and sang, "Good… morning…ladies."

"You're doing that at eight in the morning? Have you had any sleep?" Balancing Lily on her hip, Stephanie opened the refrigerator and took out a container of sliced fruit she'd cut for Lily's smoothie the night before. She looked strikingly beautiful even first thing in the morning. Her freckled fair skin framed with radiant red hair made her look like she had makeup on when she didn't.

"I was up late working on a song," Woody said. "I've got a lot going on today. I just needed a little bump to get my engine started."

Stephanie cleared space on the counter with her free hand and set Lily down. "I feel like the wife of that country singer that tied her husband's leg to hers so he couldn't sneak out and get drunk." She opened the container of fruit. "Snorting coke at eight o'clock in the morning? We've got a one-year-old baby and her father's a drug addict. I'm going to my Aikido class today. At least one of her parents has to take care of themselves. I'm getting out of shape. Yoga pants don't lie."

Woody strummed a chord and sang; "Looking good is where it's at…you think this song makes me look fat?"

She brought the plastic container down hard on the counter. "I'm serious! I'm going to class today." She took a breath to calm herself. "I honestly don't know if I can even trust you alone with her. Just wait here, sit in the living room, play your guitar, and don't take your eyes off her. She was up during the night, she'll probably fall asleep on the couch. I'll be back in an hour and a half, two at the most."

"I need to hit the music store today." Woody took a piece of sliced melon and handed it to Lily. "I need some strings and a new instrument cable. Mine's been cutting out. They've got these low-impedance cables that make a big difference in the sound. Lily always gets a kick out of the music store. I'll keep a close watch on her." He handed Lily another piece of fruit.

"Woody?"

He concentrated on helping Lily get a grip on the melon.

"Woody!"

He jerked his head up. "What? I'm right here. You don't have to yell."

Stephanie leaned back against the refrigerator and cinched her bathrobe. "You've been up all night. Just wait here with her until I get back. You've been acting so spaced out lately and…you need to take better care of yourself."

He reached into the container for another piece of fruit.

"Woody? Are you listening to me?"

"*Woody, are you listening to me?*" He gave Lily a strawberry and felt Stephanie's emerald green eyes drilling into him. "I've heard every word. I'm right here."

"You know exactly what I'm talking about, or maybe you don't. Maybe that's why I have to keep bringing it up. Coke is artificial energy, a trick with mirrors. You think you're thinking clearly, but it's fake luster, like Las Vegas or Disneyland. It actually leaches your energy."

"Doing a little dab in the morning is no different than having a cup of coffee, maybe even better for you. Caffeine's one of the most addictive things there are. People chewing coca leaves in the jungle are healthier than Americans chugging down coffee." He took a drink of coffee.

She rolled her eyes. "I've heard your rap before, thank you. You're using concentrated cocaine, not a natural leaf, to create energy you don't really have. You're out of actual fuel and burning the furniture."

"I just do a bump now and then when I need to get going so I can…"

"You do it all the time!" She glared at him. "There's always a reason. That kind of habit comes on slowly until you're too spaced out to realize how spaced out you are. Your judgment's been off-kilter," she pointed her finger at his chest, "even for you."

"I'm just trying to get a lot of things accomplished and sometimes there's a slight overlap and I just need a little boost to—"

“I’m not going to stand here and argue with you!” She cinched her bathrobe tighter. “Just stay here with Lily until I get back. There’s clean diapers on the line out back.”

“Okay, take it easy. I’m not a drug addict, I’m just busy.” He gave her a goofy grin. “I don’t actually like coke, I just like the smell of it.”

She slapped the stone counter separating them. “This is not a joke! The energy you *think* you have is running through frayed wires, ready to short-circuit. You’re not using coke, it’s using you. It hollows out your soul!”

“I told you I’m going to quit using when I finish the record. When I tell you I’m going to do something, don’t make me keep telling you.”

“Very funny!” She picked up the container of fruit, dumped it into the blender, slapped on the plastic top, and hit the high button much harder than necessary. With Woody’s ultra-sensitive ears from years of loud rock and roll, he hated the sound of the blender—and she knew it.

—

Woody sat playing the electric guitar he was planning to use at that night’s session, accompanied by Lily banging her bongo drums with both hands. The phone rang, but he ignored it. “This is crazy,” he thought, “home detention. I at least need some new guitar strings. These strings are like playing snot.” He changed up the guitar rhythm to a simple chunky beat he’d been trying with the band in the studio and, miraculously, Lily locked in with him on the bongos. Looking at her fat little hands brought a big smile to his face, and he realized how many endless hours he’d spent in recent weeks working with Billy on that beat. And during those late nights in the studio, Stephanie was always home with Lily, being the attentive mother she’d been since the day Lily was born. He immediately regretted giving Stephanie such a hard time about going to her Aikido class, one of the few breaks she allowed herself. Did he even deserve such a dedicated wife and mother while he acted like such a selfish jerk? He’d been up all night snorting coke, smoking pot, and drinking beer, and now he was complaining about giving Stephanie a break with two hours of babysitting? He could stay home with Lily, show Stephanie some respect, and figure out a way to rejuvenate his guitar strings.

Using a rag and a bottle of rubbing alcohol, he rubbed down each string. By the amount of gunk on the rag, he could tell he'd neglected that guitar. When he played it again it wasn't any better. Setting the guitar on a towel on the kitchen counter, Woody removed the strings, curled them into a saucepan of water, and set the pan on the stove. A last resort to reviving guitar strings: boil them in water. Sometimes it worked, sometimes it didn't. It was always a challenge, reinstalling the shortened strings after the ends had been snipped off.

The water started boiling over, the phone rang again, and Lily stood on his foot and reached up for the stove. He grabbed her, turned off the gas burner, took her into the bedroom laid her on her back on the bed, got down next to her, and stroked her bare stomach. "Don't move, I'm going to the backyard to get you a clean diaper."

The diapers on the clothesline were still damp. Woody looked in every drawer and cabinet for the disposable diapers Stephanie used when she was out of cloth diapers. Woody gave up his search and fashioned a diaper out of a hand towel. By the time he got it installed, with substantial difficulty, Lily had soaked it. "So what's up, sweetheart? There's a grocery store right next to the music store? Just sayin'. And everybody knows you can't play music with soggy strings *or* a soggy diaper. It's me and you girl, we're on a top-secret mission, and I know how much you love the music store. Just don't say anything to your mother and we'll be back before she even knows we were gone. We'll write her a song on our new strings. She loves music as much as anybody."

He took the bindle out of his shirt pocket, there were only crumbs left. He snorted up half of it, dressed Lily in her miniature San Francisco Giants jersey, grabbed a bottle of mother's milk Stephanie kept in the refrigerator, and in the off chance that Stephanie beat them home, he wrote her a nice note saying he'd made a quick trip out for diapers and that he'd be extra attentive to Lily. Lily giggled gleefully when he buckled her into the baby seat in the passenger seat of his convertible.

—

Having changed Lily in the car's driver's seat with a new diaper, Woody set her on the floor of the music store by a rack of shiny Zildjian cymbals, gave her a pair of drumsticks the same length as her arms, and walked to the nearby guitar section. She immediately began hitting every cymbal in sight and let out a piercing, high-pitched yelp. Woody eyed a nearby ukulele about the same size as Lily and was considering the physics of smaller bodies producing higher pitched sounds when a salesman walked up.

"Hi, Woody, it must come in handy having a drummer in the family. How's the music going?"

"It goes by itself. I just hold on."

"How about holding something really nice? It just came in." With a knowing smile, he unlocked a glass case and removed a mint-condition Gibson, semi-hollow-body electric guitar. Woody admired its finish, a dramatic sunburst of gold dissolving into fuzzy orange, then a border of tobacco brown rimmed in jet-black. Woody sat on a nearby stool and tuned up while Lily flailed her chubby arms, hitting every cymbal she could reach. He tried strumming along with the cacophony until she suddenly stopped and cocked her head toward the next aisle. He stopped and heard the music she heard. He knew Lily's hearing was much more sensitive than his.

Lily threw down her sticks and crawled off to the next aisle while Woody sat and listened to what had attracted her: classical guitar music being played with precision, obviously by a professional. Woody knew that type of accurate fretting and articulation on nylon strings took thousands of hours of practice. He assumed someone had chosen one of the store's high-quality instruments by the sound of the lush harmonics cascading from lightning-fast arpeggios and pictured a master, maybe a balding older man bent over a wide-neck nylon-stringed guitar. When he heard the high strings go abruptly off-key, Woody smiled, walked to the next aisle and, sure enough, there was Lily like a heat-seeking missile, going for the source of the music, grabbing at the strings. The guitar player was a young Chinese girl with black braided pigtails, about ten years old, smiling down at Lily.

—

Cruising with the top down on the warm breezy Marin County afternoon, Lily seemed thoroughly amused with herself, giggling and flapping her arms. Woody glanced at the dashboard clock and thought of the note he'd left for Stephanie in case she beat him home: a short poem expressing appreciation for her concern and reassurance that he'd take good care of Lily and be back soon. It also said that if she was hungry after her Aikido class, there was some pasta al dente on the stove. Walking out of the house, Woody had grabbed a jar of tomato sauce from the cupboard and set it on the stove next to the pan of curled metal guitar strings.

After so much fun at the music store, Woody knew Lily was hungry. For about the tenth time since leaving the house, he glanced at the dashboard clock. Stephanie wouldn't be home for almost an hour. He generously applied sunscreen to her arms and face, adjusted his baseball cap so it would stay on her head, and took her to Mel's Drive-in, where the waitresses were on roller skates. Lily was fascinated by their superhuman mobility. When a waitress in a red and white uniform came rolling over at top speed, spun a three-sixty at Lily's window, and handed her a complimentary mini-milkshake, Lily's eyes were wide and unblinking. She accepted the drink with both hands, tracking the waitresses' every move as she spun to Woody's window, took his order, and zoomed off.

Woody retrieved the baby bottle of milk from between the seats to exchange it for the shake, but he was too slow; Lily was already sucking on the straw, her face a portrait of delight. A minute later, when the straw slipped from her lips, Woody tried again to surreptitiously introduce the milk bottle. Lily batted it away, and during the fuss, the straw ended up repositioned on the opposite side of the cup. He resisted the urge to help her. As much as possible he left her to her own devices. Sure enough, a minute later she enjoyed the sweet taste of success, a stream of pink foam flowing through the straw. He remembered putting the tip of his little finger in Lily's mouth when she was born and being amazed at the strength of her sucking power.

After a French fry and a few sips of shake, Lily fell asleep with the straw in her mouth. Woody sat drinking her milkshake, thinking about recording the song he sang to put her to sleep. He looked at her sweet expression, rosy cheeks, pouty little mouth—would he be home from the studio tonight to play her his song? Probably not. He and Stephanie spoke often about avoiding the typical musician's pitfall of being on the road and working endless hours in the studio while they missed their kid's childhood. Trying to have his professional life conform to Lily's life, not vice-versa, there was still a lot to figure out.

When the teenage waitress scooped up their window-tray, Woody thought about how soon Lily would be that age. He sensed the healthy competition between the waitresses over who could deliver food orders with the most agility and wondered if their dads ever came and watched. He gave an extra tug on Lily's seat belt, nuzzled her neck for a hit of sweet baby-smell, started the motor, and drove off slowly, careful not to wake her. He thought of what Stephanie had said about him not being mindful with her. Actually, Lily was the only thing besides music he'd ever given undistracted attention to.

Cruising toward Mount Tam past the 7-Eleven, the last store before he got home, Woody checked the clock again and touched the near empty pack of cigarettes in his shirt pocket. He scored a shady parking spot right in front of the door. He glanced at Lily fast asleep under the baseball cap, then looked through the window at the cashier behind the candy rack ringing up two customers. He considered getting Lily a piece of chocolate for when she woke up, a rare treat. Stephanie gave her nothing but fresh organic fruit, vegetables, and mother's milk. Woody was grateful for Stephanie's commitment to health but enjoyed the conspiratorial camaraderie he and Lily shared, the explosive joy on her face when he occasionally gave her the smallest taste of chocolate. Not today, though. A French fry and milkshake were already over the top.

Woody got out of his car, gently closed the door, and went into the store, looking back at Lily as soon as he got inside.

"Woody!" A young woman and her boyfriend in matching orange and blue tie-dye T-shirts were at the cash register. "We totally love your music." The girl put her hand on her boyfriend's arm. "We heard your version of 'Stephanie' on the radio, then we went and saw you play it, and we were like, wow, he plays it even better than the record. Your guitar playing's like a rope of electricity. It *sounds* like what velvet *feels* like."

"I'm Ocean. This is my girlfriend Breeze." The young man stuck out his hand. "We really do appreciate your music."

Woody shook hands and looked to the cashier.

"Those were totally our real names before we met," Breeze giggled. "Watching you up there on stage playing, it's like...it makes me wish I could be like that."

Woody nodded. "Actually, I wish *I* could be that guy on the stage. Ninety-nine percent of my life isn't like that. It's phone calls and practicing and changing diapers. But thanks for checking out my music." He went up on his toes and looked out the window. "I just came in for a pack of smokes. I'm kind of in a hurry."

"We definitely don't mean to bug you," Breeze said. "Just saying thanks for the music."

"Totally," Ocean said. "We've got a lot of respect for musicians, we know how hard you work to do what you do."

"Thanks." Woody glanced over the candy rack, then at the Pakistani salesman and the Coke, chips, cookies, and Tampons on the counter. "Could I just get a pack of Winstons? I've got somebody waiting for me."

"Yes, of course," the salesman said in a thick Pakistani accent. "I will finish first ringing up this sale."

"You can totally let him buy his cigarettes first," Breeze pushed her items aside and knocked the box of cookies off the counter onto Woody's foot. She and Woody went to retrieve the box and bumped shoulders.

"Sorry," Breeze giggled. "Want a cookie?"

"No, thanks." Woody turned to the cashier. "Can I just get my smokes?"

"One moment please. I cannot stop the first purchase I have started."

Woody looked over the candy rack and out the window at his car. Up on his toes, he could just see the top of Lily's car seat but couldn't see her slumped down, asleep. And from his angle he couldn't see the other car that was now parked, idling, a foot from his passenger door.

"When I listen to 'Stephanie'," Breeze said, "I can feel the feelings you felt when you wrote it."

"Thanks. Glad you enjoyed it."

"I don't mean like, thanks for doing it for *me*. It's not like that." Breeze put her hands on Ocean's back and began massaging him. "It's like the things I like best about Ocean are the things he just does, not when he's trying to be nice. Stuff he doesn't even know he's doing." She pressed her thumbs into Ocean's lower back. "It's like, you put your feelings into a song, and I feel them. The music's a delivery truck for emotions."

"Music's a place where total strangers can be intimate," Ocean said.

"It feels that way *playing* the music." Woody put a five-dollar bill on the counter and pushed it toward the salesman.

"Do you like, do you visualize an actual woman named Stephanie when you play the song?" Breeze asked.

"Stephanie's my wife." Woody smiled. "Stephanie's my life." He looked over the candy rack, walked the few steps to the front door, went out to his car, and saw Lily's empty car seat.

—

Woody's heart pounded so hard he couldn't catch a full breath, he felt like he was suffocating. He braced himself against the passenger door and picked up the unfastened seatbelt. *She can't undo the seatbelt herself...someone undid it*! He scanned the parking lot, up and down the street, looked behind the seats, then dropped prone to his stomach and stuck his head under the low-slung car. Getting up, he hit his head hard on the undercarriage but didn't feel it with the rush of adrenaline coursing through his body. He ran behind the building—nothing but trash and broken glass—then back out front, across the street to a ditch littered with more trash, then into the middle of road, not realizing he was stopping traffic.

Twenty feet away on the double yellow line was an indiscernible lump of bloody flesh. The screaming synapsis from what he was seeing blew through his brain with gale force and constricted his throat. Gasping for air, he forced his leaden feet to keep moving up the road until, ten feet away, he saw the dead raccoon. He collapsed onto his hands and knees, gagging, staring down at the patch of pavement ten inches from his face. A blaring horn startled him. He got up, staggered to the shoulder, bent at the waist, and vomited in plain view of the traffic that started moving past him.

He wiped his mouth on his sleeve, ran the twenty feet back to the store, and shoved open the door. The couple was gone. Woody slapped his hands on the counter, eyes bulging. "Call the police!"

The word "police" got caught in his throat. The salesman didn't understand him.

He swallowed hard. "Call the police! Somebody kidnapped my daughter! They took her out of my car! Call the police!"

The man picked up the phone on the wall behind him and looked at it blankly. Woody ran behind the counter, grabbed the phone out of his hand, and dialed 911. "My daughter's been kidnapped! Stolen from my car at the 7-Eleven near Tam Junction! What?" Woody turned to the salesman. "What's the address?"

The man stood frozen in place.

"Hold on!" Woody ran out, looked at the address over the door, glanced at the empty car seat, and felt a paralyzing jolt of anxiety. He forced himself to keep moving, ran back behind the counter, and picked up the phone. "Nineteen Seventy-One! Nineteen Seventy-One-Shoreline Highway! What? Woody! Chester Woods! Send the police! Yes! No! I'll wait here. Hurry!"

He dropped the phone and ran out of the store—around the building again, up and down the street, fifty feet in every direction. He ended up standing at the passenger door of his car, panting, covered with sweat, looking at the empty car seat. Without thinking, he took the paper bindle of coke out of his shirt pocket—nothing left but scrapings. He held the open bindle up to his nose, inhaled, then crumpled it up and hurled it to the ground. Manically he paced back and forth in front of the car until an object behind the right front tire caught his eye. Dropping to the pavement, he reached under the car and pulled out his baseball cap Lily'd been wearing. He pressed the hat against his face, hands trembling, and inhaled the smell of Lily's hair before shrieking into the hat with every ounce of strength he had.

—

Ten minutes later a green and white Marin County Sheriff's car pulled into the parking lot and two sheriffs got out. Woody ran the ten feet to the car.

"There was a call about a missing child?"

"That was me. I was parked right here. My daughter was asleep in her car seat. I walked into the store, turned around, and she was gone. She's been gone for twenty minutes!"

One cop stood next to Woody while the other cop looked at the baby seat and shook his head.

The cop standing next to him took out a palm-size notebook. "How old is she?"

“Twelve months.”

“Name?”

“Woody…Chester Woods.”

“Her name?”

“Lily Woods.”

“Driver’s license?”

“She’s twelve months old!”

“*Your* driver’s license.”

Woody reached for his wallet in his back pocket, fumbled, almost dropped it, and handed the policeman his license, his hands shaking the entire time.

“You still live at this address?”

“Yeah.”

“The mother’s name?”

“Stephanie. Stephanie Woods.”

“Same address?”

“Yes.”

“Where were you coming from?”

“Mel’s Drive-in. We had a milkshake, she fell asleep in her seat, and I stopped here for a pack of cigarettes.” Woody opened his wallet again, produced a picture of Lily with an oversized acoustic guitar in her lap, and handed it to the cop.

He looked at the photo and back at Woody’s as if to verify the resemblance.

“She was wearing this hat.” Woody took the hat off his head and handed it to the cop, who now had his hands full.

The other officer opened the driver’s door of Woody’s car and reached into the open ashtray in the center console. He picked up a half-smoked joint and smelled it. “Is this marijuana?”

Woody felt the heat of blood rushing to his face. “Are you guys gonna radio in about a lost child or report it or what? This isn’t a drug deal. Somebody kidnapped my daughter!”

The cop next to Woody stepped closer, taking in the smell of vomit on the front of his shirt. “I know you’re worried, pal, I got kids of my own. Just calm down and help us so we can help you. Just tell us what happened.”

“I told you what happened! Nothing happened! Everything happened! I parked here, went into the store for one minute, she was asleep in her car seat with the seat belt buckled. I turned around and she was gone. She could be heading to Nevada or Mexico or…we need to do something! We need to start looking for her!"

"Where's the child's mother?"

"I don't know! Her martial arts class or home or somewhere. What're we gonna *do*?"

The officer reached into the open window of the patrol car and picked up the radio mouthpiece. "MC 273, abducted child, twelve-month-old girl…" he held up Lily's photo… "blonde curly hair, last seen"…he glanced at his watch…"approximately fourteen hundred hours at the 7-Eleven convenience store parking lot, Highway 1, Mill Valley, half-mile west of Tam Junction."

"What's she wearing?" the cop asked Woody.

"An orange Giants T-shirt, shorts, and sneakers."

The officer reported the information, looked at the photo once more, and shook his head. "Cute kid."

"Cute? She's my daughter! Let's start looking for her!"

"Request backup," the cop said quickly into the radio. He hung up and turned to Woody. "We know how upsetting this is for you. The report I called in will alert all law enforcement in the area. Every agency involved will take this very seriously, but we have procedures to follow."

"Procedures? Then let's proceed!"

The other cop walked over and held up the half joint. "This yours?"

The officers on each side of Woody were several inches taller and at least forty pounds heavier than him.

Woody looked at the joint. "What does that have to do with anything?" He held his hands out. "Don't you guys get it? My daughter's been *kidnapped*!"

"Take it easy, pal. We're just following protocol. It's illegal to possess marijuana. And it's illegal to drive under the influence—especially with a minor in the car." He put the joint in a small plastic baggie from his molded leather pouch on his belt, then went back to Woody's car and began removing items from the glove compartment.

"What's happening here?" Woody yelled at the sky, his arms spread. "There's two crimes in progress. Somebody took a puff of pot, somebody kidnapped a kid, and you're investigating the pot?"

The officer in the car examined the registration card he'd found. "Car registered to you?"

"Yes, the car's registered to me! You got it in your hand!"

The cop closed the glove compartment and looked behind the seats and on the floor, rummaging through old newspapers and the package with the guitar strings and instrument cable. He picked up the baby bottle of milk, exchanged a glance with Woody, and set it back between the seats.

Woody paced in a tight circle.

His hand on the passenger door handle of Woody's car, about to close it, the cop looked straight down and spotted the crumpled white bindle on the pavement. He picked it up, unfolded it, smelled it, and walked over to Woody. "This yours?"

"Is that *mine*? Are you *nuts*?" Woody pointed at the picture in the other cop's hand. "That little girl is mine!"

The cop put Lily's photograph and Woody's driver's license in his shirt pocket, buttoned the pocket, and squared himself toward Woody. "We'll make sure that every agency is notified and fully aware of the situation. We'd like you to come to the station with us."

"The station? For what? I'm not going anywhere except to look for my daughter!"

He put his hand around Woody's bicep. "You're coming with us."

Woody yanked his arm away. "Are you fucking kidding me? You guys are aiding and abetting the kidnappers. My daughter's gone! We've got to do something! We've got to start looking for her, set up roadblocks, do something!"

The other cop slipped the bindle into his leather pouch with the joint and unlatched the handcuffs from the back of his utility belt while the cop next to Woody stepped behind him, grabbed his arms, and pulled them behind his back. Woody struggled to get free, jerking violently from side to side, kicking at the policeman's shins. When Woody connected with a well-placed thrust into the side of the policeman's knee, he responded by wrenching Woody's skinny arm up to the top of his back, just short of the breaking point.

"Fuck!" Woody screamed in pain and collapsed, dead weight in the cop's arms.

The officers, one on each side, cuffed Woody's hands behind his back. Holding him under his armpits, they dragged him to the patrol car, the tops of his sneakers scraping on the pavement, and tossed him into the back seat and slammed the door.

There was a thick wire screen between the front and back seats and no door handles on the back doors. Woody lay on his back and began kicking a door with both feet.

While the sheriffs went into the store and spoke to the cashier, another patrol car with two Mill Valley policemen arrived. They heard the kicking, walked over to the sheriff's car, and looked down at Woody with their arms folded across their chest.

Woody's hair covered his face. With his hands cuffed behind his back, there was nothing he could do about it. He kicked the door as hard as he could.

"Wonder why they have him there," one cop said. "Thought this was about a missing child. He looks pretty out of it."

"From what I heard on the radio, the father called 911. Maybe he's the kid's father. Maybe there's a warrant out for him for something. Probably drugs."

"Probably can't see too good with all that hair covering his face. Like one of those little dogs. Probably too stoned to keep track of his own kid."

Handcuffs digging into his lower back, Woody shook his head, cleared enough hair to see the policemen looking down at him. "Hey!" he yelled to be heard through the closed window. "My twelve-month-old daughter, my baby girl's been kidnapped! Let me out so I can find her! Let me outta here!"

The cops looked at each other and back down at Woody.

"What the fuck are you looking at?" Woody screamed. "There's a missing child! Fucking do something!" He kicked the door so hard they simultaneously stepped back and turned toward the store. Just then, the sheriffs came out and the four cops huddled in the parking lot, periodically glancing at Woody who'd managed to sit up, head leaned back on the seat, staring at the ceiling. The Mill Valley police drove off and the sheriffs got in the front seat of their patrol car.

The driver picked up the radio. "Transporting subject to Civic Center." He turned around to Woody. "A bulletin's been posted about your daughter. Federal, state, and local agencies are all acting on it. Mill Valley police will begin searching the area immediately. Everything that can be done is being done right now. You're under arrest for possession of narcotics, child endangerment, and resisting arrest."

CHAPTER 5

Woody sat slumped in a brown metal folding chair at the Marin County jail, in front of a booking desk as high as a judge's bench, his hands still handcuffed behind his back. The sheriff's deputies stood on each side of him, and the heavy-set booking sergeant peered down at him without expression, her tan polyester uniform stretched to capacity. "Name?"

Woody looked like a deranged Charles Manson, missing one shoe, torn shirt, wild hair, and an angry-looking purple welt on his temple from hitting it on the underside of his car. He jerked his head from side-to-side to get his hair out of his eyes and glared up at the woman. "You have kids?"

She held her pen over the form on her desk. "Name?"

"You know where your kids are?"

"Name and current address?"

"You got my driver's license. You got everything. Everything but my daughter! Every second you spend on this you're helping the kidnappers. I could be out there looking for her. I know what she looks like, what she smells like—we have radar between us. Let me outta here!" Woody jumped to his feet. Before he could fully stand, the deputies on each side dropped their weight into his boney shoulders and slammed him back into the metal chair. Woody's body shuddered.

The booking Sergeant waited a minute for him to calm down. "Listen, pal, you're the one driving around doing drugs with a baby in the car. You can make this as hard as you want, or you can cooperate and maybe we can help. Full name and current address?"

Legs splayed apart, Woody was slumped back as far as he could while still being in the chair. He turned his head to the side and spat on the floor. "I wanna talk to my lawyer."

The woman looked at the deputies. "Give him one collect call then put him in C-14."

Woody tensed up and resisted when the cops grabbed him under his arms. They easily plucked him out of the chair, but he managed to snag a metal rung with his heel and sent the chair clanging backward onto the floor. They tightened their grip and shoved him down the hallway.

"If anybody ever tries to hurt one of your kids," Woody yelled over his shoulder, "don't bother calling the cops! They'll be too busy going after a guy for smoking a joint!" His face wet with spit and tears, he screamed, "You pigs don't give a fuck about kids...shit-eating pigs!"

The deputies manhandled Woody through a metal door into a closet-size room with a wall-mounted telephone and slammed him down into another metal chair. A deputy picked up the receiver. "Number for a collect call?"

Woody tried to get his brain working. If he called home, what could Stephanie do? She'd just call Pearlman to get him released so he could help find Lily. What would he say to her? He couldn't think.

"Listen, kid," one of the cops said, "we know you're worried about your daughter. But that don't give you the right to be an asshole. You're the one that left her in the car. You can call your wife or your lawyer or whoever you want. But if you don't cooperate, that ain't gonna help anybody."

He told the cop Jeff Pearlman's phone number.

The cop grabbed a fistful of Woody's hair to get it out of the way and put the receiver on his shoulder.

"Brenda, it's Woody. I need to talk to Jeff, it's urgent."

"Jeff isn't in right now. I can take a message or you can—"

"It's an emergency! Where is he?"

"I'm not sure if he's gone for the day."

The phone started slipping from Woody's ear down his shoulder. "Brenda! Somebody kidnapped Lily!"

"What?"

"I'm in the Marin County jail. Somebody took Lily out of my car. She's gone!"

"What? Why are *you* in jail?"

His hands still handcuffed behind his back, Woody looked up at the cop and strained to speak toward the receiver. "I can't explain right now. Find Jeff!"

"Where's Stephanie?"

"Time's almost up." The cop pulled back on Woody's hair harder than necessary and put the phone back up to his ear.

"Brenda! I can't talk right now. Find Jeff! Tell him what happened."

—

When Brenda had Pearlman paged at a North Beach cafe he frequented and gave him the news, he walked straight out the door, got his keys from the valet, and drove his Jaguar at high speed to San Rafael.

"I'm here to see Chester Woods, in custody," Pearlman said into the gray metal intercom box at the Marin County jail.

"Visiting hours are over."

"I'm an attorney, here for a contact visit."

The booking sergeant buzzed him in. Sitting at her desk under bright fluorescent lights, she looked down at Pearlman in his pleated tan slacks and pin-striped dress shirt. "ID?"

He put his driver's license and California State Bar card on the desk.

"It'll take thirty minutes to arrange for a contact visit. Have a seat."

"I'll take a visit through the glass. I need to see my client immediately, it's urgent. It's regarding a missing child."

"I'm aware of the situation. Have a seat." She picked up the black phone on her desk. "Non-contact legal with Chester Woods, C-14." She hung up and pushed a clipboard across the desk. "Fill out both sides."

"Is there any information about the child?"

"Everything that can be done is being done."

"What happened?"

She ignored him and picked up a sheet of paper off her desk. "You're a lawyer, you know I can't give out information about a pending case until the court designates you attorney of record."

Pearlman took a deep breath. "I've known the child since the day she was born. She's my goddaughter. I've been Woody's lawyer for years." He held out his hands. "Please, tell me what you know. I'm just here trying to help."

"Mr. Woods left the baby unattended in a store parking lot in a convertible with the top down. Narcotics were found at the scene: marijuana and cocaine."

"Has someone contacted the child's mother?"

"A sheriff called and left a message at the home. He didn't leave any information, just a message to please call. We have a full description of the child. A nationwide alert has been issued. The California State response team is coordinating with Federal agencies, the Marin County Sheriff and Mill Valley police. We have the baseball cap the child was wearing, it's being used with a K-9 unit in the abduction area. We're following up on every possible lead."

Woody sat clutching a telephone receiver behind inch-thick glass in a small concrete room. His skin was chalky gray, his face gaunt as if he'd been incarcerated for years.

Pearlman sat down and picked up the receiver. "You okay?"

The phone quivered against Woody's ear. "Does Stephanie know?"

"I tried calling her from my car phone. I don't think anyone's spoken to her. The desk sergeant told me every agency in the state is on it, they'll find her."

"If you don't tell Stephanie something, she'll be worried. She doesn't know where me and Lily are. But if you tell her what happened she'll…" tears started seeping out of Woody's vacant eyes.

"I might be able to get you bailed out tonight," Pearlman said. "It'll take about four hours. We need a judge's signature. If the process goes too late, they'll just hold you until your arraignment at 8:30 tomorrow morning, and I'll get you released then. If you can hang in there—sometimes it's easier that way—we get everything done in court. What happened to your head?"

Woody's voice was barely audible. "It'd be good to be with Stephanie tonight."

"What happened to your head?"

Woody reached up. "I hit it under my car looking for Lily. Then they tossed me into my cell, and I hit it on the cement floor. I can't feel anything, my head's numb."

With some effort, Pearlman averted his attention from the blood oozing out of Woody's cut to look him in the eyes. "I made some calls on my way here. The elected sheriff of Marin is a friend. He's already talked to the FBI. And I know one of the best private investigators in the country. I've hired him. He's on it. We'll find her. I left Stephanie a message to call me." Considering how he could possibly break the news to Stephanie, he blurted out, "You left her alone in the parking lot?"

"For one minute. I turned around, and she was gone."

"Where were you?"

"The 7-Eleven near Tam Junction. I was going home."

"You left her alone in your car?"

"She was asleep, buckled in her car seat. I parked right in front of the store window, where I could see her, went in for a pack of smokes, and she was gone." Woody's voice was high, razor thin. "I wasn't even in the store long enough to get my cigarettes. I watched the car the entire time." He looked down and spoke softer. "There were a couple of music fans talking to me. I guess, I...I guess I must've spaced out and forgot about her for a second."

They held each other's gaze through the thick glass, both knowing Lily had been left unattended long enough for someone to take her.

"Were you high on something?"

"No!" The trembling from Woody's phone-hand shuddered through his body.

"You weren't high on anything?"

"I took a hit of pot driving into town. One hit of pot!"

"They said something about coke."

"No!" He spoke through clenched teeth, his knuckles white from squeezing the phone. "I had a left-over bindle, scrapings. I wasn't high. I wasn't *high!*" He dropped his head into his hands and spoke softly. "It was my fault, I lost her, I lost our baby." He raised his head and looked at Pearlman. "We can't tell Stephanie. We can't. Let's wait 'til we find her...let's wait." He started sobbing. His chest heaved, the phone slipped out of his hand.

Pearlman instinctively reached for the falling phone and hit his hand into the glass. He decided to curtail the questions and give Woody time to cry. It was as if tears were pouring out of every part of him. Watching him, Pearlman was reminded of his time as a young public defender, visiting jails and prisons, feeling powerless, consumed with guilt for being able to walk outside and see the sky while his clients languished in windowless concrete cages.

"Whadda they gonna do," Woody mumbled into his hands, "put her picture on telephone poles with lost cats?" Lily's vanishing was omnipresent, hovering over them, ready to descend at any moment and crush them with pain.

"I can't hear you without the phone. Pick up the phone."

Woody looked up, his eyes rolled back under his eyelids. His head fell, and he hit his forehead on the edge of the six-inch stainless-steel shelf at the bottom of the glass.

Pearlman was on his feet. "Woody!"

Arms hanging at his sides, bony shoulders twitching, Woody lifted his head up a few inches and let the full weight of it fall again, smacking his head on the shelf.

"Woody!" Pearlman slapped the glass. "Woody! We'll find her! Get yourself together. We'll find her!"

His head on the counter, the phone dangling between his knees, Woody said, "When somebody stops living, they're frozen in time. Lily might be twelve-months old forever."

Pearlman shoved back his chair, slapping the thick glass with both hands. "Woody! Woody!"

Woody slowly looked up, reached down between his knees, picked up the receiver, and held it to his ear, rivulets of blood from his forehead suffused with tears.

"Get yourself together, man!" Pearlman commanded. "Get it together. We'll find her!"

Woody raised his left arm up over his head and placed his hand flat on the glass.

Still standing, holding the phone, Pearlman put his right palm against Woody's on the glass. "I'll look into getting you out of here in a few hours or I'll see you at the arraignment in the morning. Try to get some rest. We'll find her." Pearlman hung up the phone and turned to leave.

Woody tapped the glass and pointed to the phone. Pearlman picked it up.

"Don't tell Stephanie. Don't tell her. Not yet."

"The police already put a call into her. So did I. She needs to know. I'll talk to her." Pearlman lowered his voice. "Hang in there."

"I hope not."

Pearlman mustered a weak smile. "You're at your lowest right now. Just make it through the night, tomorrow's another day. There's no place like rock bottom to push off from." Pearlman contemplated the pool of blood and tears accumulating on the steel shelf.

"Maasai warriors die within a very short time when they're put in jail," Woody said in a dry voice, almost a whisper. "They live in the present and can't comprehend that someday they'll get out." He closed his eyes. "When Lily closes her eyes, she thinks the world disappears."

"You've got to stay strong. Lily needs you now more than she ever has."

Woody took a long deep breath. "Ever since Lily was born...it's like having my own heart going around in another body." He looked up at Pearlman; they locked eyes. "Not wanting to die is different than wanting to live."

Pearlman slowly nodded. "I love you, Woody. Stay strong."

CHAPTER 6

"I could kill your father! I could *kill* him!"

Stephanie was driving much too slowly for the flow of traffic on Miller Avenue, a main thoroughfare in Mill Valley. Cars honked, but she didn't notice. One started to veer past her on the right and she changed lanes without looking, cutting them off. Tires squealed, horns blared. Stephanie gripped the steering wheel and kept her eyes straight ahead.

"I could kill him! And when he finds out what I've done, he'll probably kill *me*. Then you won't have *any* parents!"

Lily whimpered.

Stephanie adjusted her rearview mirror for a better view of Lily in the back seat. "I'm sorry, honey. I know you just woke up. I know you're upset 'cause mommy's upset. Your father left you asleep in his car in front of a store, and I was driving by and...I waited, he didn't come out, so I took you and left. I'm sorry to put you through this, but I felt like I had to do something. I'm teaching your dad a lesson—a big lesson."

Lily started crying.

"I'm sorry, darling. We're going over to Aunt Auddie and Uncle Max's to get you something to eat, maybe take a warm bath. Maybe we'll take a bath together." Stephanie reached back between the bucket seats and held Lily's sneakered foot. "Maybe it's time for me to be candid with you, sweetheart, about your father. I've never really talked honestly to you about him, about what a space case he is. He loves you very much, but sometimes I think he's just not capable of the kind of parenting you deserve. The kind of attention you need to—" Stephanie looked down from the rearview mirror, slammed on her brakes, and skidded to within inches of a car stopped in front of her.

Lily let out a long, piercing shriek.

—

When Auddie opened the door to her condo, Stephanie was standing there holding Lily. "Sweethearts!" she said. "Sweetsheart!"

"Attorneys General," Max said from across the room.

"What a wonderful surprise." Auddie took Lily out of Stephanie's arms and left her standing at the door. Auddie was Stephanie's aunt, her best friend, and a surrogate mother to Lily.

Balancing a martini in his hand, Max walked over and gave Stephanie a hug. Her uncle was a bear of a man, with thick graying hair on his arms, the back of his hands, and curling out from the neck of his shirt. He had one continuous bushy eyebrow. Stephanie had enjoyed his furry hugs since she was a young girl. It was especially comforting today. "Been to your martial arts class?" He nodded at her workout clothes. "You okay? You seem upset."

She managed a weak smile and shrugged. "I'm okay, Uncle Max. I just...let me sit down, we'll talk."

Max nodded at his drink. "Martini?"

"Sure, why not." She walked across the living room and fell back into an armchair.

Stephanie's aunt and uncle were a lookalike couple who'd met in high school and had been married almost fifty years. He was a retired physician, she a tireless volunteer for Amnesty International, the ACLU, and the Sierra Club. Auddie was almost the identical round shape as Max, about half his size. They were at the place in their relationship where they often finished each other's sentences and could communicate by telepathy.

Auddie sat in a chair next to Stephanie, holding Lily by her waist, gently bouncing her in her lap. Being so enamored with Lily, she looked over at Stephanie's face for the first time since she'd arrived. "My God, darling, did something happen? What's wrong?"

Stephanie looked at Lily, trying to gather her thoughts and get her emotions under control. "Actually, Woody and I have been...we've been having disagreements about Lily and it's been...it's gotten out of hand."

"I've sensed something's been going on," Auddie said. "Woody seems so on-edge lately. He always looks like he hasn't slept in days, and he acts like he could just snap at any moment for no reason."

Max appeared with a professional-looking martini. He handed Stephanie her drink and raised his eyebrows. She'd seen him practically carry on a conversation just using his bushy eyebrows. Stephanie took a small sip.

"I know something's happened," Auddie said, "tell us what happened."

"I need to use your phone first."

"Of course, dear. If you'd like privacy, you can use the phone in Max's study."

"I just need to see if Woody's home or check if he left me a message." Stephanie went to the kitchen and called home. No answer. She listened to the first few words of a dozen messages, then skipped to the next, listening for Woody's voice. She hung up and stood staring at the phone until Auddie called across the room, "Would you girls like something to eat? Is Lily hungry? She's always hungry. Let me make you something."

Stephanie went back to her chair, picked up her martini, and looked at the floor. "I'm not hungry. Lily'd probably go for a piece of fruit." She sighed. "We're just juggling so many things, it's more than we can keep track of."

"Maybe get some help with housework and the baby," Auddie said. "I could certainly help more with Lily." She lifted Lily off her lap and kissed her on the cheek.

Stephanie kept her eyes down, cupping her martini with both hands. "Something's got to give. We have a child and Woody's been so, I don't know. He's been acting so erratic, sometimes I can't tell if he's—"

"Substance abuse," Max said.

"Max!" Auddie yelled, "let her finish!"

Stephanie's lower lip was quivering. "We're on overdrive, with pressure coming at Woody from every direction. He's supposed to finish his record and play shows, and there's our financial concerns and all the big personalities in his band and"—she looked over at Max—"and yes, drugs. Woody uses cocaine to make up for his lack of confidence. Then he does it to counteract how bad he feels from using it. Sometimes when I'm talking to him it's like he's not even there. It's like I'm just one of those women in his songs. And it feels like Lily"—she looked over at Lily and tears started rolling down her cheeks—"she doesn't get the attention she deserves. We're losing track of what's important in our lives, and sometimes, sometimes we even lose track of *her*." Stephanie sobbed uncontrollably, her shoulders quaking, her martini splashing on the carpet.

—

Pearlman knew they'd let Woody languish in that closet-sized telephone room while they took their sweet time moving him back to his cell. He walked slowly down the brightly lit hallway, gazing at the scuffed, well-worn floor, thinking how throughout the protracted administration of justice in America—from the arresting officer on the street to the prosecutor, judge, jury, probation officer—the person who wields the most power over a defendant's quality of life is the prison guard. In fact, for many people in America, the primary interaction they have with the thing called "government" was with cops.

Pearlman came to a locked metal door, pressed a button, and looked up at the mounted camera. After a long five minutes, a buzzer sounded and the door into the reception area unlocked. "I'll get the bail process going," he said, walking past the sergeant's desk. He thought of saying something else so as to not seem rude, but he had no words left in him. He crossed the room without looking at her and she pressed the buzzer under her desk. He was halfway out the front door.

"Mr. Pearlman?"

He turned.

"I think you should know. Stephanie, the mother of the missing child, called. The child is with her, she's fine."

Pearlman let the heavy door slam closed into his back. "Thank God," he whispered, "thank God." He took several long breaths, letting the information sink in. "Where did they find her?"

She took her time with a form on her desk and finished writing her sentence before looking up. "The mother had her the whole time. She saw the car in a parking lot with the baby unattended and took her to teach the father a lesson." She glared at Pearlman. "This entire incident was a domestic dispute."

Pearlman nodded toward the cellblock. "I need to go back and tell my client what happened."

She looked at the big school clock, the only thing on the room's four gray walls. "They're transferring him back to his cell, then the guards change shifts. It'll be forty-five minutes. Have a seat." She slid the clipboard toward him. "You'll need to fill out another form."

Pearlman considered the clipboard. "I guess it'd be faster if you could just give him the news. I'll get to work on bailing him out. Can you get word to him right away that they found his daughter, that she's safe with her mother?"

"Sure."

"Thank you for doing that. Please do it as soon as possible. I know you know how important it'll be for him. And my apologies to you and your staff for all the trouble you've been through."

She nodded, pressed the door buzzer under her desk, and went back to her paperwork.

"One more thing," Pearlman said, "my client needs medical attention. Apparently, he hit his head and he's—"

"The bruise on his head has been noted."

"He's bleeding."

"I already took it on myself to report it to medical."

Without looking up, she pressed the buzzer again and Pearlman walked out.

—

An hour later, the jail's front-door intercom buzzed. "Wally here."

The sergeant let him in.

"Hi, Helen." Wally was in uniform, there to take over nightshift booking duties. "Anything exciting?"

Helen neatened the stack of papers in front of her. "The usual craziness. A couple of DUI's, a guy in a stolen car going a hundred miles an hour the wrong way on the wrong side of 101. It's a miracle he didn't kill somebody." She patted the stack of papers. "And we have a new guest with an attitude in C14. Pot, coke, seems strung out on something. He thought his kid was kidnapped. Turns out the kid was with her mother the whole time. He's got a serious attitude." Helen collected her personal things off the desk and walked to the door. "Have a good shift, Wally." She stopped and stood looking at the door.

Wally began arranging his own personal items on the booking desk. "Forget something Helen?"

"Forgot something in C." Using the heavy cache of keys on the retractable cord on her belt, Helen made her way down the hallway, ambling side-to-side to accommodate her wide thighs. She got to the door of Woody's cell and looked in through the six-inch square window. There was a metal bench fastened to one wall, a cot fastened to the other wall with a thin mattress, no sheets, blankets or pillow, a stainless-steel sink big enough for someone to cup their hands in, and a toilet with no toilet seat. Woody sat on the bench, legs extended, arms at his sides, leaning back against the hard wall, staring into the middle distance.

She watched him for several minutes. He didn't move a muscle. It seemed like he didn't even blink. She looked down at his chest to see if he was breathing.

Below the little window at eye-level in the cell door was a four-inch opening covered by a metal plate that could be slid to the side to communicate with an inmate without having to open the door. Helen put her hand on the slider, then dropped her hand to her side. She looked up and down the hallway, even though she knew no one would be in that section without being announced by the clanging of metal doors. She adjusted her utility belt, checked her watch, and looked back through the little window. Woody hadn't moved.

Helen checked her watch again, doing the time calculations for picking up her six-year-old son from kindergarten. It was always the same decision: she could hurry home and barely have time to get a few things done, or take her time, get to the school early, and wait in the long line of cars with the other mothers. It was almost all mothers, rarely a father. She looked back through the cell door at Woody, lifeless except for the barely perceptible movement of his chest, streaks of dried blood across his forehead. She'd witnessed prisoners losing their muscle mass from lack of exercise, but that took weeks, or months. Woody looked like a straw-filled scarecrow, barely filling his clothes, all signs of vitality gone from his body. She stared at her watch, trying to imagine what it would feel like to have her child stolen. She looked back at Woody and said under her breath, "Where's your shit-eating pigs now, boy, when you need them?" Resisting one last look into the cell, she turned and walked down the hallway, let herself out through the heavy doors and said goodnight to Wally.

Woody slowly turned his head, contemplating the little window with its pattern of wire triangles embedded in the glass. He'd sensed someone there. When he stood and walked toward the door, he knew his head should hurt, but it didn't. The bloody gash on his forehead was swollen, seeping blood into his eye, but it didn't hurt. Nothing hurt. His body was trapped in this concrete coffin, but his mind was released to another dimension. His mind wasn't imprisoned, he was free. Free from this cell, free from his body.

He tentatively put his face up to the square window and looked back and forth the short distance he could see down the empty hallway. Something had been there, a presence, a spirit trying to communicate with him. He was certain it was Lily's ghost, free like him, telling him that she was okay.

"I love you, Lily," Woody said to the window. "Sorry about what happened."

"I love you, too, Daddy," he heard her say. "If your heart's free, it doesn't matter where you are."

He slowly turned back and reassumed his position on the steel bench.

—

Driving back to San Francisco, Pearlman realized that his concern for Woody and Stephanie had been so overwhelming, he hadn't acknowledged his own fears about Lily. He regretted not giving Woody the news himself, that Lily was safe...they could have processed the information together. But he knew that once Woody heard the good news, he'd be okay, nothing else mattered. Pearlman looked at his watch, he might be able to get Woody bailed out by ten o'clock tonight, or at six tomorrow morning, they'd start the long tedious process of transferring inmates to court.

As soon as he walked into his house, Pearlman made himself a stiff scotch on the rocks, called the sheriff and the investigator he'd hired, and explained that it was all a mistake. Then he got out the Marin County phone book and flipped through the yellow pages, looking for a bail bondsman he'd worked with. He finished his drink and poured himself another; if someone had to drive to the jail tonight, it wasn't going to be him. He needed to get some rest and be his best in court the next morning.

He finished his second drink, considered having a third, and thought of what awaited him in the morning. He decided to forego the third drink, forego the bail process, and get some sleep. It would save a lot of money and hassle, and there was a good possibility that if Stephanie and Lily were there in court, the judge would release Woody without bail.

He reached for the phone just as it rang.

"Hello?"

"Jeff, it's Stephanie."

"Hi, Steph. I was just about to call you. Are you and Lily okay?"

"We're fine. I'm sorry for what you've been through. I came home, got the messages, and called the jail. They told me you were there visiting Woody. Is he okay?"

"It was a difficult visit, harder for him than me."

"What did he say when you told him Lily was okay?"

"I didn't tell him myself. They told him at the jail."

"When I saw that Woody left Lily asleep in his car, I just wanted to teach him a lesson. He'd agreed to stay home with her. I never meant for things to spin out the way they did, but seeing Lily left alone in a parking lot…it was more than I could handle. I'm sorry for all the trouble you've gone through dealing with this, but Woody brought this on himself. Yes, he learned a hard lesson, but honestly, I still don't trust him."

"Did Woody actually learn his lesson? Unfortunately, I think that remains to be seen."

"I don't understand why Woody's in jail."

"They found drugs at the scene—coke and pot."

"What's going to happen to him?"

"It's just personal use amounts, but they could tack on resisting arrest or child endangerment. Depends on the DA. We could challenge the search, but it'd probably be more effective if Woody just shows remorse with the judge and we try for a deferred sentence that's ultimately dismissed. Marin's pretty good about shuttling personal-use cases to probation instead of jail. I know the judge, she's usually fair. Like any game, it's how you work the refs."

"Can he get out on bail?"

Pearlman looked at his watch. "It's pretty late to start the process. He'll be okay now that he knows Lily's okay. His arraignment's at eight thirty tomorrow, courtroom D. It always makes a good impression on the judge when the family's there. I could meet you and Lily by the main entrance at eight?"

She didn't respond.

"Steph?"

"I've been thinking," she said, "this could be a big wake-up call for Woody, for both of us. Our life's been spinning out of control with Woody's crazy schedule, up all night, the drugs...he never stops moving. Living with him is like trying to hug a tornado. It's no way to raise a family."

"I'm glad to hear you say it instead of me. Will you be there in the morning?"

"I'll sleep on it, if I can get any sleep with Woody in jail."

—

As soon as Stephanie hung up the phone, Lily awoke and reached for her breast. They got comfortable and Lily began suckling as if she were starving. She'd eaten that way since the day she was born. "You know I always try not to disturb you while you're eating, sweetheart," Stephanie said softly, "but tonight it feels like it's just you and me in this world and I don't have anyone else to talk to." She caressed Lily's silky hair. "Your father's in jail. He's probably lying awake in some cold cell, wishing he could be with us. I know how much you love your dad, how much you like spending time with him. Me too. But I think maybe it'd be better for everyone if you and I tried living on our own, at least for a little while. In some ways, we already are." Lily had fallen back to sleep with Stephanie's breast in her mouth. Stephanie watched her own teardrop fall onto Lily's cheek. "First things first," she said. "First we have to get your dad out of jail."

—

After a night of restless sleep, Pearlman stood at the entrance to the Marin County Civic Center in one of his most conservative suits, waiting for Stephanie under the gold and blue art deco archway. He glanced at his gold Rolex; he couldn't wait much longer. Trying to distract himself, Pearlman contemplated the structural engineering of the thousand-foot-long architectural tour de force. Of all the government buildings he'd been in, and he'd been in courtrooms across the country, this was by far the most aesthetically pleasing. On his first visit, he'd taken time in the sky-lit library to read its history. Frank Lloyd Wright built it in 1969 at age ninety, the ultimate expression of his organic Usonian architecture, his last and largest work. Explaining his creative process, Wright had written that most architects start with a building's shell then force their way in. He let the design unfold from the inside out, the way a plant or animal develops from a seed, always emphasizing the spirit of play and surprise in his buildings.

He wondered if Woody and Stephanie's marriage would survive this nightmare. For Lily's sake, he hoped it would. And he couldn't help but wonder how the ordeal would affect Woody's ability to create music. Pearlman looked at his watch for the tenth time in ten minutes, scanned the parking lot again, and headed inside.

It had been years since Pearlman handled a criminal case. The round, low-ceiling courtroom where they administered the criminal docket always reminded him of a Star Trek spaceship. The bizarre irony of armed sheriff's deputies in the pastel-colored, organically shaped room was not lost on him. Walking through the heavy security to the inner circle in front of the judge's bench, he wondered how Frank Lloyd Wright had grappled with the concept of people losing their freedom, sentenced against the backdrop of his colorful artistic creation to spend their years behind gray prison walls.

Pearlman took a seat with the other defense attorneys, many of whom he knew. They were exchanging stories about their cases when armed guards escorted in a dozen shackled, unshaven men in orange jumpsuits and seated them in the jury box. Woody sat in the back row with his head down, hair covering his face, looking lifeless. Pearlman kept his eyes on him, hoping to get his attention, give him an encouraging smile. When Woody struggled against the tight handcuffs, his hair fell away from his face and Pearlman got a glimpse of his ghost-like pallor and the ugly crimson welt on his forehead. He'd never seen such a dramatic physical change in someone over the course of one day.

The judge had fiery blue eyes, white hair, and was all business. Like the feathers of an angry peacock, her billowing black robe made her thin, slight body look much larger than it actually was. She brought down her gavel. "Court will come to order. Bailiff, call the cases."

As far as Pearlman could tell, Woody didn't look up once during the forty minutes it took to get through the first four cases.

"Case number CV7758," the bailiff called out, "The People of California versus Chester Woods, in custody."

Pearlman stood before the judge while a guard unfastened Woody's handcuffs and escorted him to the podium. Woody shuffled to within a couple feet of Pearlman, stopped, and stared at the floor.

"Good morning, gentlemen," the judge said. "Nice to see you, Mr. Pearlman. I haven't seen you in my courtroom in quite a while."

"Good morning, Your Honor. I've been doing mostly civil work in San Francisco. For the record, Jeff Pearlman representing Chester Woods, who is present in court." As he spoke, he reached over, pinched the arm of Woody's baggy overalls, and tugged him closer. Woody shuffled over, staring at the floor.

"Lighten up," Pearlman said quietly to Woody, "I'll get you released today. The worst you're looking at is probably a misdemeanor with probation."

"Any news?" Woody grunted. With black circles around small red eyes, he looked like he was peering out from the back of a dark cave.

"News?" Pearlman said.

"About Lily."

"They didn't tell you?"

"Gentlemen." The judge raised up her skinny arm and brought down her gavel. "Your attention, please."

"They didn't tell you at the jail?" Pearlman said to Woody.

"What?" Woody grunted.

"Mr. Pearlman," the judge said firmly, "you and your client will direct your attention to the court. There are two immediate matters to address: arraignment and the issue of bail. Our first order of business will be—"

"What?" Woody grunted more loudly at Pearlman. "What'd ya' hear?"

"Gentlemen, please," the judge tapped her gavel. "Mr. Pearlman, you will instruct your client to remain silent while we proceed. Our first issue to address is the issue of..."

Eight rows behind them, in the center of the crowded gallery, Stephanie cleared her throat and whispered loudly, "Woody!"

Woody and Pearlman both turned around.

The judge smacked her gavel hard. "Order in the court! I will not tolerate public comment in my courtroom. Mr. Pearlman, your attention, please. And you will control your client and have him face the court."

Pearlman turned around and faced the judge. Woody kept his back to her, scanning Stephanie's face for any sign of emotion.

"Mr. Woods!" The judge slammed her gavel twice in rapid succession, the folds of her robe a billowing parachute. "Mr. Woods, you will direct your attention to this court!"

Woody stood frozen, staring at Stephanie.

"Mr. Woods! You are a criminal defendant in my court facing serious allegations. You will have no communication with anyone but your counsel and will be found in contempt if you don't face this court immediately!"

Woody gave Stephanie a weak smile and started to turn back toward the judge when he heard Lily's familiar gurgle and saw the curls on top of her head emerge into view above the seatback in front of her. When Stephanie hoisted her up onto her lap and faced her forward, Lily immediately recognized Woody, let out a squeal, started flapping her arms…and Woody fainted.

The judge held her gavel in mid-air, everyone in the courtroom on the edge of their seats as Pearlman tried unsuccessfully to catch Woody before he fell and hit his head on the hard wooden floor. Two armed deputies rushed over.

Woody slowly opened his eyes to Pearlman on his knees next to him.

"She's okay." Woody's lips were trembling. "Lily's okay."

"She's fine." Pearlman looked up to the judge. "Your Honor, can we please pass this case while I consult with my client?"

"Of course, Mr. Pearlman, take all the time you need." The judge poured a glass of water from the silver pitcher on her bench and gestured to the bailiff. "Please deliver this to the defendant."

Huddled at the side of the courtroom, Pearlman watched the color return to Woody's face as he explained to him what had happened. "You sure you're up to doing this arraignment right now?"

Woody looked out at the gallery at Stephanie and Lily, Stephanie busy trying to keep Lily quiet on her lap. "With Lily here I can do anything. Let's get it over with." Woody brought his hand up to his forehead.

"That looks pretty bad," Pearlman said. "You need to see a doctor."

"I keep landing on the same spot." He massaged it with his fingertips. "My temple, my place of worship." He flinched at the whack of the judge's gavel. She was back in action, barking orders at the lawyers.

"I'll do all the talking with the judge," Pearlman said. "Okay?"

"Okay."

"Just say not guilty, nothing else—nothing. Got it?"

"Got it."

When the judge concluded the case being heard, Pearlman stood up. "Your Honor, if it pleases the court, we're prepared to proceed with the Woods matter."

"Bailiff, re-call the case."

"Case number CV7758. People of California versus Chester Woods, in custody."

Pearlman and Woody stepped to the podium. "Thank you for your consideration, Your Honor. My client has endured an extremely stressful twenty-four hours. He's now fully cognizant, prepared to proceed. I believe the first issue is bail. I respectfully request the court to release Mr. Woods on his own recognizance."

The judge turned to the Deputy District Attorney. "I've read the incident report. Mr. McClosky, your position regarding bail?"

At the podium six feet to the left, the young lawyer consulting his notes looked to Pearlman like he was wearing his father's suit and was too young to shave.

"Sean McClosky, for the People. We object to an OR at this time, Your Honor. The defendant is charged with possession of narcotics and child endangerment, both serious offenses, especially when considered together. The district attorney's office considers the allegations serious enough to justify felony charges and bail has been set at ten thousand dollars."

"Mr. Pearlman?"

"Your Honor, this is a case of a domestic misunderstanding. It's now clear that, unbeknownst to the defendant, the minor child was safely with her mother, never in harm's way. This is a personal matter. The criminal justice forum is inappropriate regarding care of the child. As for the narcotics, they're clearly personal-use amounts."

"That's the point, Your Honor," McClosky said. "Drugs and children are not a good mix. The report indicates that the defendant is perfectly capable of posting bail. Due to the seriousness—"

"If I may, Your Honor," Pearlman interrupted, "considerations regarding bail are whether Mr. Woods is a flight risk or presents a danger to the community. Everything else, including what McClosky just said, is irrelevant. Mr. Woods owns a home in Marin. He's a well-known professional musician under contract with Warner Brothers Records and currently works in a recording studio in Sausalito. Mr. Woods' wife Stephanie and their twelve-month-old baby are present in court. This righteous little family deserves to be back together as quickly as possible to address their personal issues." Pearlman took a breath to get his emotions under control.

McClosky saw the opening and piped in. "There are serious allegations that Mr. Woods acted in a manner that could be considered—"

"Don't interrupt me, McClosky!" Pearlman spoke so forcefully McClosky took a step back. "I've got a few more sentences, then you can carry on with your irrelevant gibberish." Pearlman faced the judge and cleared his throat. "I'm sorry, Your Honor, I obviously have personal feelings regarding this matter. If I may, as an officer of the court, I personally know the defendant to be a humble, nonviolent man. A threat to no one. Regarding being a potential flight risk, Mr. Woods is a well-known performing artist whose appearance is recognizable to the general public. It would be virtually impossible for him to abscond and live as a fugitive." Pearlman glanced over at the assistant DA. "The people's position on bail is their typical knee-jerk resistance to a reasonable request. It's without merit and a waste of judicial resources."

"Mr. McClosky?" the judge said.

McClosky's face was beet red. "Your Honor, the defendant is charged with serious felonies. He can clearly afford to post bail and he—"

"Your Honor," Pearlman said, "as you know, his ability to post bail has nothing to do with it! He presents no danger to the community and isn't a flight risk, period!"

"One of the charges is child endangerment," McCloskey's voice was getting high and whiney, "a serious charge with serious consequences."

"I'm aware of the allegations." The judge gestured at Stephanie and Lily. "The child appears to me to be healthy and well cared for." She brought down her gavel. "Mr. Woods will be released on his own recognizance."

"All right, judge!" A young Black man with dreadlocks in an orange jumpsuit with the other in-custody defendants raised a handcuffed fist in the air.

"Order in the court!" The judge swung her gavel with the power of a rock drummer. "Mr. Pearlman, does the defendant wave formal arraignment?"

"Yes, Your Honor."

"Waive time?"

"Time is waived."

"Mr. McClosky," the judge said, "any objection to the court accepting the defendant's plea?"

"No objection," McClosky said looking down.

The court reporter, seated on a four-inch-high stage next to the judge, cleared her throat.

"Mr. McClosky," the judge said, "speak up to be heard for the record."

McClosky snapped to attention. "No objection."

"How do you plead, Mr. Woods?"

Woody looked to Pearlman.

Pearlman leaned toward him and whispered, "Not guilty."

"Is this whole thing about a half-joint?" Woody said under his breath. "Shouldn't we say something about the search or the way they treated me?"

Pearlman bent over and spoke into Woody's ear. "Say: *not guilty.*"

"But shouldn't we at least—"

"Say those two words and nothing else!"

Woody turned to the judge. "Not guilty."

—

It took until late in the day for Pearlman to finalize the paperwork, get Woody's car out of impound, and get Woody out of jail. He watched Woody burst out the front door, hold out his arms, and tilt his head back. "A free man! I can see the sky!" He ran up to Pearlman and gave him a hug. "Sorry about putting you through all this, Jeff. Stephanie predicted I was gonna hit the wall. Thanks for scraping me off."

"We got lucky with a little soap and a squeegee, your next collision with reality could be fatal."

"You know that expression, 'I felt bad about having no shoes until I saw a man with no feet?'" Woody said. "I can't believe how much joy I feel just seeing the sky."

"That cut on your forehead looks like you might need stitches."

Woody touched the bruise and winced. He rummaged through the clear plastic bag of personal items he'd been arrested with, found his cigarettes, and lit one up. "Where's Stephanie?"

"Probably home sleeping. None of us got much sleep last night."

"Now I know what they mean when they say the worst part of being in prison is when you wake up in the morning and remember where you are." Woody couldn't stop looking at the sky. "Man, I'm glad to be out of that suffocating cell. You don't have to be deprived of freedom very long to appreciate it. And that courtroom with all that heavy security, that place is oppressive."

Pearlman contemplated the expansive adobe-colored building looming over them. "A few years ago, some Black Panthers walked into that same courtroom, duct-taped the end of a sawed-off shotgun to the judge's neck, took him outside, and blew his head off. The government tried pinning it on Angela Davis because she bought the gun. The whole event was in response to the institutionalized violence raining down on Black prisoners at Soledad. Violence breeds violence."

Woody was quiet, imagining the pandemonium that had taken place in that crowded courtroom.

"I don't like being in that courtroom any more than you do. That's why I quit doing criminal defense work." Pearlman went from calm to livid in a matter of moments, pointing his finger at Woody's chest. "And I'm not doing any more work for you—legal work, recording, nothing—until you quit doing coke." He thrust his finger with each word. "Either you quit or I quit."

Woody looked back at the sky. He knew the last twenty-four hours had been as emotional for Pearlman as it was for him and Stephanie. "When I think of doing coke, I get the same feeling in my gut I felt as when I saw Lily's empty car seat. I quit yesterday." He contemplated the clear plastic bag in his hand. Helen, the booking officer, had kept her eyes down when she handed it to him, knowing full well she could've prevented his night in hell by telling him his daughter was safe. He hadn't felt angry. He hadn't felt anything; just took the plastic bag, anxious to get outside. He looked Pearlman straight in the eyes. "I'll never do coke again. Never. I'm done."

Pearlman saw Woody's tears welling up. "I know you believe that right now. Prove it. Prove it to Lily." Pearlman took out his car keys. "There's a process in Marin County called deferred sentencing. You plead guilty to drug possession, they'll probably drop the child endangerment and put off the sentencing. Don't get in trouble for a year and the original charges get dismissed. The judge might go for it if I put my reputation on the line." He pointed at Woody's chest again and did another emotional zero-to-sixty. "If I even *smell* the vibe of coke around you, just once, I'm gone. A hit of pot to change the channel and get a different perspective on things can be helpful, but you doing coke is creativity genocide. I've seen musicians lose their family and their career behind getting strung out on coke. With you, losing your family is not just a figure of speech. If I even suspect that you're doing coke, I won't get into another discussion with you about it. I won't be your psychologist. I won't even accuse you to hear your explanation. I'll just walk out the door for good!"

"You don't get it, Jeff. I wouldn't expect you to...there's no way you could really understand. Last night for me was like..." He took a moment to wipe his eyes. "Last night I went through hell—a literal living hell. Like a living suicide. The worst night of my life times a thousand. You get burned badly enough with a hot frying pan, you'll never touch one again the same way. I thought I lost Lily. I thought she was gone." His voice was quiet and shaky. "I'll never touch cocaine again—never."

Pearlman waited until he was sure Woody was done speaking. "I hope you're right. I'm rooting for you, we all are." He tossed up his keys a few inches and snatched them out of the air. "We'll take a few days off, let me know if you need more, then let's get back in the studio and make a great record. And we're meeting with the guys from Warner Brothers next week." Turning to leave, he said over his shoulder, "Good luck with your family...be kind to Stephanie."

—

Pearlman sat in his car in the parking lot, head against the headrest, eyes closed, seeing the nightmarish images of Woody on the other side of the thick glass. They'd been gripping their telephones like lifelines, all the oxygen sucked out of the room. He opened his eyes and for the first time in a long time, he cried. Emotionally exhausted, he wept quietly for a minute, then sat up and started his car. He needed to keep moving.

When he turned on the ignition, he saw the blinking light on the car phone in his center console. There were four messages his secretary considered important enough to forward to his car. Driving out of the parking lot, he listened on the speakerphone: an American Olympic figure skater being detained at the Moscow airport; a female pop star in a concert-hall dressing room in Chicago, refusing to go on until the stage lights were right; an NBA player calling about salacious photos of him and his girlfriend in a tabloid magazine; and Bernie Siegel, vice president of Warner Brothers Records, requesting an update on Woody's album. Pearlman turned off the phone, headed down Highway 101 toward San Francisco, and slipped Woody's tape into the cassette player.

With the surround-sound six-speaker audiophile system, specially designed for the padded leather and natural wood listening environment of his vintage Jaguar, Pearlman felt like he was sitting in the middle of the band. Woody's signature electric fingerpicking soaked in high-quality reverb resonated like an orchestra of wind chimes in a big wet cave. He knew Woody was obsessive about his guitar sounds. He'd often find him on the studio floor surrounded by guitar and amplifier parts, reassembling everything his sound traveled through. Early in their relationship, he'd walked in on Woody holding a can of Brasso polish in one hand and sniffing a rag in the other, as if he was getting high on the solvent. It turned out he had a variety of guitar-cleaning rags and was just making sure he had the right one.

Pearlman reached up and cranked the volume as the other instruments joined in and the song slowly congealed into a glistening newborn with a fluttering heartbeat. The way Woody slid into the vocal was so subtle it was spooky. Pearlman rewound the tape and listened to the section again. The singing was so perfectly blended with the guitar, they were a single perceived sound until the words departed in their own rhythmic direction. Pearlman took one hand off the wheel and leaned back, immersed in the surround-sound experience, until a honking horn made him realize how slowly he was driving. The tape blended impressions as diverse as Beethoven and the Rolling Stones.

It had always been a wonder to Pearlman how Woody could make such an eclectic amalgam of music flow together so seamlessly.

Approaching the familiar streets of his San Francisco neighborhood, he turned the stereo up another notch. When the metal gate swung open to his expansive Nob Hill residence, the sight of his big dark house brought on an empty feeling that distracted him from the music. Then he noticed the little red car parked in front of his guest cottage with all the lights on. The car was a Kilowatt, one of the first production electric cars, that his tenant Orchid fondly referred to as "Kilo." A friend of a friend, Pearlman rented the cottage to her to do her art, and she'd quickly filled it with oversized canvases and art supplies. He didn't need the rental income but enjoyed having such a dedicated artist around, and he found her fascinating. Day or night, it seemed she was always painting.

Without thinking, he turned his motor off and the cassette stopped. He quickly turned the ignition back on and reclined in his seat, holding the wheel like he was still driving as the band accelerated into a high-energy foray with Woody's guitar at the head of the pack, leading the charge, the bass and drums close behind threatening to barrel over everything. A startling saxophone shriek jolted Pearlman up in his seat as the band lurched forward, reaching out musically to each other for a handhold to keep from tripping. The interplay gave the impression that the song was gaining speed, careening out of control, but the galloping drums held back on the reins with controlled aggression, rock steady, building momentum internally not externally, advancing toward an ever-receding horizon.

Sitting in his dark car, Pearlman realized he was gripping the steering wheel with both hands. He loosened his grip just as the band prepared for landing, a gradual descent until Woody played a quiet, unexpected chord followed by the sounds of muted laughter, clicking off switches, setting down drumsticks, and lighting cigarettes.

Pearlman turned off the ignition, opened his car door, and did a double take, thinking the band had started up again. The music, Stravinsky's "Rite of Spring," was coming from the guest cottage. He pictured Orchid in front of a stretched canvas taller than she was, music commandeering her paintbrush, imposing itself on the painting. He'd barely eaten all day, and it occurred to him to invite her over for dinner. He loved to cook but didn't like cooking for one. He wondered if she enjoyed his company as much as he enjoyed hers. He didn't feel like being alone but wondered whether, after such an emotional day, he should try relating to an attractive woman. Or maybe it was the perfect time. He thought of Woody, how he often seemed his most creative in the most stressful circumstances.

He walked into his house, changed out of his suit, and went straight to his wine cellar. He liked to pick his wine first, then decide on the food. He selected one of his most eclectic bottles and re-opened the front door to hear the music coming from the cottage. Amidst a crescendo of violins, horns, and timpani, he splashed a generous taste into two bowl-sized crystal wine glasses and walked to the cottage fifty feet from the house. It was an unusually warm San Francisco evening, and he stood at the open door with the two glasses, watching Orchid paint just as he'd pictured, totally absorbed in her work.

Tall and statuesque, she stood in front of a canvas a foot taller than her, dabbing at a striking portrait of the back of a naked, androgynous figure peering over its shoulder at her. She wore a lime-green, long-sleeve shirt covered with blotches of paint and an orange sarong split up the side almost to her waist, exposing a long muscular leg that resembled the painting. Proud of her Tanzanian heritage, Pearlman knew Orchid intentionally wore clothes that accentuated the color of her ebony, blue-black skin. She seemed unaware or indifferent to the fact that the tips of her copious afro were dipping into her palette of fresh oil paint, her brush strokes fluttering in synchronicity with the music. He watched her hand, not the painting.

When the music paused between sections and she looked up, she didn't react, as if she'd known he'd been standing there. She reached over and turned the music down. "Hello, Jeff, please come in."

He looked at the two wine glasses in his hands as if surprised to see them. "When I drink good wine, I prefer drinking two glasses at once."

She nodded, her expression illegible. It occurred to him that, being from a different culture, she might not know he was making a joke. He extended a glass. "It's delicious wine."

She took a sip and held the glass up to one of the small spotlights illuminating her painting. "It, as they say, has legs?"

With considerable effort, Pearlman kept his gaze on her eyes. "It's Buffalo Blood Petite Syrah, from Sonoma County."

She held it up to the light again. "Is buffalo blood the same color as human blood?"

He held his own glass up to the light. "The question never occurred to me."

"With a few blue exceptions, most creatures, even fish, have the same color blood." She took another sip, matter-of-factly dipped her brush into her wine glass, and ran the tip down the back of the figure's leg. With the oil paint on the canvas still wet, the visual effect was dramatic: a trickle of wine-colored blood running down the figure's sinuous, muscular hamstring.

The music on the tape became suddenly agitated, almost menacing, and Pearlman tensed up. The rivulet oozed down the figure's calf and over its ankle and formed a red pool in the painted field of lavender it stood in and reminded him of Woody's pool of blood and tears on the steel shelf in the jail. Pearlman realized he was holding his breath and exhaled as the orchestra transitioned to a trembling flute solo. "It's been a long couple of days," he thought.

"You could paint a picture with your own blood until you die," Orchid said. "I've painted with my own menstrual blood. The color is dramatic."

He was considering what she'd said when the music veered into another raucous clatter. "This music was composed for a ballet about a ballerina who dances herself to death," Pearlman said. He took her wine glass, poured it into a paper cup, refilled it with half of his own, handed it back, and clinked a ringing, bell-tone toast. "To art."

She clinked him back. "Life is a question, art is the answer."

He nodded at the painting. "It has such a presence, it's like there's three of us here. Is it from a live model or your imagination?"

She sipped her wine and studied the painting. "It started from a live model, then I let my imagination take over. I've been trying to decide whether human bodies are already perfect or if I should impose my idea of perfect imperfection. I guess it depends on your perspective, even where you happen to be standing. You can't even *see* a painting if you get too close to it."

The music became a cacophony of clattering percussion. "When this piece was first performed," Pearlman said, "a music critic described it as a terrifying musical hunt."

"Until lions learn to read and write, the account of the hunt will always be from the perspective of the hunter." She wrinkled her nose. "I'm a vegetarian."

"I was about to cook myself a vegetarian dinner. Feel like joining me?"

"When you walked in here tonight, Jeff, you seemed like you've had a stressful day."

He nodded.

"Are you sure you feel like having company?"

"Honestly, I'm not sure. But I'd like to try. Come over in a half hour, and I'll make us something simple to go with the wine."

—

Holding her empty glass, Orchid leaned inside Pearlman's open front door to the aroma of garlic and ginger. "Jeff?"

"In the kitchen."

Cut vegetables and jars of fresh herbs covered the counter. Pearlman stood at the stove stirring a sauce, wearing an apron that said: YOUR MESSAGE HERE.

Orchid had changed into a full-length sarong of traditional African kanga, a multi-colored fabric imprinted with Swahili phrases, wrapped in swirls from her long, graceful neck to her ankles. She was two inches taller than him in her sandals and looked so dramatic when she walked in that he had to avert his stare.

"Smells delicious, how can I help?"

"Pour us some wine."

"This wine really is lovely." She cradled the oversized crystal glass with both hands, her long fingernails the same variety of colors as her palette of paint. She took another sip. "One day while working I concluded that the color of thirst is silver, a silvery gray."

Pearlman took a slow considered small sip. "The wine is interesting but not overbearing, a genial dinner guest rather than a loud blabbermouth." Pearlman swilled his wine and brought the glass to his nose. "It's from a small family vineyard. They don't do much besides crush the grapes and let God turn it into wine. All the fancy techniques and oak barrels and Picasso labels are fun, but it's also possible for a bunch of grapes to fall into a little dent in the ground, get covered by some leaves, and ferment into the best puddle of wine you ever tasted." He stirred the sauce, adding fresh herbs and splashes of wine with two-handed dexterity. He lifted his glass. "Love the wine you're with."

She smiled and took a sip. "How have things been going at the recording studio? You're making a record with one of your clients?"

"Woody. He's also the guy I was in court with today. A band leader without followers. Maybe the most unique person I've ever met. And the most musical. He's always pointing out sounds I don't hear—background music in a restaurant, the rhythm of a motor, songs of birds, wind through trees, the trees themselves singing to us—he hears music everywhere. He definitely prefers listening to music over listening to people talk. He says music can raise thinking to the level of poetry. He creates uncanny dream worlds with his songs that at the same time have this nuts-and-bolts authenticity. When he sings it's like he's thinking out loud. He makes language sing." Pearlman turned down the heat under his sauce, minced some fresh garlic and parmesan cheese into a small dish with olive oil and balsamic vinegar, sliced some fresh bread, and slid it across the marble counter to Orchid. "Getting Woody's songs recorded is like trying to hold water in your hands. Or like mining nuggets of gold: you have to separate out all the dirt and gravel. If you look up the word 'enigma' in the dictionary, there's a picture of Woody." He stuck his little finger in the simmering sauce and tasted it. "I've often wondered how many different tastes a person can discern at one time."

Orchid dipped some bread in the olive oil and chewed thoughtfully. "Two or three? Maybe four? In the village where I grew up, life is simple. So is the food. People do one thing at a time, Pole Pole, slowly slowly. In America people do everything at once. They think, taste, talk, and listen, all at the same time. Nothing but everything is enough. Life in America is like trying to fit every color into one painting." She took another sip of wine. "Of course, just the right amount of input can be stimulating—like adding just the right amount of spice." She nodded at the sauce that was at a gentle boil. "I've just recently learned to paint while I listen to music."

"Have you ever heard the song 'Stephanie'?"

"No."

"Woody wrote a song about his wife Stephanie. While he was going through some hard times, a singer named Ray Bell stole the song and released it. The version on the radio is Bell singing. We managed to get back Woody's legal rights to the song, but it's a bone of contention for him, living off the royalties of Ray Bell's version. He wrote a song called 'Funny Bone of Contention,' he's a very funny guy." Pearlman expertly flipped a full skillet of grilled vegetables six inches off the pan, losing only one errant piece of broccoli. "Now he's under pressure to write another hit song, make a record, have a touring band. I don't know if he's got the constitution for it. He definitely punches above his weight, but he can also be pretty self-destructive. He's such a perfectionist about his playing, I wouldn't be surprised to see him fall to his knees and pull out a Samurai sword after playing some inaccurate fretting on his guitar. Sometimes I wonder if I want to invest so much of my life in his. His music is sublime, but, like many great artists, he has some deep psychological issues."

"Challenges can add authenticity to a person's art."

Pearlman considered the iron skillet of cut vegetables in his hand. "If music was a meal, Woody's music would get four Michelin stars." He shook the pan. "To play an instrument as well as he does, you have to practice a *lot*, starting at a very early age. While other kids are in the sandbox learning social skills, the prodigal musicians are home practicing. Then, when they grow up, they can play music really well, but they never learned how to relate to people, how to talk to a girlfriend or a landlord. They communicate through their instruments."

Orchid's expression was once again unreadable. Pearlman held the skillet suspended over the fire, wondering if they were having another communication breakdown.

"I spent much of my own childhood drawing pictures," she said. They were quiet while she created a design in the olive oil and vinegar with her bread. "What can I do to help besides pour wine?"

Pearlman raised his glass, "A day without wine is like…just kidding, I have no idea." He wasn't surprised to see the blank look on her face. He pointed to a cupboard. "Dishes in the cupboard, silverware in the drawer, candles above the dishes. Would you like to hear Woody's music?"

"You've piqued my interest."

Pearlman retrieved Woody's tape from his car and put it on the kitchen stereo. Orchid set the table, lit two candles, and Pearlman watched her hips swaying to one of Woody's funky jams. When Woody steered the band into a slow, sweet ballad, Pearlman took off his apron, gave the sauce a stir, and walked over to Orchid. "May I have this dance?"

"It sounds awfully slow to dance to. Is this going to be like a white man playing basketball?"

Pearlman chuckled and took her hand. "Exactly."

They slow-danced for five minutes with their eyes closed, Pearlman careful to hold the wooden spatula in his hand away from her hair. He knew Woody's drummer had mastered the difficult art of creating an infectious swing to a slow song. He felt her body moving to the groove until the song faded out.

They simultaneously opened their eyes and smelled the sauce burning.

CHAPTER 7

"You ever in touch with that guy Woody? I heard about what went down with you and him over the song 'Stephanie.'"

"Haven't heard from him." Ray looked down at the sheet music in his hand. Across the top of the page it said *"It's About Time" Words and Music by Willy Keyes*. "Play the chorus again?"

Willy turned back to the piano they were sitting at in Ray's living room.

Ray stood with one elbow on the piano and sang the song tentatively while reading the lyrics. "One more time."

Willy played it again, Ray sang.

"Go back to the chorus into the bridge," Ray said.

"Much better," Willy said after they played it.

"One more time."

Willy played the chorus into the bridge and kept playing through to the end. This time Ray belted out the song with authority.

Willy finished with a keyboard flourish, swung one of his long legs and cowboy boots over the piano bench, and sat on it like a horse. "Your voice suits the song real well."

"I'd like to record it." Ray rolled the sheet music into a tube, slapped it in his hand, and pointed it at the keyboard. "This song deserves the perfect vocal melody to go with those great lyrics."

Willy tipped back his black cowboy hat. "It's got a melody. The one I played with my right hand, the melody you just sang."

Ray tapped the piano with the rolled-up sheet music. "It sounds good, but just a little incomplete in the second part of the chorus."

Willy made a fist, pointed his index finger up into the brim of his hat, and tipped it back farther. "If you're interested, I cut a version of the song with some top cats in Nashville. It has a vocal with that melody on it, but you could easily replace the vocal with your own."

"I'd rather record it from scratch," Ray said, "see if I can round out the melody just a little, lock it in just right."

Willy brought his hat back down to above his eyes and cleared his throat. "Record it any way you want, Ray, I think the melody's fine." He swung his other long leg over the bench and stood up to his full six-foot-two height. "Record it whatever way makes you comfortable. My guy in LA does management stuff. He's got a two-page contract he'll send you, does that kind of thing all day long. I look forward to hearing what you do with my song."

Ray pointed the rolled-up sheet at the keyboard. "Mind if I at least play around with the melody just in that one middle section of the chorus? There's a few notes right there that could use a little help, add a little oomph. Like what I did with the chorus in 'Stephanie'—it's what made the song a hit."

Willy wove his long fingers together and cracked his knuckles. "I know you're trying to follow up 'Stephanie' with something strong, Ray. I was glad when you called me. Like I said, I can hear your voice and this song blending together real nice. Sounds to me like the chorus is working just fine, just the way I intended it to. A slight build up then back into the verse with a smooth landing. Take the listener on little ride, but not too bumpy."

Ray unfurled the sheet music and visualized the credits across the top: "Words and Music by Ray Bell and Willy Keyes." All the bad press about who wrote "Stephanie" was a dark cloud over his career. He needed the credibility of composing his own song, or at least co-writing one. Frustrated trying to write lyrics, plunking notes on the piano, he had bits and pieces but nothing close to a cohesive piece of music like this Willy Keyes tune. "I'm just not feeling it in the chorus. If I come up with something that might grab a listener's attention, maybe you'd be open to at least checking it out?"

"I like the melody just the way it is." Willy cleared his throat. "If you feel like fooling around with melodies, I'd prefer you do it with your own songs. I've been doing this a long time, Ray. It's been a while since I had to share writer's credits—not since I first started out and didn't know any better. Used to be I didn't have much choice in the matter, now people are waiting in line for my songs. You know that, that's why you called me. I'd rather just keep things straightforward between us. Wouldn't want any confusion like the way things went down with you and Woody."

—

Early evening, driving home from the county jail in a state of euphoric exhaustion, Woody pulled up to his house and his heart sank. Stephanie's car wasn't there and the house was dark. He knew she wasn't just not home, she was gone. She and Lily were gone.

He walked from room to room, not touching anything, feeling the emptiness, afraid to turn on a light and make the emptiness more vivid. "Stephanie's been my night light," he thought. He came to a stop at the kitchen counter. Was it possible that they were just out doing something and in his altered state from his sleepless night of torture in that jail, maybe he just wasn't thinking right? Then he saw the note on the counter in the dim fluorescent light from the fish tank across the room. Reading Stephanie's elegant cursive in near darkness seemed to make the content of the message even darker than it was.

"Woody, thank you for honoring our desire to have our own space right now. We'll be in touch soon. We love you, Stephanie and Lily."

When he looked away it felt as if he couldn't get a full breath, as if Stephanie's note was sucking the air out of the room. He reflexively turned away and went back to his slow pacing around the house from wall to wall. He ended up sitting on the floor in the living room in front of the fish tank he'd placed on a low shelf at eye level for Lily, his arms wrapped around his knees, slowly rocking back and forth.

Time passed the way it had in jail, Woody not knowing if minutes or an hour had gone by while the fish in the tank did their own perpetual laps from glass wall to glass wall. He focused on one fish in particular, a kissing fish Lily had picked out one rainy day at a pet store. She'd been ecstatic, checking out the puppies, kittens, and birds, but the fish were her favorite. He remembered the tip of her stubby index finger pressed against the glass. Wherever she put her finger, the fish tried to kiss it. Observing the bent-back angle of her first knuckle had made him wonder if she might have double-jointed guitar-player fingers.

In the blue-white reflection of the fluorescent light, he could see the smudge marks on the glass from Lily's hands and lips. Her fingerprints looked like his had looked being processed in jail, pressing his fingers on the blue ink pad then onto white paper. What if he'd kissed the ink pad then kissed the paper with his lips? What would the cop do? The randomness of it would be way outside the cop's limits of understanding. The thought of it made him queasy. He wiped his mouth with his sleeve.

Watching the fish do a U-turn at the glass, Woody estimated the length of the fish, two or three inches, then stretched out his thumb and finger across the tank, measuring its length. The size of his hands relative to his body had been a topic of discussion his whole life. "Musician's hands," people said. As a teenager, he could reach to the tenth note of a scale on a piano. He'd read that Rachmaninoff could reach the thirteenth.

The tank was three hands, a little over two feel long. Somewhere in the middle of the harrowing night in his jail cell with its always-on fluorescent light like the fish tank, he'd paced the length of his cell. He did the math. Relative to their size, the room the fish had in the tank wasn't much different than what he'd had in jail. He'd been locked up for twenty-four hours. There were so many fish in tanks, birds in cages, animals in zoos, and so many people around the world sentenced to confinement. "Someday I'll take Lily to the Sierra Mountains," he thought. "We'll bring the kissing fish in a fishbowl and release them into a mountain lake." He pictured a rocky beach at the edge of the clear shallow water, submerging the bowl, the fish darting away to freedom. Woody knew he wouldn't be watching the fish. As with everything, he'd be watching Lily. He felt sure she understood the concept of freedom.

He thought of getting up, turning on the lights, turning on the heat in the cold house, getting something to eat. Then more time would pass and he hadn't moved, paralyzed with depression and he knew it. He looked at his yellow acoustic guitar leaning against the couch, barely visible across the room. Would he ever muster the energy to play music with Stephanie gone? It would test his will to live. She was present in every square inch of his life. He knew it was futile to try to know himself by knowing her, a cul-de-sac thinking process that always dead-ended, as if she could be an antidote for everything he disliked about himself.

Notebooks with hand-written song lyrics were scattered around the house. He took one off a low shelf and, for an hour or two, maybe three, he experimented with song lines, moved words around, crossed them out, wrote and rewrote. Eventually, he got up and got his guitar and played a staccato rhythm with a repeating melody he'd been working on, singing what he'd written by the light of the fish tank:

ME AND YOU
FOR YEARS
FOUR EARS
FOUR EYES
TWENTY TOES
TWENTY FINGERS
TWO HEARTS
TEN THOUSAND THOUGHTS
SOME FLOWERS
ONE LIFE
TOGETHER

He paused and played a major chord, letting it ring to silence.

Woody put down his guitar. Now what? Where could the song go…where could *he* go? To bed? He was beyond exhaustion. Maybe he should try to sleep. He knew that sometimes, being in this state of exhaustion is when his best lyrics appeared, and sometimes nothing but frustration happened. He picked up his notebook and forced himself to write more, one painful word at a time: He wrote "modulate up a whole step." and kept writing, forcefully pushing his pencil:

THIS SONG
THIS SONG
WHERE CAN IT GO
IT WAS OVER
FOUR LINES AGO

Woody flung his pencil across the room and laid his guitar down on the carpet. Sunlight was now seeping into the house, he'd been sitting there a long time. Thinking about writing about how solitude compares to loneliness, and without consciously deciding to get up, he found himself across the room with the telephone in his hand, staring at the clock. 7:20 a.m. *They must be at Max and Auddie's, and they're probably awake.* He dialed their number and listened to their answering machine, then turned around, walked out the door, and got in his car. Virtually no food or sleep for a day and a half, his head throbbing, he glanced at his gas gauge…running on empty like everything else. He left two strips of smoking rubber peeling out of his driveway, then did it again shifting from second gear to third, a getaway driver from pain.

—

Woody knocked on the door at Max and Auddie's condo. He heard people talking inside, put his ear up to the door, then there was silence. He walked in a circle on the small cement porch, raised his hand to knock again, heard a sharp verbal exchange, and then Auddie, in her bathrobe, partially opened the door, their faces inches apart. Startled, Auddie recoiled back, replanted her feet, and stood squarely in the opening.

"Hi, Auddie, sorry to scare you. Sorry to put you and Max in the middle of my family stuff. I know Stephanie's here. Her car's out front. I need to talk to her."

"Stephanie and Lily are asleep."

"Please, Auddie, I have to talk to her. It's a matter of…I *have* to talk to her." Driving in the morning fog with his convertible top down, Woody hadn't thought to put on a coat and stood there in his T-shirt, wet and shivering.

"I'm sorry Woody, she doesn't want to see you right now." She started to close the door.

"Auddie. Please. I need to…I have to explain something to her. She doesn't know what really happened. Let me talk to her. Just let me see Lily. If I don't see them," he tucked his hands under his armpits, trying to control his shivering, "I won't be able to breathe."

Woody saw the muscles in Auddie's jaw slacken and felt a glimmer of hope. Then she bit her lower lip and shook her head. "No. She's made it clear. I'm sorry, but she needs her space right now." Auddie started to close the door again and Woody stuck the toe of his sneaker in the last inch. "Where's Max? Let me talk to Max. He'll understand."

"I'm not here," Max said from behind the door.

"Max. Please. I *have* to see them. It's really important—for all of us."

Max swung open the door in his open bathrobe over boxer shorts and a thicket of chest hair. "This isn't our choice, it's Stephanie's. She'll be in touch with you when she's ready. She's made her intentions clear. How about showing her some respect and thinking about somebody's needs besides your own?" The veins in Max's neck were taut as cables. "Leave her alone; you're not welcome here. And see a doctor about that gash on your head." He kicked away the toe of Woody's sneaker, closed the door, and locked it.

Woody hit the door with his fist. "I'll be camped out on your front porch, waiting for my family!" He turned around, fell back against the door, slid down, and collapsed sideways onto the rubber doormat. Exhaustion overwhelmed him. His eyes closed of their own accord, and he fell asleep dreaming about a song with icy lyrics so graphic it would make a listener cold. Twenty minutes later he woke shivering, a spike of pain in his forehead. He got up, put his hands on the closed door, hung his head between his arms, and wept.

—

Heading up the road to Mt. Tam, the thought of walking into his empty house made him nauseous. He did a U–turn and headed toward San Francisco. Woody's friend Murray still lived in their old apartment building. Working the graveyard shift at the all-night video-rental store, he'd be home during the day. Like a big furry dog with his tail always wagging, Murray was always a comfort to be around. Woody thought of him as if he was born an old man.

Woody climbed the narrow stairs of the building on Ashbury Street. The bare light bulbs, scuffed-marked walls, and moldy smells created a bristly sensation on his skin, an acidic taste in the back of his throat and a cascade of memories. He stopped on the second floor and stood in front of his old apartment door, which was pockmarked with a thousand holes from thumbtacked notes and splintered at the bottom where he'd kicked it when his landlord padlocked him out for overdue rent. It reminded him of the gory remains of a battlefield disfigured by mortar shells. Surviving in that apartment had been like hand-to-hand combat, getting out like clawing his way out of a muddy foxhole. He walked up the next narrow flight of stairs to Murray's apartment.

"Woody, what's going on?"

"Thought I'd stop by, see what you're up to."

"I'm just getting ready to go to work," Murray said with his eyes closed. "What happened to your head?"

"Stephanie and Lily moved out."

"Stephanie and Lily moved out?"

"You know, Murray, I don't think I've ever said anything to you that you didn't repeat back to me."

"I didn't repeat back to you? What're you talking about? Did you come here just to get on my case? What's happening with Stephanie?"

Woody ducked under Murray's arm that was across the doorway and flopped down on Murray's familiar brown couch. "Stephanie took Lily out of my car when I was parked at a 7-Eleven. I didn't know she did it; I called the cops, got in a big hassle." Woody rested his elbows on his knees and hung his head. "It's a long story, man."

"Stephanie moved out?"

"Yeah."

"She's gone?"

"She's gone."

Murray shuffled around in a little circle. "What happened to your forehead?"

Woody leaned back and slapped the couch with both hands. "I don't know what happened." He slapped the couch again. "I *do* know what's happened! She left me 'cause I'm such a fucking space case. She left 'cause I'm *me*. Who'd wanna live with someone with my pinball machine brain? Not me. I'd move out in a second!"

"Are you high on something?" Murray said with his eyes closed. He had a habit of closing his eyes whenever he spoke directly to someone.

"What?" Woody scooted to the front edge of the couch. "I haven't slept for a couple days and my wife just left me, if that's what you mean. How exactly do you expect me to be? How would *you* be?"

"Whoa." Murray dug his hands into his pockets. "I'm just saying lately you've been like, like I don't know what. I know you're normally spaced out. Everybody that knows you knows that. But that's not what I'm talking about." He looked directly at Woody, something he rarely did. "It's like, a fire sucks in oxygen and radiates heat in some kind of balance. But if you throw on gasoline it explodes and burns out. You doing coke is like throwing gasoline on a fire that's already raging."

Woody shook his head. "You been reading Shakespeare or something?"

"You asked me and I'm telling you. You've been snorting coke and smoking pot like… like you're not just getting a buzz going to feel good. It's like you're getting too blotto to feel *anything*." Murray dug his hands farther into his pockets and locked his elbows. "I'm just sayin' maybe that's what Stephanie picked up on." He shrugged. "Sorry you're going through all this. I really gotta get going to work. You can hang out if you need a place to hang out or whatever. I really gotta get going."

Woody wanted nothing more than to close his eyes and lie down the length of the soft, brown corduroy couch. He stood up and headed toward the door. "Thanks, Murray."

"Before you try fixing what's going on inside your head, maybe try fixing that bump on the outside of your head."

"Thanks, Shakespeare."

—

After spending the night dazed in front of the fish tank, Woody woke up fully dressed under a blanket on his living room couch, the house dark. At least he'd had it together to get himself a blanket, though he couldn't remember doing it. He went to the kitchen and looked at the clock: 5:45. In a few hours he'd go back to Max and Auddie's and try again. He hadn't seen Lily since he'd parked at the 7-Eleven. A searing pain radiated from his temple to the back of his head. He collapsed onto a stool and almost fell over backward, catching himself by slapping his hands on the kitchen counter. He traced the contour of the welt on his forehead. It was too sensitive to touch. He should at least check it out in the mirror, but he was afraid to even look at himself, the guy who lost his family. Twenty-four hours ago he thought he'd lost Lily. Now he'd lost Stephanie, too.

A random, horrific image manifested at the front his mind, a story he'd read about The Reign of Terror during the French Revolution. The worst resistors were put under the guillotine face-up rather than face-down. He instinctively pressed the bruise on his forehead until the sharp pain obliterated every thought but the pain. Holding his finger there, he cringed, emitting a distended animal sound across the roof of his mouth that vibrated his skull. Within moments it became intolerable. He dropped his hand to his side and made the intentional choice to try the opposite tack. He closed his eyes and tried being quiet, still, focusing on his breath. He put up an image on his mental screen of a serene mountain lake, gently rippling water reflecting Lily's smiling pink face. It seemed to help slightly.

At least Lily was safe. And she had a great mom. He'd have weekend visitations while Stephanie dated any number of guys who found her as achingly beautiful as he did. He thought of how early on in their relationship it sometimes hurt to even look at her because it called up the possibility that she might not always be there. Now it had happened. The guys she'd date would be cool dudes, not nearly as scatterbrained as him. They might even like kids. She'd never be with a guy that didn't like kids. But Lily would know how much he cared about her. He pictured himself in his little apartment in San Francisco playing his guitar, sending soundwaves across the ethers, Lily's little pink ears receiving the music vibrations. Would Stephanie let him see her? Was she even thinking straight, stealing her from his car, knowing how devastating it would be for him?

He looked up and saw that the house was no longer dark. Time was playing tricks on him. He decided he'd go back to Max and Auddie's, look in the guest-room window, see Lily's face, at least get to watch her sleep. Maybe she'd feel his vibe through the window and wake up. Or maybe the curtain would be closed. An abysmal sense of hopelessness coursed through his body like a shot of heroin, and he became aware of the high-pitched tinnitus he'd developed through the years of loud music. It was always worse when he didn't get enough sleep. The ringing in his ears and the sharp pain from his forehead forged into one piercing sensation.

Almost running to the bedroom, he flicked on the light and dug an old backpack out of his closet. At the bottom of the backpack was his exit-strategy pill bottle: a large prescription bottle of pain pills and pieces of pills that he'd saved over the years that he could swallow in two or three gulps and go to sleep forever. He used to think about it often, sometimes carry it around with him, but he hadn't considered it since the day Stephanie told him she was pregnant.

He went to the bathroom, took two pills, and chewed them. They tasted bad but worked faster that way. He drank some water and considered the pill bottle. It would take about ten seconds to pour the contents down his throat and be done with everything, just lie down and go to sleep. No drama, just quiet efficiency. Infinitely easier than starting a new life without Stephanie. Practically every moment-to-moment decision he made in his life, he considered her thoughtful, grounded perspective. He didn't have to ask her what she thought, he already knew. He'd be half a man without her, a crazy out-of-control motorboat going around in circles with no rudder. The lighthouse that always guided him home had gone dark. And that fucking song. It'd be impossible to sing it again. He held the pill bottle at his side, looked at the floor. His eyes landed on Lily's little four-inch cowboy boots, the ones Stephanie had bought for her first birthday. She had just barely learned to walk, and Stephanie only got them because she knew he would get a kick out of them. He remembered that day, Stephanie had decorated the living room and baked a cake and there were a half dozen toddlers and a few parents. When the frenetic activity died down, the last child left was one of Lily's older friends, six-year-old Chloe. Lily and Chloe were best buds. Woody offered to give her a ride home. As they'd wound through the neighborhood and approached Chloe's house, there was girl about her age on the sidewalk out front walking a dog. "Is she a friend of yours?" Woody had asked Chloe.

"She's my neighbor," Chloe said matter-of-factly. "She's the girl whose father killed himself."

Now, staring down at those cowboy boots, Woody knew at that moment he'd endure life's worst rather than leave Lily with that title. "I can't even die my way out of this," he thought.

He upended the pill bottle into the toilet and flushed the contents.

Looking in the mirror, he put the tips of his fingers under cold water and gently dabbed the edge of his wound, his eye halfway swollen shut. He should deal with it, go to a doctor, especially if he'd be seeing Max again. If he didn't, he'd look like a total loser.

Averting his attention from the mirror, he walked back to the bedroom to his closet, took off his clothes, and realized how badly he needed a shower. He hadn't had one since his night in jail. It wouldn't matter how bad he smelled if he lived alone, but if he did get to see Stephanie today, it definitely wouldn't help.

The clock next to the bed said another hour had passed. Time was acting strange.

He went back to the bathroom, got in the shower, and let cool water run over his head. When he noticed Lily's lavender baby shampoo, the thought of her curly angel-hair produced a stream of tears commingling with the water.

A towel around his waist, Woody walked back across the bedroom to his closet and took out a shirt Stephanie had ironed and put neatly on a hanger. A surrealistic image of his own skeletal body on a clothes hanger flashed before him. Then he pictured the pile of clothes on the floor of his closet in his San Francisco apartment and swore to himself he'd never throw a shirt on a closet floor again. It was time to stop trying to change Stephanie, time to change himself.

He held the shirt at eye level. She'd buttoned every other button. His chest constricted at the thought of never getting that kind of caring and kindness from her again. When he lowered the hangered shirt, he caught a glimpse of a shape across the room that sent an electric jolt through his body, and he jerked the shirt back up, blocking the view. No food, no sleep, maybe a concussion, his mind seemed to be departing on a vision quest of its own. His hand trembling, he tentatively peered back over the shoulder of the shirt. It was some kind of delirium, hallucinating the fantasy he so desperately yearned for. He stood staring at it, dripping wet hair stuck to his face, unable to keep the hanger from shaking. He dropped the shirt to his side and tried bringing into focus the shapes under the covers in his bed.

Could it be? Stephanie and Lily in bed, asleep?

Without taking his eyes off them, he ran his hand down the wall behind him and turned off the bedroom light. They were still there, a white stripe of sunlight from where the curtains weren't quite closed illuminating the side of Stephanie's face, Lily's body in the shape of a crescent moon, draped across the top of Stephanie's pillow like a baby hat.

Woody carefully hung up the shirt, went to the bed, and stood there, tears rolling down his cheeks, realizing that tears of joy tasted the same as tears of pain. He still couldn't believe his eyes. Stephanie and Lily must've come home in the middle of the night and gone to bed while he slept on the couch. Stephanie must've put that blanket on him. He'd been walking back and forth past them with the bedroom light on, not even seeing them when he'd checked the clock six inches from the bed.

He stood silently weeping, savoring the unbelievable sight then, as carefully as he could, dried himself off and slipped into bed. Stephanie opened her eyes, their faces inches apart under their comingled curly hair.

He inhaled the organic smell of her sleep and ran the back of his finger across her cheek.

She blinked slowly. "Lily made me come home."

Tears welled up in both their eyes. "I cried for both of us when I was in jail," he whispered.

"Me too," she whispered back. "What happened to your head?"

"Some sense got knocked into it."

Untangling her hand from the sheets, she went to touch it but didn't. "Does it hurt?"

"You and Lily are here. Nothing hurts. One drop of love cures an ocean of pain."

They held each other's teary gaze for so long it reminded them both of the five-day tantric workshop they'd attended early in their relationship. They'd sat in a lotus position facing one another, knees touching, staring into each other's eyes in silence for ten minutes every morning and every night, the remainder of the day spent working in the garden side by side in silence—the deepest interpersonal connection they'd ever shared.

"Namaste," Woody finally said.

She smiled. It was the single word they'd spoken each morning at the retreat. "Namaste," she said softly, "I honor the place in you where the entire universe dwells."

They held each other's gaze for another long minute.

"The only way out of this is through it," she said. "For us to make it to the other side, I'm afraid we'll have to talk." She closed her eyes, compressing out the tears. "But not now."

When he brushed her hair back from her face a minute later, she was already asleep.

—

An hour later, Lily now sleeping at the top corner of the bed, Woody and Stephanie woke up at almost the same moment and, as they often did, reached out under the covers. Naked, lying on their sides, they caressed each other with sleepy, languid strokes. He was hard and dry, she was soft and wet, both in the slow dreamy process of ascending to the surface of consciousness. Virtually sleep-walking, Stephanie gently scooped up Lily, carried her to her own bedroom, laid her down in her bed, and returned to Woody, who'd half-fallen back to sleep. She gradually moved her face down across his chest and stomach, scintillating curls of her hair fanning over him. She took him in her mouth and, minutes later, he heard the most gentle, beautiful music he'd ever heard in his life. She was faintly humming the melody to "Stephanie."

When she came to the chorus, her motion became more deliberate, her humming less audible until she turned back in the direction she'd come from, up across his chest, buried her face in his neck and, lying full length on top of him, guided him inside her with her hand.

They slowly moved together to an ethereal climax and drifted back to sleep, Stephanie still lying on top of him.

CHAPTER 8

Sitting at her apartment kitchen table in a white terrycloth bathrobe, hair wrapped in a white towel turban, Maria Angel, Ray Bell's attorney, looked like a mummy with eyes peering out of a brown layer of dried facial cream. Two cheap cassette players sat side-by-side on the table in front of her: one with a tape of Ray's highly produced version of "Stephanie" with a full orchestra that was still being played on the radio, and the other with Woody's minimalistic rendition, him singing and playing acoustic guitar.

She pressed play, listened to one line of Ray's version, then the same line of Woody's version, referencing a column of handwritten notes on a legal pad. She dug deep, listening, rewinding and replaying both tapes, homing in on a phrase, a word, even a syllable. It was a tedious process, listening for any anomaly or deviation between the versions. To a casual listener, the performances were pretty much the same, but on closer inspection there were departures. Were the differences enough to convince a jury that what Ray added to his version amounted to co-writing?

When she got to the final chorus of Woody's version, she let it play. She'd heard it many times and—as always—was moved when Woody belted out his final emotive "Stephanie!" Something about the plea in Woody's voice, his beseeching, plaintiff call to the love of his life, made it both authentic and disturbing, as real as art could be. Ray's smooth delivery was effortless to relate to, perfectly understated, powerful without being overbearing. His voice had a natural dynamism, its commercial attraction to mass-market music fans a given. Woody's singing felt intimate, compelling, but often erratic, on the verge of being out of control, leaving a listener feeling off-balance. It was impossible to relax listening to Woody sing.

She replayed Woody's last chorus again, then Ray's. Something was different. On the fourth playback, she figured out where it happened: the melody hook Ray added with his voice on the last line. Pouring herself another cup of coffee in her small kitchen, she sat back down and smiled at the cassette players. After endless hours of digging, she felt like she'd struck a vein of gold. With renewed energy, she played every chorus from both versions of the song; the hooky melody line on every one of Ray's choruses was lacking in Woody's. The difference was most pronounced in the last chorus, but she'd failed to recognize it before because Woody's singing in the last chorus was so emotive, it had always distracted her.

When she hit the stop button, a flake of dried face cream fell onto the tape player. She wiped it off, put both cassette players aside, and considered the piles of legal books and papers in front of her. The complexities of legal theories in the case would be challenging for a jury, but they could understand this simple *la-di-da* melody.

Maria patted the management agreement she had with Ray. In exchange for getting his record deal and handling his legal work, Ray agreed in writing to give Maria half of all royalties from "Stephanie."

She picked up another legal pad with an outline of her theory of the case: Woody solicited Ray to collaborate on the song, they worked on it together, but it was never finished. Then Ray recorded his own version and added his melody. Ray wasn't claiming to be the sole composer, only reasonably claiming he'd added part of it—the part that made the song a hit.

The biggest factual challenge was a tape that was rolling when Ray and Woody were working on the song in Woody's apartment. With the recorder on, Ray had said, "Stephanie's your song. Stephanie's your girlfriend, you've got every note and word figured out. I'm not singing somebody else's song without a budget." The night Ray was set to perform "Stephanie" at the Grammys and receive the award for best song of the year, Pearlman had threatened to play that tape for the television audience of millions unless Maria and Ray signed a release giving up rights to the song. They'd signed, but Maria felt confident a court would find it was signed under duress. As for the substance of the tape, their position was that it was irrelevant, Ray changed the song after that rehearsal when the tape was rolling, and he made it into a hit. They also had the fact that Woody's acoustic version that was released later sold only a small fraction of what Ray's sold. The reason: Woody's version didn't contain Ray's hooky melody line.

Granted, Woody had composed the original song-sketch about his girlfriend, now his wife. But at the time the song was written, Stephanie was working as a topless dancer at a club Ray frequented, and their relationship was open to speculation. Ray clearly could have been motivated to write a song about her.

She wrote "STEPHANIE'S BREASTS" in capitals at the top of the page and drew circles around each word with two check marks pointing sideways. The strongest leverage she had to get an out-of-court settlement wasn't a legal argument, it was Woody's jealousy about Stephanie having been a stripper. Pearlman would kick and scream, saying Stephanie's personal life was irrelevant and could never get to the jury, but there were ways to surreptitiously get things into court and still avoid a mistrial. And they all knew it wasn't about getting Stephanie's past history to the jury, it was about getting it to the press covering the trial—that's what would disturb Woody the most.

She dabbed at her face with a damp washcloth and flipped the pages of her legal pad to a page with CONFIDENTIAL written across the top. In an abundance of caution, she'd researched the penalties for suborning perjury. Did Ray really have permission to release the song in the first place, or had he actually stolen the words and music from the tape of that rehearsal session in Woody's apartment? Was she complicit? If details about music theory, notes, and chord structure came up at trial, did Ray know enough about music to defend his position that he was a co-writer? She knew Ray to be ninety percent showman, ten percent musician. And if the issue of perjury or her knowledge and participation in it ever did come up, she knew Ray'd sell her out in a heartbeat if it made him less culpable.

Maria's research was clear that besides exposure of up to three years in prison, an attorney could face permanent disbarment for perjury. But one defense was "if an attorney reasonably believed what their client told them to be true." Her thoughts spun out with the ramifications of being disbarred, including a ninety percent cut in pay if she went back to the waitressing she did in law school. She laid her hand on the bible-thick tome on the corner of her table: *Intellectual Property, Copyright, and Derivative Works*. "The truth, the whole truth, and nothing but the truth, so help me God." She quickly withdrew her hand; it felt odd talking out loud to herself.

She picked up the demand letter to Pearlman, her fourth draft threatening a lawsuit. It still wasn't right. She knew she'd never get it right because it was the wrong first move. She should just file a lawsuit, not send an obsequious letter. She'd worked at Pearlman's law firm for two years when she first passed the bar and always remembered him saying, "If someone sends you a letter threatening to file a lawsuit, they have a weak case, otherwise they'd just file."

She walked to the kitchen window. Arms folded, holding her coffee cup, she contemplated the traffic two stories below and wondered how she could possibly prevail against an opponent like Jeff Pearlman. He had a reputation of being one of the best trial lawyers in San Francisco, handling some of the most high-profile cases. He'd relish taking this case to trial. Her hope was that Woody would want to avoid press about Stephanie's past and Ray would want to avoid more negative press about who wrote the song…they'd both be ready to settle out of court. Bottom line, she badly needed the money. There was too much at stake not to try.

—

A square gauze bandage taped on his forehead, Woody stood at the window of Pearlman's corner office on the forty-fourth floor of San Francisco's Transamerica Pyramid Building. He looked past Alcatraz and the Golden Gate Bridge to the hills where he lived on Mount Tamalpais, trying to wrap his mind around the upcoming meeting with the vice president of Warner Brothers Records.

"How's your head?" Pearlman said.

"Empty."

"Things okay with you and Stephanie?"

"Things are thawing at the speed of a glacier. We have marriage on eggshells for breakfast. She still doesn't trust me with Lily."

"You can be right, or you can be married."

"Oddly enough, ever since I thought she left, if she does something that used to bug me, now it makes me happy 'cause it means she's still around."

"When I called the house, she asked if I knew about any modeling or acting jobs," Pearlman said. "She's worried about your finances. Royalties from 'Stephanie' are tapering off."

Woody put the tip of his nose and the toes of his sneakers against the window and looked down eight hundred feet, thinking about the pot he'd smoked in the parking lot. He thought that taking one puff might help him relax, ease the pain in his head. *Big mistake.* This hairline crack in his confidence would probably become a fissure when he got to the meeting. "Look sincere and budget your eye contact," he thought. "Pearlman will do the talking."

"Warner Brothers is betting a lot of money you can produce another hit without Ray Bell," Pearlman said.

The statement landed in Woody's stomach, enhancing the queasy vertigo from watching the jerky movements of the tiny cars almost a quarter mile below. Like dialing back the wrong end of a telescope, he brought his focus up to his red Converse sneakers. "Write a song without Ray Bell? I already did that. Ray stole it."

"We need another one as good as that. Tell you the truth, I don't think Warner Brothers record execs even *like* music. The bottom line: hit songs, that's what it's all about."

Woody raised one foot off the floor and danced a little twist. "You put your right foot in, you put your right foot out, do the hokey pokey, and turn yourself around...*that's what it's all about.*"

Pearlman smiled. "Sounds like a hit."

Woody turned back to the window. "Why's everyone in such a big hurry for this record? I thought people like their games going into overtime. Can't everyone just chill for a minute?"

"Record companies don't have patience. It's not in their contract *or* their vocabulary."

"Stephanie says patience is a form of action," Woody said to his sneakers. "Musicians have the time, record companies have the clocks." He looked across the room at Pearlman. "You know time is actually a man-made invention."

"Please, don't get all esoteric on me right now. It definitely won't get you anywhere with these record guys. If you're not up for doing this meeting today we can just—"

"They want me to write Ray Bell music?" Woody stepped back from the window. He dropped his hands and sighed. "My music doesn't have perfect teeth and a hundred-dollar haircut. This major-label thing feels like some kind of pilgrimage to nowhere. How am I supposed to get there when I don't even know where *there* is? It's like when a dog chasing a car catches the car...then what? The business of music, it's an oxymoron." He shrugged. "Me and these record guys speak different languages."

Pearlman leaned back in his big desk chair, folded his hands, and sighed. "So, let me try to unpack what you're saying. You prefer to go back to playing in crummy bars because you don't feel like talking to the vice president of Warner Brothers Records?"

"I just don't feel like I'm helpful at meetings." Woody began pacing. "Getting a group of people to communicate by playing music isn't easy, but it's way easier than getting a group of people to *talk* to each other. When I talk to those record guys it's like…it feels like I'm talking to somebody with their pants on backwards." He stopped pacing. "If by some miracle I do manage to write another hit song, who'd make more money from it—me or them?"

"It'd be close."

"People who work sitting down make more money." Woody sat in the closest chair. "I thought me and you had a kind of delegation of duties: you talk, I play music."

"They wanted to meet you. I thought, okay, let's give them something since we haven't given them a record." Pearlman picked up an eight-by-twelve glossy photograph, leaned back, and put his feet on his desk. "You really expect me to give this to Bernie?" It was a glossy black and white close-up of Woody with two ballpoint pens in his nose, pencils in his ears, paper clips for earrings, and the open end of a stapler protruding from his mouth.

"We were stoned, somebody said band photo. It's a joke. We'll get a proper one." Woody went back to pacing. Head down, long curly hair covering his face, each time he reached the end of the room Pearlman thought he might run his bandaged forehead into the wall of law books. Woody stopped. "I feel like I'm about to hit the wall."

Pearlman smiled, then saw Woody's troubled expression. "Those songs on that tape you gave me, they're beautiful, but they're unpredictable. Before they finish a complete thought, they move on to the next. Sound familiar? People want music they can trust."

"They say write about what you know. These days all I know is exhaustion. Sometimes I'm so busy, I don't have time to finish taking a piss. My mind's filled with static like a car radio." Woody collapsed into a chair in another sitting area in the expansive office. "It feels like I'm writing uphill. Whatever I do, I'm fucking up not doing something else. If I pick up my guitar, I'm not calling somebody back. It's weird. Me actually working on music doesn't get acknowledged the way a phone call or a meeting does. It's like I've got everything but time. I'm not a human *being*, I'm a human *doing*. I feel like I've lost my fastball." He sighed. "Am I making any sense?"

"You're thrown off balance with new responsibilities. A new baby, new house, new record deal. When I first met you, you were making a simple life complicated. Now the complications are piling on."

"It seems like accomplishments get less attention than failures, as if what could have happened is more important than what did happen."

Pearlman nodded thoughtfully. "Do one thing at a time. Finish one song."

"Last night I worked on a song until about five this morning, then counted the ten most important people and things I deal with these days. Then I took ten quarters and threw them on the table a hundred times to see what the chances are of everything coming up heads. No chance, zero." Woody looked out across the bay. "Hey, you can see my house from here."

Pearlman took his feet off his desk and looked out.

Woody pointed. "That part of Mount Tam they call 'The Sleeping Lady.' You can see my back deck by that clump of trees by her knees."

"You're right. I never realized that."

"Duh," Woody said, "I can see the top of this building from there." He snapped his fingers. "I got it. I've got an extra-long phone cord at home. For our next meeting, I'll stand there on my deck, a quarter inch tall, and talk to you and Bernie." He gave a little wave. "We can wave to each other."

The intercom on Pearlman's desk crackled on. "Jeff, the gentlemen from Burbank are here. They're in the conference room."

"Thanks, Brenda." Pearlman stood up, unsmiling. "This isn't just about you, Woody. A lot of people are invested in this—your band, your family, your fans, me. Even Lily wants you to make this work. The life you ordered has arrived." He contemplated Woody's thick file folder of contracts and correspondence on his desk. "What you bring to this meeting will determine what you get out of it." Pearlman picked up a blank yellow legal pad, Woody picked up his guitar. "And what you say isn't as important as how you say it."

—

Bernie Siegel, VP of Warner Brothers Records, had staked out his position at the head of the boat-shaped, polished-oak table with two young men in sport coats and skinny ties sitting to his right, one from accounting, one from A&R. He was a burly, chinless slab of man, his neck spilling over his collar with a ruddy, alcoholic's complexion and a helmet of gray hair ten years out of style with the sculpted look of a plastic model from the top of a wedding cake.

Pearlman took a seat at the opposite end and gestured to Woody to sit next to him. Woody walked past to a high-backed chair off to the side by the window, took his guitar out of its case, leaned back, strummed a soft chord, and gave everyone a little wave.

Introductions were made, and Pearlman gestured at the panorama of the city. "Thanks for coming up to the enlightened half of the state. Would you guys like some coffee or a cold drink?"

"We're fine," Bernie said without asking his associates.

"Hash, grash, acid?" Woody said. "Lick a frog?" Before anyone could react, Woody added, "Just kidding. Welcome to San Francisco. Thanks for coming up here to support my music."

"Who doesn't like San Francisco?" Bernie said. "The Fillmore, Haight-Ashbury, The Hookers Ball?" He tented the fingers of his big hands and cleared his throat. "Jeff, let's get right to the point of why we're here."

Pearlman leaned back. "What've you got, Bernie?"

"Woody's acoustic version of 'Stephanie' is sliding off the charts." He glanced to the young man to his right and got a quick affirmation. "As predicted, it was strong coming out of the gate, but sales are flat, or worse. Our bean counters are concerned." He glanced at Woody, who was incrementally swiveling his high-back chair toward the window. "The sales we *did* get from Woody's version came on the coattails of Ray Bell's hit. All the press about the authorship dispute only helped, but we expected Woody's version to have more legs." Bernie automatically went to his usual mannerism of massaging his temples, glanced at Woody's bandaged forehead and put his hands back on the table. "Pollstar numbers of Woody's live performances are impressive, but we need new, catchy songs. With those Pollstar numbers and a good record, we'd be right as rain. We need a record, and we need it yesterday. It's key, it's our primary promotion tool." With the progressing movement of Woody's chair toward the window, Bernie was now talking to the side of his face. Trying to hold the last periphery of his attention, Bernie quickly added, "I know the creative process doesn't always coincide with the schedule of the business model. We need to develop a teamwork dynamic that works for everyone."

Woody nudged his chair around another inch.

Bernie spoke quickly. "Bottom line, if the business model doesn't fly, the music doesn't get off the ground."

Woody was revisiting his regrets about smoking pot. Every word spoken weighed a hundred pounds. These record execs looked like cartoon caricatures. The robotic-looking suits next to Bernie were oddly two-dimensional, like they'd been sent over from central casting, and Bernie was an animated bobblehead with a bulbous R. Crumb nose. "Pearlman should be handling this," Woody thought. "I should be home writing songs. I could write a song about Bernie."

"Bernie," Pearlman said, "maybe it's unrealistic to expect a second wave of sales from an acoustic song on the heels of a highly produced mega-hit. Besides the excellent new songs Woody's working on in the studio, there's a healthy tape-trading network of live shows that boosts his attendance. We need to tailor our approach to the artist, not vice-versa."

"Since you've brought it up, our top brass in distribution are concerned about the way Woody allows taping at his shows. He's literally giving away his music. Warners has the exclusive right to distribute Woody's music. We've paid handsomely for that right." Bernie glanced toward Woody and cleared his throat. "We don't know what made 'Stephanie' so popular, the song itself or Ray's singing. It's a well-constructed song, but there's no way to really know. We need to keep our options open. Woody might consider a songwriting career rather than recording, bring in someone like Ray Bell to sing."

"I suppose we could try something like that," Woody said looking down at the table. "But it might be like dissecting a frog. You get some good information, but the frog dies."

While he considered how to respond, Bernie thought he heard some faint music and scanned the ceiling for hidden speakers. "We need to anticipate trends, stay ahead of the curve. Everything these days has that catchy disco beat. Now I'm not suggesting—" Bernie stopped midsentence and glared in the direction of Woody, who was lightly strumming his strings with the edge of his thumb, barely audible. Bernie could now only see his long curly hair hanging over the back of his chair. He slapped a meaty hand on the table. "Woody!"

Woody deadened his strings and swung his chair around. The two young men next to Bernie kept their eyes down, the points of their pens pressing into their legal pads.

Bernie pushed his open hands forward on the table, his forehead wadded into corrugated lumps. "We're talking about your *career*. That's what we came all the way up here for." He pulled out a handkerchief and mopped his brow. "If you think this is some kind of futile exercise we can just—"

"Bernie." Pearlman leaned in. "I'm representing Woody here. If you have something to say…"

"I've said what I have to say. Legal tells me Woody's already breached the recording schedule in his contract. There's been nothing but delays and piling up studio costs." He punched his fist into his hand. "We want this to work, but the reality is, we've got a thousand talented singer-songwriters beating down our doors ready to make a record at a moment's notice."

Pearlman leaned in, matching Bernie's energy. "Woody wrote a mega-hit. There are plenty of record companies eager to release his next song. When Woody's on, it's as good as it gets. He's got an album's worth of solid songs with commercial potential close to being finalized."

"Give me a date."

"Soon. The recording process isn't linear."

"What about the band?" Bernie kept his eyes on Pearlman while he gestured at Woody. "We've put his supposedly crackerjack band into a top-notch studio and word has it there's more socializing going on than actual work. If you want things to stay the way they are, something has to change." He slapped the table. "Close to being finalized? Not linear? What's all that gibberish supposed to mean? We need song release dates!"

Woody played a soft chord. "It feels weird, you guys talking about me like I'm not here."

Pearlman nodded at him. "You've got the floor maestro."

Woody met everyone's eyes one by one. "My music pretty much says everything I have to say. It's like…the only way I know how to speak honestly is through my music." He strummed a chord, let it die out, and what came to mind was something he'd read about Asian cultures pausing between phrases while Americans feel compelled to fill in every void. Asian people take an average of eight seconds to respond to a sentence—twice, or even three times, as long as Americans. He decided to wait and an unsettling silence took hold, growing exponentially more uncomfortable with each passing moment. Everyone reflexively reverted to their go-to body language. Bernie cleared his throat, leaned in, and clasped his hands; Pearlman leaned back and folded his arms across his chest; accounting and A&R doodled in the margins of their legal pads. The deafening silence quickly reached a breaking point when Woody and Bernie both spoke at the same time.

"I'm not sure I should be here—"

"If you think we came up here—"

They both stopped mid-sentence, waited a few seconds, then started to speak again at the same moment.

"Music and conference rooms—"

"Musicians and meetings—"

Bernie demurred with a nod, leaned back, and folded his hands across his large midsection.

Woody lowered his shoulders, rested his hand on top of his guitar, and for a few seconds everyone thought he was going to allow the silence to return. Bernie re-centered his weight and leaned in, about to speak, when Woody dropped his hand across a soft minor chord. "Before I say anything at all," he said, "let me say this: I can't not be myself…I have no choice in the matter." He swiveled his chair to face Bernie directly. "It may not seem like it, but I actually appreciate you coming up here, trying to figure me out, trying to figure what to do with my music." He took a deep breath and exhaled. "I came to this meeting empty, open to whatever the universe brings. As far as what I have to offer, all I have is my music. Making plans about how, when, where it gets played—I don't have a clue; that's your department. My songwriting process is like…sometimes doing nothing is doing something." He gestured at the window. "While we're sitting here, the earth is spinning at a thousand miles an hour, but it feels like we're standing still. I stay on my toes, stay vigilant, so that when a song is ready to be born, I'm there in the delivery room with a guitar in my hands." He played the first six notes of "Happy Birthday to You."

The sweaty speed bumps reappeared on Bernie's forehead.

The young man from accounting ran his fingertips across the binding at the top of his pad, and the A&R man two seats from Bernie, whose job was to recognize potential hit songs, spoke for the first time. "Sounds like a hit."

No one knew what he meant until Woody re-played the first Happy Birthday notes and there were chuckles and a palpable release of tension in the room.

Bernie dropped his shoulders and brought out his first smile. "I'd sure like to hear what you've been recording."

"The birth of my new songs is imminent," Woody said. "The contractions are coming closer together. Depending on the key, some of them might need a C-section." Everyone smiled, the gravity in the room reduced by half.

"I look forward to hearing them," Bernie said.

"We'll get you some rough mixes within one week," Pearlman said. "You have my word. Want to show me those accounting statements?"

Bernie nodded to accounting on his right. Without skipping a beat, the man opened a manila folder and put down four pages of spreadsheets in front of Bernie, snapping down the corner of each page like a blackjack dealer.

Woody stood up. "Gentlemen, if you'll excuse me, I've got to drop a couple of kids off at the pool." He gave a little bow over his guitar and walked out.

Bernie looked at Pearlman and raised his eyebrows.

Pearlman smiled. "He's going to the bathroom."

The A&R man and accountant both chuckled.

Bernie shook his head. "What is it with that guy? I can't figure him out."

"It's deeper than you or I will ever understand," Pearlman said. "He's so deep into music, English is his second language. He eats, drinks, and shits music."

—

While Bernie and his assistants gathered their papers, Pearlman thanked them and walked out through the reception area, where Brenda, the receptionist, was on the phone. Pearlman peeled the stack of pink phone messages off the metal spike on her desk and leafed through them as he walked down the hallway.

"Mr. Pearlman?"

He turned and continued sorting the messages.

"While you concluded your meeting, Woody used the restroom then went into your office. I tried telling him your office was private, with confidential documents. He said something about attorney-client privilege and his music-archive suppository, which I didn't think was funny, then went into your office and closed the door."

"Thanks, Brenda."

Pearlman opened his office door and saw Woody sitting across the room, playing and singing into a telephone receiver lying on a side table. Pearlman leaned against the door and listened. The song was a melodic rock ballad with poignant lyrics about a family of squirrels trying to make it through a harsh winter, using their tails as toboggans, the mother squirrel getting nourishment just from the act of feeding her children. Pearlman was still listening when Bernie and his assistants came through the lobby. Bernie heard the music, walked over, and stood next to Pearlman, his assistants almost walking into his back.

Woody repeated the final chorus and picked up the phone. "She asleep? No? Okay, I'll try a couple of verses of 'I Will Love You.' She likes that one." Woody sang in almost a whisper.

Through the long long night
When daylight fails
And the beasts of the forest
Wrap themselves in their tails
To sleep through winter
Awake with the spring
And the valley of danger
With birdsongs rings

I will love you
I will
Love you

Through the false tribulations
And the true actual pain
Through the torrents of cloud
With their fingers of rain
That beat on the shutters
And creep under the door
Leave signatures in sediment
That seep across the floor

I will love you
I will
Love you

Woody sang progressively softer:

Through the moral situations
When both my hands are tied
And either way I waver
Seems to be the losing side

Through the things I bring upon myself
And those that come for free
I will keep my faith in you
If you will keep your faith in me

I will love you
I will love you
I will
Love you

"Okay? Great," Woody said. "See you tonight." He gently hung up, turned, and saw his small audience.

"Nice song," Bernie said, "beautiful melody hook. What's it called?"

"'A Baby's Coefficient of Friction.'"

"Well, it's—"

"Just kidding," Woody said, "It's called 'I Will Love You.' It's a Robert Hunter song I found in an old songbook. My wife Stephanie was having trouble getting our twelve-month-old daughter to sleep for her afternoon nap. That song usually does the trick. Stephanie says for Lily it's like kissing a cloud."

"Get me a demo of it," Bernie said. "It's got a hook that could catch a whale."

CHAPTER 9

Ray gripped the sides of his bathroom sink and stared at himself in the harsh fluorescent light. The skin on his face seemed to be losing its shape, drooping from its scaffolding. *Now what? Back to bed for more dream torture?* It was 9:00 a.m. He'd woken up covered in sweat, the sheets soaked. A towel around his waist, he walked around the house, kicking empty cardboard boxes, his head throbbing. How many drinks had it taken to finally get to sleep at five this morning?

He stopped in front of his piano. What was that melody that sounded so intriguing last night? Still standing, he plunked some notes, tried humming along, and couldn't remember what he'd played. He picked up a scrap of paper with lyric ideas he'd scribbled watching the sun coming up over the city.

no love/no hate
no wife/no strife/no life
no sleep/no rest/arrest
dreams
screams
crashing beams

If he could remember the melody, maybe the words would make sense. He slapped the paper down on the piano. He needed some coffee, or a drink, or both. He went to the kitchen, made a cup of instant coffee, added a healthy shot from a bottle of vodka, picked up the phone, and dialed the number he knew well.

"A&M Records, good morning."

"Ray Bell for Marty Levine."

"Please hold while I transfer you."

"Marty Levine's office."

"Greta, it's Ray."

"Hello, Ray. Marty's on the phone, can I take a message?"

"I left two messages this week, I need to talk to him."

"I gave him your messages, Ray. He's on the phone, and he has someone waiting."

"I'll hold."

"Suit yourself, it could be a while."

Five minutes later, "Ray?"

"Hi, Marty. How're you doing? I've been trying to reach you, and I thought maybe we could—"

"Hold on, Ray, I need to put you on hold."

Another five minutes, "Standby, Ray, one more call and I'm all yours."

Ray made himself another cup of coffee.

"Ray?"

"I'm all yours."

"Sorry, it's been nuts around here. You sound terrible. You have gravel for breakfast?"

"I left you a couple messages."

"I've been totally jammed. You got me now. What've you been doing with yourself?"

"Writing songs. I'm ready to make a new record."

"You have an album's worth of original songs?"

"Some of my own, some others."

"Your catalogue's been flagging, Ray. You need another single like 'Stephanie.' I thought we agreed on that last time we spoke. You said you were co-writing. Get me something to listen to."

"I'm on it, Marty. Put me in the studio."

"When the material's ready, not before. The days of fat recording budgets for musicians to jerk off in the studio for a month are gone the way of horse-drawn wagons."

"How about a gig opening for one of your big-shot acts? That new diva on A&M—Chevy? She's got the voice. She's topping all the charts."

"It's not that easy, Ray. There's big competition for those opening slots. Bands are paying *us* to get a chance to open the shows. I have to put you on hold for one more sec; I've been waiting for this call all week. Standby."

Ten minutes passed while Ray gazed out the window at the Golden Gate Bridge, finishing his coffee and grinding his teeth. "Ray?"

"Still here."

"Sorry about that. I've been waiting for that call forever. If you ever wonder if you should judge somebody by what they say or what they do, always go by what they do. Now, what were you saying?"

"Me and Chevy would make a great double bill. We could sing a duet to close the show. She's one of the few singers out there with a voice as strong as mine. Singing together, we'd kill it."

"Maybe I could get you a date with her instead of a date *singing* with her. Knowing you, that's probably what you're after anyway. Those opening act slots are gold, Ray. I can't just snap my fingers and—"

"I'm looking for a break, Marty. After all I've done for A&M's bottom line?"

"That was several years ago. Things change fast in the music business. Ray, as a friend, let me be straight with you. Word has it you're not taking care of yourself. A certain horn player described you as a vampire living on left-over groupies and vodka. Is it true you're actually selling your toenail clippings through your fan club? I mean, c'mon Ray, you know how this works. Record sales, ticket sales: that's what talks, everybody else walks…hold on…Greta, tell Lindsey I'll be with him in five. Ray, have you been in touch with Harvey? He's working a matinee in Vegas. I heard it's decent money."

"Harvey? Vegas? I'm not ready for casinos."

"One sec, Ray. Greta, we better put off Stevie 'til later this afternoon. I don't want her bumping into Lindsey in the lobby. Last time those two were on a stage together there was broken furniture in the dressing room. Ray, listen, I gotta split. Get me a cassette of your new songs."

"I'm working on it, Marty. In the meantime, I gotta get something going."

"In the meantime, *I* gotta get something going…*me*. Bubbala, we'll be in touch, get me a cassette, and careful with that vampire stuff, I heard type-O can be contagious."

Ray hung up and stared at the phone. There was about an inch of vodka in the bottle on the kitchen table. He mixed it with some orange juice from the refrigerator and drank it down in one gulp. Who could he call for a gig? He'd already tried calling the major touring bands he knew and had resorted to sitting in with local bar bands, looking for any decent-paying gig. Word traveled fast of his heavy drinking and the fact that he'd fallen off a two-foot stage into an audience. He knew his only avenue toward any modicum of success was another hit song. Eying the empty vodka bottle, he knew that's what had erased the catchy melody he had at the piano last night. Or just as likely, the vodka had created a hallucination of a catchy melody. His new plan: hit the liquor store today and drink enough to float a melody but not enough to drown it.

—

Murray glanced around the crowded restaurant where he and Woody were having lunch. He only went to upscale places like this with Woody. It wasn't long ago that, for both of them, going out for a meal meant a burrito or a slice of pizza. Now they were the only ones in the upscale restaurant in flannel shirts and faded jeans. "What time's your recording session?" Murray said.

"Two o'clock."

Murray glanced at his watch. "It's almost two thirty."

"I guess we should get going." Woody took a forkful of salad. "I wanted to give the energy a chance to gel before I get there." He noticed how close Murray kept his face to his plate when he ate, and the large pool of ketchup on his plate. "Ketchup soup?"

"No. Yeah. It's how I like it." Murray said with his eyes closed. "What's with you always being so judgmental about other people's condiments?" He picked up the bottle of ketchup. "It's like you're some kind of condiment cop." Murray mopped up extra ketchup with some fries, tucking the aberrant ends of long ones into his mouth. "It's like you think there's some God-given perfect amount of condiments. I'm not one of those guys in your band that's supposed to play what *you* think they're supposed to play." Murray shrugged. "I just like ketchup. What's your trip about it?" He picked up the saltshaker and shook it extra hard on his fries. "And I don't even wanna hear about how much salt I use."

"I get it," Woody said. "There's salt and pepper on every table on the planet. European white guys practically conquered the world just because of the difference between potatoes with salt and no salt."

Woody ate thoughtfully for a couple of minutes. "Maybe it's a pack-animal thing."

"What?"

"About your question, why *I* care about *your* condiments." Woody pointed his fork at Murray's plate. "That pool of ketchup triggers something in me. I'm just speculating here, but maybe I just instinctually want what's best for the herd. A zebra that wanders off by herself is vulnerable. Deviant behavior is dangerous."

"Deviant ketchup?"

A young woman coming toward them from across the room caught Woody's eye. From thirty feet away he could tell she had a bead on him. Estimating the timing of her trajectory, he turned to Murray and spoke quickly. "It's like the way everybody's judgmental about how everybody else makes a fire. Everything's about survival. We're all part of the same web. There's not individual trees or even individual forests, the earth is covered with one big tree. And a band doesn't happen by one guy telling another guy how to play, it happens by breathing the same air."

The young woman in an ankle-length dress and fringed leather vest approached their table. "Excuse me, Woody, sorry to disturb you while you're eating."

Woody inhaled the thick aroma of patchouli oil. She had sparkles on her cheeks, a surplus of bracelets and necklaces, and waist-length hair drawn back with two life-size butterfly hairpins.

She acknowledged Murray and turned to Woody. "Really sorry to bother you. I saw you through the window and like, me and my boyfriend, actually my fiancé, we love your song 'Stephanie' so much we named our daughter Stephanie. Sorry to barge in on you and everything but, do you think I could get your autograph to give it to Stephanie for when she's old enough to appreciate it?"

Woody picked up his napkin and wiped his mouth. "Actually, I'm just having lunch. I don't really have a piece of pen or paper or anything and...I'm kind of busy at the moment."

With a chime of rattling bracelets, she retrieved a pen from her beaded purse and gestured to the white cloth napkin in Woody's hand. "It'll only take a sec. I know this seems rude and everything, but it's like, Stephanie will have it when she grows up. She'll have it for the rest of her life." She looked to Murray for support.

Murray looked at his plate.

She made another gesture toward Woody's napkin. "Maybe if you could just like take a sec and like…" she shrugged.

Woody looked at the soiled napkin in his hand. "You're serious?"

She glanced around at the nearby tables then leaned in. "I know I'm being a pushy mom." She gripped her pen with her thumb-ring made from a spoon handle. "Who else would do this?"

Woody shook his head and smiled. "Motherly love, the most powerful force in the known universe." He smoothed out his napkin on the table and opened his hand. "Can I borrow your pen?"

Her face turned red.

Woody took a moment to find a clean spot. With difficulty he applied the ballpoint pen to the cloth and signed his name… *To Stephanie.*

She kissed him on the cheek and walked out clutching the napkin.

He watched her weave through the restaurant, long hair swaying across her hips like a horse's tail. "Women carry a gene that makes them want to make the world a better place for children, and that makes the world a better place. The women are smarter." He went to take a forkful of salad with the woman's pen and smiled. "I'll eat later. Let's split."

—

The valet parking attendant saw the guys coming and within minutes was at the curb with the Corvette, top down. Woody gave him five dollars and drove off, chirping his tires.

Murray's head snapped back, he grabbed his baseball cap. "I think just drop me off at my place."

"You don't like music?"

"The music's great when you actually play. When you go over the same song a hundred times it gets kinda boring. Could you slow down a little?"

Woody stayed behind the car he was about to pass. "Billy might be bringing one of those Thai sticks."

"You think Amber will be there?"

"Neolithic tree resin? Could get sticky."

"You know who I mean."

"That sweet chick with the dreads?"

"Yeah," Murray said with his eyes closed. "I've never really talked to her."

Woody felt as if he could mechanically close Murray's eyes by asking him a question. "Eyelids are maybe the most authoritative function of the human body," he said.

Murry shrugged. "I can think better with my eyes closed. That girl Amber seems pretty shy. Between the two of us, we'll probably never talk."

"Our tiny speck-of-dust-size planet is not the center of the universe, and talking to a shy girl isn't the end of the world. You're a national treasure, Murray—she'll like you."

Murray looked like a dog that just had its head scratched. Woody put his hand on the chrome gear-shifter but resisted shifting. "There's a lot of people hanging around the sessions lately, which is okay. I like the buffer between the sharp edges of the band. It's amazing the difference an audience makes—even one person in the corner reading a book. Think Yoko Ono." The car in front of them slowed, and Woody downshifted and accelerated around it. "But it's getting hard to get stuff done. The studio's become one big party."

"I think just drop me off at my place," Murray said. "I have cleaning stuff I do on my day off."

"Cleaning? Your place is the neatest place I've ever seen."

"It's good for constipation."

"We come from dust and return to dust," Woody said. "I try not to dust too much, it could be someone I know."

"Could you please slow down?"

Woody let off on the gas, took out a half-joint out of the ashtray, lit up, and passed it to Murray. "That's cool about Jimmy Carter pardoning the draft dodgers. What's your number?"

"Number?"

"Your draft number."

"4-F. Flat feet."

"Flat feet?"

"Yeah, flat feet."

It was the first time Woody had considered Murray's feet. Now that he mentioned it, Murray did often seem to be padding around in clown shoes.

Overweight, round shoulders, and a bad complexion, he knew Murray couldn't care less about his personal appearance. He had the simple virtues of someone who spends most of their time alone…and people who live alone appreciate their friends. Hanging out with him was a breeze compared to his exhausting relationships with neurotic musicians.

"That's a lucky break, not going to Vietnam," Woody said. "I got a 4-F by going mental in my interview with a combat sergeant. I took some acid, blurted out a tirade of random stuff, then told him I had a secret to tell him and stuck my tongue in his ear. I can taste it to this day. Like sticking your tongue in a hairy bottle of warm Elmer's Glue."

"Whenever you start talking, you start speeding up."

Woody took his foot off the gas. "Sorry, I guess I spaced out."

Murray passed back the joint. "You have a full pardon."

CHAPTER 10

The Record Plant, Northern California's premier recording facility, was one of the first professional studios in the country to transition from an antiseptic, business-like environment to an adult playground designed to foster creativity. Traditionally, studios were officious, florescent-lit affairs with amenities that amounted to a coffee pot, an ashtray, and a couch. The Record Plant took the recording experience in the opposite direction, with a creativity-enhancing environment so fun and friendly that clients would enjoy just hanging out on the clock at four hundred dollars an hour. It featured an attractive female staff, soft mood lighting, cushy furniture with pinball machines, ping-pong and pool tables, a hot tub, sauna, in-house masseuse, and beer in the soda machine. It could take Woody an hour just to find his band and assemble them in one room. Tonight was no exception. Everyone was finally assembled at their instruments, ready to play.

Malcolm, the keyboard player, picked up the sheet music on his piano. "'If God Took Acid She'd See People?' What kind of song is this? I get the cute play on words, but maybe your personal view of spirituality doesn't represent the whole band."

His electric guitar hanging from his neck, Woody took his time lighting a cigarette. "So you're saying what? The existence of atheists proves there's a God?"

Malcolm ran the back of his knuckles across his piano keys and banged a dissonant chord. "How about a little respect is all I'm saying."

"Easy there, cowboy. The concept of soul is man-made." Woody wedged his burning cigarette between two strings in the headstock of his guitar, put on his headphones, and said into his microphone, "Those devil notes you just played were once banned by the church."

Billy tilted his head back and yelled into the overhead microphones above his drums; "In London, they use those notes for police sirens to get people's attention." His bulky headphones were secured on his head by a wide strip of silver duct tape. "Besides, mates, it was James Brown that invented soul."

"Whatever," Malcolm said, "let's play something." He snapped his headphones over his knit cap with a Christian fish-symbol on it.

"Okay," Woody said, "we'll try a different song, but don't tell the other song we're working on this one."

"Sounds like adultery, which most songs are about anyway." Billy took a drink of beer. "Let's 'ear the groove, mate."

"I thought no drinking when we're recording," Malcolm said.

"I thought no *thinking* when we're recording." Billy raised his beer in a toast. "No worries, mate, it's a medical thing. I'm just nursin' me drink."

"This song's in G," Woody said, "the people's key, a rock ballad." He went into the chord changes.

Billy laid down a relaxed ballad beat, hitting the snare at the last millisecond of each measure, creating a tension that made the song feel like it was slowing down when it wasn't. Within four bars, the bass player and keyboard player came in as if they'd played the song before and the tenor sax blew a shimmering melody.

Woody started singing "Song For Lily"—poignant verses about a mother squirrel as a metaphor for parental love, a microcosm of universal love. While Woody sang softly, the other musicians looked down at their instruments. They all knew what had happened with Lily.

Woody replaced the vocals with a melodic guitar run, weaving in an instrumental aviary of fluttering notes, then transitioned back to the repeating lullaby lyrics until they all dissolved into silence and sat listening to each other breathing in their headphones.

"Betty?" Woody said into his microphone.

"Got it," she said from the control room. Betty Spitalnik, with her yellow corn-silk hair and coke-bottle-thick glasses with red plastic frames, was one of the best audio engineers in Northern California. Woody loved working with her. "You want to listen back or do another one?"

The glass separating them reminded Woody of sitting behind the thick glass in the jail. He wondered if looking through glass like that would always produce that same memory. He took the guitar off his neck. "Let's take a break. I'll come in and check out the last take." He pushed open the heavy insulated door to the control room and sat in the high-backed producer's chair. Betty rewound the two-inch tape and hit the big green "play" button.

"Beautiful song," Betty said when it was over. "Has Pearlman heard this one?"

"Once, in his office, on my acoustic guitar."

"The band plays well with everyone in the same room, but the drums bleed into the vocal mic. It'll be hard mixing vocals with drums on the track. Feel like putting down another vocal by yourself?"

"Not really," Woody said, "but give me a track, I'll give it a try."

The rest of the band retired to the lounge and Woody pushed open the vault-like door into the vocal booth, a soundproof closet with wall-to-wall foam padding. His head of curly hair turned into a wildly shaped bouffant when he put on the big headphones. "Betty, you there?"

"I'm one big ear. How's your level?"

"Check, check. Let me hear it with the band."

The music started. "Give me a little reverb, and more high end. Treble's my middle name."

Woody sang a verse and stopped. Betty stopped the tape. "What's up?"

"Some stuff recently went down between me and my daughter. I sing this song when I put her to sleep, not in a claustrophobic vocal booth."

Betty knew what had happened with Lily. "Got a picture?"

"A picture?"

"Of your daughter."

"Good idea." Woody took a picture of Lily out of his wallet and wedged it eye-level on the microphone stand. It was the picture he'd shown the cop and later found wrinkled at the bottom of the bag of his personal items from the jail. "Roll it, Betty."

"That was better, but a bit forced. Do another take?"

"When did 'take' become a noun?"

"Are we doing vocals or semantics?

Woody did his best to relax and let the words flow out of his body. When he took another break, Pearlman was sitting at the board.

"Well?"

Pearlman folded his hands in his lap, which Woody didn't take as a good sign. "Take your time," Pearlman said. "It's a lullaby. You're trying to make the aperitif the entrée."

"How about I go home and get Lily and her bed," Woody said. "I'll bring her into the vocal booth and sing until she's asleep. That's how we'll know when we've got it. You had lunch yet?"

"Not yet."

"I had a cigarette for breakfast." Woody put his hand on the door to the vocal booth. "I'll try one more. I'll pretend I'm putting Lily to sleep, you pretend you're eating a sandwich."

Woody sang it again, gave it his soulful best, but wasn't feeling it.

"How was your sandwich?" he said into the mic.

Pearlman pressed the talkback button. "I don't know why, but I'm still hungry."

—

With the band occupied playing pool, Woody and Pearlman went five minutes down the street to the Trident restaurant for its good food and outdoor deck overlooking the Bay. They scored their favorite table by the railing.

With just enough fog to moderate the summer temperature and enough light wind to keep the hundreds of sailboats on the bay tacking out of each other's way, Marin County weather was at its best. Pearlman gazed out across the water. "'Song for Lily' is a beautiful song."

"We need to re-do the sax licks so they land in between the vocal phrases, not on them. Jupiter plays some soulful stuff, but sometimes he gets musical incontinence."

Pearlman looked across the bay at the Transamerica Building, trying to make out which window was his forty-fourth-floor office. "It's not the sax."

Woody raised his eyebrows.

"Honestly, it's the singing. It's about your core energy, or lack of it right now. Maybe it's about what went down with Lily and Stephanie. When you sing from your heart and play guitar straight out your fingertips without stumbling over your thoughts, a listener can hear it, whether they know it or not."

Woody looked for a waitress. Four in the afternoon, the deck was an amalgam of tourists having a late lunch and musicians having Bloody Marys for breakfast. A dramatic-looking woman a few tables away with bleach-blonde hair and thick-mascaraed eyes caught Woody's attention. She had what looked like four bloody gashes on the side of her face. When she moved her head and her hair fell away, he realized he was seeing four ultra-long, blood-red fingernails of the hand her head rested on. He drained his water glass.

Pearlman turned to see what he was looking at. "You looking at that blonde in the back?"

"She looked like her face was bleeding. It was her red fingernails."

"Today probably wasn't a good day to try recording."

"After all that went down with Lily, I had a feeling it'd either be the perfect time to get an emotional performance or impossible. Good music happens like rain. You live your life, do your best—sometimes it rains, sometimes it doesn't."

"Things any better at home?"

"Stephanie said we needed to talk, it'd be like taking out a splinter, painful in the short term but necessary. Our conversation turned into yelling. Lily didn't like it. So then we tried a no-talking day. As usual, Lily was doing most of the blabbing, we just responded with smiles and watched her slowly pick up on the silence. She doesn't learn from what we say, she learns by example. It was far out, two adults and a twelve-month-old, taking walks, cooking, eating meals, all in total silence."

The noise level from conversation in the restaurant grew louder. Pearlman leaned in. "You think you and Steph will be okay?"

Woody shrugged. He looked for their waitress, he was hungry. "She talks about patience and I'm always in a hurry. She says everything will be alright in the end. If it's not alright, it's not the end." Woody stared out at the bay. "Stephanie's the only one I've ever met that understands that when I stare into space I'm actually working. One positive thing about this mess, it's made me more aware of the feminine side of music."

"I got a call from a TV producer looking for a mother-daughter for a baby-food commercial, the kind of natural product Stephanie might like. Lily'd look great on television, so would Stephanie. She could make some money, get out of the house, might be fun."

"We don't even have a TV," Woody said. "Stephanie says it's child abuse to let a child watch it. People with TV relationships couldn't survive in the real world, it's not something kids should be exposed to." He looked around the restaurant. "Our waitress is probably outside smoking a joint."

"Speaking of which, that band of yours smokes a lot of pot. They're pretty scattered, it's like you're herding cats."

Woody saw a super-tanker heading directly into a sailboat with a woman sailor arched backward over the side, the full weight of her body on the line of her mainsail. The sailboat narrowly avoided the collision and Woody took a breath. "When we finally do gather the band and it clicks…it's worth the trouble. It's like, one note can be nice, but it gets boring pretty quick. Combinations of notes is what make things happen. A high note, low note, sad note, happy note—same with musicians. When one guy in the band is sad, one guy's hungry, one has the flu, and one's been depressed his whole life, the sound of that chaos is interesting. You might end up with a circular firing squad, but it's interesting. Being in a band doesn't build character, it reveals it. Like you said, the listener hears the source whether they know it or not."

"The way Bernie sees it, he's spending thousands of dollars for a group of dysfunctional guys to have a place to smoke pot and play pool. I don't think you get how serious this is. Bernie's one of a small handful of guys that can actually make things happen…or not happen. You blow this deal with him, it could impact everything in your life. You could end up back…" Pearlman stopped and rubbed his neck. "Bernie's like a screaming thermometer, indicating what's actually going on in the music industry at any given time. You can ignore the thermometer, but it doesn't change what's happening." He went back to rubbing his neck. "I need some coffee."

A waitress walked up to their table in a short skirt, platform shoes, and a paisley headband barely containing the curly blonde afro hanging over her eyes. She glanced at Woody's like-minded hair, tilted her head sideways in acknowledgement, and held up her pad and pen.

"We don't have menus," Pearlman said.

She looked over the top of her pad. "Sorry, guys, you're not the only ones out to lunch today." Her voice was ultra-high and squeaky like a Betty Boop cartoon. "It's my real voice." She turned to leave.

"Eggs benedict," Woody said.

She spun like a ballerina and raised her pad. "You're gonna improvise?"

Woody smiled. "And coffee."

She nodded at Pearlman. "Sir?

He gave her a peace sign.

She returned it. "Peace, brother, what'll you have?"

"Make it two eggs benedict and coffee."

She jotted down the order with a flourish like scrawling an autograph, ended with a hard point period with her pen, curtsied, and started to walk away.

"Did you put vocals on anything?" Pearlman said to Woody.

The waitress spun back around and raise her pad. "Vocals on eggs benedict will cost extra." She held her deadpan look for a long moment, broke into a smile, did another curtsy, and walked away.

"I talked to Bernie again before he left town," Pearlman said. "Your acoustic version of 'Stephanie' did even fewer sales than he thought."

Woody turned and gestured to the waitress a few feet away.

She changed course and walked over. "Craving more attention?"

"Can I get a Bloody Mary, with a splash of vocals?"

"One Bloody Mary, blended three-part harmony." She raised her eyebrows. "I know what you're thinking. It's the voice I was born with…for real." She spun a pirouette and walked off.

"Have you heard the new Bee Gees record?" Pearlman said. "Bernie says disco's infectious beat is the direction radio's going, replacing rock, replacing everything."

"Three young white guys sounding like three old black women and a drum machine." Woody shrugged. "The grooves *are* pretty catchy. I guess it's where de-evolution ends up."

"De-evolution?"

"Ever see a bird's nest full of junk cars? Humans are obviously at the bottom of the evolutionary ladder, the bottom rung is a drum machine.'

"Bernie's just trying to stay relevant. He studies radio charts, anticipates people's tastes. He's very successful at what he does."

"P.T. Barnum said you can't go broke underestimating the taste of Americans."

The waitress brought Woody an exotic Bloody Mary concoction in an extra-large glass with celery, olives, a cooked shrimp, slice of crispy bacon, and a skewered marijuana bud on a plastic toothpick. From the elevation of her platform shoes, she had to bend over almost in half to set the drink down. "My partner's the bartender. When you take a drink you get a whiff of the bud, it's her specialty." She smiled and skittered away on her clacking high heels.

Pearlman nodded at the drink. "I've met her partner, nice ladies, a couple of swingers. They call it stunt garnish."

Woody maneuvered the floating pastiche with his celery stick and looked out over the water. "Generally, I think gay people are more hip. Great minds drink alike."

Pearman smiled. "Seems like when either of us says something, we look out at the water."

Woody smiled. "To see if it floats?" He took a drink. "Bob Marley's music's done more for peace and justice in the world than all the books and politicians and soldiers combined. They call people like that artistic leaders, they speak to us beyond our minds. Authentic music has its own built-in natural power…a lot of it's played at the same tempo as our heartbeat."

"So?"

"So I predict the Berlin Wall's gonna come down someday soon because German kids want Beatles records. That's powerful. Roger Waters or Pete Townshend singing from experience about boys being abused under cover of religion? That stuff resonates with a generation. I'm not interested in some record company's idea of the latest disco fad. Good stuff endures. Piebald art never lasts. The good shit isn't about what happened, it's about what's happening."

"And how do you know what's good?"

"It's in the eye of the beholder. If it resonates with you, it's good art."

"Like what the Supreme Court said about obscenity? They can't define it but they know it when they see it?"

"It kind of *is* that simple," Woody said, stirring his drink. "The Mona Lisa, about the most valuable piece of art ever created, is a simple painting of a smile, a portrait of calmness. I can't even tell if she's really smiling. People have recognized the quality for four hundred years. Bernie would've said it's not flashy enough, it'll never be a hit."

Pearlman shrugged. "People don't dance to paintings."

The waitress appeared at their table and sang, "*I know who you both are, a couple of locals, I could season your songs with backup vocals.*" She went up an octave, which seemed impossible. "*I can sing even higher, make your songs objects of desire.*" She set down two plates and did a hip-bump toward Woody so animated he jerked back in his seat and the three of them laughed.

They ate in silence for a few minutes, Pearlman enjoying the way Woody manipulated his knife and fork with his tactile guitar-player hands. "Two thousand years ago Epicurus said who you eat with is more important than what you eat," Woody said.

"I'll join you any time," Pearlman said, "but Bernie isn't going to keep buying lunch if he doesn't see results. I've seen a lot of artists get a taste of success, a nice house, a comfortable lifestyle, then lose it all."

Woody gestured at the Bay. "I don't mean to be whining, sitting here in a nice restaurant. I'm thankful every day I don't live in my crummy apartment with the landlord banging on the door. I'm just trying to understand the relationship between music and money. Truth is: I hate money."

"Its value will become abundantly clear when royalties from 'Stephanie' dry up."

Woody slowly stirred his drink.

"I've got an idea," Pearlman said, "how about we send the whole entourage home for a couple days and just me and you see what we can do with some of your songs. We've got some good basics, we just need vocals. Maybe use tracks we have, maybe re-record with acoustic guitar and vocals, whatever. You play, I'll record. We've got to get Bernie something to listen to—it's now or never."

Woody finished his last bites of breakfast. "If I could let my mind off its leash, I could sing fine. Bernie wants music that reaches the most people, but I can't sing to everybody." He pointed at the water. "My voice goes from here to there." He put both hands on the table and leaned back. "You really think it's a good idea putting Lily and Stephanie on TV?"

"Stephanie has good intuition, especially with Lily. Maybe let *her* decide?"

The waitress set their check on the table, Pearlman picked it up. "My treat."

"Maybe she'd like your autograph," Woody said. "Salvador Dali does little drawings on his checks 'cause he knows people won't cash 'em."

When Pearlman opened the black vinyl folder a bright-pink business card fell out: *Allison Wonderland, vocals and beyond.* He handed the card to Woody.

Woody smiled. "A lot of musicians don't get as much attention as waitresses. She's got an unusual voice. We should try her on backup vocals."

CHAPTER 11

Wearing black wraparound sunglasses and last night's wrinkled clothes, Ray made a late-morning trip to the liquor store after a particularly brutal bout with nightmares. Afraid of the recurring dreams about being on a concert stage engulfed in flames, he'd taken to drinking himself to sleep, then drinking with his morning coffee. His drink of choice, a Screwdriver, had gotten progressively stronger until he began skipping the orange juice altogether.

Driving home past the big white houses of Seacliff, his tony neighborhood in San Francisco, Ray wondered if the size of the houses made the people inside any happier. He came around the corner, saw two cars in his driveway, his front door wide open.

He drove his black Mercedes up on the lawn and jumped out, a brown paper bag with a quart-size bottle of vodka in hand. "Hello? Who's here?"

"We're in the kitchen."

A curvaceous middle-aged woman in a wine-colored satin pantsuit as form-fitting as a bathing suit stood in the breakfast nook with an Asian couple and their young son.

"Hello, Ray." The woman stepped forward and gestured to herself with her clipboard. "I'm Beverly Rosen with Wynthall Rosen Real Estate. Did you get my message? We have an appointment to show the house today at eleven." She pointed her clipboard at the couple. "This is Doctor Ni; his wife, Shamru; and their son, Niko. They're relocating from Los Angeles. Doctor Ni is a cardiologist. They're interested in purchasing a Seacliff home. Dr. Ni," she gestured her clipboard toward Ray, "this is Ray Bell, former owner of the property."

Dr. Ni extended his hand. "Nice to meet you. This is a very attractive location you have overlooking the ocean."

Ray ignored him and turned to Beverley. "*Former* owner?"

The doctor dropped his hand and stepped back next to his wife.

"Dr. Ni," Beverly said, "why don't you and Shamru and Niko check out the lovely view from the patio? I'd like to have a word with Ray in private." She walked to the living room, Ray following. "You were supposed to have this place cleaned up and suitable to show a potential buyer." She slapped her thigh with her clipboard and waved it at the piles of moving boxes. "How am I supposed to show people this mess?"

"I've been a little busy packing." Ray opened the vodka and took a swig. "I didn't get your message."

She pinched the sides of her pantsuit and tugged it down. "My office has contracted to represent the property. You executed the paperwork; you're responsible for keeping the place presentable for—"

"Don't come in my house and start lecturing me first thing in the morning." He took another drink.

Beverly looked at her watch. "It's not first thing in the morning, and it's not your house anymore." She reached into the large leather purse on her shoulder, took out a piece of pink paper. "This was posted on your front door when we arrived."

FORECLOSURE. 30-DAY NOTICE TO QUIT OCCUPANCY.

The paper was covered on both sides with small print. Ray held it at arm's length and squinted at it.

"You don't own this home anymore, Mr. Bell. The bank owns it. In the future, I'll make arrangements directly with the bank. Dr. Ni is a very attractive potential buyer."

Ray looked her up and down. Her sheer pantsuit left little to the imagination. "Does that thing between your legs bite?"

She recoiled back, eyes wide. "You're the obnoxious bastard everyone says you are!"

"That's right, lady." He gulped down another drink. "And it's this bastard's house for another thirty days, so why don't you and your attractive buyer clear the fuck out!" Ray spun around, walked into an empty cardboard box, and kicked it across the room.

—

When Maria drove up an hour later, the front door was still wide open. "Ray? You home?" She heard a tinkle of piano keys.

Ray was at his white piano in the living room, the bottle of vodka in one hand, a half-loaf of French bread in the other. She watched him tear off a chunk with his teeth, plunk out a one-finger melody holding the bread, and wash it down with vodka.

"That breakfast looks delicious. Did you prepare it yourself or order takeout from a gourmet restaurant?"

"Wanna hear my new song?"

"Sure." She set her briefcase down and sat on the couch next to the piano, the only seat in the room not covered with moving boxes. "What's it called?"

"Be On Me."

"Beyond Me?"

"Be *On* Me."

She gave him a condescending smile. "Wasn't your last song called 'I Wanna Be On You?'"

Ray set the bread and vodka on the piano, played a simple 1-4-5 major chord progression, sang two verses, banged the last chord, and turned and glared at her, daring her to say something.

"Interesting," she said.

"Small words, big emotions." He picked up the vodka and bread and extended them to her. "Hungry? You look awfully sexy in that short skirt."

"Is that you or the liquor talking?"

He gave her a goofy grin. "It's me talking to the liquor."

"Very funny. And that's a funny way you parked your car on the front lawn. Your car door's open and the wipers were on. The key was on. I turned it off."

"Fog," Ray said.

"Frog?"

"Fog. Why the wipers were on."

She slid her briefcase closer and took out a ten-page document.

Ray noticed the handle of her pistol sticking out from under a legal pad in the briefcase. "You still carry that gun around?"

"I like carrying it. It makes me feel...I like carrying it."

"You always have it with you when we're together?"

"Like I said, I like carrying it. And it's my business what I do with it." She straightened her skirt, set the legal document on her knees, and patted it. "This is the complaint I want to file. I'm confident we can get partial royalties from 'Stephanie.'" She lifted it off her knees. "Want to take a look at it?"

He jerked back like it was a block of kryptonite. She dropped it back in her lap. "Are you okay?"

"I'm great. I'm losing my house, I'm losing everything, I'm fucking great!"

"No need to yell." She patted the complaint. "That's what this lawsuit's for."

"I thought you were gonna get my career going, get me a national tour."

"We've been over this, Ray. Promoters don't even return my calls. We need new material to work with."

Ray glanced back at the piano.

"I'm glad you're working on new songs. Maybe consider working with a co-writer. A lyricist. Arranging a simple hit song can be more complicated than it appears. You know that." She lowered her voice. "Ray, is there a reason you're so agitated? Drinking in the morning? You've been acting like—"

"Like my life's falling apart?"

"This lawsuit can get us some money." She picked it up again. "It addresses everything we've talked about."

He leaned back and banged his elbows on the keyboard. "I don't speak legalese. There's a hit song on the radio with me singing. Can't we go forward instead of backward?"

"That's my point. Your voice made that song a hit. A jury will know it the minute they hear your version compared to Woody's. There's no way we should have signed our rights away. We were coerced."

"I just wish I didn't need a lawyer to do my fighting for me. And the last place I want to fight this is in the press. Fucking journalists, they'd rather write about people fighting than about music." He set down the bottle between his legs and dropped his hands onto the piano bench, his eyelids drooping.

"Ninety percent of cases like this settle. Yes, if it goes to trial it'll cause a stir in the press." She pushed up her sleeves. "But this time we'll be ready. Woody will want to settle if he thinks that stuff about Stephanie being a stripper might come out."

Ray took another long drink, slammed the bottle down next to him on the bench, and lurched over to the couch, knocking his shoulder into Maria's. "That

Stephanie really does know how to dance. Who wouldn't wanna write a song about those tits?" He slapped the papers on Maria's knees. "Let's quit talking this legal bullshit. Wasn't there something else we used to do?" He ran his hand under the document and up her skirt.

"Ray! You're drunk!" She clamped her hand on his forearm and yanked his arm away. "You've been drunk for days! I can tell when we talk on the phone." She stood up and tugged down her skirt. "Let me know when you want to file this and do something with your life besides feeling sorry for yourself!" She put the complaint in her briefcase, slammed it closed, and headed toward the door. When she looked back Ray's head was cocked at an odd angle on the back of the couch, eyes closed, his mouth hanging open.

—

"Hi, Ray, hope it's okay I stopped by." Ray was still where Maria had left him, passed out drunk on the couch.

"Zoe?" He said with his eyes closed. The word barely crawled out of his throat.

"I was just like cruising by the beach, and I thought, wonder what Ray's up to, and your gate's open, your car door's open, your front door's open, and I thought, 'open house.'"

Ray stretched his neck and rubbed his eyes, trying to bring Zoe into focus with her rainbow-colored hair and sunglasses the size of a snorkel mask.

"I just popped by to say hi. Hope it's okay. I'm all like, my astrologer's sick and not writing her column, so I'm flying on instruments." She giggled. "I brought you an apple from the farmer's market." She proudly displayed the apple, an open can of beer in her other hand. "I was just, like, cruising by the beach, wondering if maybe you felt like hanging out," she giggled, "or whatever."

Ray tried straightening himself up and winced.

She stepped around a cardboard box, sat down on the piano bench next to Ray's vodka, and turned the bottle around. "Vodka. That looks fun." She crossed her legs in her skin-tight jeans, dangling a leather sandal up and down on the tip of her painted big toe. She took a cigarette out of her purse, put it in her mouth, and kept talking, the cigarette bouncing up and down in synchronicity with her sandal while she tried to catch the end with a lit match. "What's up with all these boxes? Are you, like, moving or something?" She lit up and exhaled out the corner of her mouth. "Last time I was here, you were like saying about getting your music trip going and talking about some trip you're having with money?"

Her pouty lips sent a perfect smoke ring swirling across the room. Ray watched the Mobius strip of smoke cut a path through the air and break apart against a picture window. The sweeping view from Ray's living room windows went west to the distant green humps of the Farallon Islands and east to the Golden Gate Bridge, Alcatraz, and the white concrete city. Zoe's voice was bouncing around the room like in a reverberating echo chamber. Ray put the heel of his hand against the side of his head and tried stretching out the kink in his neck from the awkward position he fell asleep in. The last thing he remembered was Maria's short skirt, getting shoved back onto the couch, now waking up to Zoe's echoing voice. He retrieved the vodka, fell back onto the couch, and took a drink.

"I heard you've been, like, working with songwriters, writing songs that sound like 'Stephanie.' Your voice totally matches that kind of vibe." Zoe took an ashtray off the floor and set it on the uneven folded top of a cardboard box. "I mean, like, anything you sing sounds great, but that kind of song with that deep meaning and everything is, like, totally like rad."

Her voice sounded helium-tinged, as if it could be coming out of the stereo speakers across the room. When the next smoke ring from her bee-stung lips collided with the window, the Golden Gate Bridge appeared unnaturally close, sagging in the middle, the thick suspension cables stretching like rubber bands. Ray squeezed his eyes closed and reopened them. Had that really happened? He could barely make out a tiny figure, a man, his shoulders shrouded in gray fog, standing on the railing of the bridge. The figure looked eerily familiar, then he recognized himself, wet wind sweeping through his hair, looking back across the bay at his house on the cliff. He looked back through his own eyes and could see his miniature picture window and into his living room with Zoe blowing smoke rings. He rubbed his eyes. The image vanished and there was the usual distant bridge.

"Wow, what's that?" Zoe said.

Ray looked at her like he was seeing her for the first time, bulimic, crossed insectile legs, alternating sips of beer with drags on her cigarette.

"Did you draw that?" Zoe pointed her cigarette at the artist's pad on the floor. "That's really heavy."

Looking down at the drawing, Ray felt as if he were being sucked into the drawn image of the suffocating smoke-filled dream. He remembered trying to run from under a collapsing wall, like his feet were buried in cement; the harder he ran, the slower he went. He'd looked back at the audience and saw a sea of strewn corpses with a man in aviator goggles and combat boots in a wide stance atop a pile of bodies, pointing a bazooka-size flame thrower at him, setting his hair ablaze. The multi-angled glass of the man's goggles was a refracting prism, splitting the man's eyeballs in two. The expression on his face reminded Ray of someone he knew. Then, from the freakishly tranquil calmness behind four flame-throwing eyes, Ray recognized Woody.

"Did you draw that?" Zoe said.

Ray ran his hands through his hair, his eyes wide.

Zoe finished her beer and folded a stick of chewing gum into her mouth. "I didn't know you were like an artist *and* a musician, which I guess is, like, all totally art anyway. That picture…it's so heavy. It makes you feel like running for your life."

Working her molars and cracking her gum, the concussive sounds popped in Ray's eardrums like tiny gunshots. He shook his head side-to-side. "It's a drawing of a dream."

"That's far out, you expressing yourself in other ways besides music." His distressed expression staring at the drawing made her uncomfortable, and she doubled down on her chewing gum. "Anyway, I was just in the hood, just seeing what you were up to. I heard Woody's recording at the Record Plant. I heard he's got some like major label recording budget with a hot tub and catering and everything like right in the studio. Are you in touch with him? You guys have such a totally musical connection, it'd be a crime if you didn't like, whatever. I mean, you're like Lennon and McCartney or something."

Standing up, Ray grabbed the vodka, the apple, and his wraparound sunglasses. He walked past Zoe as if she wasn't there.

She leaned out of his way, hugging her elbows. "Where you going, Ray?"

"To see Woody."

—

Swigging vodka, Ray drove to the Golden Gate Bridge, parked in the north parking lot, and walked through the underground walkway to the ocean side and the center of the bridge. Looking back at his house on the cliff, he expected to see himself sitting on his couch. Instead, the window of his living room was a tiny speck of reflected sunlight. The unexpected optics made him feel unsteady on his feet, like the bridge was swaying. Maybe it was. He ran all the way back to the parking lot.

Hands flat on the roof of his car, out of breath, head hanging between his arms, he reached into his pocket—no keys. He went through every pocket, scanned the ground and looked back at the bridge. He must've dropped them, maybe in the water. He tried the car door. it was open, the vodka on the passenger seat, the keys in the ignition. He sat down, took a drink, started the motor, and slammed it into gear.

He took the Mill Valley exit and headed up Mount Tam, abusing the suspension of his heavy Mercedes on the tight turns until he came to the ridgetop and slowed, looking for Woody's house. Ray was familiar with that area of the Panoramic Highway where local rock stars lived. From what he'd heard about Woody's new house, he lived on this two-mile stretch of road. It seemed like everywhere he went, people felt compelled to keep him updated about Woody.

Private homes on the east side overlooked the ocean, the west was an expanse of National Seashore grassy hills, rocky cliffs, and beaches. It was getting dark as Ray began a methodical search, looking up every driveway, looking for the silver Corvette he'd seen parked at the Record Plant.

He pulled into a driveway, drove up the narrow macadam lane through tall pampas grass, and came to a ten-foot-high gate. Should he jump over? Jump over every gate he came to? What exactly did he want with Woody? He took a drink and slammed his car in reverse.

As it grew darker, his search took on a manic edge. He parked in front of one metal gate, left his car running, and squeezed around the edge of a stone pillar, thick blackberry brambles wrapping around his neck. He ran up the driveway, the house completely dark, no cars in front. After another bout with the brambles, he got back in his car, wiped his neck, and saw blood on his hand.

He poured vodka on his fingertips and rubbed it on the cuts. The burning sensation felt good, woke him up. He took another drink.

After a half-dozen more driveways, he was considering giving up when he spotted Woody's car in front of a redwood house perched on a hill, soft yellow lights coming from the windows. He parked in front, turned off his car, and wondered why he was breathing so hard. What would he say to Woody? His mind froze. What the hell was he doing here? His eyes landed on Zoe's red apple between the seats. He came all the way up here to give Woody an apple? He took another drink, the quart of vodka three-quarters gone. He tossed the bottle onto the floor, picked up the apple, walked up to the house, and knocked on the carved wooden door. No answer. When he knocked again, he heard a soft knocking like an echo. Was he hearing things? He tapped softly again with one knuckle and heard a responding tap. Somebody inside must have seen him drive up and was fucking with him. He tried the door, it was unlocked, opened it slowly a few inches, looked down, and saw a baby on her knees, her little chubby hand on the bottom of the door. He bent down and handed her the apple.

"Lily, how'd you get that door open?" a woman's voice called from across the room. "Come back over here."

Ray opened the door tentatively, just enough to take a small step inside.

Stephanie, standing at the kitchen counter with a glass of water in her hand, saw a man step inside the door in a torn sleeveless T-shirt, blood dripping from his neck, Lily at his feet. She dropped the glass, smashing it on the tile kitchen floor.

Woody, in a living room chair with a guitar in his lap, his back to the door, heard the glass break and saw the expression on Stephanie's face. The next moment, Woody and Stephanie both bolted toward Lily. Stephanie made it there first, scooped her off the floor, backed across the room, and held Lily tightly against her chest.

"Stephanie, it's me, Ray. I came to talk to Woody."

"Ray?" Woody stood ten feet away holding his acoustic guitar at his side. "What the hell are you doing here?"

"Did you call, or even knock on the door?" Stephanie said.

"I came to talk to Woody."

Woody looked at the blood dripping from Ray's neck onto the carpet. The last time he'd seen Ray was at the Grammy Award Ceremonies in Los Angeles over a year ago.

Ray looked across the room at Stephanie clutching Lily. "I *did* knock."

"What do you want?" Woody said.

"I heard you've been recording." Ray's chest was heaving. "Let me see what I can do with your songs." He took some quick shallow breaths, trying to get his voice under control. "You got the songs. I got the voice. We could work together." He rubbed his neck and looked at the blood on his hand. "Whaddya say?"

"You tried stealing my song."

"I didn't steal it. I added what it needed."

"You stole it."

"It was my voice, my melody that made it a hit!"

"What're you doing here in my house, yelling at me?"

Ray held out his hands. "I just wanted to talk to you, man. Talk about music. I didn't come up here to get in a hassle."

"You could've called or something instead of just barging in here. What happened to your neck? You're bleeding."

"I just wanna make music. And I didn't steal it, I sang it. You ended up with this house, the song, Stephanie—what else do you want?" He took an unsteady step forward. "I've got the voice. It's *my* voice that made that song a song, and I can do it again. Give me some lyrics, get me in the studio, try me on a gig, I can sing anything!" He clenched his hands into fists at his side, veins in his neck bulging, blood swelling out of the cuts.

"You're drunk, Ray. And now you come in here yelling at me and…I don't have to deal with this."

"Deal with it, man! It's about time you dealt with the truth. I got the voice!" He turned to Stephanie. "He sings like shit, and you know it! He's not pitchy, he's flat! Why won't anybody fucking admit it?" Ray took a step toward her, almost fell forward, and caught himself.

Stephanie clutched Lily closer and stepped back.

Woody wrapped his hands around the neck of his guitar and brought it over his shoulder like a baseball bat. "What the fuck are you doing here, scaring the shit out of everybody?" He raised the guitar, hands shaking, his face screwed up into a ball of anger. "You're drunk! Get out!"

"Maybe I'm drunk, but she doesn't have to be a stripper anymore 'cause of my *singing*!" He pointed at Stephanie, leaned back as a cantilever to his outstretched arm, almost fell over backward, caught himself again, and gave Woody a crooked smile. "Anybody ever tell you your wife's got nice tits?"

"Fuck you, asshole!" Stephanie screamed across the room, turning Lily's head away to not scream in her ear. "Get out of our house!" Spinning around, Stephanie stalked away, set Lily on the bed in her bedroom, put her favorite stuffed animal in her lap, closed the door, and picked up the phone in the kitchen. "Ray, if you're not out of here in five seconds, I'm calling the cops! And by the way, you couldn't write decent a song if your life depended on it!" She put her finger on the phone dial. "Five! Four! Three!"

Woody stepped in closer to Ray, the guitar quivering over his head. "Get... The...Fuck...Outtta Here!"

"Whoa, everybody." Ray held his hands up, palms out, looking back and forth at Stephanie and Woody, then dropped them to his sides and scanned the room wide-eyed as if he didn't know where he was. "I just came to talk about music...about singing...singing music!" He did a wobbly about-face like on a ship's deck on a rough sea and lurched out the door, slamming it closed. Woody heard him yelling to himself, "*I got the voice! I got the fucking voice! Why doesn't anybody get that?*"

Woody went to the window, watched Ray drive away, then quickly crossed the room to Stephanie. They hugged and went and sat with Lily on her bed.

"He's not okay." Stephanie was breathing hard, shaking her head from side to side. "He really scared me. It was like he was in some kind of trance. His eyes weren't tracking."

"I've heard he's been broke, going through some hard times, but that was off the hook."

"I hope he can drive." Stephanie wiped her forehead with her sleeve. "I hope he doesn't hurt someone."

"He's pretty drunk."

"It's deeper than that. Drugs or alcohol would be a less scary explanation. There's a storm raging inside him."

Woody rubbed Lily's back thoughtfully. "I have to admit, a couple times this week, when I couldn't get the vocals the way I wanted, it occurred to me to see how Ray's voice might sound on my stuff."

Stephanie's eyebrows shot up.

Woody shrugged. "Just making a musical observation."

"I'd stay away from him right now. He's definitely in no shape to work. And by the way, I love your singing."

"If Ray could ever let go of what people think of him and just focus on the music, he could be great. People who want other people to know who they are don't know who they are. He's all hat and no cattle."

Lily emitted a high, monosyllabic sound that Woody and Stephanie both knew meant she was hungry. "*She's* got the voice," Woody said, "mezzo soprano." He picked her up, carried her to the kitchen counter, peeled a banana, and handed her a piece. Lily squeezed it in her fist and mashed it half in her mouth, half on her face.

Stephanie walked into the room. "Maybe try a spoon?"

"Fifty percent reached its intended destination, up from twenty percent a couple months ago. It's a fun way to eat for now, she'll be using a spoon for the next ninety years." He cleaned off Lily's cheeks with a kitchen towel. "I first asked Ray to sing 'Stephanie' because he was Ray Bell. Then, when I actually heard him sing...he knows how to deliver a song. He's got the vocal chops, I don't."

"You're singing is who you are. Your music is a true expression of a beautiful human being." Stephanie looked toward the front door. "Ray's not okay."

"He's always been kind of a hero in his own mind, now he's losing his mind," Woody said.

"He's a hollow shell of a man with pleasant-sounding vocal cords, that's it. And from what I saw tonight, he's a suicide waiting to happen."

CHAPTER 12

Woody drove to the Record Plant the next morning and went straight to the kitchen for coffee. Stirring in cream and sugar, he thought about the day's songs. Yesterday had been slow going. They'd tried focusing on one tune. Pearlman wrote out the lyrics on a legal pad and Woody sang multiple takes of each phrase, sometimes going through a verse ten times to get the right feel. When he finished, Pearlman listened back, auditioned every performance of every line, sometimes every word, rated them, and spent four hours assembling a composite version of the best takes. When they listened to the finished product it sounded like the botched-together mix that it was. Their new plan for today was to have Woody come in fresh, sing the whole song straight through, and nail it.

Woody remembered reading about a man who'd started piano lessons before he ended up in prison. While he was doing his time, the man dedicated part of every day to mentally practice without a piano and came out three years later an accomplished pianist. Woody tried singing one of his songs in his mind. It sounded flat, maybe Ray was right. He tried another song, same thing. He decided to leave it up to Pearlman to figure out what worked and what didn't. He sipped his coffee and spread out that morning's *San Francisco Chronicle* on the kitchen table.

A FALLING STAR
SINGER RAY BELL'S BLOODY SUICIDE NOTE
YOU GOT THE SONG, YOU GOT STEPHANIE, YOU GOT IT ALL!

Underneath the headline was a photograph of Ray's Mercedes, the only car parked in the north parking lot of the Golden Gate Bridge, the driver's door wide open, the handwritten suicide note lying on the passenger seat, an empty bottle of vodka on the floor.

Woody choked, coffee spurted out of his nose and mouth, and he hurled his cup against the wall. He swept the paper off the table with the back of his shaking hand and watched the milky-brown liquid make its way down the wall and over the mounted speakerphone, thin rivulets dripping in through the molded plastic slits and onto the two-inch paper speaker. Woody looked at the newspaper at his feet and visualized Ray ten feet below the surface of the water screaming a garbled suffocating wail. Suddenly, the wet speakerphone crackled to life with garbled unintelligible words from a female voice.

Woody picked up the receiver and hit the red intercom button. "Marilyn? That you? Marilyn?"

"Woody? Where are you? Are you in the kitchen?"

"I'm here."

"Stephanie's on line two. She says it's urgent."

Woody pressed the line two button. "Steph?" Nothing. He stabbed every button, getting dial tones until he hit the line-two button again and got silence. "Steph?"

"Woody?"

"It's me. You okay?"

"Did you hear about Ray?"

"I saw it in the paper. I can't believe it. I knew he was stressed out, but I can't believe he'd actually—"

"Woody?"

"Did you ever think he'd really…"

"Woody. The police are here."

"Police? Where?"

"Here. At the house. They want to talk to you. Will you come home?"

He watched the dribbles of coffee reach the floor and form a small brown puddle. "What? What are the police doing—"

"Woody. Listen to me. I'm in our living room with Lily and two Marin County Sheriffs. They said they're going to wait here until you get here."

—

Woody made it home from the Record Plant in record time and parked next to the green and white patrol car. He looked at the wire-mesh screen between the seats and wondered if they were the same cops that had arrested him at the 7-Eleven.

Two deputies he didn't recognize sat at his kitchen table drinking coffee with Stephanie in the living room with Lily in her lap, flipping pages of a picture book. The cops were like bookends, in similar bent-over positions, fingers in the handles of their cups. One cop was young with buffed biceps under his uniform shirt, light-blond hair shaved so short it looked transparent. The other cop was older and stocky. With their tan uniforms, pants tucked into black combat boots, and utility belts loaded with walkie-talkies, handcuffs, holsters, and grip-handled pistols, they were an ominous presence in the room.

Stephanie hugged Woody and put the side of her head against his chest. He wrapped his arm around her shoulders and said to the cops, "What's going on here?"

The deputies set down their cups and stood up in unison. "I'm officer Shannon," the older cop said, "this is officer Hannah. We'd like to ask you a couple of questions about Ray Bell."

"Excuse me," Stephanie said. "I need to change the baby's diaper, and if you don't mind, I'd like to talk to my husband in private for a minute." She looked at Woody and tilted her head toward the bedroom.

The officers exchanged glances. "The questions we have will be brief." Officer Shannon stepped closer. "Was Ray Bell here yesterday? Yesterday evening to be more precise?"

"I'd like to speak with my husband for just a minute." She hefted Lily up, grabbed Woody by the arm, and tugged him toward the bedroom.

Officer Shannon stepped to the side, instinctively keeping a line of sight to see if there was a back door to the bedroom. Like most homes in the area built on the hillside, the back bedroom was ten feet off the ground.

—

"Shouldn't we talk to a lawyer?" Stephanie whispered as soon as she shut the door. "Those policemen are nice enough, but we should be careful what we say. I called Jeff and left a message."

"Careful what we say? What're you whispering for? We've got nothing to hide, let's not act like we do."

Stephanie set Lily on the bed and put her fingertips on Woody's lips. "You're talking too loud."

"Talking too loud?" Woody opened his hands. "How do they even know Ray was here last night?"

"They interviewed the last person to see him, some woman at Ray's house. She told them Ray said he was coming over here. And they noticed the fresh blood on the carpet by the front door. One cop pointed it out to the other when they walked in."

Lily started whining. A human mood ring, her antennae picked up on any tension between Woody and Stephanie.

Stephanie sat on the bed and rubbed her back. "When they started asking questions, it felt like they were accusing me of something."

Woody sat down and took Stephanie's hands in his. "I think you're being paranoid, we didn't do anything wrong. But if it'll make you more comfortable, we can talk to Jeff first. I'm not going to let these guys mess with my family." Woody rubbed Lily's head, walked out of the bedroom, and over to the cops. "Do you guys have a warrant or anything? My wife and daughter are pretty upset about everything that happened with Ray and everything and…why are *we* being questioned?"

"There's a missing person, a possible fatality," Officer Shannon said. "We have reason to believe the last place Ray Bell was before he went to the Golden Gate Bridge was here in your home. We'd like to ask you a few questions about his state of mind, what he said, how he was acting."

"Am I under suspicion for something? Am I supposed to get my Miranda rights or a lawyer or what?"

The sheriff hooked his thumbs in his belt. "We have reason to believe the incident involves a suicide. You're not a suspect to a crime, we're just gathering information. If you'll agree to cooperate, we just need to clarify a few things. First of all, we'd like to narrow down the time parameters."

There was a knock on the front door, the phone started ringing, and Stephanie walked out of the bedroom holding Lily. Stephanie answered the phone, and Woody answered the door. It was Murray. "Hey, Woody. I heard about Ray on the news. Did you hear about it? What's going on? There's a police car parked in your—" He looked over Woody's shoulder and saw the two sheriffs.

"Woody," Stephanie said, "Jeff's on the phone."

"Maybe I should come back another time," Murray said.

"Yeah, it's kinda crazy around here at the moment," Woody said.

Officer Hannah walked over to Murray. "Are you a friend of Woody's?"

Murray glanced at Woody. "Yeah, kinda…I guess."

"Do you know Ray Bell?"

"I know who he is."

"When was the last time you saw Woody and Ray Bell together?"

Murry stuck his hands in his pockets, closed his eyes and his face turned red. "I don't know if I've ever really—"

"Woody," Stephanie said from across the room, "Jeff's on the phone."

"Hang tight for a sec, Murray, until I talk to my lawyer." Woody walked quickly across the room and took the phone from Stephanie. "Hello?"

"Woody, it's Jeff. Are the police there?"

"Yeah."

"Are they in the same room as you?"

"Yeah."

"Can you go somewhere private to talk?"

Woody took the kitchen phone with its long chord into the bathroom and closed the door. "What the hell's going on here? Why am I acting like I have something to hide?"

"Are they asking questions about Ray?"

"Yeah."

"Have you said anything?"

"Yeah."

"What did you say?"

"Nothing."

"Did Stephanie say anything?"

"No, I don't know."

"Tell them you you'd like to cooperate with their investigation but your lawyer said don't talk to them until he's with you. Be polite, tell them I'll call and set up a time for an interview."

"But I didn't *do* anything. Why do I even *need* a lawyer?"

"Trust me on this."

"The guy jumped off the bridge. I didn't push him. I didn't *do* anything."

"You're not a lawyer, Woody. I can think of several scenarios that could be problematic. What if an autopsy shows Ray was high on something? Where's the last place he could've gotten drugs? Whatever you have to say to the cops, you can say another time in a controlled setting. What's the downside of waiting? Blame it on me, but don't say anything. Nothing."

"I'll call you back." Woody opened the bathroom door and heard one of the cops say to Murray, "If you're a friend of Woody's you must know Ray Bell. We're just trying to establish a timeline. When was the last time you saw Ray and Woody together?"

Murray gave them what looked like a constipated smile, his face in a knot, eyes closed.

Woody quickly walked over to Officer Shannon. "Listen, Officer, that was my lawyer on the phone. He's a total control freak. Sorry, but he wants to be here before anybody answers any more questions. So if you wouldn't mind—"

"Like I said," Officer Shannon said, "you're not a suspect in a crime. We're not alleging any wrongdoing, just trying to fill in the blanks. Was Ray alone when he was here last night?"

Woody turned to Murray. "Murray, read me back the last thing I said."

Murray's face went slack.

Shannon closed the distance between him and Woody. "What did you just say to him?"

"I was checking on what I said to *you*."

"Wait, what?" Shannon said. "*I'm* asking the questions here. We're doing an investigation about a possible fatality. If you're refusing to cooperate, we can—"

"Excuse me, gentlemen," Stephanie walked over. "Officer Shannon, we'll make ourselves available to answer all your questions at another time. The news about Ray Bell has been very upsetting for our family. We're much too upset right now to have accurate recollections about anything. So, if you wouldn't mind, give us some time to collect our thoughts, we'd prefer to be left alone right now."

Shannon took a card out of his shirt pocket and handed it to Woody. "I'll expect a call from your attorney by tomorrow morning, or we'll be back with a warrant."

When the sheriffs approached the front door, Officer Shannon knelt down on one knee, took out a white handkerchief, rubbed it across the blotches of

Ray's blood, and folded the handkerchief into the molded leather pouch on his belt.

—

The next day Pearlman called the Marin County Sheriff and explained that Woody and Stephanie had no helpful information regarding Ray Bell's suicide.

"Jeff," the sheriff said, "is this the same guy you called about a couple weeks ago that thought his kid had been kidnapped?"

"It is. The two incidents are unrelated."

"Your friend's been using the services of the Marin County sheriff quite a bit. I'll put the matter of him being a witness regarding Ray Bell on hold for now, but mention to your client that our annual fundraising drive is this month."

"Will do."

—

Pearlman called Woody. "You and Stephanie are off the hook for now. Unless Ray's autopsy turns up something unusual, when all the excitement in the press settles down, they'll probably forget about talking to you, especially if you make a nice donation to the sheriff's fundraising drive."

"Donate to the cops? Let me think about that one. You feel like going back to the studio tonight? Maybe take a pass at some of those vocals?"

"With everything that's been going on, I wouldn't expect you to be in the mood to sing."

"When I'm feeling good, I feel like playing music. When I'm feeling bad, I feel like playing music. After all the stuff that's gone down with Ray and the cops, I'll just be home bouncing off the walls."

When Woody got to the studio, Pearlman was waiting in the lounge, drinking coffee.

"We should talk about what song we're going to do." Pearlman gestured to a chair, and they sat listening to John Coltrane coming out of hidden speakers in the ceiling. "I don't have many friends I can just sit quietly with," Pearlman said.

When the song ended, they sat in silence for another minute. "The quieter you are, the more you hear," Woody said. "Silence for a musician is like a canvas for a painter. And silence is hard to come by—loud people, cars, planes, refrigerators, tinnitus, screaming thoughts. My mind's especially loud today." Woody crossed and uncrossed his legs and adjusted himself in his seat. "I'm always on the lookout for chairs with no arms, 'cause it's easier for playing guitar. But just sitting in chairs with no arms and no guitar," he squirmed side-to-side, "there's too much freedom."

"What was it like, seeing Ray?"

"He brings out the worst in me. I should've been more kind." Woody pictured Ray sitting in the audience at the topless place where Stephanie had worked, him and everyone else in the room watching her undress. He shook his head, shaking out the thoughts. "He was possessed, on some kind of mission. His anxiety was contagious. Lily must've heard Ray at the front door and crawled across the room. Ray came in, Stephanie freaked out, I freaked out about Stephanie freaking out, and things spun out from there. He was pretty drunk and couldn't figure out how to express himself. He actually just came to say let's play some music. Just looking for a little love, like everybody. There's no sense holding grudges. It hurts the grudger more than the grudgee. I just wish I'd been a little nicer to him. Maybe Ray didn't have the right to put out 'Stephanie,' but he made the song a hit. I don't know if he's got family, but if he does, and they need some money from song royalties, maybe we should help them out. Let me know if you hear anything about a funeral." Woody considered the cigarette in his hand. "I'm trying this new approach, doing everything with my cigarette except lighting it. It's not working out too well. These days I feel more like smoking than singing." He stood up and lit up. "I'm gonna split. Sorry for asking you to drive over here. I'm not really up for recording, but it was good to talk. Once I get a mental bead on it, the physical part of singing should be close behind."

"We'll record any time you're ready. As Picasso says, the muse doesn't always show up, but when she does, she needs to find you working."

Woody squeezed Pearlman's shoulder as he walked past him.

"Woody," Pearlman said, "Ray was on his own path, you're on yours. You're not responsible for what happened."

Woody gave him a weak smile. "It's never too late to be kind...until it is."

—

Woody manually flipped down his convertible top and left Sausalito heading north in the slow lane of Highway 101, trying to clear his mind by focusing on the percolating rhythm of his motor. The Corvette always did exactly what he expected. He liked looking at its beautifully sculpted body style as much as he liked driving it. Sometimes he enjoyed tapping into the car's potential, winding out the high-performance 327 motor to 7,000 RPM with enough torque to burn rubber in all gears. And there were times like tonight when he appreciated the understated, deep-throated power the car had at low RPM's, enough to accelerate smoothly in fourth gear from a standing start.

Cruising through Mill Valley, Woody stopped at the Sweetwater for a nightcap before heading up the mountain. The popular local bar was usually quiet on weeknights with no band playing. One beer and he'd head home. Stephanie expected him to be working late. She and Lily were probably asleep.

—

Sitting alone at the polished-wood bar, halfway through his beer, Woody set down a ten-dollar bill. The pretty barmaid in an embroidered white cotton blouse and black pigtails walked over and pushed the ten back. "Seven already covered it."

Woody slid it over again. "Keep it, Alex."

"Thanks, Woody. We've been missing you. Guess you got too popular to play our humble little room."

Seven, the six-foot-four manager, walked up and leaned on his elbows on the bar down to Woody's height. "Wussup, Woody? Join me for a shot of tequila?"

"One shot. I gotta drive up the mountain."

Seven gave a peace sign to Alex, she knew what it meant.

Alex set a bottle of chestnut-colored Don Julio Reposado on the oak bar with two shot glasses, some cut limes, and a saltshaker. Seven poured. "To the music." They did their shots. "Heard you've been recording," he said. "How's it going?"

"Lately it feels like throwing a hot dog down a hallway."

Seven looked straight ahead. "That's pretty tough about Ray."

"I guess that's what people do—they die. I wouldn't know, I've never tried it. It's always somebody else that dies."

"But doing it like that? Leaving that crummy suicide note?"

"Suicide used to be on my list of things to do." Woody contemplated his glass. "I saw Ray the night before last."

Seven looked into the side of Woody's face. "The night he jumped?"

Woody watched Alex polishing the rows of liquor bottles reflected in the bar's ornate mirror. "Ray came by my house. He'd never been there before."

"You two guys being together *any* time is far out." Seven hunkered down lower and flipped his long blond ponytail over his shoulder. "You and Ray actually hung out that night?"

"He stopped by to see if I wanted to play some music sometime. He was pretty drunk."

"That's too much, you two guys finally getting together the night before he checks out."

Woody contemplated his empty shot glass. "People get larger than life right after they die. The life they've accumulated erupts like a volcano and incinerates their mistakes. Death brings forgiveness." He turned to Seven. "The night I saw him, Ray was approaching liftoff to his big bang in the universe. Now his particles are floating in the ethers. They're probably playing his music on the radio in Tokyo, New York, Mexico City—I'm gonna miss the thrill of hating him."

"They're probably playing your song 'Stephanie.'" Seven shook his big head. "He must've been having a pretty hard time."

"He was wrestling with his karma. It had him in a full nelson. I'm not sure what made him snap. Sometimes things make more sense looking forward than looking backward. There are a lot of things in the universe waiting to be known."

As he often did with Woody, Seven paused to let what he'd said sink in. "Ray stopped in now and then," Seven said. "He always asked about you. He sat in with the Sunday night house-band once, and they played 'Stephanie.'"

Woody looked straight ahead. "How'd it sound?"

"Great. That guy has the pipes." Seven poured himself another drink. The shot glass looked like a toy in Seven's oversized fist. He offered the bottle to Woody.

"I'd better cool it to drive home. I probably could've acted more kind with Ray. He was one of those people who had a kind of distant relationship with lots of people, but wasn't really close with anybody. Thousands of fans who saw him perform felt a kinship with him, but they were all strangers."

Seven looked at his watch. "If you change your mind about another shot, there's no cops on the road in Mill Valley when they change shifts at nine thirty. I got the inside tip, one of my waitresses dates a cop. Ever heard of a band called Stone Pillow?"

"Sounds like the night I spent in jail."

"It's a band from LA. They play weird instruments that expand their sound in the room. It's not loud, it's wide, like the music spreads out and fills in the corners. Anyway, their singer fell off a horse, canceled their gig next Friday. Wanna play?"

He looked at Seven's friendly belly being supported by the bar. "Well, normally I wouldn't, but for a smooth talker like you..."

Seven let out a yelp and slapped Woody on the back harder than he meant to. "Sorry, man. Hey, Alex," Seven called out, "get us a couple of glasses of soda water and some popcorn, Woody's gotta drive home." He turned to Woody. "No kidding? You'll play here next Friday?"

"I've got a couple new songs that haven't been out of the house. It might motivate them to get dressed up, get out more," he said. "We could dedicate the show to Ray."

Seven clapped his big hands together loud enough to hurt Woody's ears. "You gonna play with a band or play by yourself?"

Woody took a moment. "We have some shows coming up in the Northwest, I think I'll play this one by myself. Getting the band together on short notice is more about phone calls than music."

Alex set down two soda waters and a basket of popcorn. "Hey, Alex," Seven plunged his catcher's-mitt-size hand into the basket. "Woody's gonna play here next Friday."

"What? Really?" Alex looked back and forth from Woody to Seven. "What happened to Stone Pillow?"

"They canceled. Woody's gonna play solo acoustic." Seven leaned in. "Alex, listen, I want this show to be totally unannounced. Keep it to yourself, got it?"

"Totally. Friday's my night off, but I'll be here. Wow! That's awesome!"

Seven took another fistful of popcorn when Alex walked away. "That'll be my only promotion for the show, telling Alex not to tell anyone. They'll be lined up around the block."

CHAPTER 13

The next morning, Pearlman was late getting to work. Brenda was at her reception desk, dabbing her red eyes with a tissue. When Pearlman approached, without looking up, she said; "He was a total jerk! Sooner or later somebody would've killed him if he didn't do it himself! What's amazing about the whole thing is that that coward actually got up the nerve to jump!"

"I'm sorry, Brenda. I know you two were close."

"Close? That asshole hasn't even bothered to call me since…" She put her head down on her folded arms and sobbed.

Pearlman reached over and put his hand on hers. "Take the rest of the day off if you want." He started to walk away.

"Mr. Pearlman? Marty Levine from A&M Records called, he says it's important."

"Thanks, Brenda."

Pearlman picked up the phone on his desk and made the call without sitting down.

"Jeff?"

"How are you, Marty? Sorry about Ray, I assume you two became friends since he's been on your label for what…two years?"

"We did business together, we weren't friends. The guy was a jerk. He acted like a jerk with all my employees, always trying to feel up the secretaries. He rode the elevators alone, they made sure of that."

"No sense in dredging up the sludge. He was a good singer, that's all his thousands of fans cared about. He's gone, Marty. But that's not what you called about."

"Did you ever meet Ray's mother?"

"No."

"Her name's Connie, she's a real sweetheart. She's got a serious drinking problem, but Ray didn't care. He had us send her a check every month, but not enough to get too drunk on. Those checks and a little social security are what she's been living on. We know you got the writer's credit for 'Stephanie'—that's where most of the money from Ray's hit record goes."

"What's your point?"

"Our promotion guys are looking for a way to capitalize on Ray's swan dive. Maybe Woody could acknowledge Ray's musical contribution to 'Stephanie' and kick down a little for Connie. Not only would it help record sales, it'd be the righteous thing to do. Not only for Connie, but for Ray's legacy."

"Ray's legacy of singing other people's songs and claiming he wrote them?"

"I thought we were done with the sludge," Marty said.

"Does Maria Angel still represent Ray?"

"I assume you mean Ray's estate. I don't know."

"Didn't she used to work for you?"

"That was quite a while ago. She's a real piece of work."

"She told me she owns half the rights to 'Stephanie.'"

"He had a contract with her, a contract that *she* wrote. Half of nothing is nothing." They were both quiet for a long pause. "I'll talk to Woody," Pearlman said, "see if he's ok with helping out Ray's mom. I doubt he'll want to put it out there that he's doing it because Ray deserves songwriting credits."

—

Maria took the previous attorney's business cards from the holder on her desk and replaced them with her own. Then she replaced the framed law school diploma and California State Bar certificate. The last thing she did before sitting at her desk was hang up the Jackson Pollock painting she kept behind the file cabinet. The other attorneys who rented the "virtual" office by the hour wouldn't go for it, said it was too distracting in such a small space. She admired the three by five-foot painting with its dramatic bold red and yellow slashes, the one item of value she'd been allowed to take when she'd left Pearlman's law firm. "It'll remind me of you and your scheming," Pearlman had said, "get it out of here. It's worth a lot of money, call it your termination package."

Maria often thought of selling it since she'd gone into private practice, but she was determined to keep it and refused to even have it appraised. She imagined someday having a nice office of her own and getting a visit from Jeff Pearlman. An avid art collector, he'd probably regret giving it away.

That afternoon she consulted with three clients in four hours, all elderly women she'd met at her apartment building wanting estate planning advice. It was an area she wasn't very interested in or even knew much about, but one woman told a friend who told another and things were working out so Maria could pay her bills, barely.

The day went by with one boring task after another until she took a break, switched to decaf coffee, and finally got around to reading the day's newspaper and saw the headline about Ray. She walked to the window to give herself a few minutes to digest what had happened before she read more.

Almost an hour later she was still reading and rereading the stories about Ray: concerts, drugs, exotic cars, women, almost like a life designed for a movie or TV series of what other people thought a life of celebrity was like. Still emersed in the stories, her office door swung open, and Ray walked in and collapsed in the chair in front of her desk. He had filthy bare feet, a torn sleeveless T-shirt, and stripes of dried blood and black soot on his face like a face-painted warrior returning from battle.

"Ray!"

He slumped way back, arms hanging at his sides, fingertips almost touching the floor.

"I thought you—what happened to you? How'd you get here?"

He raised himself up enough to get an upside-down view of the front page open on her desk: his car in the bridge parking lot and a view of his handwritten suicide note. He fell back in the chair and let his head fall back, eyes wide, staring at the ceiling.

"Ray? Where've you been? How'd you get here?"

"I swam."

She actually looked to see if his clothes were wet.

With some effort, Ray sat up slightly and gazed at his chalky blue feet extending into the darkness under her desk as if they belonged to someone else. Beyond his feet, in the desk's shadow, he saw the bottomless black water under the Golden Gate Bridge. Ray's head flopped back over the back of the chair in front of Maria's desk, he closed his eyes and remembered finishing the last of the vodka, tossing the bottle on the car floor, and taking the pedestrian pathway to the west railing of the bridge facing the ocean. Looking straight down, he'd started taking things out of his pockets and hurling them at the water. He took out his wallet and broadcast a fistful of bills, a flock of fluttering green wings descending out of sight then rising back up momentarily in gusts of fog. Then he'd tossed his entire wallet, dug the coins out of his pocket, picked out a penny, tossed it over the railing, and thought to make a wish. Make a wish?

He emitted a forced laugh, like a cough.

"Ray?" Maria was concerned. She thought he might be choking. "Ray? Are you okay?"

He saw a thousand little reflections of Maria's wavy black hair undulating in the choppy water. Toss a penny, make a wish? Wish for what? His entire life was about to end, the past, the future, everything. Everyone would be relieved. Woody would be thankful for no more bullshit lawsuits about 'Stephanie.' Who'd miss him...his mother? Her worst fear was that she'd outlive him. He'd always dismissed her concerns..."what's the worst that can happen mom?"

"It's about the natural order of things, Ray." Then she'd tell the story she'd repeated many times about the ancient Chinese emperor who summoned a Buddhist priest to his castle to give him a blessing.

"Your parents die," the priest said to the emperor, "then you die, then your children die."

"What kind of blessing is that?" the emperor demanded. "That's not a blessing."

"Yes, it is," said the priest.

Ray pictured his frail mother with her scrapbooks of newspaper clippings spanning his music career. She'd get over the loss. She had her own life, his was to do with as he pleased, including cutting it short. Where did that concept come from, that you can't die healthy? He spat over the railing, and it disappeared in an instant—the way *he* would. He took off his shoes, loafers with no socks, and flung them one at a time out to sea, stripped off his jacket and hurled it, its empty arms flailing, hugging itself. In a sleeveless T-shirt, slacks, and bare feet, the cuts on the side of his face dripping blood, he stepped up onto the cold steel beam beneath the wet railing, reached into his pockets, and felt the last thing left: his car keys. This was his last chance to change his mind. By tossing his keys, he'd commit. He took them out and considered them in his open hand. He knew the longer he waited, the harder it would get. He threw them as hard as he could straight out at the horizon and looked down at the tiny splash on the water's surface, so meager he couldn't tell if he'd imagined it. That's how quickly his life was about to be extinguished.

Moments of his life streaked by, flashes of people's faces disappearing the instant he recognized them. A blur of women, fans, musicians. He couldn't slow his mind down enough to see a face, as if the tape had snapped on the movie projector, frames playing at a hundred miles an hour. He pictured himself trying to grab the spinning wheels of the projector, a ten-foot tail of brown film flapping in the wind, growing longer by the second, coiling around him, wrapping him in giant loops. He saw himself hanging ten feet below the bridge, swaddled in rubber like the Michelin Man, a bungee jumper bobbing up and down with appendages of stretchy brown videotape. Why jump? Why not? Nothing awaited him but nothingness—below the water or above the water, it was all the same. His gaze landed on his house perched on the cliff across the bay with its warm yellow lights. He suddenly felt a bone-chilling cold and, at the same moment, felt relieved by the simplicity. Within minutes he became so cold that all that mattered was relief from the cold. Shivering, he reached into his pockets, no car keys, he began walking toward the glowing warmth of his house. He didn't decide not to jump, he didn't decide anything, he was just drawn toward the warmth, not even aware he was walking until he came to the San Francisco end of the bridge and looked back to where he'd been standing and looked down at his ashen feet under Maria's desk.

"Ray?"

Confused, Ray looked up, surprised to see her.

"Where the have you been, Ray? You walked here from the Golden Gate Bridge?"

"I came for my appointment."

"We have an appointment scheduled for tomorrow," she said softly, "to talk about the lawsuit."

"I thought it *was* tomorrow."

"Our appointment's for Wednesday...tomorrow."

He slumped down farther in his chair, looking dejected, mumbling, "Tomorrow never comes, it's always today."

"What happened to your face, Ray? How did you get those cuts on your neck? Maybe you should get cleaned up. Get some rest. Does anyone know you're here?"

"Who cares where I am?"

Maria folded the newspaper on her desk, set it aside, and said under her breath, "You swam here."

Ray rubbed his bare feet into the office carpet, trying to stimulate some circulation, his thoughts reeling back to walking from the bridge on the craggy trail along the cliffs toward the warmth of his home. He heard the bark of sea lions on the beach below, saw a tall, teepee-shaped bonfire and automatically veered off toward the heat, the trail steep and rocky, cutting his feet. He finally reached the edge of the cold sand and gravitated to the blaze of driftwood logs as big as trees. The fire was surrounded by young men and women with long hair, some naked, some holding hands in a circle, two guitar players sitting in the sand strumming and singing, dogs weaving in and out of everyone's legs. Ray got close to the fire and held out his hands. Heat, relief from cold, such a simple concept. He felt a soft touch on his arm and saw an attractive young woman naked above the waist extending a sweet-smelling joint to him.

Ray shook his head. "No, thanks."

"It's peace, brother."

"Not tonight."

She stepped closer with a soft, disarming smile. "It's elastic, it can bend colors. It's laced. It will make you a hero."

"Laced?"

She twirled her arms in flowing figure eights over her head "It's a liquid dream. One puff will show you the world as it really is." She took a long, lung-expanding hit and slowly exhaled, blowing the smoke up and down Ray's body, from the top of his head to his feet. Then she turned the joint around, put the lit end in her mouth, and blew a jet stream of smoke into Ray's nose and mouth.

He inhaled the pungent taste of licorice. When he took another breath, she gave him a second big hit, then started slowly spinning in place, arms straight out. Another shirtless woman came over and puffed deeply on the joint. Then the two women intertwined their arms above their heads, turned with their backs against each other, and slowly extended their bare feet out step by step. They slid their feet out until just the back tops of their shoulders were touching, and they collapsed onto the sand laughing.

Through the shimmering sounds of people laughing and strumming guitars, Ray recognized the Bob Dylan song the two men in the sand were playing, took a step closer, and joined in, quietly harmonizing. Soon everyone joined in, singing and swaying, ending with a round of applause for themselves, collapsing onto the beach in a pile of tangled limbs and hair.

The guitar player sitting next to Ray looked up. "You sing really good."

Ray nodded.

"No kidding, man, you sound like a professional singer."

"Wow!" a young woman lying on her back yelled out. "Check out the light show!"

"Trippy!"

"Awesome!"

Myriad red, blue, and yellow lights flashed from a half-dozen police cars and emergency vehicles on the span of the bridge above them. In the middle of the activity, a flatbed truck with a large revolving spotlight scanned the surface of the water, a coast guard cutter below also cast a white searchlight beam.

The array of blinking lights that was like a psychedelic expansion of the fountain of sparks pouring skyward from the bonfire. Some of those still standing craned their necks so far back they fell backward onto the sand. While everyone looked up at the bridge, Ray looked up at the cliffs behind them at Seacliff. He couldn't see his house, but he could see the eerie reflection of flashing lights and knew that police cars were at his house. He didn't know where he should be, he was in suspended animation, between life and death, a walking ghost. He didn't want to be anywhere. He looked down at the burning embers on a driftwood log covered with white and orange worms, a collage of pulsing color like the whirling lights on the bridge, like the glowing complexion of the girl standing next to him, her eyes ablaze.

"Ray?"

He looked up across the desk at Maria.

"Can I make you a cup of tea or get you some food? There's an executive gym in the basement with a shower and towels if you'd like to clean up. You're bleeding."

He ran his hand down the side of his neck, looked at the blood on his fingers, and remembered the girl on the beach touching him, showing him the blood on her fingers and painting stripes on both their cheeks.

He'd stayed at the beach until the fire became a breathing mound of coals and the emergency lights on the bridge were fewer than before.

"Seems like everyone's pretty much gone." It was the girl who gave him the hits of pot. "Are you cold?" She nodded at the bedroll under her arm. "I've got a sleeping bag." She turned and headed down the beach, looking over her shoulder with an inviting smile.

Ray followed.

She made them a bed in the sand at the base of the cliff and they both lay down.

"What's your name?"

"Ray."

"I'm Amanda." She waited for him to say something, he didn't. "Do you live around here?"

Ray was on his back with his hands folded behind his head, looking up at the bridge. "Those emergency lights? The emergency's over. Everyone can go home. Everyone but me. I've got one foot on the boat and one foot on the dock." He pointed up at the cliff behind them, keeping his gaze on the bridge. "That's where I used to live, before the lights came on."

She gazed up.

"Some memories, I choose whether or not to think about them," Ray said. "Some memories I have no choice. They hang around like the old clothes in my closet I never wear. But I never remember things I don't understand. It's like trying to have thoughts I don't know how to have."

"I remember everything," Amanda said.

"Sometimes you think you can't bear to go on living," Ray said, "then you always do. But you can't survive death."

She nodded at his index finger still pointing in the air. "Hoping for a miracle? A Grateful Dead ticket?" She licked her own index finger and held it in the air. "Checking for wind direction." She barely got the words out before she cracked up laughing.

He kept his finger erect, gave her a deadpan look, and started laughing with her.

When their laughing died down, she laid her head on his shoulder, wrapped her hand into a small fist around his still-erect finger, and began gently massaging it up and down.

He gazed into her eyes. "I used to live up there, above us, in a house on the cliff. Now I live down here on the beach with you. Both places have a view of the bridge, the place up there has a hot shower."

They burst out laughing again. When she naturally quieted down, he didn't. He kept laughing—a gruff, forced laugh. When she removed her hand from his and nudged a few inches away, he abruptly stopped laughing and folded his hands back behind his head. They listened to the sound of the small waves lapping on the shore and fog horns moaning in a slow, repeating pattern, guiding in cargo ships from China and notifying San Francisco residents that the fog was arriving. A fuzzy veil of mist cloaked the remaining emergency lights on the bridge.

Amanda gently rubbed Ray's shoulder. "Even flowers that get stepped on spring back."

She moved closer and ran her fingertips across his chest, over his stomach, and up and down his inner thigh. When she put her leg over his and pressed her tight bell-bottoms against him, he began humming in unison with the foghorns. It took Amanda a minute for the sound to register. She stopped moving and listened. Ray was humming a mournful dirge, modulating up from the horns a minor third, a fifth, then back to unison, an ancient sorrow emanating from deep within his chest.

She put one hand on his heart and one on her own. "You have a beautiful voice."

She fell into a slow undulating movement, rubbing up and down against his leg in cadence with the oscillation of the horns and his voice. As Ray went deeper into his circular breathing, sustaining notes through the long intervals between the sounding horns, she rubbed against him with more pressure, her breathing becoming more pronounced until she emitted a chirp and slid her hand all the way up the inside of his thigh. She felt that he was completely unaroused and he abruptly stopped humming. The naked foghorn blared on like an aberrant saxophone blowing after the band stopped.

Amanda rolled onto her back.

He waited until her breathing slowed. "I don't think I've ever slept with a woman I didn't have sex with." He rolled toward her on his side. "I've been lonely, but compared to how I feel now, it feels like I've never been lonely before. Like, I'm not even really here." He rolled back over on his back and gazed up at the bridge. "You're sweet, Samantha."

"You're sweet, too. My name's Amanda."

"When I saw the front page of today's paper—"

Ray jerked his head up at Maria.

"—it was the first time I've really understood how much emotional pain you've been in Ray."

Ray abruptly stood up, walked to Maria's second-floor window, and looked down at the thick traffic. Maria noticed again how discolored his feet were.

"I guess I just needed to take a walk," he said to the window, "to clear my head." There was a long pause. "When I was singing 'Stephanie' at that Greek Theater concert last year, Woody was sleeping in the dirt out back, lying in a pile of trash. My limo driver spotted him in the headlights when we were leaving. I heard the driver mention it, but I was too busy getting head in the back seat of the limo." Ray shook his head lightly. "I'd gotten a message that Woody was at the backstage door, trying to get in. I ignored it, a slight irritant washed away by the ocean of adulation I was getting. I made about forty grand for that show. The only reason I even had a gig like that was because 'Stephanie' was such a big hit." He turned to Maria sitting at her desk across the small office. "I could've helped Woody that night. I could've given him some money, given him a ride. Hell, I could've brought him up on stage to sing his song with me. To sing *his* song. And now…I went over to his house last night and asked *him* to help *me* and he threw me out. I don't blame him." He looked down at his feet. "I walked here from the bridge. Four miles, no money for even a bus." He looked down. "My feet are a mess."

Maria waited to see if he was going anywhere with his train of thought. His intentions were usually transparent, easy to read; she'd never seen him act so random. "You're in an interesting position right now, Ray. You can sit back and literally watch the rest of the world sum up your life. Everything you've ever done will be unraveled in the press by one journalist or another."

He stood staring out the window. "Maybe I'll take the time to figure out my own goddamn life."

"Would you like a ride home?"

"Home?" He seemed perplexed by the question. "There were cops at my house last night. I definitely don't feel like dealing with cops or reporters."

"What are you going to do? You can't just....are you going to tell people you're alive?"

"Why do I have to tell anybody anything?"

The intercom on Maria's desk came on. "Ms. Angel, sorry to interrupt, I know you have someone with you. Marty Levine from A&M records is on line two; he says it's important. It's about Ray Bell. Would you like to take his call?"

Maria looked at Ray by the window. "I don't have to take this right now."

He walked over and sat in front of her desk. "Go for it."

"You sure?'

He nodded.

"Should I tell him...what should I tell him?"

"Let *him* do the talking."

She was surprised at how clear and articulate Ray had suddenly become. "Put the call through," she said, and left the speakerphone on. "Hello, Marty."

"Hello, Maria. Thank you for taking my call. I assume you've heard about Ray?"

Maria and Ray locked eyes across her desk. "It's on the front page, Marty."

"It's sad it had to end like this. He was a tremendous talent, always beating himself up about his lack of songwriter ability. He had a voice to die for."

Maria cleared her throat.

"Sorry, that wasn't very tactful. You know what I'm saying. He always resented the fact that his first hit song was written by someone else, then the issue about the authorship of 'Stephanie'...no sense revisiting all that now. It's a shame he wasn't satisfied just being a great singer. Elvis Presley didn't write his own songs but look at the impact *he* had on popular music."

Maria tried to think of something to say.

"Maria?"

"I'm here."

"I'm sorry to be calling you today. If it's too distressing for you to talk right now, I completely understand."

When Ray adjusted himself in his seat, she thought he was going to speak. He stayed silent, lips pursed, his eyes riveted on the speakerphone.

"Maria?"

"Still here."

"Actually, I called for a reason. I know the timing's not ideal, but I have a responsibility to both my artists and my shareholders. As you know, A&M controls Ray's catalogue. I've fielded no less than twenty phone calls today from press and industry people. Right now, because of all the attention being given to Ray's career, there's a unique window of opportunity to exploit the renewed interest in Ray's music. Before I go any further, Maria, I assume you'll be handling legal matters for Ray's estate going forward?"

She looked across her desk. Ray seemed completely mesmerized by the speakerphone.

"Maria, I know this is all very sudden. It doesn't sound like you're up for talking about business right now, which is completely understandable. I just have a responsibility to act in a professional manner. My company has the contractual authority, and we're perfectly capable of doing what needs to be done regarding distribution of Ray's catalogue. There are other matters to address, but all I need to know for the time being is the status of legal representation of Ray's estate. If by notifying you of our intention to continue distributing the catalogue, I can assume Ray's estate has been notified, then there's nothing else that needs to be discussed at the moment."

Maria thought she saw Ray nod. It was the most nuanced up and down movement, but she felt sure she'd gotten an affirmation. Her eyes still on Ray, Maria said, "I'll confirm with Connie Bell, Ray's mother, that she wants me to continue my representation and I'll get back to you."

"Thank you, Maria. One more matter. I spoke with Jeff Pearlman today. I suggested that, under the dramatically changed circumstances Woody might want to acknowledge Ray's compositional participation in the song 'Stephanie' and contribute some amount of the song's royalties going forward to Ray's estate. I'm told that the entirety of Ray's estate will go to his mother, he has no other surviving family. Again, I'm sorry for being so officious. I know you understand that time is of the essence. The music business moves fast. I'll wait to hear from you."

Maria hung up, leaned back, and exhaled. "That was the spookiest phone call I've ever had."

Ray kept staring at the phone.

"Ray?" she said softly. "Do you want me to call your mother?"

Without looking up he said, "Call her."

Maria cleared her throat. "You sure you want to make this decision right now? We'll be perpetuating a sham. It could be considered fraud. You don't *have* an estate, you're here."

"I'm *not* here. Call her." Ray's voice was flat. "Just ask if it's okay to represent my estate. Keep it simple. She'll be upset, but she'll be okay while we sell some records. It'll help her, too. Tough love."

"On the speakerphone?"

Ray nodded.

"Hello?"

"Connie, it's Maria Angelista."

"Hello, Maria. I thought I might be hearing from you."

Ray pictured his mother sitting in her living room in Redwood City, gaunt, frail, silver-white hair in a bun, chain-smoking cigarettes with red lipstick smudges on the white filters. On an average afternoon she'd be on her second or even third martini. Today would be above average.

"I'm very sorry about what happened," Maria glanced up at Ray. "We're all in shock. Everyone that's known Ray or known his music is in shock." She rested her forehead in her hand, making an effort to get the words out. "You have my deepest condolences, Connie. I wish I could find the right words that would..."

"Words are meaningless, Maria. Less than meaningless. Please, I'd prefer not to try to understand this. Not today. Maybe I never will. I know that the only possible solace will come from the passage of time."

Maria waited a full minute. "I'm sorry to bring this up today but, as you know, I've been Ray's attorney regarding his music business matters. I'm calling to ask if you'd like me to continue my legal representation to include Ray's estate. I believe you are his only heir."

"Legal representation? Oh dear, I haven't considered anything like that. I haven't even come to grips with what happened."

"Again, I apologize for calling about a business matter on a day like this. At some point, we should get together in person to discuss this. There is one other matter I feel compelled to notify you of...a bit of positive news. Woody, the singer-songwriter who composed the song 'Stephanie'....who *helped* compose *parts* of the song, has offered to contribute songwriting royalties from the song to your retirement savings, seeing as how you are Ray's only remaining heir."

"My child...my beautiful son! He made me feel...."

"If it's too difficult for you to discuss on the phone, perhaps we can—"

"...he made me so proud. I can't...I can't imagine a world without him!"

There was a smashing sound, a high-pitched wail, then quiet weeping. Ray knew his mother was trying to muffle the sound of her crying with one of her frilly white embroidered handkerchiefs.

Maria looked up, not sure what had happened. Ray knew exactly what they'd heard; his mother's martini glass slipping out of her shaking hand and falling onto the polished mahogany coffee table in her living room.

Ray and Maria sat listening to the soft sobbing on the speakerphone, Maria unsure what to say. After another minute, she cleared her throat. "Connie, again, I want to apologize for—"

"Mom?"

"Ahh! What was that?"

"It's me, Mom."

"Ray?"

"Yes, it's me."

"Is that really you?"

"It's me Mom. I'm fine."

"Oh my God, Ray. You're *alive*! I can't believe you're alive. I thought I was hearing a ghost."

"I'm okay, Mom. The newspapers made a mistake. It was all a mistake. I'm fine. Sorry for the scare. I love you, Mom."

"To hear your voice. I'm always glad to hear from you, but to hear from you today— it's a miracle. Thank God. Thank God you're okay. I keep thinking I'm I going to wake up from a dream."

"I'm really all right, mom. I'll explain everything. In fact, I'll come down and see you. I'll come see you today."

"That would be lovely, Ray, that would be lovely."

"I love you, Mom. I'll see you a little later."

Ray nodded, Maria hung up the phone, and they both sat looking at it.

"I couldn't do that to my mother," Ray said.

"I understand." She thought for a moment. "Shouldn't we make some kind of announcement? Put out a press release, tell people you're alive?"

"I went to the bridge to check out the sunset and lost my car keys. What's the big deal? If the press wants to make a story out of it, let 'em."

"You wrote a suicide note and went to the railing of the bridge to do what?"

"To take a walk and get some space from all the bullshit in my life!" He shoved his chair back, stood up, and headed for the door.

"Ray? Where are you going?"

"I don't know." He looked confused. "I can't go home, not right now. I'll go to my mother's house. She could use some comforting. So could I."

"Are you going to walk there?"

Ray's mother lived in Redwood City, thirty miles south of San Francisco. He reached into his pockets and remembered he had no money, no wallet. He looked down, no shoes. He shrugged, walked back to his spot by the window, and looked into the fluorescent-lit offices across the street. "Lawyers."

Maria went over and looked at what he was looking at. "Lawyers?"

"Those offices are probably full of lawyers."

"Actually, I think it's an insurance company."

"What do lawyers do for people anyway?" He pointed down with a sour look on his face. "That suit on the phone in the corner office, I bet he's a lawyer talking to another lawyer, costing people a thousand dollars an hour. I get that carpenters build shelves, musicians make music, a doctor stitches a cut. What do lawyers actually *do* for people?"

"If two people disagree about something, they can settle it with a physical fight and the biggest, meanest person wins—survival of the unfittest. Or lawyers can do what they're trained to do and have civilized dispute resolution. It's called evolution."

"Big animals eat small animals, big fish eat small fish, but sometimes the smart little guy outsmarts the big tough guy."

She waited for him to finish his thought and connect the dots, but he didn't. "I know something tangible a lawyer can do for you right now; give you a ride to your mother's house."

—

"Want the heater on for your feet?"

"I don't care."

She turned on the heater and they rode for ten minutes in silence, until she said, "Is it your financial problems, is that what's causing all your stress, Ray?"

"It doesn't help."

"I imagine you'd be in a more musically creative space if you weren't about to lose your house."

"Duh."

She had the feeling that if she didn't say anything, neither would he, as if he weren't present, not even aware of being in her car. "I don't know if you're up for talking about this right now, Ray, but we could file that lawsuit, possibly get a settlement, and save your house."

Ray slightly swayed side to side in his seat as if with the movement of the car, but the car wasn't swaying. "File it."

"Ray?"

"You heard me. What've I got to lose? Nothing. Maybe I can keep my nice house I can't even go to. As soon as you file it, everyone will know I'm alive. I'm tired of thinking about what people think about me. I'm tired of thinking."

She waited a few minutes. "I heard Woody's playing at the Sweetwater this Friday. I can get the complaint filed and serve him at the show. I know the right process server for the job."

"He's probably trying to call me right now about what songs we're going to play."

"What?" Maria looked over at him. "You're playing with Woody at the Sweetwater on Friday?"

"Just kidding," Ray turned and spoke to the passenger window. "When I was at Woody's house, I asked him about sitting in at one of his gigs. He wouldn't call me in a million years." He turned back. "You're going to serve Woody at his gig? That seems pretty harsh, even for that little punk. I thought you serve these lawsuits on lawyers."

"Lawyers have people personally served all the time. It might make Woody want to settle and avoid litigation."

CHAPTER 14

Four houses from Ray's mother's, they saw the white van with CHANNEL 4 TELEVISION printed on the back, the side door open with a camera on a tripod pointed at the house. Maria pulled over.

"Keep driving," Ray said. "When you get to the end of the street take a left, then a left into the first alley."

Maria glanced over at him, his calm, calculated manner as unexpected as everything else that day. When she pulled into the alley, Ray's eyes darted around. "That's the back door of her house. Go past a few more houses, slow down, I'll jump out, you keep driving. Thanks for the ride. Put it on my bill."

Keeping his head down, Ray walked quickly, almost running down the narrow alley to his mother's house.

"Ray! What are you doing at the back door?"

"Unlock the door, Mom."

When he got inside and kissed her cheek, she wrapped her arms around him and held on, sobbing. He smelled the alcohol on her breath. "Sorry for the scare."

She held on, her thin arms shaking. "I can't believe you're here. I thought I'd never see you again. I was so upset I couldn't—"

"I'm fine, Mom. I really am. Let's go in the living room. Make me a drink of whatever you're having."

Connie Bell lived alone in the tidy 1950s suburban tract home Ray bought for her with royalties from his first hit record. The house was filled with cabinets of China and ceramic knick-knacks, the walls covered with framed Ray Bell concert posters. She made them each a martini, and they sat in the living room where she'd been watching television.

"I haven't heard from you, Ray. When I don't hear from you it often means you're not doing well. I was just thinking about you yesterday and then I turned on the television and the news came on with your car on the bridge and pictures of you and…I couldn't watch. Now I can't unsee those images."

She sipped her drink and Ray saw the familiar thin blue veins and tremor of her delicate pale white hand. Throughout his childhood it seemed as if she always had a drink in her hand, often shaking on the verge of spilling. By the second or third drink, early evening, her hand steadied, and so did her temperament. He remembered as a child being relieved when the martinis appeared, and he knew that no matter what he'd done to displease her that day, she'd soon be in a better mood. In recent years, when he came to visit, it seemed as if all they did was get drunk together and watch TV.

"I've been meaning to call you, Mom. I've just been tangled up in my mind with my own problems."

"I didn't know you were so unhappy. You should've called me."

He saw her tears welling up. "I just stopped on the bridge for a minute to check out the sunset and lost my car keys. That was it. The press tries to make a big thing about everything to sell newspapers."

She gave him a weak smile. They turned their attention to the TV and sipped their drinks.

When a commercial came on, she said, "What happened to your neck? How did you get all those cuts?"

He raised his hand and felt the dried blood. "I was on a walking trail near where I live. I got too close to some blackberry brambles." He finished his drink and saw she'd finished hers. "You've really perfected your martinis, Mom. How about making us another one?"

"Are you hungry? I can make you something. You must be hungry."

"I'm fine."

She took their glasses to the kitchen. The next TV commercial came on, a birds-eye-view of acres of new cars at a Redwood City Ford dealership.

"Where are your shoes, Ray?" his mother called from the kitchen. "Aren't your feet cold? They look like they're cold. I might still have an old pair of your father's socks somewhere."

"I forgot my shoes. I left them in my car."

"I can't really hear you very well. You know my hearing's going. I'll come in there in a minute. I should call my friends and let them know you're all right.

Everyone called when they heard the news. They're going to start coming by with the casserole parade."

The TV commercial segued into the evening news with an image of Ray's suicide note. Ray held his breath. Millions of people were seeing the spastic-looking handwriting scrawled by a madman. Ray's mother had confident-looking, neat handwriting and always encouraged him to take notice of people's handwriting and what it might say about them. He remembered scribbling the note in his car on the bridge, pressing his pen into a scrap of paper on the soft leather passenger seat. When drops of blood fell off his face onto the note, he thought it added a dramatic touch, a validation of his feelings. Now it was making great news.

A handsome, glossy-skinned television reporter with a solemn expression appeared with a photo of Ray in a high-collar white shirt open almost to his waist singing to an audience of thousands. "And now we take you to Ray Bell's luxury mansion in Seacliff, California, one of San Francisco's most exclusive neighborhoods. Rob Portman is with us live, talking with Zoe Schoenfeld, Ray's live-in girlfriend."

"Live-in girlfriend?" Ray said to the TV.

"What did you say?" his mother called from the kitchen.

Sitting in Ray's living room surrounded by cardboard boxes, a reporter extended an oversized foam-covered microphone toward Zoe. She was taking a cigarette in and out of her mouth so fast it looked like the film had been sped up.

"Thank you, Phil. I'm sitting in this lovely Seacliff home with Zoe Schoenfeld. Zoe, I imagine this must be a very difficult time for you. This is where you've lived with Ray Bell?"

"We've been, like, we're best friends and do practically everything together and…I, like, I can't believe this is happening." When she started blowing smoke at the camera, the cameraman's hand came into view, waving her to turn away. She quickly turned her head and exhaled. "Sorry, I've never like been on TV before. I, like, don't even know what he could've been thinking. This whole thing is like totally, like…I've never had a friend that didn't want to live." She looked down at her lap. When she looked up, she was crying, her cigarette singeing the split ends of her hair.

Ray stood up, hands on his hips, moving closer to his mother's television set.

"Ray," his mother called from the kitchen, "Did you say something? I think my hearing's getting worse."

"You were with Ray yesterday?" the reporter said to Zoe, "the day he leapt from the Golden Gate Bridge?"

She brushed away the strands of hair, maneuvering her cigarette with two fingers. "Yeah. We were like totally together, hanging out and everything, and then he just, like...he just disappeared."

"This must be quite a shock for you."

"Oh my God. I'm *totally* in shock. I don't even know what to say. Besides being my *boy*friend, Ray was like, he was my friend. And his incredible voice, his singing could make me orgasm just hearing it." She gave a nervous laugh. "Sorry. I forgot we're on TV. I'm just, like, I totally don't know what to say."

"With all these cardboard boxes throughout the house, it looks as if you and Ray were moving in or moving out. How long have you and Ray lived here?"

She waved her cigarette around the room and rattled on. "Actually, he's moving out. I mean he *was* moving out. See, Ray wrote this song 'Stephanie,' and this guy named Woody took it back from him because he was all like jealous because his girlfriend who's now his wife is named Stephanie. Ray's been working with different songwriters trying to get another song that's all like, like 'Stephanie' so he can have another hit."

Ray raised his hand as if he could reach into to the TV.

"I don't mean a song *like* 'Stephanie,' I mean a good *song* like 'Stephanie.'" She giggled. "I say 'like' a lot when I'm nervous."

Ray took four quick steps across the living room, reached up with both hands, shoved open his mother's heavy insulated curtains and stood facing the window, a fistful of curtain in each hand.

"I mean Ray's like one of the greatest singers...*was* one of the greatest singers, that anybody ever..."

The reporter quickly put the tip of his finger up to his right ear. "Thank you, Zoe. We're now going to our mobile reporter Zack Schanaker with a live update from Redwood City, California. He's currently at the home of Connie Bell, mother of the late Ray Bell. What've you got, Zack?"

"Well, Rob, unbelievably, standing in the living room window of Ms. Bell's Redwood City home seems to be none other than—are you ready for this?—a person who looks exactly like Ray Bell. We're trying to get a close-up for our live audience. As you know Rob, Ray Bell's appearance is quite familiar to many of our television viewers."

Ray's mother walked into the living room balancing two over-filled martini glasses, saw a full-screen close-up on the TV of Ray standing at her living room window, then looked at Ray at the window, back at the TV, and walked over and stood next to him, the two trembling drinks spilling over.

Ray knew the foot-long zoom-lens camera in the van in front of the house was broadcasting a magnified close-up of his face around the world. He became aware of his mother extending a martini glass to him, looked across the room at the image of him and his mother on the television, spun back around, reached up, and whipped the curtains closed.

"Rob, this has been an amazing evening of revelations. We're here at Connie Bell's home in Redwood City where, by all appearances, her son Ray Bell was seen just moments ago. The lights in the home are on, the curtains are now closed, and it looks like generous happy hour martinis are being served at the Bell residence. We were able to see a man who looked very much like Ray Bell for only a matter of seconds. I'm guessing ten to twenty seconds. I'm sure a replay is being prepared so our viewing audience can decide for themselves what they were witnessing. Back to you, Rob, in Seacliff."

Rob and Zoe were in Ray's living room watching TV, seeing the image of themselves watching TV. They'd both seen the screenshot of Ray at the window of his mother's house. Rob extended the microphone to Zoe as the cameraman panned to a close-up. She was trying to understand the concept of looking at herself on TV, like looking at a mirror but every move she made moved backward.

"We're back at Ray Bell's Seacliff mansion with Zoe Schoenfeld, Ray's live-in girlfriend. The world-renowned pop singer was thought to have committed suicide, to have jumped from the Golden Gate Bridge. Now, a complete surprise to everyone, Ray, or someone looking a lot like Ray, was seen by our viewers to be alive and well at his mother's home in Redwood City, California. Zoe, I'm sure our viewers would like to hear your thoughts on this latest development. It looked like Ray Bell to me, did it to you?"

Zoe squirmed in her seat, her eyes glued to the screen. "Oh my God. *Oh my God*!"

"All indications are that Ray Bell is alive, but at this moment we can't be certain. Knowing Ray as well as you do, can you speculate on what might have happened? Sitting here, do you believe Ray is alive?"

"I'm just, like…oh my *God*."

"Being so close to Ray, can you tell us what you're feeling right now?"

"I'm just like totally, like…*oh…my…God*!"

"Thank you, Zoe. We now go to Gretchen Ghirardelli at our San Francisco newsroom. Gretchen, can you summarize for our viewers the information we have to date? Are emergency workers still searching for Ray Bell's body under the Golden Gate Bridge?"

—

Early the next morning, Ray thrashed his way to consciousness in his mother's guest room. He bolted up in the narrow bed in his mother's guest room, breathing hard, tasting the metallic stomach acid he'd thrown up in his mouth from all the gin he drank last night. He belched, farted, fell back onto the hard bed, and tried rubbing the dream from his eyes.

Evenly spaced rows of framed black and white photos slowly came into focus on the walls surrounding him; his mom and dad taking him to his first singing audition at age six; his dad, Ray Sr., playing saxophone on a small jazz club stage; Ray sitting in, singing with the band at age seven. The smell of his father's always present cologne always made him queasy. Then his eyes landed on a family favorite, a glossy photo of him, eight years old, in his first suit and tie, standing next to Elvis Presley, Elvis' hand on his shoulder and the silver flourish of an autograph in the bottom corner of the photo. He remembered what Elvis said to him that day: *"I don't really know much about music. In my line of work, you don't have to."*

Then, in chronological order across another wall, pictures of him and his mother after his father's death, at school plays and talent shows, everyone else in the pictures with both their parents.

His father had been found in his car with another woman, parked on the side of the road in the middle of winter, the motor running, both of them asphyxiated. People talked about alcohol, infidelity, suicide, maybe a double suicide, and he remembered trying to wrap his nine-year-old brain around the concept. Exactly where had his dad gone? Into that fake-looking body in that casket with all the hushed talk about his mom saying no to a double funeral? What happened to his dad? Did he stay the same age? His dad had left him alone to figure out everything for himself with his alcoholic mother.

Ray flung off his blanket. The sheets were tucked in so military-tight, he had to struggle to extricate himself from the bed. His mother kept a fanatically neat house, ironing sheets, hand towels, even his boxer shorts when he was a kid. He remembered one day leaving for school, her at the ironing board. She noticed his fistful of school-lunch one-dollar bills, took them from him, and ironed them crisp. She'd seemed to become even more obsessively neat after his father died.

He sat up on the edge of the bed. He didn't want to be there. He needed coffee, and a drink, and a ride—to anywhere. What were his options? No money, no credit card, no driver's license—like starting his life over from scratch, like when his father left him. Anyone he contacted would want to know what happened on the bridge. It'd be impossible to act like nothing happened. TV cameras and reporters were probably waiting at his house, probably still in front of his mother's house. Maybe it *was* time to start over, dye his hair, move to Canada, get a job singing in a blues band.

In the living room, the TV was still on, showing a fast-food hamburger commercial that turned his stomach. He started toward the kitchen when a split-screen comparison came on of his first album cover and him standing at his mother's window last night. A fast-talking TV personality with sculpted amber waves of hair speculated on whether or not Ray was alive. The photo of Ray from last night was barely discernable; a spooky, ghost-like mystery-guest suspended in the backlight of his mother's living room. Ray flicked off the TV.

He found a plate of fresh muffins and a pot of coffee in the kitchen and thought about what his mother had been going through in recent days, how she'd shown him nothing but unconditional love his entire life.

He looked at the phone. Maria and his mother were the only ones that knew for certain he was alive. He picked up the phone and called Maria.

"Good morning, law offices."

"Maria, I need you to do something for me."

"Ray?"

"How many clients do you have? Can you go over to my house and see what's going on?"

"I know what's going on. Your live-in girlfriend Zoe is holding a press conference."

"What?"

"She's on TV on your front lawn with enough microphones to be the president in the rose garden. She's making a personal plea. 'Ray, for your fans around the world, if you can hear me, please, if you're alive…call home. We love you.' The press is eating it up."

"What?"

"Is that the only word you know? You could put the brakes on this whole thing right now: just walk out the front door of your mother's house."

Ray parted the small lace curtain over the kitchen sink. All he could see was the house next door.

"What're you going to do, Ray?"

"I had too many martinis last night. I can't even think. Is there any way you can go to my house and get Zoe and everybody out of there?"

"To tell you the truth, Ray, I don't feel like dealing with your *live-in* girlfriend."

"She's not my girlfriend and you know it. She's a dingbat groupie trying to be on TV."

"Whatever. She must have at least spent the night to call herself live-in. Your latest crush is your problem, not mine. There's a picture in today's paper of an empty vodka bottle on the floor of your car. How about a press release saying you're alive and in rehab—something like that?"

Ray's mother walked in and busied herself cleaning the white tile counter, which was already immaculate. "Good morning, Ray. I'm going out to the store, can I get you anything? Oh, I didn't see you were on the phone."

"Maria?"

"Still here."

"I'll stay here with my mom for a couple more days until I figure out a plan."

"I got an interesting offer today. A promoter from Caesar's Palace in Tahoe said if you're alive, he wants to promote a concert, 'Ray Bell Alive.' Twenty thousand dollars for a three-night engagement—all amenities, the house band, and the Emperor's Penthouse suite. I thought you could use some good news."

Ray heard the front door slam, and his mother call out, "Ray! There are men with cameras on my front lawn. I can't even get to my car. What should I do? They're standing on my tulips. Ray?"

CHAPTER 15

Maria drew circles around the date on her desk calendar: *Woody/File complaint/ Process Server/Sweetwater/9pm show*. She'd stayed up late making revisions to the complaint and couldn't resist playing up the sympathy factor; Ray's financial stress from Woody refusing to acknowledge his musical contribution to "Stephanie," sending him to the brink, to the railing of the bridge. And she couldn't resist the juicy opportunity to have Woody personally served in the middle of his gig at the Sweetwater.

The next day, Maria drove to the Federal Building in San Francisco, paid the seventy-five-dollar fee, filed the complaint, and went straight to the Sweetwater in Mill Valley to purchase a ticket for her process server for that night's show. She was in line at the box office when the bleary-eyed man behind the glass announced, "We've got ten tickets left. That's it, folks."

Maria counted sixteen people in front of her. "Sorry," the man in the box office said to a young man holding a baby, "we don't take food stamps."

"Why not? They're as good as money. Just ask Woody; he's been on food stamps, he'll okay it."

Maria quickly stepped to the front of the line. "Excuse me, I can help solve this problem." She slipped a twenty under the window. "I'll cover his ticket and take one for myself."

"Wow, thanks, lady," the man with the baby said.

The ticket-taker slid two tickets under the window. "Enjoy the show."

—

Five o'clock sound-check, Woody figured he wouldn't have to deal with any fans for the nine o'clock show. When he saw the crowd out front, he circled the block and knocked on the back metal door. Seven swung it open. "I expected you back here. We're sold out. Doors at eight. Betty's doing sound like you requested. Food and drinks in the dressing room. Let me know if you need anything."

Woody walked onto the stage and sat on a wooden chair in front of two microphones—one for guitar, one for vocals. "Let me know what you need," Betty said from the back sound booth. "It should be pretty close."

"You know the routine: make everything louder than everything else."

—

Soundcheck was Woody's favorite part of the gig: his audience was a handful of employees washing glasses, sweeping the floor, and polishing the bar. He'd heard of bands making records entirely from sound-checks, when everyone was most relaxed. Stopping in the middle of a song at a gig with a live audience would be like bucking a force of nature with the inertia of a fast-moving river. At sound check he could play anything and stop any time to fix something.

He was warming up his hands playing jazz chords when his guitar began playing a Woody Guthrie song he remembered and sang a verse:

I got a woman at home with her door left open for me
I got a woman at home with her gate wide open for me.

I'm a high ballad man, I'm a folk singer too
I sing about the good things men and women do

"Sound okay in the house Betty?"

"Perfect. How's it on stage?"

"Perfect."

"Give me a sign if you need any adjustments during the show."

"I'll swallow."

—

Seven had posted a security guy at the door to the downstairs dressing room, but with persistence and ingenuity, people were finding their way in. Woody sat in a corner doing his usual warm-up regimen on guitar. Like swinging a lead bat, he played a series of scales that challenged the limits of his dexterity.

After a few people came over and sat down and tried striking up a conversation, Woody put his backpack on the chair next to him.

Ten minutes later, a tall, lanky man with a blond ponytail, cowboy boots, and a tailored cowboy shirt with pearl snaps, crouched down in front of him, elbows on his knees.

Woody zeroed in on the extra-large turquoise stone on the man's ring and kept playing.

He waited until Woody took a break. "I'm psyched to hear the show tonight." He had clear blue eyes and a friendly, engaging smile. "Mind if I ask you a couple of questions?"

"Sure," Woody said, "what's the second one?" He noticed the man's ease of motion retrieving a leather-bound notebook from the back pocket of his jeans and knew the guy was a pro.

"That's some crazy stuff that's been going down with Ray Bell. The papers reported he jumped off the bridge and left a suicide note about 'Stephanie,' now he's been spotted at his mother's house."

"That's not a question." Woody played a super-human flurry of notes and slapped four fingers across his strings. "Who do you work for?"

"*Rolling Stone*. I was hoping to get your take on the whole Ray Bell thing. There's an entry in the Marin County sheriff's log that indicates they went to your house asking about Ray. Word has it Ray was at your house the night he didn't jump off the bridge."

"The night he didn't jump off the bridge? Every night of his life?"

"Have you been served with Ray's lawsuit?"

"Lawsuit?"

"Filed today in Federal Court in San Francisco. You haven't heard about it? Does that mean Ray's alive?"

Woody slapped the top of his guitar. "The fucker's alive! I knew it! I knew it when I saw those shots of him on TV at his mother's house." Woody shook his head. "The guy can be a real asshole, but I'm glad he hung in there. He sings too good to stop now." Woody's mind took off racing. Another lawsuit? He glanced at his cigarettes on the chair next to him. This was the exact kind of distraction he hated when he was trying to get mentally prepared to play. And here comes more of the mind-fuck morass lawyers always bring.

"Did you guys talk about a pending lawsuit when Ray was at your house?"

Woody dialed his attention back to the rhinestone Rolling Stone cowboy kneeling in front of him. "You don't get my relationship with Ray. You write this story in your magazine, Ray reads it, that's how we communicate. He lives in my head rent free." Woody played another fluid scale. "I didn't get your name."

"RJ"

"I've got an idea, RJ. You know that psychological technique where two people trade places to see what the other person's thinking? Let's try it."

RJ looked up from his notebook. "Try *what*?"

"You be Woody and say what you think I'd say. I'll be RJ, I'll say what I think you'd say. Ready? Here goes. Hi, Woody, my name's RJ. How're you feeling about tonight's show?"

RJ adjusted his position. "Nervous?"

"How do you feel when people ask you how you feel?"

"Nervous?"

"What're you nervous about?" Woody said. "You're playing for people who like your music. What's the worst that can happen? Nobody's gonna die if you play a wrong note."

Still crouching, RJ dropped his notebook to his side and thought for a moment. "The audience just sits there staring at me. When I go see a gig, I check out every move the band makes, so I figure they're checking out every move *I* make. I don't know what to do with my face when I'm playing."

"What if you turn off all the lights and do the gig in the dark? Then they'll *listen* instead of *watching*?"

RJ thought about that one. "There's reasons why performing's scary. Nobody buys a ticket to see somebody walk across a tightrope with no net that's an inch off the ground."

"That's what you signed up for," Woody shot back, "playing music with no net."

RJ looked down at his boots. "What if I shit my pants on stage?"

Woody smiled. "You catch on pretty fast for a music writer. Wasn't it Mark Twain that said writing about music is like dancing about architecture?"

"What do you think was in Ray's mind when he was standing on the Golden Gate Bridge?"

"He was probably thinking about dying. Being dead's like being stupid, it only bothers other people."

RJ closed his leather notebook. "Did Ray Bell have any part in writing 'Stephanie'?"

Woody's smile disappeared. Things were getting way too confusing, and he needed to focus on his show coming up in ten minutes. "You're askin' me about the genesis of that song right now, when I'm getting ready to go on stage? Who do *you* think writes a song? The guy that played bongos? The guy that rolls joints at the recording session? The guy that gave you a place to stay or money for guitar strings? The woman that gave you a blow job when you had writer's block?"

Stephanie walked up in a black, flowing dress with a white silk scarf, her copper-colored curls pouring over her shoulders, everything accented with silver jewelry that seemed to light up the room. After a long embrace, Woody nodded at RJ.

"Stephanie, meet RJ."

"Pleasure to meet Stephanie in the flesh."

Stephanie glanced at the notebook in RJ's hand and immediately recognized him as a journalist.

"I assume you've met many of the musicians your husband knows," RJ said. "Do you know Ray Bell?"

"I'm not a character in one of my husband's songs, Mr. J I'm an actual woman, as you say," she poked her arm, "in the flesh, with thoughts and feelings of my own. Many of them not about Woody. I doubt that you're genuinely interested in who *I* am. In any case, I don't do interviews."

Just then Seven came down the creaking stairs and yelled across the room, "Ten minutes!" He walked up to Woody. "Ready to go on?"

Stephanie looked to Woody. "Do you have a set list?"

Woody shrugged.

"What're you going to start with?"

Woody turned to Seven. "How about clearing out the dressing room so the band can get their shit together?"

Seven placed himself between Woody and RJ. "All right, everyone," he called out to the empty room, "let's give the band some space."

RJ sidestepped Seven. "Woody, are you going to play 'Stephanie' tonight? You think people will react to it differently after what happened with Ray?"

Seven walked straight into RJ. "Time to clear the dressing room."

RJ stumbled backward, headed up the stairs, and called over his shoulder, "Have a good show, Woody!"

Woody, Seven, and Stephanie stood in a little circle. Seven clapped his big hands together. "It's gonna be a great show. You feelin' okay?"

"I'm pretty tired," Woody said, "I was up all night practicing."

Seven glanced around surreptitiously and touched the side of his nose. "How about a little something to wake you up?"

Woody raised his eyebrows. Seven suddenly slapped Woody across the face with his open hand, strong enough to be almost real but light enough to be a joke. It took Woody and Stephanie a moment to get it, then the three of them burst out laughing. "Ready to go on?" Seven asked.

"Approaching liftoff." Woody slipped his guitar strap over his neck. "How about a cup of coffee? Straight black."

"Coffee'll be here in a minute. We need to get going. I tried not selling too many tickets but with friends of staff, friends of friends of friends, the place is about to burst. That kind of crush is okay when the music's playing, not when people are waiting around." Seven headed up the stairs, leaving Woody and Stephanie alone in the dressing room.

"How's Lily?"

"Auddie's with her at the house with a major finger-painting project in the works."

"What should I start with?"

"'Stephanie'?"

Woody strummed the opening chord. "That's all anybody asks me about."

"That's all anybody asks *me* about. Everyone's expecting it. Maybe play it first, get it out of the way, and concentrate on your new songs. Otherwise, everything you play will be *not* 'Stephanie.'" She glanced up at the ceiling. The wooden floor of the small club was creaking under the weight of the over-capacity crowd. "The people up there are thirsty for your music."

Woody smiled. "I read somewhere that it takes twenty minutes for a drink of water to reach your bloodstream, but your brain knows it's coming, so you're satisfied with the first sip. Opening with 'Stephanie' might do the trick." He strummed a minor chord. "Or I could take it in another direction and sing a line from Ray's suicide note."

She grimaced. "Forget about Ray, forget about everything. Just go on stage and listen to the music you're playing."

"You mean like…tell me when you're not thinking of an elephant?"

She smiled. "Something like that."

"If I knew I was going to have to play 'Stephanie' for the rest of my life, I would've kept it to myself. It feels too personal for public consumption."

"It's funny how that works—the more personal the song, the more universal its appeal. Play it for *me*."

Woody dug through his pockets with both hands, jostling the guitar up and down on his neck.

"Did you look behind your ear?" Stephanie reached up and magically produced a guitar pick from behind Woody's ear. "I found it on the floor."

He kissed her, took off his guitar, leaned it against the back of a chair, and started to walk away.

"Where you going?"

"To wash my hands."

She put a hand on his shoulder. "You'll do great tonight. They'll love whatever you do. They just appreciate you doing it."

He looked into her emerald eyes, one of his favorite things to do. "People come to my gigs for the same reason they go to car races: to see the crashes."

"Then drive carefully, but don't get a ticket for sitting at a green light." She smiled, her eyes smiled too. "There's only one person who brings what you bring to the world. There isn't anything you can do to mess this up, except not doing it. Schedule some time to worry later."

Seven came down the stairs with Woody's coffee. "Where is he?"

"Washing his hands."

He set the coffee down, splashing some in the saucer, and looked at his watch. "We're a half-hour past start time. It's getting crazy up there."

"Sometimes he gets a bad case of stage fright, like he's going in front of a firing squad." She wrapped her scarf around her shoulders, contemplating the closed bathroom door. "The harder you push him, the slower he moves. Let's go upstairs. When he comes out, he'll be down here alone. That'll get old fast, he'll have nothing to do but come up and play."

Seven didn't look too thrilled with the plan.

"He's actually very shy," she said. "He feels like performing music is the only time he's really heard, and that makes him self-conscious. He says singing his own words in public is as naked as he can get."

Seven nodded his big head. "Musicians are funny that way. The ones that play here, they get up on stage and perform their hearts out. But when you actually get to know them, they're usually pretty shy."

"When people talk to Woody and they think he's listening, he's not, he's listening to a song in his head." She looked toward the bathroom. "Let's go upstairs. If that plan doesn't work, I'll come back down and get him."

Once upstairs, it took Seven several minutes to make his way through the dense crowd to the stage. "Check," he said into the microphone. "Check, one, two. Thanks for your patience, folks. We've had some technical difficulties, but we've got them sorted out. It'll just be a few more minutes—it'll be worth your wait."

Seven shaded his eyes from the stage lights and looked toward the dressing room…no sign of Woody. He went back to the microphone. "Bunny to the stage, please."

Five minutes later a huge man with long, straight black hair, stevedore arms, and a leather Hell's Angel vest walked up. Seven, himself a large man, was eclipsed by Bunny in every dimension.

"Wussup, boss?" Bunny said. "Every minute I'm not at the front door people are leaking in the cracks. There ain't room in here for a sardine."

"I'll watch the front door. Go downstairs and get Woody up here, pronto. The place is gonna explode if we don't get the music happening."

—

Woody finished washing his hands and walked around the dressing room trying out the first few measures of different songs. Nothing seemed right to open with. He made his way to the foot of the steep, narrow stairway half hidden from sight by an overhanging abutment of the ceiling. He instinctively started playing the guitar introduction to "Stairway to Heaven" by Led Zeppelin. Then he heard the steps creaking and saw a descending pair of black engineer boots followed by two log-size legs in grease-stained jeans that looked like the legs of a giant. Then came a T-shirted stomach hanging like a sack of feed over a rectangular-shaped silver belt buckle, its top edge digging into the protruding gut in a way that looked painful. Thick-soled engineer boots dangerously bent each wooden step as the man's expansive midsection continued to expose itself. Woody visualized a fairy-tale giant descending a wobbly beanstalk unable to support the giant's weight.

When Bunny got to the bottom, Woody involuntarily took a step back. They sized each other up and Bunny scanned the room. "Looks like a party, bro." He strode over to a cooler overflowing with beer cans and a deli-tray of sliced meat, cheese, and bread that looked like it had been left out in the sun. He folded a piece of white bread around a handful of salami and cheese and popped opened a can of beer while Woody scanned the red letters on white background across the top of his expansive back; HELLS ANGELS over a white skull with gold wings and OAKLAND written across the bottom.

"You should talk to Seven about the catering," Bunny said through a fistful of food. "Maybe next time ask for ribs." He drained his beer in three gulps, crushed the can, and tossed it in the trash. "A party without a cake is just a meeting."

Woody stood with his hand across his strings. Bunny was the largest human being he'd ever seen. He was wondering if the missing apostrophe in HELLS ANGELS was intentional when Bunny turned around and started walking toward him, his head about to collide with a low pipe in the ceiling, then ducking at the last moment with an agility that seemed incongruous for his size. "Looks like it's show time." He did an exaggerated bow and extended his open hand toward the stairs. "Senor?"

"I gotta get a couple things together before I go on," Woody said.

"Whuddya need, pal?"

"I need to figure out my set list, what song to start with, stuff like that."

"How about alphabetical order? Start with a song about an Aardvark." Bunny waved at the stairs again. "*Si vous plait*?"

Woody's feet wouldn't move.

"Need a little encouragement?" Bunny put his hand on Woody's lower back and nudged him toward the stairs like an elephant prodding a kitten.

Woody tripped forward, caught himself, and turned around. "I need my backpack with my extra strings and stuff."

Bunny took three long strides across the room, picked up Woody's backpack, and stuck it under his arm. "Gotcha covered, boss." When Bunny went to give Woody another push, Woody headed up the stairs. The crowd was so tightly packed they could barely get one step inside the room.

"Woody!" a young man yelled in Woody's face. "You gonna play 'Stephanie'?"

Woody inched forward, holding his guitar vertically in front of him, got past the young man, and was confronted by a woman whose eyes seemed out of focus. "Woody? Is that really you?" She turned to the girl next to her. "Lydia! It's Woody!"

Bunny took Woody's hand and placed it on his back. "Grab onto my belt and don't let go." With Woody in tow, Bunny moved like a snowplow, forcing people into spaces where there were none. The crowd became so dense a few feet from the stage, Woody lost his grip. Bunny reached back over two people, stuck his hand under Woody's armpit, and gingerly lifted him and his guitar off the ground and onto the steps to the stage. The crowd exploded. "Let me know if you need anything, bro," Bunny yelled in Woody's ear.

—

Parked across the street from the Sweetwater in her black BMW, Maria Angel turned to her passenger, a short, buffed young man with a military haircut in a tight, tie-dye T-shirt, and tie-dye pants. "Go up to the front of the stage where everyone can see you and hand the papers to Woody. Do it in the middle of a song."

The man looked out the passenger window at the crowd at the front door. "Look at all those stoned-out freaks. How the hell am I supposed to get in? I don't even have a ticket."

Maria handed him a ticket to the show and two copies of the summons and complaint. "There's an extra copy."

"I thought these lawsuits get served on lawyers. The guy's represented by Jeff Pearlman, right?"

Maria leaned in closer. "We've been over this. Doing it this way will get Woody's attention—he'll put pressure on his lawyer to settle. You're getting paid, don't question me!"

"Hey, take it easy, lady."

She sat back, gripped the steering wheel, and stared straight ahead like she was driving. "You know what to do. That's why I hired you. Get in there!"

When he got out, she considered what it would be like inside. She was curious to see one of Woody's shows, but not this one. It didn't look like there was enough room in there to breathe.

—

Woody took his seat on the stage, adjusted the microphones, and the crowd exploded. When he played his first chord the noise plummeted like a startled frog pond and he leaned into the mic. "Here's a song about an aardvark that I wrote on my way to the stage." He went into a fingerpicking pattern with a relaxed, swinging cadence until the chord changes morphed into something vaguely familiar. After a few minutes, there was a communal sigh when everyone in the room recognized the melody to "Stairway to Heaven." A minute later he segued into the instrumental chorus of "Stephanie" to a burst of applause.

Everyone was anticipating the lyrics, but Woody played the song instrumentally. When he brought it down for the final chorus, the audience sang the words. So caught up in the communal choir, they didn't notice that Woody had incrementally decreased the volume of his guitar playing until he was moving his fingers a millimeter above the strings, not actually playing at all.

—

The tie-dye-clad process server pushed his way through the crowd at the front door and kept moving, extending his ticket to Bunny.

Bunny clamped his huge hand on the man's shoulder. "Whoa there, buddy, not so fast. There's other people tryin' to get in too."

He put his ticket in Bunny's face. "I pre-paid, dude. The show's already started." He tried to keep going.

Bunny kept his grip on the man's shoulder. "Wait your turn, pal. You can go in when somebody comes out. We're past capacity, don't want the fire marshal bustin' us."

"I paid for a ticket, I'm goin' in." When the man tried peeling Bunny's hand off his shoulder, it was like it was bolted in place. "Get your fucking mitt off my shoulder!"

"Sorry...forgot it was there." Bunny squeezed harder.

The man bent sideways under the pressure. "Hey, goon! What the fuck you think you're doing?"

The more the man struggled, the harder Bunny's grip. After a few seconds, the man stopped resisting, and Bunny released him. "Wait over there, pal, away from the door. I'll let you know when your number comes up. The more you bug me, the longer it'll take."

The man rubbed his shoulder and glared at him. "You just committed assault and battery, asshole!"

"It was self-defense. Call your lawyer or go wait over there."

Bunny opened the door, let someone out, and waved a young woman in. The woman took a half step forward, and there was nowhere to go. Bunny put his hand on her back, gently pushed her in, and closed the door behind her.

Five minutes later a large woman came up and put her arms around Bunny's waist. He bent down and kissed the top of her head. "Hi, Sally, I was hoping you'd show up. Wanna go in and check it out?" He patted her on the butt and opened the door. The previous young woman was still standing just inside.

"Where am I supposed to go?"

"Where there's love, there's room." Bunny reached to the shoulder of the woman he'd just let in, gently guided her to the side, and Sally took the vacant space.

The process server walked up. "I thought you said somebody had to come out. Why'd you let *her* in?"

"Fuck you, that's why."

—

Woody transitioned out of "Stephanie" into free-form rubato space music, haphazard chords and notes that seemingly out of nowhere congealed into a familiar groove, an *ah-ha!* moment for the audience recognizing the funky disco rhythm with a taste of melody from "Stayin' Alive" by the Bee Gees. People were dancing where there was no room to dance. Woody went full steam for an hour, taking the audience on a roller coaster ride through rock and roll power chords, poignant slow ballads, and funky grooves.

Woody took a break to tune. "Thanks everyone for joining me on this musical journey. I've been thinking it's a chance in a million that I ended up here playing music for you people tonight. Here's a new Robert Hunter song." He went into an infectious simple chord progression that immediately got everyone who wasn't already standing up on their feet:

Chance in a million, might as well try
Chance in a million to do it or die
Chance in a million to call your own shot
Better believe it, it's all that you've got

Opportunity don't really knock
Just ticks loud like a dynamite clock
Chance in a million, stay with the beat
Get all I got, it was coming to me

Woody modulated up a full step to a higher key. It literally lifted the energy in the room.

Nine hundred ninety nine thousand goodbyes
Don't make one hello, you got to improvise
One in a million to turn it around
Follow that hunch, baby, follow that sound

He played a short single-note solo and went back to the chords:

Star-struck, hazy, caught up in lies
Burned-out, crazy, tears in my eyes
Chance in a million's better than none
Sink into madness or reach for the sun

Nine hundred ninety nine thousand goodbyes
Don't make one hello, you got to improvise
One in a million to turn it around
Follow that hunch, baby, follow that sound

Chance in a million, winner take all
Chance in a million to follow that call
Better than zero divided by one
Chance in a million is better than none

Chance in a million
Chance in a million
Chance in a MILLION!

Woody took some deep breaths as the applause died down, and he began strumming and singing softly, segueing into his new song, "Song for Lily," everyone straining to hear every nuance of every word.

CHAPTER 16

The moment Seven opened the back metal door to let in some fresh air, the man in tie-dye walked in, waving his ticket.

"Hey!" Seven said.

The man kept moving through the doorway.

"Just a minute, buddy, you need to go to the front door."

"The gorilla at the front door isn't letting people in. I've got a pre-paid ticket, I already missed half the show. I'm goin' in!"

Seven took a closer look. It was unusual to see such a buffed-up short-haired guy wearing head-to-toe tie-dye.

The man took another step forward and Seven grabbed his shoulder on the same spot Bunny had grabbed it. The man violently yanked his shoulder out of Seven's grip. "Hey, asshole, I've waited long enough. I paid for a ticket, I'm goin' in!"

Seven waited until he took another step forward then extended his arm across the doorway and let him run into his forearm, a clothesline across his throat. The man choked, and his demeanor changed. "Look, bro, I don't mean to give you a hard time. I just wanna see the show. I'm a paying customer and my girlfriend's waiting inside. We're huge Woody fans."

Just then Woody finished his guitar solo, the audience noise swelled, and a young woman started to slip in the door.

"Hey, lady! You got a ticket?"

She gave a sheepish smile, a full body shrug, and kept going. When Seven reached for her, the tie-dye man saw his window and disappeared into the crowd.

—

Woody went into the final repeating choruses of "Song for Lily." The audience swayed to the slow-swinging rhythm like one connected body while Woody sang the chorus... *"Being in love with being in love."* Betty the sound engineer did a masterful job of blending Woody's voice with the resonance of his guitar, making it sound as if Woody were playing in the middle of the audience.

The man in tie-dye made his way toward the stage, rudely wedging himself through the blissed-out crowd, jolting people out of their euphoria with a shoulder or sharp elbow, legal papers in each back pocket. A few rows from the foot-high stage, he took out a set of papers, held them over his head, and pressed forward, roughly shoving a slight young woman out of his way. She fell backward into the man behind her, who set her back upright, and she laid her open hand on the process server's chest. "Hey, brother, chill out. There's room here for everyone."

"Outta my way, hippie." He slapped her forearm to the side and took another step toward the stage. A skinny shirtless man put a hand on his shoulder. "Hey, man, be mellow. We're all brothers and sisters here. Dig the music, go with the flow, we can all groove together."

The tie-dye man hit him with a well-placed jab to the solar plexus and the shirtless man crumpled in half. Two fans jumped on the tie-dyed man's back from behind. When he began flailing his elbows, four more people piled on, and he collapsed under the weight, face down onto the wooden floor.

Everyone in the front rows turned around, and Woody stopped playing. When Seven arrived on the scene from the back door and Bunny from the front, there were six people sitting on the tie-dye man's back, arms, and legs. The petite girl he'd first shoved sat on top of the pile with her hands raised in two peace signs.

"Okay, folks, everybody back off." Seven peeled off the people one by one.

As soon as he was able, the tie-dye man violently threw the last two people off, stood up, and faced Seven, fists clenched, the side of his face creased with deep red lines from being pressed into the floorboards. "What the fuck! What the fuck's going on here?"

"You're outta here, asshole, that's what's going on." Seven pointed toward the back door.

He spit in Seven's face, drew his fist back, and started to throw a punch. Bunny, standing right behind him, wrapped his huge hand around the man's fist like it was a golf ball, corkscrewed his arm up behind his back, and lifted him straight up. Seven grabbed the man's other arm and they raised him a foot off the ground and carried him out, the man pedaling like a roadrunner cartoon.

Seven kicked open the back metal door. "One. Two. Heave…Ho!"

They tossed him out onto the paved parking lot like a rag doll. The petite girl who'd been in the scuffle came out and handed Seven the crumpled legal papers she'd found on the dance floor. *Proof of Service, Summons and Complaint.* Seven glanced at the papers, tore them in half then in half again, and tossed the scraps over the man lying on his back on the pavement. "This is called *self-*service, asshole. If I ever see your fake tie-dyed ass around here again, I'll tear you up like those papers."

Seven went back in and found Woody standing by the side of the stage with Stephanie, the audience emitting an agitated low-pitched rumble. "You need to play something," Seven said.

"Play something?"

"Yeah, you know, music."

"I can't play after all that."

"This ain't the time for me to make an announcement," Seven said. "There's only one person that can put this scene back together."

Woody looked to Stephanie.

"You can't leave the energy scattered like this," she said. "These people need some musical healing." She nodded at the guitar in his hands. "Doctor?"

Woody instinctively strummed a few soft chords and the musical calmness spread in concentric circles to people close by. Still playing, Woody walked up the two steps to the stage and sat down on the chair that had ended up a foot back from the microphone. The faint sound of the off-mic guitar sounded like he was playing in the distance. As he slowly leaned closer to the mic, the audience recognized the ebullient chord changes and everyone in the room joined in, singing John Lennon's "Imagine."

—

"Might as well revisit that bottle of Tequila where this all started," Seven said. It was two thirty in the morning, and the doors to the Sweetwater were locked. Woody, Seven, Stephanie, Betty the sound engineer, and Alex the barmaid were the only ones left in the place. Alex set them up with limes, salt, and generous shots. She wasn't drinking tonight, wasn't even officially working.

Seven raised his glass. "To the healing power of music."

They threw down their shots.

"Who's the designated driver?" Stephanie said.

Alex looked at her watch. "The local cops have a shift change coming up. There's no cops patrolling in Mill Valley from three to three thirty every morning. That's our window."

"Time out. Time out." Woody leaned back on his stool, waving his hands flat like an umpire. "Last time we sat here, Seven said the window was nine to nine thirty."

Alex looked at Seven. "Nine o'clock? Why would they change shifts when everybody's driving home drunk from dinner? They do it at three in the morning, when there's no cars on the road. Hello?" Alex lit a joint and passed it to Woody.

Stephanie put her hand on Woody's shoulder and whispered in his ear. "I can drive you home. We can come back tomorrow and get your car."

"One shot of tequila, that's it for me, I'll be fine."

"Okay, one shot max for those curvy mountain roads." She kissed him on the cheek. "You played great." She gave a little bow to Alex, Seven, and Betty. "Goodnight, everyone. Thanks for making this happen. Without people like you, musicians like Woody would be singing in the shower." She reached over and ruffled Woody's hair. "I'm not saying he doesn't sing well in the shower."

Twenty minutes later Woody pointed at the clock over the bar. "Don't want to miss my window of opportunity. Thanks for the big fun, everyone." Walking through the back parking lot, he spotted a police car parked across the street, half-hidden in a stand of trees. When he went back in and reported his finding to the group, he saw Seven look at Alex, a sparkle in her eye.

"Had anything to drink tonight?"

Alex gave a knowing smile. "Not a drop."

Seven stood up and clapped his big hands. "Okay folks, somebody forgot to tell the cop he's supposed to go home, so we're going for plan B. Alex is the designated drunk."

While everyone waited and watched by the back door, Alex walked around the parking lot, tried her keys in three different cars before she found her own, got in, turned the windshield wipers on and off twice, turned the headlights on and off and on again, drove two feet backward, two feet forward, two feet backward, stopped, then ultra-slowly exited the parking lot. While she drove down the street and got pulled over by the cop, the rest of the group got in their cars and headed the other way up the street.

—

Woody's car felt as if it were stationary with the road rolling under him and the scenery streaming by. He often felt that way about his life, a pillar of existence while time and space sped past him at the speed of his thoughts. His convertible top down on a cool Marin County night, making his way up the curvy residential roads of the east slope of Mount Tamalpais with houses built on stilts on impossibly steep hillsides, he replayed the gig in his mind, second-guessing every musical decision. He mentally zeroed in on the last minutes of the extended solo of the third song, when he'd been struggling to plant his feet and gain a purchase that could provide the needed lift to a crescendo. Gaining altitude, he'd just noticed how thick the fog on Mt. Tam had become when he hit a wet patch going forty into a twenty-mile-per-hour curve and suddenly the world was spinning. The car fishtailed, the rear end came around even with the front, four wheels skidding sideways toward the trunk of a giant Eucalyptus tree. Everything slowed in suspended animation while Woody considered his choices: go over a steep embankment or hit the tree. The sound of squealing rubber snapped time back to now, and he made an instantaneous decision to switch from brakes to gas, power-shifted from third to first, skipping second, swung the wheel, floored it, and righted the car out of the curve, his rear bumper just kissing the loose shards of bark protruding from the tree trunk.

Rushing with adrenaline, he shifted to second, slowed to thirty, and kept it there, realizing that mentally replaying the solo in his mind was what sent him careening into the curve. He took some deep breaths, placed his hands at ten and two o'clock on the wood-veneered steering wheel, and made a conscious effort to let his weight sink into his seat. A few quiet miles later his mind did an involuntarily U-turn back to the spot in the guitar solo where he'd tried to make something happen that wasn't happening. He remembered what Stephanie said before the show about scheduling time to worry. Was now the time?

Woody remembered the flushed feeling when he finally managed to bend an old melody into a new shape, locking it into place like a Rubik's Cube. Just when he'd settled into that simple little melody, a repose on a high-altitude plateau, he'd caught a glimpse of a higher, snow-covered peak off in the distance and went for it, leaping across a chasm and found himself out on a musical limb, scrambling for a grip on the slippery melodic slope. And he'd taken that leap of faith on the third fucking song! No sooner had he tipped his hat to the God of melodic symmetry, for some egotistical, look-what-I-can-do masturbatory reason, he went for the octave and played the exact same thing again, only louder, as if playing louder would carry the day. It fell flat on its face like pushing on after an orgasm, everyone in the room knowing he'd forced the solo to go where there was nowhere to go.

"When it's time to shut up," he thought, "just shut up."

He swung his head toward his empty passenger seat and yelled out loud, "No! *You* shut up!"

—

Six o'clock the next morning. Woody'd been asleep for about two hours when he woke to a loud knocking on his front door. Squinting at the morning light in his bedroom, he looked over at Stephanie, sound asleep, then at Lily on the floor next to the bed arranging a pile of grapes and guitar picks. Another hard knock on the door catalyzed what Woody was looking at through his nascent consciousness. He'd been trying to be more mindful about leaving guitar picks lying around that Lily could swallow, they must have fallen out of his pants pocket. His life was forever littered with guitar picks.

Woody threw the covers off, slipped into his bathrobe, draped Lily backward over his shoulder naked, grabbed a half-cup of yesterday's cold coffee on his way through the kitchen, took a gulp, and swung open the front door. The man standing there looked vaguely familiar.

"Woody?"

Woody blinked hard. "Yeah."

When the man took the sheaf of papers out of his back pocket, Woody recognized him as the guy in the audience last night that had tried to serve him in the middle of a song. No longer dressed in tie-dye, he wore a black T-shirt, black pants, and an angry scrape on his face from when Bunny and Seven tossed him out the back door.

The man held the papers up at shoulder height with a diabolical smile. "Hope I'm not disturbing you."

Woody squeezed his eyes closed and reopened them. "What're you doing here at six in the fucking morning? You know I have a lawyer. You know he'll accept service at his office. What the fuck are you doing here?"

The man snapped a sharp military salute. "Reporting for service, sir." He saw that Woody's hands were full, holding Lily backward on his shoulder, the coffee cup in his other hand. He took the six-page summons and complaint, folded it in half the long way, wedged the edge of the papers in the crack of Lily's butt, and took a step back. "You've been personally served…asshole."

Tightening his hold on Lily, Woody instinctively whipped up his bare right foot and kicked the man hard in the balls. The man grunted loudly and doubled over. "You ever come around here again or touch my daughter, I'll fucking kill you…asshole!" Woody spun around and slammed the door closed behind him.

—

Woody set Lily up with fruit salad and coloring books and played his guitar until Pearlman's office opened at 9:00 a.m.

"Read me what it says," Pearlman said.

Woody flattened out the papers on the kitchen counter. "Aren't they supposed to serve your lawyer instead of going to your house? I thought that's what you have a lawyer for. That fucking jerk tried to serve me last night right in the middle of a song, then he comes here pounding on my door at six in the fucking morning." He slapped the papers. "I guess this means Ray's definitely alive and kicking?"

"Just read me what it says."

"You are hereby notified per Federal Rule 4 of Civil Procedure that at the time and place referenced—"

"Just the causes of action."

"Copyright infringement, unfair business practice, fraudulent inducement, defamation of character, intentional infliction of emotional distress…what is all this shit?"

"They call it a kitchen sink complaint: throw in everything and see what sticks. It's a bunch of bullshit, but it'll take a lot of work to answer it. I'm jammed today. Come over to my office tomorrow, bring the papers."

"My bank account's hemorrhaging. I've got house payments, car payments, taxes, insurance—does Ray actually have a chance of winning this?"

"We'll figure it out. At best it'll be a huge drain of time and energy. At worse it could be worse. Want to do something positive? Finish your record."

A paper fell on the floor. "There's one more page. 'Motion For Temporary Restraining Order, Injunctive Relief To Freeze Royalty Assets.' Freeze my assets? Sounds cold. What the fuck is this?"

"It's a TRO, we'll deal with it."

"TRO? Is that some kind of tractor pull contest?"

"Temporary Restraining Order. Come over tomorrow, bring the papers, bring Stephanie, I'll explain everything."

Ten minutes later, Woody was making a fresh pot of coffee when the phone rang. "Hello?"

"Morning, mate, it's yer favorite drummer. Sorry ta be phonin' ya so early."

"What's up, Billy? You caught me in the middle of dealing with some shit."

"We back in the studio tomorrow night?"

"Yeah."

"It's about bloody time. I been itchin' to play. Sorry to bother you about this, mate—I need an advance."

"Advance? On what? You got your advance and per diem from the record company."

"I need a few extra quid right now."

"A few extra? For what? I've got so many hands in my pockets these days, I can't keep my pants up."

"What happened was, Twig came by last night and we kinda made up and had a few for old times' sake. We were in that sweet spot between two and three drinks and things were heating up, if ya know what I mean, and I was just roundin' third base and slidin' into home when, with his perfect fookin' timing, Malcolm calls. And he ain't callin' for me, mind ya, his bloody bandmate. Oh *no*, he's callin' for *her*. I mean what the stink is that? And of course, as would be bloody expected, me and Twig got into it big time and she storms out and backs her goddamn pickup truck into me bloody car and hits it so hard she pushes the front grill through me radiator and into me bloody motor, so now I'm bloody…"

Woody set the phone down on the counter, picked up his guitar and played along with the sing-songy, up and down pitch of Billy's cockney accent: squeaky ascensions, then the precipitous fall back to the second or third note of the scale at the end of each phrase. The more excited Billy got, the more musical his yelling became. It was always hard to take him seriously with that accent.

"… and why she needs a pickup truck with giant bloody tires is beyond me. Her bumpers are so bloody high she went clean through me radiator without putting a scratch on her goddamn truck. She thinks she's some kinda fookin' cowgirl! I'm not sayin' it was intentional, mind you, but she bloody knows where me car is parked and was in such a tizzy and…that fookin' Malcom, it's bollocks assholery! When I look across the stage at him with his skinny arse on the bench and that ham-fisted pawing motion he does, it's like watching a bloody dog play the piano!"

Woody picked up the phone. "Billy. I can't talk about this right now."

"…the bloke couldn't figure out how to pour water from a bucket if the instructions were printed on the bloody bottom. And when Twig goes off about Malcom talkin' about Jesus—Jesus! She doesn't come up for air, I can't get a word in sidewise, and when she…"

"You got one mouth and two ears Billy, play the odds. I'll see you tomorrow at the studio. Closed sessions, nobody but the band."

"And how am I supposed to bloody get there?"

"I'm your guitar player, not your mother. Figure it out."

"And what about me bloody car? How am I supposed to—"

"Life's tough, Billy. I hate having to go to the bathroom. Maybe get a teardrop tattoo to match your other ones."

CHAPTER 17

"Ms. Angel is not available. Can I take a message?"

"Is she there?"

"Ms. Angel is unavailable, can I take a message?"

"Tell her Ray Bell's on the phone, it's important."

"Ray?"

"Maria Angel?

"I changed my last name to Angel. I've told you that before, Ray Bellini. Where are you?"

"Still at my mother's."

"You haven't gone outside?"

"I haven't left the house, just watching the news."

"There's lots of speculation, but the still shots on TV of you at the window are pretty conclusive. Everyone knows you're alive, otherwise the lawsuit would've been filed under 'estate of.'"

"I saw a thing on the news about a guy trying to serve Woody at his gig last night. A reporter from *Rolling Stone* caught the whole thing. Was that our lawsuit?"

"I told you we were doing that."

"A guy almost jumps off the bridge then files a lawsuit? Sounds like it was planned. What happened at Woody's gig?"

"Nothing. The show was so crowded the process server couldn't get to the stage. He served Woody this morning at his house."

"Woody must've loved that."

"Welcome to the world of litigation."

"Now what?"

"Now we see if Pearlman will settle." She had the complaint in her hand marked FILED. "I decided to mention the strip club issue right up front, we'll see what Woody thinks of that."

"Are you allowed to do that?"

"It's a factual basis explaining why you'd write a song about Stephanie. Woody wasn't the only one who had a relationship with her."

"I saw her dance at a topless place a couple times, what's the big deal? Woody *married* her."

"Does Woody want that in the press?"

"Is this a lawsuit about music or about Stephanie being a stripper?"

"We have a valid claim about the melody you added; we'll use whatever means it takes to resolve that claim."

"So when can I get some money out of this?"

"They're not going to call us tomorrow and ask where to send a check. We need to put something out, a press release, make it official you're alive. What about that offer from Caesar's Palace? A nice room, good money. Put off the bank from taking your house while we try to settle."

"A casino gig? Slot machines and a ten-dollar buffet with novelty-has-been Ray Bell?"

"It's up to you Ray. Three nights, twenty thousand dollars, a penthouse suite overlooking the lake. They want to call it 'Ray Bell Alive.'"

"How about 'Ray Bell Dead or Alive'? How about a gig at the wax museum, or tickets to see me on a diving board on the bridge? I've become a fucking freak show."

Ray's mother walked into the kitchen. "Can I make you some lunch, Ray? Oh dear, I didn't see you were on the phone. My hearing really *is* going."

Ray turned his back to her. "What about that company that gives loans on lawsuits?

"No one's going to lend money to a dead person. It's time to put out a press release."

"What would it say?"

"It's your life, Ray, what do you want it to say?"

"It was all a mistake. I took a walk on the bridge like a thousand other people a day, and the press tried making something out of it."

"What about the bloody suicide note?"

"I cut myself on a blackberry bush and was bleeding, that's the truth. That note was a lyric idea for a song."

"I think we should be more honest, go for the sympathy angle. It could help the lawsuit."

"Just put something out. I don't give a shit what it says."

—

Lily squealed with glee, holding onto Stephanie's hand and pumping her knees, experimenting with gravity in the high-speed elevator traveling up forty floors to Pearlman's office. Everyone on Pearlman's staff knew her.

"Hello, Lily. thanks for coming to the city to visit us."

"You look lovely today, Lily. That bow in your hair is stunning."

"I have an apple for you, Lily. I know you love fruit."

When they went into Pearlman's office, he was on the phone. Lily crawled to the floor-to-ceiling window and gazed down at the miniature cars with the same fascination her dad always had when he was there. Woody sat down in front of Pearlman, set down his guitar case, and slid the legal papers across the expansive desk.

Pearlman scanned the papers while he finished his call. Woody had watched him multitask many times—read, write, and talk at the same time, somehow giving attention to each task.

"Jelly," Pearlman said into the phone, "I've got someone waiting for me. If you guys can't even agree on what songs to play, how're you going to be on the road, where you have to practically live together? It'll be a knife fight in a phone booth. A lawyer can't legislate that people get along. Aerosmith hired a psychologist to travel with the band, think about doing that. I think your music's great, I wouldn't represent you if I didn't. I'm late for a meeting with another musician."

He hung up and looked across his desk at Woody. "General Motors has a hundred thousand employees. Do they have disagreements? Of course. But they get cars made for fifty years. A hundred thousand people agree how to work together, but five people in a band can't agree on *anything*. Go figure." He slapped the legal papers. "We've got thirty days to deal with this."

"Thirty days?"

"Our answer's due in thirty days, they have ten days to reply, then we go to court. First thing to deal with is their request for a temporary injunction. They want to freeze your bank account receiving royalty payments from 'Stephanie.'"

Woody took his beat-up beach guitar out of its soft case. "They could actually freeze my bank account?"

Pearlman nodded at Woody's guitar. "They say you've got to live the blues to play the blues."

Wood strummed a blues chord and sang, "I'd love to go out with you tonight, love to treat you right. But I'm already married, I'm already married to the blues."

"Nice song."

"It's by Joe New, a Memphis blues guy. Is Ray trying to steal my song again, or is he bypassing that and straight up stealing my money?"

Pearlman went back to reading the legal papers. "Almost everything in this complaint is bullshit. Did you read it?"

"Not the whole thing."

Pearlman looked at Stephanie. "Have you read it?"

"No."

Pearlman cleared his throat, glanced at Lily, and read, "Page five, paragraph six." He cleared his throat again. "Plaintiff Bell acknowledges that defendant Woods created an original song sketch, the subject being his romantic partner, now wife, Stephanie. Plaintiff avers according to proof that he also had a personal relationship with Stephanie, which provided the impetus for him to compose additional melody to the song 'Stephanie.' To wit: Plaintiff patronized a business where Stephanie was employed. Said business employed women to disrobe for the enjoyment of male patrons."

Woody slapped the arms of his chair. "Fucking great!"

Stephanie bit her lower lip, stood up, and walked to the window, her voice quivering. "I can't believe we're even talking about this. I thought this lawsuit was about music."

"What do they want?" Woody said.

"Fifty percent of the royalties," Pearlman said. "This stuff about Stephanie has nothing to do with anything. It's irrelevant and prejudicial. Any attempt to get it to the jury would be grounds for a mistrial. It was designed to do what it's doing: rile you up and get you to settle."

Woody slapped his chair again. "It worked, let's settle."

Stephanie stood looking out the window, Lily next to her with her hands flat on the glass. "I thought Ray and Maria gave up their claim to song royalties. They signed that release over a year ago at the Grammys."

"They claim they signed under duress," Pearlman said. "It's true we didn't let them know we had that cassette until right before Ray's performance. I cued up the part where Ray says Woody wrote the song and I threatened to play it for the television audience. Ray had the choice of signing the release or being publicly humiliated." Pearlman folded his hands behind his neck. "It worked like a charm, but a court might conclude I was being a little too shrewd. Bottom line, it'll take a lot to litigate the issue, and we could lose."

Stephanie turned toward them, her arms folded tightly at her chest. "Ray admitted on tape that it's Woody's song."

"They claim Ray and Woody were working on the song together, then Ray added the melody later—the melody that made it a hit. They want fifty percent."

"This lawsuit is a huge distraction," Woody said.

"Losing fifty percent of your income might be a little distracting," Pearlman said, a dry irritation in his voice.

Woody glared at Stephanie. "Can they bring up at trial that my wife's a stripper?"

"I'm *not* a stripper!" Stephanie's face was beet red. "My past is my past. I've made peace with it—will you ever?"

Woody turned back to Pearlman. "Can they bring it up at trial or not?"

"I told you, there's no way."

"A hundred percent?"

"Ninety-five percent."

No one spoke. Lily crawled over to a bookshelf, pulled a law book onto the floor, flipped the pages, and began babbling like she was reading it.

"Ray added what he added to the song," Woody said. "Why not give credit where credit's due and just settle the fucking thing?"

"He...stole...your...song!" Stephanie said. "This case is not about *me*!"

"Great. We go to court and have Ray talk about writing songs about strippers he knows?"

"I had nothing to do with Ray, nothing! We've been over it a thousand times. If you have to keep talking about it, we'll talk about it later. I don't want to expose Lily to this negativity."

"My guess is it's Ray's lawyer making this happen," Pearlman said calmly, trying to bring down the temperature in the room. "I don't think it ever *was* Ray. He knows he got caught stealing the song. They're just looking for a settlement."

"Ray's no dummy," Woody said, "just ask him. The complaint says something about defamation of character? Is that some kind of screenplay thing?"

Pearlman opened his hands. "Ding dong, steal my song? Ray Bell, go to hell?"

"I was goofing around on the mic at a gig. Somebody had a tape recorder, a local radio station got the tape." Woody dropped his hand across his strings and played a minor chord.

Stephanie kneeled next to Lily and rubbed the top of her head. "Your dad's a musician, sweetheart. The only thing he knows how to do is play music. When his lawyer talks to him about money, he just plays his guitar. Do you like salami? Your dad's music is nice, but the only food they have for the band in dressing rooms is salami and cheese. But no worries, they also have beer, which is like eating a salad."

Pearlman rapped his knuckles on his desk. "This meeting has lost its focus, and I've got another one to get to. Here's the plan: I'll prepare an answer to this complaint, you finish your album. You've got out-of-town gigs coming up. Playing the songs live can give them the juice they need. We'll schedule sessions for when you get back." He looked from Woody to Stephanie and back. "This is not a drill. I work with record companies every day. They're like ponderous prehistoric animals, hulking buildings of marketing nerds with guys like Bernie as their tiny brains, pulverizing everything in their path." He pointed at Woody. "I can feel the ground shaking. Throw popcorn at the screen all you want, it's not going to change the movie. It's time to deliver a record."

"So you're saying *when* is more important than *what*?" Woody leaned his head against the back of his chair and closed his eyes. "It's always darkest before it goes pitch black."

Brenda knocked on the door and stuck her head in. "Jeff, you asked me to let you know when Anthony Polanski calls. He's on line one."

"I'll take the call, and call Hal at Paramount and tell him I'm running late. Thanks, Brenda." Pearlman picked up the phone. "Anthony? I got your message, and I've got your cast of characters right here in my office: one-year-old Lily, the most beautiful child you've ever laid eyes on, and her elegant red-haired mother. Let me talk to them about your project and call you back." He hung up and looked across the room at Stephanie. "Anthony's a producer doing a commercial for an all-natural baby food. They need a cute baby and her good-looking mother. They usually use identical twin babies and switch off because of union rules about a baby's working hours, but Anthony agreed to give Lily a try. A few days' work, five thousand dollars plus residuals. Lily, would you like to start saving for college?"

"Lily's never even seen a TV," Woody said. "Family rule."

"She doesn't have to watch TV," Pearlman said, "she just has to sit in front of a camera, eat some baby food, and smile."

"Sounds interesting," Stephanie said. "I'd like to see what the working conditions are for her."

"A TV commercial?" Woody said. "You wanna expose Lily to that idiocy?"

"Can we afford to pass up five thousand dollars?" Stephanie said. "Royalties from 'Stephanie' barely cover our mortgage anymore, not to mention the payments on your fancy car. Half the record contract advance went up your nose. Remind me again, when exactly is your new record going to be done?"

"Anthony wants to run a screen test next week at the Warner Brothers lot in Burbank," Pearlman said. "It'd be a way to find out if it's a good fit for everybody."

"Warner Brothers?" Woody strummed an up and down *ta-dum* chord. "They control my music, now they want my wife and first-born?"

"Warner Brothers film studio and Warner Brothers Records are different companies run by different people."

Woody turned to Stephanie. "Lily in LA? Wouldn't camping in Yosemite be more enlightening?"

"You can come with us."

"I've got those out-of-town gigs coming up."

"Maybe Lily and I can have our own gig."

Woody held his hands out toward her. "You tapping into your own creativity, having a career in modern dance like you've always talked about? I support that, and I'll do what it takes to help make it happen, including helping more with Lily or just staying out of the way." He dropped his hands to his sides. "It's just that fake Hollywood glamor thing. I thought we agreed it's not what we want Lily exposed to."

"I appreciate you offering to support my creativity," Stephanie said firmly. "Me and Lily will be careful, but we're going down to LA and see firsthand what it's like. Please trust me to make the right decisions."

CHAPTER 18

Wanting to road test their new songs, Woody's band booked a ten-day tour of nightclubs and small theaters in the Pacific Northwest. Due to the three-dimensional-chess challenge of scheduling ten days' worth of gigs at venues that were juggling the schedules of thirty other bands, the roadmap of the trip resembled a W. They called it the W tour.

After a seven-hour drive from Bend, Oregon, Woody and his roadie pulled their yellow Ryder equipment truck into the parking lot of the Hercreator Theater in Arcata, California. The rest of the band, including Billy's girlfriend Twig, their new road manager, were in a rental car a couple of hours behind. Billy had gotten into a fight with Twig just as everyone was getting in the car, and they had a late start after Billy walked off saying it would benefit the music that night if he took ten minutes alone and got himself a cup of coffee. Twenty minutes later, when he hadn't returned, the rest of the band, one by one, peeled off in search of their own coffee. The next hour and a half was a Marx Brothers' movie of people coming and going.

Presently, Woody's trusted roadie Block did a pro job of backing the truck up to the theater's loading dock and stepped out of the high cab. Woody stayed and watched him walk around the venue trying all the doors. Block's baggy jeans, weighted down with a key ring, trucker's wallet, and Buck knife, rode low, exposing the top few inches of the crack of his butt. Woody felt sure Block was aware of how his pants fit.

They first met at a gig in San Francisco in an over-crowded dressing room. The band ready to go on, Woody had gone over to the security guard by the door where a constant stream of people were coming and going. The short stocky guard had a bottle of beer in one hand, a burning joint in the other, and seemed to be thoroughly enjoying himself.

"Excuse me," Woody said to him, "you think we could cut down on the traffic while the band gets ready to go on?"

The guard stepped to the side and planted himself in front of the door. "You know what my name is?"

"What?"

"Block. Steve Block."

Sitting in the truck, Woody smiled to himself. It looked like Block was wearing the same sagging jeans, T-shirt, and leather vest he'd been wearing when Woody met him.

Every door to the theater was locked. Block sauntered back to the truck, stepped up on the running board, and rested his forearms on the open window. "Two o'clock load-in, four o'clock sound-check. It's three thirty. The rest of the band'll be here pretty soon. Whuddya wanna do, boss?"

"I'll walk to a phone booth and call the promoter. You wait here for the band." Woody put his hand on the door handle. "Got any quarters?"

"Does a chicken have lips?" Block pulled a fistful of coins out of his pocket.

Walking to the corner, Woody wondered if Block's jeans would be riding any higher without the coins. He called the promoter, who informed him that things were running late, then he called home.

"Hi, sweetheart."

"I was hoping it was you."

"I was hoping it was you."

They listened to each other's quiet breathing for a comfortable thirty-second silence, a habit they'd fallen into when he was traveling; a brief, wordless heart connection before they launched into the details of their lives.

Woody broke the silence. "Being on the road is a lot like being on the street."

"How's the music?"

"Funny you should ask. Sometimes I forget I'm out here to make music. I get so tangled up in traveling and personalities and setlists and guest lists and...careful what you ask for when you ask how I'm doing. Tell me something about Lily."

"Last night she saw her first fire." Lily pulled herself up onto Stephanie's lap. She seemed to always know when her dad was on the phone. "I made a fire in the backyard, first of the season. The last fire she saw, she was just a few months old. She actually saw this one, crawled right up to it, stopped, and put up her hands. She was born with an innate understanding of fire, it's hardwired in."

"You sound relaxed."

"We're enjoying the peace and quiet. People somehow know when you're not here. No one stops by, the phone stops ringing. How's the band holding up?"

"We follow the ten commandments of rock and roll: single out absent band members for criticism, destroy yourself physically and mentally and encourage others to do the same, stuff like that."

"Sounds delightful."

"I started riding in the truck with Block. In the car, Billy's always talking. He reads every billboard out loud. His English accent makes it a little more tolerable, but the guy never shuts up. He reports on his bowel movements when he gets back in the car."

"Some people are like that."

"They say you can get used to anything, even hanging."

"Then hang in there."

"I get paid for traveling, rehearsing, moving gear, and making phone calls, then I play music for free. I miss you." Woody took a photograph of Stephanie and Lily out of his wallet.

"Lily keeps looking around the house for you. When I put on a tape of one of your shows, she looks for you in the living room speakers."

"I'll call you tomorrow, I love you."

"I love you too. Don't forget to enjoy the music…and don't forget me and Lily are going to LA on Thursday for that baby food commercial."

"You're sure that's the kind of reality we want for Lily? That fake television world?"

"It's five thousand dollars. What if we lose the court case?"

"Let's settle that stupid case."

"It's not right to give up what's rightfully yours."

"I don't want the world thinking of my wife as a stripper."

"Jeff says it won't come up, and what if it does? We're being blackmailed about something that doesn't even matter."

"It matters to me, that's what matters."

They fell into a long silence.

"I love you," she said softly.

"I love you too," he said, "be careful, stop at yellow lights."

Stephanie hung up and looked at Lily asleep on the couch with a ukulele on her stomach. At twelve months old Lily had never watched television. It was always an issue when they visited friends and insisted they turn their TV off. Even Max and Auddie obliged, and Max was an obsessive sports fan.

Stephanie gently lifted the ukulele off Lily, covered her with her baby-size quilt, and tried picturing her pudgy pink face on a television screen. Woody was right—it wouldn't be possible for Lily to be on TV and not end up watching TV. They often talked about the way television surreptitiously enabled an unconscious acceptance of fake relationships, violence, and abrupt interruptions by rude commercials.

She glanced down at the book she'd been reading to Lily, a picture book about a tribe of Native Americans who adopted a white girl whose parents had died of smallpox. The book was replete with hand-drawn images of brown-skinned children showing the white girl how to hunt, fish, tend a fire, and sit in a prayer circle. One print showed a white man trying to photograph them with the Indians covering their faces because of their belief that photographing someone steals their soul. "If there's a grain of truth to that," Stephanie thought, "what would making a TV commercial with endless reruns do to a person's soul?"

—

By the time Woody finished his sixteen-quarter call at the phone booth, the truck had been unloaded. Block was setting up the stage, and Billy and Twig were at the bar drinking beer. Chewy changed the strings on his electric bass, the instrument on its back on a round cocktail table. In a booth, Malcolm read his Bible, and Jupiter was taking advantage of the reflective wet tiles, practicing scales in the recently cleaned ammonia-smelling men's room with the door held open by an orange cone.

Woody took his acoustic guitar out of its case, swung the strap over his head, and walked down the theater aisle plucking strings and twisting tuning pegs, tuning to the echoing bray of the sax. By the time he reached the men's room, he was in tune with Jupiter and the splashy wet blend of the instruments put smiles on both musicians' faces.

Billy heard the sound echoing through the empty theater, took out a pair of drumsticks, and joined them in the bathroom with paradiddles on the water pipes. Twig came in, sat clapping along on the edge of a sink, and Chewy held the headstock of his electric bass against the hollow wooden door, playing it like a sonorous bass reverberator.

When the makeshift jam meandered to a natural conclusion, everyone singing *ooh-oohs* in off-key harmony, Twig pulled the handle of a urinal for the finale, and they shared a congenial laugh.

Walking to the front of the three-foot-high stage, Woody tried to visualize the optimal positioning of the amps, instruments, and microphone stands. Block had the gear out of its travel cases and generally arrayed across the stage. He knew to wait for the final placement for Woody to intuit the vibe of the room.

Woody hopped up on the stage and perused the remains of last night's show on the dirty worn carpet, trying to divine what kind of music had been played. There were strips of silver duct tape with the edges peeling up, an empty Marlboro pack, a beer bottle, guitar pick, unopened condom, chord chart, hotel key, a stepped-on pair of aviator sunglasses, a queen of hearts, a dirty white athletic sock, and an actual brown ponytail with a hair tie.

Woody smiled at the selection of objects, thinking how metaphysical and free music is compared to physical things like musical instruments and human bodies. Material objects exist in some base, pedestrian dimension, unable to extricate themselves from fly-paper gravity, burdened with constraints of time, space, and wear and tear. Playing a song a thousand times just makes it sturdier while the associated tendons, muscles, eardrums, and guitar strings incessantly disintegrate. Woody flexed his punished hands. His right hand had been injured two years ago and was especially tender. He wondered how many more years he could play guitar the way he did for hours every day. Human bodies come and go, he thought, while good songs endure for generations, new ways to sing love songs informing new ways to be in love.

He made a mental note to survey the stage that night after the show, with the musical vibrations still bouncing around the empty theater and telltale droppings on the stage as if the invisible man had played there.

—

Gazing out the dirty truck windshield on the way to their fifth gig in six days, Woody was thinking how even the most bizarre routines can become routine.

They'd drive for four or five hours, the jittery rental truck doing its maximum fifty-five miles per hour, load in the gear, play an hour soundcheck, take an hour break for bar food, do two ninety-minute sets, load up the truck, drink beer and smoke pot in one of the guys' motel rooms until four in the morning, and get up and do it again. On the one night they had off near the California-Oregon border, they went to the club they'd be playing the next night, checked out the house band, and stayed up until four drinking beer and smoking pot with the other band.

—

Woody called Stephanie every morning from his motel room.

"Where are you?"

"I don't know." Woody looked around at the flowered bedspread, orange carpet, and paintings of flowers that clashed with the bedspread.

Stephanie was on the couch in their living room, reading to Lily. She picked up Woody's itinerary. "You're in South Lake Tahoe."

"It's all coming back to me. Twig got some deal for two nights at the same motel, so we drove all night after the gig. Nevada's like a foreign country. I was thinking of getting a cowboy hat."

"Sounds like Twig keeps things moving."

"She's on it. She books hotels, gets the band onstage, offstage, meals, drink tickets, guest lists, wakeup calls, bowling balls."

"Are Billy and Twig getting along okay?"

"They're a peach of a pair. It's like there's a foundational crack below the surface of their relationship that shows up in superficial tremors. It's hard to tell when the big bang's gonna come. Sometimes they groove, sometimes she blames him when it rains."

"Is there something going on between Twig and Malcolm?"

"Honestly, I think Malcolm prefers men. Whatever it takes to keep the music interesting. A couple nights ago Twig wore a T-shirt that said, "drummers are better in bed" and Billy played the best I've heard him play. She says she's going to write a book—'How to Talk to a Drummer.'"

"The music's been good?"

"I'm like a referee at a food fight. It's been sleep-deprivation camp, which either makes the music great or it's fingernails on a blackboard. Billy drinks every night, his personality's a half-bubble off plumb, but he lays down the musical floor that everybody stands on. That fat-back drummer can groove. He's late showing up for almost everything, but his playing's perfectly punctual. You just have to be careful what you ask for when you say something like 'hit it' going into a chorus…it's like saying mush to a sled dog."

"Is Malcolm holding up okay?"

"Some people just aren't good at being happy. He plays beautiful keyboards when he's not complaining about driving directions or God. I'm personally okay having God in the band. It isn't where I would've thought to look for her, but we need all the help we can get. The band's coming together and coming apart at the same time. When life fractures, that's when the beauty is exposed."

Lily recognized Woody's voice on the phone, grabbed the cord, and yelled, "Woody!"

"Lily just said your name! It's a historic day." Stephanie held the phone up to her ear.

"Hello, Lily," Woody said. "I'm singing my way home."

She squealed, let herself down off the couch, and crawled off toward the fish tank.

"You can call her on her shell phone. How's Jupiter holding up?"

"The poise and elegance of his soloing continues to amaze me. He tracks my melodies like a homing pigeon. It's fun traveling with a big black guy. He kicks down knowledge from a different cultural perspective. The other day he said to me, 'they don't call you the guy that changes his mind for nothin' for nothin.'"

Stephanie chuckled. "I can relate."

"I've learned a lot hanging out with him in places like Oregon and Nevada. White people think of racism as some kind of fad we went through like hula-hoops or pet rocks. Like, hey, remember that goofy stuff we used to do, lynching black people? I can feel him feel it when we're at a truck stop and he's the only black guy around for fifty miles. He's got scars you can't see."

Stephanie and Woody both switched their phones from one ear to the other.

"Block's probably waiting in the truck and someone's waiting to ask me for ten bucks." Woody visualized approaching the band car in the morning like approaching a cave of bears waking up from a six-month hibernation with hideously bad breath, starving for breakfast. "I should get going."

"Woody?"

"I'm here."

"How many tours like this have you done?"

"I don't know—twenty?"

"How many turned out okay?"

"Twenty."

"Don't be afraid of being vulnerable. And remember, you're playing music you love, with people you love, for people you love."

CHAPTER 19

Stephanie pulled up to the front gate of Warner Brothers Studios in Burbank with Lily asleep in her car seat. She showed the guard her driver's license, got her pass, and drove through the lot past gigantic buildings of soundstages, wondering if any of the four original Warner brothers were still alive. It takes the energy of four brothers, she thought, to bring a project like this to fruition. She remembered reading that Bette Davis was considered the fifth Warner brother, her movies financially sustaining the company. She glanced back at Lily and thought, "Someday soon sisters will create enterprises like this, and a woman will be elected president."

She drove through an old west town with horse-drawn wagons and wooden sidewalks, past miniature Egyptian Pyramids, Mount Rushmore, the Coliseum, and Times Square. Lily was now wide awake, as fascinated with the scenery as Stephanie. When they arrived at their shooting location, the entrance doors to the gigantic building looked as miniature and unreal as everything else.

Inside were scenes of partial living rooms, bedrooms, and streets lined with parked cars. When they came to the cafeteria, Stephanie decided to get something for herself, wondering if she should keep Lily hungry for the baby food. The tables were filled with carpenters, electricians, cowboys, space aliens, and Roman soldiers with swords clanking against their chairs.

The man in line behind them spoke to Lily like a duck. "Wuth your name, thweety? I'm Daffy. You look juth like a weal baby." He puffed up his cheeks and poked her gently in the stomach. "Quack."

Lily giggled and flapped her arms.

"What are you lovely ladies doing in a place like this?"

"We're here to make a baby food commercial."

"Phood made out of babies? Quack."

They found their studio, a brightly lit partial kitchen with shiny white appliances, the floor covered with a labyrinth of thick black cables. A man with coiffed blond hair, a copper-brown tan, and a gleaming white smile walked up to them. "Hello, darling, you must be Stephanie. I'm Anthony Polanski."

"Nice to meet you."

"And this must be Lily. She's more beautiful than Jeff described. And her mom," Anthony looked Stephanie up and down, "the cameras are going to love you both. Your matching freckles will gleam like glowing orbs. Have you already been to makeup or is that your natural hair color?"

"We just got here."

Anthony produced a lollipop in a clear plastic wrapper. "I have something for you, Lily."

Lily looked at him blankly.

"It's a lollipop," Anthony said. "Kids love lollipops."

"Thanks for the thought," Stephanie said. "Lily doesn't eat candy. She doesn't really eat much packaged food. Do you have kids?"

"No, but I have a niece named Candy."

"For something sweet, she likes fresh fruit."

"All right, Lily, I think we've got something you'll like…Nature's Peach Tummi Yumi. Let's get wardrobe, makeup, get everyone situated, and get started."

With the help of two assistants, Stephanie and Lily donned colorful casual wear, Lily was seated with a bib in a wooden highchair and a young man in an apron with large square pockets walked up to them. "Hello, darling, you must be Lily. My name's Benji. How about a kiss?" He took a silver-wrapped Hershey's Chocolate Kiss out of his pocket and extended it to Lily.

"She can't really undo wrappers," Stephanie said. "Actually, she doesn't have teeth."

Benji shrugged. "Let's get to work on those miniature cheeks." He opened a plastic fishing tackle box with a colorful array of powders, pencils, and brushes. When he brushed Lily's cheeks with a fluffy round brush, she started squirming and sneezed.

"Please slow down a little," Stephanie said, "all these bright lights and makeup seem to be upsetting her."

"*Bonjour, Mademoiselle*, you must be Stephanie." A woman with a thick French accent walked up to them. "I am Ruthie, here to do your makeup. Your hairs, they are stunning."

Stephanie reached into her pocket for a tissue when Lily sneezed again.

Ruthie set her own tackle box on the counter, flipped it open, chose a brush, and went to apply it to the side of Stephanie's face at the same time Benji went back at Lily's face with his brush. Lily sneezed harder, rubbed her eyes, shook her head, and let out a yelp.

With a lightning-quick Aikido move she'd practiced a thousand times in class, Stephanie thrust her open right hand between Lily's face and Benji's brush at the same instant she raised her left elbow up to within a quarter inch of Ruthie's chin.

Everyone froze, Lily sneezed.

Stephanie draped the tissue over Lily's nose, squeezed out the snot, and neatly folded the tissue in half, in half again, and tucked it into her back pocket. "Sorry to interrupt the process, I think we need to be more mindful of Lily's sensitivities."

Benji and Ruthie held their little round brushes in mid-air.

"Before we go any further with the makeup, Lily would probably like something to eat." Stephanie produced a banana from her purse.

"Pardon moi," Ruthie said, "will she still be hungry for the baby food?"

"She has a great appetite."

Anthony Polanski came over with another, older man with a wavy bouffant of platinum hair. "Stephanie, meet Marc Short, our director."

"Pleasure to meet you, ladies. I have marvelous news. After getting a good look at you both, we've decided to bypass the screen test. You passed the audition. Everyone is confident you'll both look fabulous on camera. We'll proceed with the shooting, and it'll save us a day. Ready to get started?"

"Lily doesn't seem to like makeup," Stephanie said.

Marc took a long look at Lily and her banana. "I've never done a shoot without makeup, but this rosy-cheeked baby is brimming with living color. Let's give it a try and let the camera decide." Marc looked Stephanie up and down. "You're quite colorful yourself, but if you wouldn't mind just a little makeup?"

"I don't mind, it's just Lily."

Ruthie went back to work on Stephanie's face.

"We'll get a take of Lily enjoying the food," Marc said, "then a take of your face enjoying Lily's face. We've got a hand actor to work the spoon and deliver the baby food."

After a half-hour of people scampering around adjusting the lighting, Venus, a slender woman with a plastic glove on her right hand, stepped up, took off the glove, picked up a shiny silver spoon, scooped a half-teaspoon of baby food out of a jar, and held it for the camera.

"Cut," Marc said. "The food color's a little dull."

Gloria, the food stylist, produced a half-size can of spray paint, shielded the spoonful of baby food with her hand, and applied a quick squirt of semi-gloss, peach-colored enamel.

"What's that?" Stephanie said.

"No worries," Marc said. "It's just for the few inches of movement from the jar to Lily's mouth. We'll cut it in later. She won't be eating it."

"Venus extended the spoon toward Lily's mouth and stopped just short of her lips. She repeated the movement a half-dozen times while Marc said, "roll, cut, stop."

Lily, in a polished wooden highchair, staring into the bright spotlights, looked confused, beads of sweat forming on her forehead.

"Okay," Marc said, "ready for live action. Let's get this baby fed." Gloria produced a new jar of baby food, set it on the counter, and turned the label toward the camera. Venus scooped a spoonful and delivered it to Lily's lips. Lily had never been offered a spoonful of food by anyone other than Stephanie, Woody, Aunt Auddie, or Uncle Max. She kept her mouth shut tight.

After several attempts, Stephanie said, "let me try priming the pump." She took the spoon and, without thinking, as she did with everything she fed Lily, tasted the baby food. She wrinkled her nose, picked up the short glass jar, and read the ingredients. "All natural? This is full of high fructose corn syrup and preservatives. Where's Anthony?"

Anthony caught the whole thing from behind the camera and was there in a flash. He put his hand on Stephanie's shoulder. "Darling, we can address any concerns you have."

"I was told this product was all natural."

"It's made from peaches."

"Have you read the ingredients?"

"Actually, I haven't, but I know it to be a reputable company."

Stephanie took the jar off the counter and read: "One, two, three, four, five, six...twenty-six ingredients. High fructose corn syrup, four kinds of artificial coloring, preservatives, monophosphate number five, peach *flavoring*—it's just chemicals and sugar!"

"A simple fix," Anthony said. "We'll put whatever you want in the jar and feed it to Lily."

"It won't be the right color," Marc Short said.

"We'll use that banana she has," Anthony said. "We'll mash it up, put it in a jar of banana-flavored baby food, and we've got it."

"Peach is the new flavor the company's pushing," Marc said. He turned to Stephanie. "Do you really think one teaspoon of this stuff will hurt her? Thousands of babies eat it every day."

Stephanie felt exhausted. All she could think of right now was being home. Could she afford to pass up five thousand dollars? Was Woody ever going to finish his album, or was that just a dream? Could he ever finish anything? Looking around at the expectant faces, she realized that Marc and Anthony were wearing as much makeup as she was, and they weren't even on camera. Everyone and everything in sight was fake. The kitchen was fake, the people were fake, and the food was fake. She flashed back to the man in the cafeteria... *phood made from babies.*

"Thank you, everyone." Stephanie scooped Lily out of the high chair. "I'm sorry, but this is not a product we care to endorse."

"You can't just walk out," Anthony threw up his hands. "We have over twenty people here working on this, we have a contract. You can't just decide on a whim to leave."

Stephanie untied Lily's bib. "Sweetheart, did you see that lovely monophosphate number five peach-flavored tree in the garden?"

"This is not a joking matter. We have a production schedule."

"Talk to my all-natural lawyer, Jeff Pearlman."

—

Stephanie and Lily quickly changed into their street clothes, made their way through the catacomb of sound stages to the parking lot, and were getting in their car when Ruthie, the makeup lady, walked up.

"*S'il vous plait,* I am so sorry that was not okay for you. I know you traveled a long way."

"Thanks for trying," Stephanie said.

"Anthony is very excitable, but he will deal with it. Delays and casting changes happen all the time. I appreciate the way you care about your daughter's health. I have two young boys."

"Thank you. I don't think Lily and I are suited for Hollywood."

"Do you know who Richard Donner is?"

"No."

"He's a dear friend of mine. We met in Paris, and he's making a movie in the next building. I couldn't help but notice…do you do martial arts?"

"I've trained in Aikido, although I've missed a lot of training since Lily was born. Why do you ask?"

"I've been in the movie business a long time, watching people's movements. I noticed the way you moved when you stopped the makeup process with your daughter. Your movements are very fluid and, honestly, your red hairs and green eyes are quite dramatic. As we say, *magnifique.*"

"Thank you."

"The reason I followed you out here: yesterday, I was speaking with Richard. He is having trouble finding an actress for a brief non-speaking part in his new movie. The woman should be very attractive and also know how to move like a martial artist. All the women he tried have been attractive but do not, as they say, have the moves. His production schedule has come to a halt…*viennent à l'arrêt.* Would you possibly be interested in meeting him?"

"We've had a very long day. We're both exhausted, and honestly, I don't know if this type of work is right for us."

"Do you know who the actor Christopher Reeve is?"

"No. My husband and I don't watch TV or go to the movies much."

"He also goes by the name Superman."

Stephanie smiled and rubbed Lily's head. "Lily has a Superman comic book, she loves it."

"I cannot guarantee you'll get the part, but I can assure you that the working conditions and compensation are much better than the baby food commercial. Since you have come all the way down here, would you like to just meet Richard? It is only a short walk from here. *S'il vous plait?*"

—

Stephanie, Ruthie, and Lily walked to another warehouse with sixty-foot ceilings and a miniature skyscraper inside. A myriad of technicians, actors, and stand-ins were bustling around what seemed to be the power center of four people gathered in the middle of the expansive set, one of them Superman.

Ruthie led Stephanie over to the group. "Richard, this is Stephanie and her *bon fille,* Lily. They were shooting a commercial and I thought possibly Stephanie might be a good fit for that scene you were so much talking about yesterday. She has training in the martial arts and knows how to move quickly."

"Pleasure to meet you, Stephanie. Hello, Lily—meet Superman."

Lily's eyes were bugging out of her head at the sight of the ultra-bright red, yellow, and blue costume like the cover of her comic book.

Richard looked Stephanie up and down. "Well, you certainly look camera friendly." He gestured to the man standing next to him. "This is my cinematographer, George."

Stephanie smiled and nodded.

The fourth person standing in the small circle was a heavy-set older man, arms folded, looking at the floor with furrowed eyebrows as if deep in thought.

"Stephanie, this is Superman's father, Marlon Brando."

Marlon nodded, barely looking up.

A man walked up behind Richard and said something that seemed urgent. Richard spoke to him in a hushed tone. The man quickly left and Richard stood with his back to the group, flipping pages on a clipboard. He stopped on one page, seemingly engrossed with something, then suddenly dropped the clipboard to his side, swung back around, and reached up as if to smack Lily on the side of her head with his open hand. The move was sudden, totally unexpected.

Stephanie reacted instantly, planting her feet, moving Lily just out of harm's way and, with one fluid motion that focused the power of her entire body, she rotated her hips and thrust the knife edge of her free hand so forcefully into the meaty part of Richard's forearm, it flung his arm violently behind his back.

Everyone in the circle jerked back a step.

"Forgive me for startling you," Richard said, rubbing his forearm. "I wasn't going to actually touch Lily or hurt her in any way. I've got about fifty people working here, all on standby, everyone waiting for my next move, and I just needed to get to the point. And, well, you just passed the audition. We need someone for a small but important part in our film. We need a woman who is beautiful and who moves like an accomplished martial artist. You've got all the elements. If you'd like the part, it's yours."

Marlon Brando cleared his throat and looked up at her. "I'd be honored if you'd consider taking care of my son the way you take care of your daughter." He had an unreadable expression and spoke as if he was sucking on his cheeks.

Stephanie looked at him quizzically.

Marlon gestured to Superman. "My son."

Richard explained, "Lois Lane, our leading lady you haven't met yet, gets shoved out of an office building window by a bad guy robbing the office safe. Louis falls forty floors when Superman comes to the rescue. He scoops her up in his arms just before she hits the pavement, delivers her back to her office, ties up the bad guy, and flies away. Minutes later Lois's office boy, Clark Kent, walks in on the other side of the office. Lois is standing by the open window, looking up at the sky for her vanished hero. When she looks down forty floors and pictures her trajectory minutes before, her head tilts back, her eyelids close halfway, she faints and begins to fall out the open window again. Clark Kent is frozen in place by his predicament—he can't reveal the super-human powers it would take to get to Lois in time. Just then, a bespectacled secretary, prim and proper in a skirt and blouse, hair in a bun, walks by cradling a stack of papers in her arms, takes in the scene, sees that no one else is reacting, and at the last possible moment, she drops the papers, reaches out the window behind Louis' back with agile dexterity, walks her across the room, and sits her down safely in an office chair. Everyone, including Clark Kent, breathes a sigh of relief, the secretary gathers the papers off the floor and continues on with her chore, delivering the documents to her boss." He paused. "Are you interested in playing the part of the secretary?"

"I don't have to say anything?"

"Please have a seat," Marlon mumbled.

Stephanie hefted up Lily and looked around behind her for a chair. "Actually, I'm fine, thanks."

Marlon's expression softened and he exhibited his first sign of a smile. "That's your one speaking line, when you lead Lois to the chair."

Stephanie gestured to an invisible chair next to her. "Please, have a seat."

"Perfect," Richard said, still rubbing his forearm. "We'll shoot a take first thing tomorrow morning."

By the time Stephanie and Lily got to their hotel room, Woody was already at his gig. She left a message and decided she'd call him in the morning.

—

The next day Stephanie gave consistent professional performances while various cast and crew members, including four different Supermen, the real one and three stuntmen, all took turns occupying Lily until she fell asleep in the back seat of a miniature car parked in front of the miniature skyscraper.

After calling it quits for the day, Richard, the director, walked up to Stephanie. "Your part's perfect. It's not a big part, but it's critical for showing the limits of Clark Kent's superpowers. I might expand it a little and include more of Clark Kent's reaction to your actions. Perhaps you and Clark could exchange a few lines? Can you stay for another day or two?"

Stephanie looked thoughtful but didn't answer.

"Is there a problem?"

A circle of technicians, actors, and two Supermen were waiting their turn to bring up their own scheduling issues with Richard.

Stephanie sensed that her thoughtfulness wasn't working with the Hollywood high-speed, back-and-forth sound bite way of communicating she'd been hearing all day. She thought again about how much this work would help with family finances: the part paid over three times the pay for the baby food commercial, more if she added speaking lines.

Richard glanced around, acknowledged the people waiting, and looked back to her.

"I very much appreciate the offer," she said. "The work is just new to us, and I can tell Lily's uncomfortable with the bright lights. I'd like to discuss this with my husband."

"I can move you and Lily to a nicer hotel with extra compensation. One more day, two at the most?"

Stephanie smiled but didn't answer.

"How about this? Starting tomorrow, Ruthie the makeup person will be here all day to watch Lily. She's an experienced mom and Lily will be away from the lights but never more than ten or twenty feet from you." Richard's eyes darted around at the expanding circle of people. Stephanie took a slow, audible breath and watched Richard's mirror neurons induce him to take his own deep breath. She'd practiced the technique in Aikido class.

Stephanie turned to Lily. "Having fun, sweetheart?" Lily giggled and slapped Stephanie's chest. "We'll stay and finish what we started. Thank you for the opportunity."

Richard smiled. "I'll have our legal department contact Jeff Pearlman." He shrugged. "Who knows, it could be the start of a new career. Superwoman? Do you by chance know how to fly?"

As if on cue, Lily flapped her arms.

CHAPTER 20

Crossing the border from California to Nevada for the second time that week, Woody and Block had breakfast at a truck stop where everyone, including the cooks and waitresses, wore cowboy hats. Block had "The Breakfast that Peterbilt"—three eggs, biscuits and gravy, steak, sausage, bacon, home fries, and a pie. Woody had yogurt and granola. After breakfast, driving around the sparkling blue lake surrounded by snow-capped mountains, Block smoked cigarettes and recited a brief history of the lake. He often surprised Woody with his knowledge of esoteric historical facts.

"Lake Tahoe, the jewel of the Sierras. It's so deep they couldn't find the bottom for a couple hundred years until some guys filled a champagne bottle with lead, tied it to a rope, and let it down a third of a mile. Of course, the white guys outright stole the lake from the Indians, mispronounced the Indian name, Da Ow, then fought over it among themselves. State militias of Nevada and California actually exchanged gunfire over rights to the lake. Then they just cut the baby in half."

Making their way to their South Lake Tahoe gig, they approached the main drag with big casinos and traffic got progressively slower. Woody watched Block pushing on the rental truck's steering wheel the way he often did in traffic, pushing so hard he bent it.

The sidewalks were packed with lily-white, overweight tourists in Bermuda shorts on gambling junkets from the Midwest. The Nevada gaming industry thrived on people coming from around the country to play the slot machines, lose four hundred dollars, and take their one-in-a-million chance at hitting a jackpot. Except to take advantage of jobs in the casinos, the locals, attracted to the area for its natural beauty, mostly avoided the gambling scene. People that actually worked in the casinos knew that sooner or later every gambler lost.

As Woody and Block came within sight of the Caesar's Palace billboard, the biggest on a strip bloated with them, Block was the first to see it and read out loud; "Ray Bell Alive. Two Shows Nightly."

"Ray Bell Alive?" Woody said. "Pull over. I gotta check this out."

"Isn't Ray Bell the guy that's suing your ass over 'Stephanie'?" Block pulled the dirty yellow truck up to Caesar's valet parking full of shiny Lincoln Continentals, Cadillacs, and BMWs.

"I wanna see what kind of stuff he's playing. Park the truck; I'll check out a couple songs." Woody jumped out and went from bright daylight into the semi-dark windowless world of whirling lights and a cacophony of bells and whistles. There was a vast sea of slot machines. People with drinks and cigarettes in hand, were yanking the arms of one-armed bandits as fast as they could, trying to impose their will on spinning wheels of cartoon images of plums, sevens, and bunches of cherries. Woody wove his way through the maze of machines and into an expanse of lush green blackjack, roulette, and craps tables. Passing a spinning roulette wheel, he touched the money in his pocket from last night's gig and considered putting it on the black and doubling it for the band. He stopped and watched the white ball bounce erratically, pop out of a black slot, and land on the red. Statistically, the next roll might be more likely to come up black. He shook his head and kept moving, knowing each spin had the same likelihood of coming up black or not—a little less than fifty percent because there were two green pockets.

He followed white-lit arrows to the ballroom, paid fifteen dollars for a general admission ticket, went in, and stood in the back. There was a ten-piece band on the stage; drums, bass, grand piano, a four-piece horn section, three women backup singers in long black gowns, and Ray out front in a white tuxedo singing Frank Sinatra's "That's Life."

Transfixed by the scene, Woody leaned against the back wall. The concert hall was mostly filled, four or five hundred people at small tables, eating, drinking, and talking while Ray crooned. Woody had always been a Frank Sinatra fan and thoroughly enjoyed Ray's vocal interpretation. There were countless singers, both men and women, whose voices were fuller, more resonant than Sinatra's. Frank was often on the verge of merely talking when he sang, but he employed such finesse and understated emotion, he was recognized as one of the world's greatest singers. Ray had a full, resounding voice, but he held back, applying Sinatra's restrained control, adding tasteful shards of the power and melody he had at his disposal. Ray finished the song with a tasty personal touch, an unmistakable Ray Bell melodic note that reminded Woody of Ray's notes on the final chorus of "Stephanie." On cue, the band jumped into an unusual upbeat, James Brown–style rendition of "Sittin' on the Dock of the Bay." Woody was thoroughly enjoying the show when a waitress carrying a cocktail tray of drinks came up and placed herself directly in his sightline of the band.

"There's a two-drink minimum. What can I get you?" She was dressed like the Emperor Caesar's concubine in a chocolate-brown mini-dress bordered with gold lamiae curlicues and a fake diamond tiara in her hair, expertly balancing her loaded tray of drinks at shoulder height. The form-fitting, low-cut top of her uniform pushed her large breasts up so high her chin was almost in her cleavage.

Woody wasn't sure where to look.

"There's a two-drink minimum," she repeated. "What'll you have?"

"Two pickets to titsburg?"

She blinked her extra-long fake eyelashes. "Sir?"

"I don't really feel like drinking."

"There's a two-drink minimum during the show." She adjusted the heavy tray. "Can I please take your order?"

"How long does the band play?"

"Two shows a night: five to seven and eight to ten."

"Do they play the same songs every show?"

"I don't really know, I'm always busy working." She transferred the tray to her other hand. "I'm actually working right now. What'll you have?"

"Can I just pay for two drinks?"

Before she could answer, Woody took out a ten-dollar bill and put it on the tray. "Keep the change."

"Thanks, pal." She spun on her gold high heels, starting to walk away. "Sure you don't want a Coke or something?"

"I'm fine."

Woody stayed until the end of the set, impressed with the band's professionalism. The players were top-notch but seemed bored. They could probably play their parts in their sleep. The repertoire became corny at times, but the show was all about the singing, and Ray managed to keep it interesting. Winding his way back through the casino after the last song, Woody wondered if he'd ever have control over his vocal cords the way Ray did.

—

Ray stepped off of the stage and into the dressing room like a sweaty boxer stepping out of the ring, a white towel with a gold-embossed Caesar's Palace emblem around his neck. He sat down next to Maria.

"Very nice show." She crossed her black-stockinged legs and sipped her glass of red wine. Her tight black dress was ultra-short and low-cut. She glanced across the room at the band; she knew they all had their eyes on her legs.

"It's hard to mess up Frank Sinatra or Otis Redding." He wiped his forehead. "Those guys did all the work, creating those killer vocal parts. It'd be nice to mix in some new original material."

"You should perform 'Stephanie.' That's what the audience wants to hear."

The musicians across the room, now helping themselves to the generous buffet, all heard Maria's comment.

"The audience isn't even paying attention," Ray said, "they're too busy with their cocktails and roast beef. I'm sick of that song."

Maria sipped her wine and re-crossed her legs. "Woody was here for the show."

"Woody was here?" He looked at her in disbelief. "He was here at *my* show tonight?"

"I saw him standing in the back of the room. His band's playing at a club a few miles away."

—

The Tahoe Yahoo Club was a two-hundred-seat music venue in Zephyr Cove, Nevada, five miles from the casinos. The hippies came out of the mountains to see the quality rock bands the Yahoo brought in from California, and tickets for Woody's show were sold out.

When Woody and Block pulled up to the club, Twig was standing half in, half out of a phone booth by the front door, yelling into the phone and waving a notebook, turning half-circles until the metal phone cord wrapped around her shoulders then un-winding like a yo-yo. "Dude!" she yelled into the phone, "you told me you'd cover the rooms for two nights, that's why we drove five hours after the show last night! I want our guarantee plus four hundred eighty bucks for the rooms before the band plays. And what about the points? It's sold out, we're into percentage. You already got the cash for the tickets. The band's gonna stand off-stage, where the sold-out crowd can see them, and not play a note until I have the cash in my hand. Got it?"

Woody tapped Twig on the shoulder and snapped his pack of Winstons so a cigarette protruded. Twig took one, and he lit it for her. "Go, girl," he said, and walked into the club.

One step inside, the smell of the empty nightclub seemed particularly pungent with the vinegary edge of beer, stale cigarette smoke, bleach, and rancid French fry oil. The walls and ceiling, covered with sound-absorbent material, also absorbed the smell of last night's two hundred sweaty dancers. Woody took a reluctant breath and walked to the stage, a guitar case in each hand.

—

Two hours later, with the doors still closed to the public, the band was set up and started playing a song to check the room's sound. Woody, on the microphone, raised his hand, stopped the band, and yelled to the soundman in the back of the room. "I can't hear myself."

"Then turn down," the soundman yelled.

"Who?"

"Everybody."

"It'll sound better when those sound-absorbing sacks of water fill the dance floor," Billy said from the drums.

"Having people in the room'll help," the soundman said, "it's still too loud."

Woody turned and faced the band. "You know how when you're walking in the woods and you step on a muddy patch, you step gingerly like you can defy gravity? Let's try doing that with our sound. Gravity's overrated."

"Can we skip the philosophy and just bloody play something?" Billy said.

"Are they giving us dinner or do we have to go out?" Malcolm said. "I've got a clunky key on my Wurlitzer I need to fix."

Twig saw what was happening and knew everyone was hungry and over-tired from last night's drive. She hurried onto the stage and handed each musician a menu. "The band can order from the sandwich menu or get half-off on anything else."

Having trouble adjusting his reed, Jupiter bent over his horn, blew a startling shrill note, and without thinking Billy responded by whacking his snare drum. Woody tossed his menu onto the floor. "It's too loud to eat. I'll get my half-off nourishment from the music." He set his guitar in its stand signaling the end of sound-check. "My hands aren't working right, I need a break. My fingers are all thumbs."

While the guys ate hamburgers, Woody took the truck back to the motel to try calling Stephanie and maybe get some rest. When he got back to his room there was a message on his phone from Stephanie saying she was staying in LA an extra day or two and she'd try calling tomorrow. He laid down and listened to the high-pitched tinnitus ringing in his ears. Woody visualized the string section of a symphony orchestra energetically sawing horsehair bows across their strings and tried getting relief by mentally lowering the pitch. He drifted off to sleep and woke with a start, afraid he'd slept through his gig. He'd been asleep for twenty minutes—time to go to work.

—

Three hours later, the band in the middle of a rollicking, high-energy second set, everyone in the room hung on every note of Woody's soaring guitar solo. He went longer than usual, exploring new spaces and sounds, the crowd pressing in, listening for clues in the moment-to-moment musical treasure hunt. Everyone, Woody included, waited patiently for the perfect procession of notes to validate the journey. For the fans, those sublime jewels provided the justification for buying tickets, traveling, waiting in long lines. For the band, they justified the endless hours of practicing, driving, and schlepping gear.

Woody knew it didn't really matter what note he played, it was the notes he played before and after. He'd started his solo with a repeating, ostinato figure, then took things further out with musical explorations that spanned the spectrum from spelunking to mountain climbing. He considered the recurring question of how long a guitar solo could go. How many licks does it take to get to the center of a Tootsie Roll Pop? What if he kept playing until the sun came up and didn't stop? He thought of something he'd read about standing Hindu Baba, a sect of worshippers in India who take an oath to remain standing for twelve years. He shook his head. "Stop thinking, listen to what you're playing, be the music."

When the band went into the last song, Block stepped out the backstage door for some fresh air. Ray was standing there, Block didn't recognize him.

"There aren't any tickets," Ray said. "I guess they're sold out."

Block just nodded. After a few minutes, he reached behind him and opened the metal door a few inches so Ray could hear better.

"Thanks," Ray said, "the band sounds good."

"This band sounds great on their worst nights. Tonight's off the charts. Sometimes no sleep and hassles with each other ends up making the best music." They stood listening until the band crescendoed to a dramatic ending and the audience exploded with applause.

"Thank you for coming, or however you responded," Woody said into the microphone. When the band walked off stage the audience grew louder, clapping and stomping on the wooden floor as if they might have the communal power to take down the building.

Woody came back on stage with the band close behind. "Thanks, everyone. I guess we're all hungry for more. You are what you eat." He went into a song the audience didn't recognize but were clearly open to discovering, some cupping their hands behind their ears to amplify the sound. One tall, skinny young man was dancing with a soup spoon, holding it up facing the stage.

Block pushed open the back door and nodded at Ray. "Go ahead in and check out the encore if you want."

Ray made his way through the thick crowd to the back of the room and leaned against the wall. He'd always wanted to see Woody's band, see what his gigs were like, check out his songs, but he'd been worried that people would recognize him. No one seemed to care about anything except what was happening on the stage, the polar opposite of Ray's audience at Caesars Palace, where people were more interested in each other than the band. Unlike Caesar's ornate, impersonal, high-ceiling ballroom, this little shoebox of a room was packed with the moist heat of gyrating bodies and wall-to-wall sound. There wasn't a single crossover; not one person at Ray's show patronized Woody's show. And except for an occasional space traveler on acid enjoying the spinning lights, hippies didn't go to Caesars Palace. They were parallel universes.

Woody's band played an experimental version of an obscure Frank Sinatra tune, "The Night We Called It A Day," with Jupiter teasing a soprano saxophone interpretation of the vocal melody. Ray was surprised to hear a Sinatra song, not at all what he expected.

Ray stayed until the last note, slipped out the door, and went back to the Emperor's Suite on the top floor of Caesars Palace. He walked across his spacious room, pulled open the wall of curtains overlooking Lake Tahoe, and softly sang the words he knew to the Sinatra song.

You kissed me and went on your way
There wasn't a thing left to say
The night we called it a day

—

With the truck loaded, Block and Woody, physically and mentally exhausted, drove back to the motel, smoking in silence. Woody usually had his acoustic guitar that he played while they drove. For once he was giving his sore hands a break. When he went to crush out his cigarette, the ashtray was so full, butts overflowed onto the floor. He thought about how much more he smoked when he was with Block. He had a kind of spiritual relationship with smoking, mindful about when and where he did it, using it as a mini-meditation, a five-minute Sabbath. It caused him to step outside his current space, literally or figuratively, to pause and reflect.

But it was time to quit, again. It was affecting his singing. As much as he enjoyed the transitory rush of a good smoke, he also appreciated in kind of a sadistic way, the bigger stimulating swings of smoking, quitting, and taking up smoking again. He'd done it many times before and made a mental note to put it on his list of things to do. It took time, and almost all his attention. Whenever he did decide to quit, pretty much the only activity he could do for a week or two was not smoke.

Block smoked cigarettes the way a dog pees on trees, marking notable locations and events. He lit a cigarette when they got in the truck, lit up when they arrived somewhere, smoked before he ate, after he ate, at the inception of a new topic of conversation or to acknowledge a stretch of time without conversation.

At just such a time, halfway back to the motel when he and Woody had been driving in silence, Block lit up. "There was a guy outside hanging around the back door tonight, he couldn't get in."

"He didn't have any money?"

"It was sold out. The guy didn't appear to be hurtin' for money."

"Whuddya mean?"

"I mean he was dressed pretty slick compared to most people that come to your shows. Nice shirt and slacks and stuff, and the way he carried himself. Kinda cocky, like he didn't wanna be hangin' around a back door. The kinda guy that women would probably pick up on his self-confidence or whatever, but probably not the women at your gigs with their hairy armpits and everything."

"Did he have an upper deck of big white teeth and a slick Elvis haircut?"

"That was him. You know him?"

"I'll bet you anything it was Ray Bell coming to check out my gig. How'd he smell?"

"Like a gallon of Old Spice."

"I wonder how he liked the music."

—

In the motel bathroom, Woody took a leak, splashed water on his face, and looked in the mirror. The jittery white fluorescent light was jarring. It brought to mind a comment Stephanie made when he'd come home from another road trip like this. "Those bags under your eyes wouldn't fit in an overhead compartment." The thought of her created an ache in his chest. Stephanie and Lily, on their first solo trip, in crazy Los Angeles. It was hard enough missing them when he traveled, and they were home safe and sound, now his feelings were a ball of confusion. He hadn't been able to reach Stephanie for almost two days. The day before, she'd left him a message that she was staying an extra two days and switching hotels, but when he called the new hotel, she was always out. He'd tried calling before his show. Now it was four in the morning, he'd try again tomorrow.

With only scraps of sleep over the past several days, Woody was beyond exhaustion. He flicked off the bathroom light and, without bothering to turn on the bedroom light, stripped off his clothes in the neon glow from the motel sign coming through the curtains, and lay down full length on a man asleep in his bed.

Twig had neglected to book Woody's room for the second night and the motel manager had taken Woody's suitcase to the lobby and re-booked the room.

Naked except for his guitar that he'd grabbed while being chased out of the room, Woody held the case by its handle horizontally in front of himself and pounded on the door to Twig and Billy's room. He heard movement, voices, then Billy opened the door in jeans with the belt undone, his zipper down, and no shirt and no shoes.

Billy looked Woody up and down. "What's up mate, feelin' lonely?"

"I need to talk to Twig."

Twig came up behind Billy, wearing only Billy's long-sleeve shirt, shielding her eyes from the bare light bulb outside the door. "Woody? What're you doing walking around like that?" She rubbed her eyes. "Where's your clothes?"

"What the hell, mate?" Billy grabbed his pants that were slipping down. "It's four o'clock in the bloody morning. That guitar case does resemble the shape of a woman but...honestly, mate, have you gone fookin' barmy?"

"I'd like to trade rooms with you guys."

"What?"

"Woody," Twig said, "are you serious? What're you doing walking around like that? You must be cold."

Woody shrugged. "It's actually kinda nice out. In fact it's so nice out, I think I'll leave it out." He stepped back and looked down intently at something on the oil-spotted pavement by the cement parking berm in front of their room. "Hey, you guys, check this out. You gotta check this out." Still half-asleep, they both stepped outside and looked down at the pavement to see what Woody was looking at.

Woody quickly stepped around them, went into their room, and slammed the door.

Billy and Twig were still standing in a daze staring at their closed door when, a minute later, Woody opened it a crack. "Your room's real nice. Let's trade. My room's twenty-seven, a few doors down. You won't need a key, just knock. There's a nice friendly chap there maybe you can share the room with."

—

Twenty minutes later Woody heard a light tapping and opened the door. Twig was standing there in Billy's shirt, a towel around her waist, dangling a key at shoulder height, Billy behind her holding Woody's clothes and his suitcase.

"I got you a new room," Twig said. "The Yahoo club paid for it, all the rooms are under their name." She shrugged. "Your new room has a bathtub."

—

The next morning Woody sat on the bed with its gaudy bedspread, trying to call Stephanie. He left messages at home, at her new hotel, and for the supervisor of commercials at Warner Brothers Studios.

—

Stephanie stood in the phone booth outside of the soundstage in Burbank, balancing Lily, a handful of quarters, and a sheet of paper with Woody's itinerary. She was in full makeup in her secretary skirt and blouse, on a ten-minute break from her shoot with Clark Kent and Louis Lane.

"I'm sorry, ma'am," the motel operator said, "there was a man staying in room twenty-seven who checked out yesterday. There's another gentleman staying there, and he's made it clear he doesn't want to be disturbed."

"I know Woody's staying there, he left me a message with his room number." Lily squirmed and started whining to be put down. "He's my husband."

"As I explained, he checked out yesterday."

A young man walked up to the phone booth. "Stephanie, Mr. Donner asked me to come find you. He said to tell you that the cast is waiting and that if you don't come back immediately, Superman will fly out here and pick you up."

Stephanie pictured her, Lily, and Superman, arms spread, holding hands, flying like Dorothy in *The Wizard of Oz*.

"Stephanie," the young man said, "we really need to—"

"Hello?" the operator said, "are you there, ma'am?"

Stephanie held up her finger to the man. "How about Twig Twillinger? Is there a room under her name?"

"I'm sorry, there's no Twig Twillinger registered here."

Lily pushed on Stephanie's chest, wanting to be put down.

"Can I leave a message for my husband?"

"I can't take a message for a non-guest."

Lily almost managed to squirm out of Stephanie's arms. She dropped the phone and walked back inside.

—

Woody called Pearlman's office. "Jeff, have you heard from Stephanie? She left me a message that she was staying in LA some extra days and I can't get ahold of her."

"I got a call from Warner's lawyer. They offered her a generous deal for a small part in a feature film. They say she's a natural."

"Feature film?"

"The baby food commercial didn't pan out, she's working on the new Superman movie. They're probably shooting today."

"Can you get a message to her to get Superman to fly her home, or at least call me?"

"I'll try. How's the band holding up?"

"Nothing like no sleep, bad food, cheap booze, and a bunch of tension to bring out the best in everyone. What's happening with Ray's lawsuit?"

"I spoke with Maria yesterday. She called to tell me how strong her case is, which means it isn't. She says she's not necessarily attached to the idea of settling, which means she is—a total amateur at negotiating. Sounds like she's coming unglued. She can barely say your name without choking on it."

A pickup truck with a bad muffler started up outside Woody's ground level motel room. He held the phone tighter, put his hand over his other ear, and pictured Pearlman at his polished-wood desk, looking out over his forty-story view.

"Maria mentioned that it would be a shame if the subject came up of Ray's past relationship with Stephanie at the strip club. She says it's relevant to the case."

The truck revved its engine. "What?" Woody walked away from the door and pulled the telephone onto the floor, setting off the bell. "Can they actually do that?"

"There's no way that stuff should be allowed to get to the jury, but honestly, anything can happen."

Outside, the truck revved its engine again.

"What the hell's all that noise?" Pearlman asked.

"It's my head exploding. *Anything* can happen? What's that supposed to mean?"

"She's betting on your jealousy, and you're playing right into it. Can't you let go of that old jealousy stuff?"

The truck drove off with a roar, and on his way back to the bed, Woody stubbed his toe hard on the phone that was still on the floor. "*You're* lecturing *me* about jealousy stuff? You ever think about my wife's tits? Seems like everybody else does."

"Whoa! Easy does it there, pal! I've never shown you and your family anything but respect and I expect the same from you, and so does your wife, and she deserves it! Have you had any sleep?"

"I see a movie on the back of my eyelids when I close my eyes."

There was long pause.

"You seem pretty on edge," Pearlman said. "Try getting some sleep, and we'll talk about the case when you're in a civil mood."

"Are you saying we could actually lose at trial?"

"Anything can happen with a San Francisco jury. Ray and his lawyer are broke, they have nothing to lose. And now Ray's got sympathy after that stunt on the bridge, which I don't think was a stunt."

"He came to my gig last night."

"What?"

"He's doing a run at Caesars Palace. I checked out his gig, he's singing great. Then he came and checked out my gig—battle of the bands."

"Did he mention the lawsuit?"

"I didn't even find out he was there until later."

Brenda stuck her head in Pearlman's door. "Stephanie's on line three, asking if you've heard from Woody."

"One second, Brenda. Woody, where are you?"

"Worst Western, South Lake Tahoe. Room thirty-two."

"Stephanie's on the other line, I'll see if Brenda can connect the calls."

—

"Where are you?"

"We're still in LA. The baby food commercial didn't work out. I got a small part in a Superman movie. I've been trying to call you."

"I've been trying to call *you*."

They both knew to take a break and were quiet for a moment. "I miss you," Woody said softly. "I dreamt last night that your hair was Niagara Falls, or Niagara Falls was your hair. I was surfing down it naked, using my guitar as a surfboard. I live two separate lives: my dream life and my waking life."

"A third of your life is spent sleeping, might as well enjoy it. In some ways it's when you're the most aware, free of time and space. During the day we're stuck in our ego, we think time's constant. In a lucid dream, anything can happen but nothing can harm you, like Superman. I'm looking forward to our heads being inches apart again, doing dream yoga together. Lily and I will be home tomorrow night."

"I'll be home tomorrow night, then back in the studio."

"Woody?"

"Yeah?"

"Let's take the weekend off."

"Let's do it."

"We'll tell everyone we won't be home for a few more days, unplug the phone, take walks. You wouldn't believe the catering they have here for the actors. I've got some new recipes I want to cook for you."

"How does Lily like Superman?"

"Except for his costume, he's kind of boring. You're her Superman," she said. "We'll see you tomorrow night."

"See you tomorrow night. What do you want to do second?"

CHAPTER 21

Woody and Stephanie arrived home within a couple hours of each other. While Lily slept, Stephanie cooked dinner and Woody sat on the couch serenading her with his nylon-string acoustic guitar. When he went into a lively Flamenco groove, she clapped her hands twice and walked over in front of him in a whirling interpretive dance, whipping the hem of her skirt like a matador. He could see she wasn't wearing underwear. He hit the body of the guitar with his thumb in between chords and flammed his fingers, adding maracas, timbales, and marimbas—a one-man mariachi band. She twirled to a stop in front him, their knees touching, and she saw he was bursting out of his jeans. They'd been apart for almost two weeks. She took his guitar out of his hands, set it aside, sat down in his lap, and wrapped her sweaty arms around his neck. They made love on the couch until they both smelled the dinner burning.

—

When Woody arrived at the studio on Monday, Pearlman was waiting out front sipping from a coffee mug that said THE RECORD PLANT with a picture of a potted tomato plant.

"The band's already here. We need to talk."

"I could see that from a mile away," Woody said.

"I got a call from Bernie. Get some coffee and meet me out back."

Woody and Pearlman often gravitated to a small outdoor area with lawn chairs and ashtrays where Woody went to smoke. Pearlman got straight to the point. "Bernie called this morning. He was in a terrible mood."

The bass player stuck his head in the door. "Don't shoot the messenger, but everybody wants to know how long you guys are gonna be."

"Ten minutes," Pearlman said.

"It's funny they sent Chewy," Woody said when he left. "He's probably the only guy in the band that doesn't really care how long we'll be. He's a gem of a musician and a real gentleman. You don't find that combination very often. I wish I could bottle it."

Pearlman considered the closed door. "Bernie wants me to fire your band and hire some studio players."

"He wants *you* to fire *my* band? That's a hot piece of shit."

"I guess I could've said it more artfully. He asked me to broach the subject of hiring some top-notch studio cats to knock out a record. Or two, or three if you have the songs. Bernie thinks quantity has a certain quality. You once told me you can write a song in five minutes."

"After I think about it for five years. *I* write the songs, but they really belong to the listener."

"From what Bernie hears from the studio staff here, he thinks your band's dysfunctional. Maybe it's you, but you're the given."

"Being different is what we have in common." Woody did a lap around his chair. "I'm supposed to work with some technically perfect studio cats who park their personalities at the door? Make musical decisions based on personality fluff and that's what you get, namby-pamby marshmallow music instead of something that burns going down."

"You're right, you and Bernie speak different languages. This conversation would sound like Chinese to him. He just wants results."

"Hurry up and make a record nobody'll listen to? You can't push a river. And you can't impose change on a band from the outside." Woody clamped his left hand over his right and squeezed it into a fist. "You don't use your left hand to make your right hand into a fist. You move it from within…you *will* it to happen."

Pearlman had always been intrigued by the size of Woody's hands. The length of his guitar-player fingers seemed twice what they should be in relation to his body.

"Music fans gravitate toward the tension they sense between the musicians," Woody said, "the band chemistry. The Beatles, Stones, Grateful Dead, Pink Floyd? A bunch of space cadets learning as they go, making magic, taking music to places other people didn't even know existed. Sure, you could find a session player better than anybody in those bands, and it might kill the magic. You wanna get a bunch of perfectly skilled studio cats to play my songs? There's session guys in town that can make a song sing. Or we might lose the chemistry the band has and kill the magic. Do you want a photograph or a painting?"

Pearlman rubbed the back of his neck. "The personalities in your band are taking over; the inmates are running the asylum. You're like a small guy walking a large dog." Pearlman leaned in, elbows on his knees "I get how attached you are to playing with these same guys. But from the outside, it looks like an old guy on a little-league team trying not to swing too hard. I'm just telling you what Bernie said. Hiring studio musicians is probably his last-ditch effort before he pulls the plug on your recording budget." He sat up and held out his hands. "Like Chewy said, don't shoot the messenger."

Woody's next thoughts knocked him into the closest chair, his mind spinning out to the possibility of losing his recording contract and his only income coming from constant touring like the grueling one he just did—then to an image of his little family in his last squalid apartment in San Francisco, his wife taking another job as a stripper. "I feel like I'm watching a wave of water rolling backwards, exposing an old coastline." He quickly stood up and put his hand on the doorknob. "Fire the band? When this band's on fire you can smell it. I've been working on something new—a new song, a new groove, a different approach. My band will think I'm nuts, but that's fine with me. They already think I'm nuts, call me the Lone Arranger." He opened the door and looked back at Pearlman. "You'll hear the results right away if it works…or it'll be like five guys trying to fuck a football."

—

Back in the studio, Woody went straight for his guitar and started an unusual, Latin-flavored slow rock rhythm, singing repeating counter-point lyrics that were brimming with emotion. He was digging into the groove, enjoying himself, when he was interrupted by a heated conversation going on between Billy and Twig in the corner of the studio, both of them leaning forward at the waist, their faces red.

Woody tried to ignore them and kept playing.

Billy took a bite of a burrito he had in his hand and yelled at Twig while he chewed.

"I've always hated the way you eat," she yelled back at him.

Billy stopped chewing, opened his hand, and let the half burrito fall, splattering rice and beans on Twig's shoe. He spun around, went to his drums, and launched into a driving rock beat way ahead of where Woody had carefully established the tempo he wanted. The song he'd been working on for a month, called "Back To Now," had a swampy, half-time Samba feel. It had a poignant lyrical portrayal of a young man on a cold sidewalk looking through a fancy restaurant window, watching his ex-girlfriend having dinner with her new rich boyfriend…a true story for Woody.

The lyrics were as if they were welded to the melody. Singing to himself, Woody looked for alternative phrasing that could work with what Billy was playing. It felt impossible. Billy was agitated and Woody knew there was nothing he could do about it. He yelled "fuck" in his head and stopped playing. Everyone stopped.

"What's up, mate?" Billy said. "We were just diggin' on the swanky new groove."

"*We* were digging the groove?" Woody said. "I was floating something new, and you dove in with a bellyflop and started splashing around." Woody looked down at his guitar. "Everybody's playing affects everything else. There's no peeing section in a swimming pool."

"Roger that," Billy said. "How 'bout this?"

He went into a beat that, to Woody, sounded exactly the same as the previous one. When Woody tried playing along, he felt like he was sitting on top of a moving train, pretending he was driving. He changed guitars. He picked up one with a green sparkle finish he knew Stephanie liked that made him think of her that made him think of her yoga pants. His next thought was of her with her leg raised, her knee almost touching her nose, swinging her arms, and spinning in one of her graceful no-resistance Aikido moves meant to capture an opponent's energy. "Use the prevailing energy to your advantage," Woody thought. "Go with the flow. Let Billy go where he goes and stop resisting." When he stepped up to the microphone, the words came out sounding half-time because the song had doubled in speed. Counterintuitively, the new feel gave the lyrics more breathing room, creating space around the words.

When the other guys joined in, things began to gel. Since he'd started writing the song, Woody had trepidation about singing a lyrical description of a woman eating, about putting a personal physical activity into words. Now the rolling groove became the focus and his shyness about the lyrics became incidental. He sang with confidence and Billy responded with punchy, upbeat accents further emboldening Woody to kick out the phrases. When the bass, sax, and keys hit Billy's accents, the song gained its own momentum. Woody felt the hair on the back of his neck raise when he recognized the added bonus: he didn't have to choose among the multiple verses he'd written, they all fit in with the song galloping along.

It soon became apparent that it was time for something to happen, time for a chorus or bridge, but the song had left the station before Woody'd finished making his travel plans. He glanced through the glass to the control room, saw Betty and Pearlman's heads bobbing, turned to the band, held up two fingers, they changed chords, then four fingers, then five, then back to the one. He waved his hand in a circle, signaling to repeat the progression. The chords instantly became a chorus, the tenor sax blowing a thick, sumptuous harmony between the vocal phrases; groove, words and melody melding together like spicy ingredients of a simmering stew. Woody tapped the top of his nose, signaling the bridge, stuck three fingers out sideways for an E chord, then patted the top of his head to take it to the top.

When Woody finished singing the story of how pain caused by love creates desire for more love, the band went into an instrumental improvisation and Billy took things in a whole new direction with a thumping, Native American tom-tom beat. Woody looked through the window, winked at Pearlman, and sang: "When the band's on fire, don't fire the band. When the band's on fire, fire *up* the band."

"Getting all this?" Pearlman said to Betty, knowing she was.

Betty kept her eyes on the band. "I always record everything. I even came in early the first day and mic'd up the whole building, every room. When Woody tries something new on his acoustic guitar in the kitchen with Billy tapping on the counter, I get it on tape."

Without a glance or cue, the band ended the song together.

Woody put down his guitar and Pearlman pulled open the thick padded control room door. They stood looking at each other, Woody breathing hard, dripping sweat.

"Great song," Pearlman said.

"Don't fire the band, fire *up* the band."

—

Preparing for trial was the worst time to let her receptionist go, but she had no choice, her bank account was running on fumes. She picked up her office phone. "Maria Angel, good morning."

"It's Ray. We going to trial next week?"

"Yes. We won the MSJ."

"MSJ?"

"Motion for Summary Judgment. Pearlman filed a motion saying they should win without a trial because of the release we signed. The judge ruled that the validity of the release is a question of fact for the jury. It's great news."

"Great news? Going to trial? I thought you said the case would settle on the courthouse steps."

"I haven't heard from Pearlman. But settling on the courthouse steps is not a myth. In the meantime, we need to work on your testimony."

"Why don't you call him and see what it'll take to settle?"

"He knows where to reach me."

Ray slammed down the phone and kicked a cardboard box across his living room.

—

"I know you're busy, Mr. Pearlman—it's Woody, on line two."

"Thanks, Brenda. Wussup, Woody? I'm busy preparing for trial."

"So the trial's happening?"

"Yes. We lost the MSJ. We need to go over your testimony."

"Heard from Maria?"

"No. I can't wait to get that bitch into court with her thumbless grasp of the law. I could eat a can of Campbell's soup and shit a better legal argument than her."

"You said the case could settle. Why don't you call her and see if you can work something out? I thought we have a record to finish."

"The record will have to be put on hold for a week. Maria knows where to reach me."

Woody hung up the phone and slammed his fist on the kitchen counter.

CHAPTER 22

Tripping up the skinny stone steps to the courthouse, Woody said to Pearlman, "Were people smaller when they built these steps?"

Pearlman looked up at the ominous building he'd been in many times and didn't answer. He had a million things on his mind.

The largest federal government building west of the Mississippi covered an entire city block of downtown San Francisco. The six-hundred-thousand-square-foot structure was home to the Department of Justice, FBI, DEA, IRS, and the district courts. For the second half of every day, the eighteen-story mass of glass, steel, and political power cast a dark shadow over the eastern part of the city. Offices of the United States attorneys, enforcers of federal law, were located behind the same type of security scanners, bulletproof glass, and automatic-locking metal doors as the prisoners they succeeded in prosecuting. During the forty or fifty hours of a work week, both prosecutors and prisoners were in fluorescent-lit, ten-by-ten high-security rooms. One room was called an office, the other a cell. The critical difference: the lawyers got to go home nights and weekends.

Pearlman tried keeping Woody in the center of their small entourage that included Stephanie and Lily and waved the reporters away.

When they went single file into the courthouse, a reporter with a camera got close to Woody. "Woody, are you legally entitled to a hundred percent of the song royalties of 'Stephanie'?" The reporter's flashbulb popped three times.

Momentarily blinded, Woody shaded his eyes. "Legally entitled? I don't really get the connection between law and music."

"Why do you think Ray took himself to the bridge over the song?"

"Bridge?" Woody said. "I thought this whole thing was about the chorus."

Pearlman kept Woody moving into the crowded hallway and through the ten-foot-tall wooden doors. Cameras weren't allowed inside.

The federal courtroom, designed to exude authority, reminded Woody of a church with its ultra-high ceilings and foreboding, elevated seat for the judge on high, peering down at the minions and common folk.

—

Halfway up the granite steps, Ray and Maria stopped to give reporters a photo-op and answer questions about the lawsuit.

"Ray, was it you or Woody that wrote 'Stephanie'?"

"We both did."

"Did you know Stephanie well enough to write a song about her?"

He looked to Maria, she nodded.

"We both did," Ray said.

"Are you saying you both…"

Maria leaned into Ray's ear. "Leave it at that for now, keep your powder dry." She kept Ray moving up the stairs, anxious to get inside, stake out her space in the courtroom, and organize her thoughts.

Two week earlier, Maria had come and watched a trial in that same courtroom, where justice had been meted out to the likes of Patty Hearst, Huey Newton, and Fatty Arbuckle. She'd wanted to check out the vibe of the room—and, more importantly, the vibe of the judge.

Another reporter walked a few steps past them and stopped, blocking their path. "Was 'Stephanie' playing in your head when you stood on the Golden Gate Bridge?"

Marie put her hand on Ray's arm and nudged him forward.

"Ray, is this case about the song 'Stephanie' or the real Stephanie?"

"No more questions," Maria said. "It's time to focus on the work at hand: a trial to get to the truth."

—

Maria and Ray were at the plaintiff's table, on the left side of the room, closest to the jury box. The two of them had all the makings of movie stars in a legal thriller, Maria in a charcoal-gray skirt, jacket, and white blouse, Ray in a bespoke sport coat, dress shirt, and a hundred-dollar haircut.

Pearlman, in his stylish navy-blue suit and colorful tie, chatted with the court reporter and clerks and marshals; he knew them all. Woody sat by himself at the defendant's table under his umbrella of curly hair, wearing a sport coat, slacks, and dress shirt that Stephanie bought him and Pearlman insisted he wear. Pearlman had mentioned they'd be sitting at the table farthest to the right, a holdover from criminal trials where they kept potentially dangerous defendants away from the jury.

Woody kept his attention on his hands folded on the table. Stephanie and Lily sat one row behind him in the gallery, Lily checking out everything. Seated next to them were Orchid, Max, and Auddie. Ray's mother, Connie, sat behind Ray and Maria.

A few minutes later the judge walked in.

The clerk stood and announced, "All rise, United States District Court for the Northern District of California is now in session, the Honorable Elizabeth Vega presiding."

The judge was a stern African American woman who both Ray and Woody had been warned about by their attorneys. A recent Jimmy Carter appointee, the only Black woman on the federal bench in the western United States, she was strict and all business, determined to minimize mistakes and avoid being overturned on appeal. From her leather chair that extended two-feet above her head, she perused the courtroom, the noisy, full-to-capacity gallery a mixed crowd of musicians, tie-dyed music fans, music-business impresarios, and journalists. The only empty seat in the house was the witness stand.

Pearlman noticed Marty Levine, president of Ray's record label, A&M records, and the young A&R man from Warner Brothers. And in the back row were the guys from Woody's band, including Jupiter who looked like a giant on the skinny wooden bench.

Woody forced himself to unfold his hands and spread them on the table. He ventured a look around. Everyone seemed to be looking at him. "Trial by ordeal," he thought. "Prove your innocence by retrieving a stone from a cauldron of boiling water with your bare hand. Easy compared to this. Pearlman told him the jury would be checking him out like he was on stage and he should try to look comfortable and confidant, the opposite of how he felt. He made an effort to relax his shoulders and concentrate on his breathing the way Stephanie taught him. He noticed that the muted rumble of conversation in the room was low in pitch and somber compared to the trebly excited clamor of music fans waiting for a show.

The judge smacked her gavel. "Counsel will approach the bench." She told Maria and Pearlman that she ran a tight ship, admonished them against anything that would cause delay, and called in the prospective jurors.

Picking a jury, questioning during voir dire, was Pearlman's forte and where Maria had the least experience. Pearlman perused the panel, on the lookout for jurors who might relate to Woody, someone with a smile, a sense of humor, not particularly prim and proper. Anyone with a slouch, a two-day growth of beard, or maybe a protective mother or grandmother would do. The one type of juror he decided to avoid was a chic-looking, fashionable woman. That kind of woman would no doubt find Ray Bell, Mr. Dapper, more attractive, and—accordingly—more credible.

Pearlman tried to maintain as much control over the courtroom as possible, never asking a juror or a witness a question he didn't know the answer to. Putting Woody on the witness stand would be risky. He was bound to say something random, something that might seem odd to a straight person. For Pearlman, it was an exercise in letting go. Woody was going to be Woody and there was nothing he could do about it. His eccentric demeanor could seem almost heretical, and he often had the appearance of someone who hadn't showered in a week even though Pearlman knew him to be attentive to his personal hygiene. He also knew that jurors relied on intuition more than rationality and that if Woody didn't testify, they'd wonder why not. And there was always a chance that Woody would say or do something so poignant it would ring true with the jurors and hit the case out of the park.

As was common in federal trials, the judge questioned the jurors before the lawyers did. She kept everyone bored with questions about marital status, occupation, and past experience, if any, with litigation. But when she addressed some of the substantive issues, the answers took Pearlman by surprise, temporarily knocking him off his game.

"I'd be interested to know if any of you folks are familiar with the song at issue in this case," the judge said. "Please raise your hand if you've heard the song 'Stephanie'?"

All twelve jurors and the alternates seated behind them raised their hands.

The judge looked at counsel to be sure they were paying attention. "Are any of you familiar with the music of the plaintiff, Ray Bell?"

Everyone raised their hands.

"Are any of you familiar with the music of defendant, Chester Woods, also known as Woody?"

One young woman and one young man, both with long hair, raised their hands.

When Pearlman got to ask his own questions, he phrased them open-ended in a way that would allow a juror to answer in a narrative instead of just yes or no, giving him a bit of insight into the person. It became clear that most jurors were already under the impression that it was Ray's song, and they were unfamiliar with the concept of one person composing a song and another recording it.

"Please raise your hand if you think Elvis Presley wrote his own songs," Pearlman said.

They all raised their hands.

"Please raise your hand if you'd be surprised to hear that Elvis Presley didn't write *any* of his songs."

Maria jumped to her feet. "Objection."

The jurors tentatively left their hands at half-mast.

The judge waited a few seconds. "The basis of your objection?"

When Maria hesitated, Pearlman quickly interjected, "I'll withdraw the question, Your Honor."

Some observers in the courtroom knew it was a slick move on Pearlman's part, acting like he was being accommodating when in fact the way he stated the question *was* objectionable, but the jurors had heard it.

Most jurors acknowledged that they listened to the radio in their home, car, or at work virtually every day. Pearlman used all his preemptory challenges, including dismissing two young women jurors who said they were Ray Bell fans and that "Stephanie" was one of their favorite songs. He knew from experience to dismiss the worst potential jurors and settle for what was left. Maria used her challenges to dismiss two jurors who were unemployed, two musicians and one lawyer. After both attorneys exhausted their challenges, what remained was a twelve-person jury of eight blue-collar working men and women, an accountant, an insurance salesman, a retired policeman, and a stock trader.

—

During her opening statement, Maria continuously gestured to Ray while Ray did his best to look pleasant, attentive, even humble. She told the jury that the evidence and testimony would demonstrate that Ray's musical contribution had made "Stephanie" a worldwide hit. She said she'd bolster her argument by showing that Woody's own acoustic version of the song was a commercial failure due to the fact that it didn't contain Ray's signature melody hook in the choruses.

She expounded on Ray's reputation as a performing and recording artist as opposed to Woody, whom she portrayed as a jealous, drug-saturated, mentally unstable former street musician trying to get more money than he deserved from a song he was lucky enough to get Ray to co-write and sing.

"Objection, Your Honor." Pearlman knew it was unusual for opposing counsel to object during opening argument, but she was drifting too far outside her lane. "Counsel is imputing motivation to the defendant."

"Objection sustained."

Maria's face reddened. She consulted her notes and quickly finished her argument.

Pearlman spoke slowly and confidently, making eye contact with each juror, portraying Woody as a hard-working musician being prayed upon by a powerful celebrity plagiarizing musical ideas from a defenseless artist because he didn't have creative ideas of his own. He explained that a hit song, one as commercially as successful as "Stephanie," was very often the target of frivolous copyright-infringement lawsuits.

—

When the presentation of evidence began, Maria called a small parade of music industry executives and rock stars to the stand. The jurors watched with rapt attention, seeming to enjoy their presence. The witnesses all testified to Ray's stellar musicianship. In their professional opinion, Ray Bell's recorded performance of the song "Stephanie" had the earmarks of Ray's distinctive musical style.

Pearlman kept most of his cross-examination of these witnesses to one question:

"Isn't it true that you're a close personal friend of Ray Bell's?"

"Yes."

"No further questions."

—

Maria had spent a full day the previous week with her music theory expert, a UCLA music professor, reviewing Ray and Woody's versions of the song. The expert had gone to a recording studio and prepared a composite recording of sections of the two versions.

"The plaintiff calls Dr. Stephen Turer."

After Dr. Turer was sworn in, Maria asked, "What type of work do you do?"

"I'm a professor of music theory at UCLA."

"How long have you held that position?"

"I've been a tenured professor for twenty-six years."

"Please tell us about your work."

"While at UCLA I've published eighteen papers on song composition. Before that I was a classically trained concert pianist and I—"

Pearlman stood up at the defense table. "The defense stipulates to the witnesses' qualifications as a music theorist."

Pearlman quickly sat down and started leafing through some papers, guessing that Maria didn't know she could object to the stipulation and be allowed to reel off Dr. Turer's impressive qualifications for the jury. Pearlman was right.

"Ms. Angel," the judge said, "if there is no objection to Mr. Pearlman's proposed stipulation, please proceed to the subject matter."

Maria rolled a metal table on wheels up to the witness stand with a professional reel-to-reel tape machine and two large external speakers. She asked Dr. Turer to play the two recorded versions of "Stephanie" and point out the differences to the jury.

The witness, a bifocaled man in a plaid suit and clashing plaid bowtie, stood up and adjusted the metal table so the speakers faced the jury. He first played the two complete versions of the song, pointing out the choruses, then focused on ten-second snippets he'd prepared that demonstrated the melody of the last four bars of each chorus.

Dr. Turer opined that, unlike Woody's version of the song, the vocal melody in Ray's version had the compelling sound that made it appealing to the general public, the sound that made it a hit. It was, he explained, the signature hook, the "musical fingerprints" that listeners associate with the song and identify after hearing just a few notes, that it often replayed in their head after hearing it whether they intentionally chose to mentally replay it or not. "It is referred to in the industry as 'ear candy' that, to use the term metaphorically, gets music fans *addicted* to a song. They repeatedly listen to a song in the same way they go back again and again to experience the taste of, say, a particular brand of candy bar. They may also associate a song with an emotion or experience, for example heartbreak or unfulfilled longing. A song may also serve as a reminder of a cathartic event that occurred while hearing the song, for example a first kiss."

"And isn't it true, Dr. Turer," Maria said, "that the hard work it takes to create those memorable musical moments is legally protected?"

"Yes. Case law terms it 'sweat of the brow' protection. Ownership rights. It's designed to encourage creative expression."

"In your professional opinion, doctor," Maria asked, "are the words or the music more important in what makes a quality piece of music?"

"As an academic scholar, that is a complicated question." Doctor Turer took out a neatly folded plaid handkerchief, blew his nose, and refolded it into his suit pocket. "Please excuse me, my allergies are always bad this time of year." He cleared his throat. "Words and music work as a kind of team, expressing things together that they couldn't express by themselves. Their relationship is a sliding scale: the better the music, the less necessary it is to have superlative lyrics, and vice versa. Of course, there are many examples of songs with both high-quality lyrics and music that, as the saying goes, does the trick for a listener. In a metaphorical sense, the music serves to lift the words off the page. Without music, words are just that—words. It can be said that music is beyond the reach of language. For example, a listener can easily enjoy a song in a foreign language, or for that matter an instrumental song with no words at all. However, that listener would not likely enjoy a speech or simple recitation of words with no music that was in a foreign language they didn't understand." He stopped talking for a moment, held up a finger, pressed his lips together, and resisted a sneeze in a way that turned his face red. "Please, excuse me. Now, of course, we haven't addressed the other half of the equation: the subjective state of the listener. Deaf or blind people perceive music in certain ways. Even minor environmental elements can affect a person's taste in music, such as how they're feeling that day." Turer let out a sudden explosive sneeze and reached for his handkerchief. When he finished blowing his nose and resettled himself, he gave a kind of mischievous smile. "The analysis of subjectivity is limitless. For example, during allergy season a music theorist might render a particularly subjective opinion about music."

Turer's attempt at humor was met with silence.

Maria consulted her notes, unsure if her next prepared question was still appropriate.

The judge held her gavel.

Turer cleared his throat.

"Ms. Angel," the judge said, "please proceed."

"In your expert opinion, Dr. Turer, would you consider Ray Bell a contributing composer, a co-writer of the song 'Stephanie'?"

"Yes."

"No further questions, Your Honor."

"Questions for the witness, Mr. Pearlman?" the judge said.

"Yes, just a couple of questions, Your Honor. Dr. Turer, I'd like to keep this as simple as possible for us all to understand. Many quote 'hit' rock and roll songs have similar chords in similar progressions, is that correct?"

"Yes."

"What are those chord progressions?"

"There are a small handful. Referring to the numerical nomenclature of chord designation in a particular key, one-four-five, one-five-four, two-five-one, or one-five-six are common. There are other similar variations. They're the building blocks of popular music."

"In your expert opinion, Dr. Turer, what percentage of quote 'hit' songs contain those same common chord progressions?"

"I'd estimate that roughly eighty-five percent of hit rock and pop songs have similar chord progressions."

"Does the song 'Stephanie' have those common chord progressions?"

"No."

"How so?"

"The verses, choruses, and bridge of the song 'Stephanie' are actually constructed of unusual chords and combinations of chords."

"Are you familiar with the songs on Ray Bell's first album?"

"Yes, I am."

"Are the songs on that album made up of the common chord progressions you described earlier?"

Dr. Turer cleared his throat. "Yes, they are."

"All of them?"

He cleared his throat again. "Yes."

Pearlman quickly cleared his own throat in a way that left it ambiguous whether or not he was mimicking Dr. Turer. "Dr. Turer, are you familiar with the song 'I Get By With A Little Help From My Friends'?"

"I am."

"Who wrote that song?"

"Ringo Starr."

"Are you familiar with the recorded version by the singer Joe Cocker?"

"I am."

"Do you agree that Mr. Cocker performed an excellent vocal rendition of the song?"

"Yes."

"Did that excellent singing legally entitle Joe Cocker to any rights as a composer of the song?"

Dr. Turer cleared his throat and hesitated.

Pearlman cleared his own throat, this time clearly mimicking Turer. "Dr. Turer, your answer please?"

"No, that would not entitle Mr. Cocker to rights as a composer."

"No further questions."

CHAPTER 23

Eight o'clock that night, Pearlman was enjoying the one shot of a sixteen-year-old scotch he allowed himself when he was in trial. He was reading over Maria's witness list when the phone rang.

It was Maria.

"Sorry to call you at home. Am I disturbing you, Jeff?"

"I had to get up anyway to answer the phone." He smiled. He'd been expecting her to call when things weren't going well for her at trial. "What's up, Maria?"

"I'm calling Ray as my first witness tomorrow."

"So?"

"To show Ray's motivation to compose parts of the *song* 'Stephanie,' I'll establish as foundation his prior personal relationship with the *woman* Stephanie."

"So?"

"Where he met her is bound to come up. I thought your client might consider settling to avoid that eventuality."

"You're talking about Stephanie working at that topless joint?"

"Exactly."

"So why didn't you just say so? How much do you want?"

"Fifty percent of past and future royalties. Woody pays our attorney's fees."

"You want fifty percent of everything and attorney's fees for those couple of notes on the chorus?"

"Those notes are the gold."

Pearlman sipped his scotch and waited.

"Well?"

He waited, enjoying the tension.

"The attorney's fees might be negotiable," she said.

He took another slow sip of scotch. "So, let me get this straight—that prima donna client of yours doesn't know shit about music, so your strategy is to embarrass my client's wife? Is that what you're saying?"

"There's an evidentiary basis to bring up any relevant—"

"My client's wife's past employment has absolutely no relevance to the music at issue here. None. Bringing up something prejudicial in court that has no relevance is grounds for a mistrial. This could be considered extortion, Maria. Be careful what you say, you're getting way over your skis."

"You can't extort someone by threatening to tell the truth."

"Stephanie's past has nothing to do with anything, and you know it."

"You're ethically required to bring settlement offers to your client. Let me know what Woody says."

"Don't tell me how to practice law, Maria. Judging by how I'm feeling right now, I'll try to put my counteroffer to you as gently as possible: Go to hell, I'll see you in court."

He hung up the phone and poured himself another scotch.

Pearlman stayed up late trying to decide whether or not to tell Woody about Maria's phone call. There was really nothing new in Maria's offer, just the same unreasonable numbers she'd mentioned before. The threat about Stephanie and the strip club wasn't new, either. She'd put it in her complaint. It was public record. His primary responsibility was client control. If he brought up Maria's threat again, Woody'd be a mess in court. Besides, he had his plans for Ray on the witness stand tomorrow.

—

The next morning, when Woody and Pearlman were climbing the courthouse steps, Woody looked up at the building, took a deep breath, and said, "My grandmother used to say you can get used to anything, even hanging."

After the lawyers huddled in front of the bench, the judge again admonishing them to keep things moving, she tapped her gavel. "We are reconvened in the case of Bell versus Woods. The record will reflect that the parties and jurors are present. Ms. Angel, call your next witness."

"I call the plaintiff, Ray Bell."

Ray's erect, confidant stride to the witness stand was like he was going to receive an award. Virtually everyone in the room, including the jurors, straightened themselves up slightly.

Maria walked Ray, step by step, through his music career starting at age six when he performed with his father's band. The direct examination was drifting into a casual conversation when Pearlman objected. "The relevance of this line of questioning is tenuous."

"Objection sustained," the judge said. "Ms. Angel, please limit the witness's testimony to issues central to the case and move things along as we discussed."

Maria went into Ray's more recent career accomplishments, focusing on the accolades and commercial success he garnered from his first hit song.

Woody kept his eyes on his folded hands, thinking how much different this cerebral process was compared to performing music. If he or Ray messed up the words performing a song at a concert, the song just kept going with virtually no consequences. If they messed up in a recording studio, they could fix it before anyone heard it. Messing up words on the witness stand could cost a lifetime of song royalties.

When Maria went further into the details of Ray's accomplishments, Pearlman objected. "Irrelevant. What does this have to do with the issue at hand?"

"Your Honor, it has everything to do with the issue." Maria put hands on her hips. "I'm demonstrating Mr. Bell's qualifications as a professional musician."

"Objection overruled. Proceed with your direct examination, Ms. Angel."

Pearlman's planned strategy was to appear as if he were trying to obstruct this line of Maria's argument so she'd push harder in that direction, digging herself deeper into the hole of touting Ray's superior music qualifications. She took the bait, enlightening the jury about Ray's illustrious career and musical skills. When Ray boasted about his qualifications as an accomplished musician, Pearlman just looked down at his notes and let him go on.

"Thank you for your forthright testimony today." Maria walked a few steps away from the witness stand, then stopped and turned back. "One more thing, Mr. Bell. Do you recognize the woman with red hair seated directly behind the defendant?"

"That's Stephanie."

"Do you know her well enough that you might cowrite a song about her?"

"You mean know her in the biblical sense?" Ray's smirk was blatant. "She used to work at a strip club I went to, so I guess you could say our relationship was kind of intimate."

Pearlman was on his feet. "Objection! Irrelevant! This line of questioning has nothing—"

Ray kept talking over him. "—I definitely recognize her, but she looks different with her clothes on."

Woody slapped the table hard with both hands. "What the hell!"

"Objection! Non-responsive!" Pearlman yelled, but by the gasps and rumbling in the courtroom, it was clear that everyone had heard what Ray said.

Woody stood, shoving his chair back, and took a step toward the witness stand. Pearlman grabbed him by the arm.

The judge smacked her gavel. "Quiet in the courtroom! Objection sustained. The defendant will remain seated, counsel will approach the bench!" She slammed her gavel down twice. "Order in this court!" As soon as they arrived the judge tore into Maria. "Your client is out of control, Ms. Angel! That was potentially grounds for a mistrial, even sanctions. If you expect to—"

"It was a spontaneous declaration by the witness, Your Honor, and it actually goes to the factual basis of the recognition he was speaking of. I didn't anticipate that he would—"

"That's ridiculous!" Pearlman said. "It's grounds for a mistrial."

"It was an emotional moment for the witness," Maria said. "A contemporaneous emittance that, if I may, Your Honor—"

"You may not, Ms. Angel!" the judge barked. "This is a court of law, and you'll obey the law, control your witness, and not introduce irrelevant prejudicial evidence. Sleight-of-hand, sneaking in irrelevant facts to the jury, cannot only get your case thrown out and sanctions imposed, you could be disbarred for that type of activity!"

Pearlman knew to wait a few moments, then said, "I hereby make a formal motion to the court to declare a mistrial."

"Your Honor, if I may," Maria said in a soft voice, "the factual issue at hand is whether or not the plaintiff had a relationship with the person Stephanie which would establish the foundation for his motivation to contribute to writing the song 'Stephanie.'"

Pearlman looked directly at the judge with his finger pointed at Maria. "She isn't practicing law judge, she's presenting the jury with irrelevant gossip."

"It's not irrelevant." Maria's voice got loud, almost out of control. "It goes to the heart of the matter. After everything we and the jury have been through, it would not serve justice to abort the entire process over one sarcastic remark."

By the look on the judge's face, both Maria and Pearlman knew the energy had shifted. The judge told Maria to control her witness or risk having her case dismissed. She said Pearlman could address the truth of any of Ray's statements on cross-examination and she would then make a ruling on his request for mistrial. The lawyers returned to their tables and the judge instructed the jury to ignore Ray's out-of-order statement, but Pearlman knew the horse was out of the corral.

"Mr. Pearlman, do you have questions for the witness?"

"I do, Your Honor."

"You may proceed. Mr. Bell, as a reminder, you're still under oath."

Pearlman stood up and stayed at the defense table next to Woody rather than approach the witness. "Mr. Bell, I have questions regarding two subjects: your relationship to the person Stephanie and your relationship to the song 'Stephanie.' Regarding the person Stephanie seated in the courtroom today, did you ever have an intimate physical relationship with her?"

Ray cracked his ingratiating smile. "Well, I guess you might say—"

Pearlman quickly interrupted, "I'm not asking for speculation or insinuation, I'm just interested in facts. Did you ever have sex with Stephanie? Yes or no?"

Ray glanced at the jury and at his lawyer.

"Yes or no, Mr. Bell." Pearlman raised his voice.

"No."

Pearlman exhaled. "Thank you for being forthright regarding any previous irrelevant insinuations. Now, regarding the actual key issue in this case: music, about which you apparently consider yourself an expert. We've heard about your illustrious music career today. I don't think it's necessary to belabor the issue, but just to summarize, before the release of the song 'Stephanie,' at issue here, you had one hit song in your career. Is that correct?"

Maria was on her feet. "Objection for vagueness as to what a 'hit' song is. The witness cannot respond without knowing how the term is being used or—"

"Let me rephrase the question. Mr. Bell, are you familiar with the concept that a quote 'hit' record is commonly considered to be a gold record, two-hundred-fifty thousand units in sales?"

Ray nodded.

Pearlman looked to the judge.

"Mr. Bell, you're required to answer verbally."

"Yeah," Ray said.

Pearlman continued. "And how many gold records have you achieved in your life?"

"Including 'Stephanie'?"

"*Not* including 'Stephanie.'"

Ray gave another one of his obsequious smiles. "One."

"That one hit song was called 'Baby Don't Be A Baby.' Is that correct?"

Ray nodded.

"Is that a yes?"

"Yeah."

"A songwriter named Dana Rohrabacher was hired to write that song for you. You didn't write it yourself. Is that correct?"

Ray shook his head.

"Mr. Bell." The judge tapped her gavel. "The court reporter cannot record—"

Ray adjusted his position in his seat. "Yeah, Dana wrote that song."

"The album that contained the song 'Baby Don't Be A Baby' had a total of thirteen songs on it, is that correct?" Pearlman asked.

"I don't remember."

Pearlman picked up the record album next to him on the defense table. "Your Honor," he held up the shrink-wrapped album with a photograph of Ray on the cover, his hair slicked back like Elvis Presley. "I'd like to offer this as exhibit seven, the eponymous album *Ray Bell.*"

The marshal took the album from Pearlman and walked it to the judge's bench. He had a long history in federal courtrooms with Jeff Pearlman. They were old buddies, often exchanging information about their families and personal lives. As he walked it to the judge's bench, the marshal held the record album by one corner at his side, his head turned away almost as if it smelled bad.

The judge took a minute to look at the album front and back. "Any objection?"

"No objection," Maria said.

"The record album will be admitted as exhibit seven."

The marshal marked it with a sticker, gave it to Pearlman, and he extended it to Ray. "Is this your album?"

Ray sat with his hands in his lap. "I remember now, it had thirteen songs."

"How many of the songs on it did *you* write?"

"One."

"And what was the name of that song?"

"'I Wanna Be On You,'" Ray mumbled.

Pearlman was back at the defense table. "I didn't hear your response, Mr. Bell."

"I Wanna Be On You!"

"Of the thirteen songs on the album, ten were released as singles, and the single that sold the least was 'I Wanna Be On You.' Is that correct?"

"I wouldn't know. I don't keep tabs on that kind of stuff."

Pearlman picked up a Billboard Magazine off the table. "Your Honor, I'd like to offer this issue of Billboard Magazine as exhibit eight."

The marshal shuttled the magazine back and forth.

"Mr. Bell, an article entitled 'Ray Bell Wants to Be on You' in this issue of Billboard says—"

"I know what it says," Ray glared at Pearlman. "You made your point."

"The article is critical of the song's musical structure and lyrics and says it had the poorest sales performance of any song on the record. Is that—"

"You made your point!"

The judge slammed her gavel. "Mr. Bell, you will allow counsel to finish stating his question."

Pearlman pointed the magazine at Ray. "I'll withdraw the question." Pearlman turned away then turned back. "Do you play guitar?"

"No, I leave that to the experts."

Pearlman looked down at his notes. Without looking up he said. "On what instrument do you compose?"

"Piano."

"The parts of the song 'Stephanie' that you are claiming you composed, you composed them on the piano. Is that correct?"

Ray readjusted his position in his hard seat wooden. "Woody showed me his idea for a sketch of the song. I added my melody."

"Using a piano?"

"Yeah."

"You played the song on the piano, then you added your melody…on the piano. Is that correct?"

"Objection," Maria said. "Asked and answered. Counsel is badgering the witness."

"Objection overruled," the judge said. "Mr. Bell, you may answer the question."

"What's the question?" Ray asked.

"It's a very simple question," Pearlman said. "You've stated that you created your compositional contribution to the song 'Stephanie' while you played the song on the piano. Is that correct?"

"Yeah, I played it on the piano. What's your point?"

The judge tapped her gavel. "Mr. Bell, you will simply answer the questions being posed."

Pearlman pressed forward, unruffled. "During the songwriting process, Mr. Bell, how many times would you typically play a song on the piano?"

"A lot."

"Could you be more specific?"

"You don't keep track. Sometimes you end up staying up all night playing the song over and over. Songwriting's hard work."

"Your Honor, may I approach the bench?"

The judge waved Pearlman forward to the judge's bench. Maria met him there once again. Pearlman spoke in a low even tone. "Your Honor, I've made arrangements to have a piano brought into the courtroom to allow Mr. Bell to demonstrate to the jury his ability to compose on the instrument."

Maria glanced around the courtroom. "Piano?"

"There's a piano on wheels in the hallway, ready to be brought in," Pearlman said. "I've made all the arrangements in advance with the marshal."

"There've been no arrangements made with opposing counsel," Maria said. "Your Honor, demonstrative evidence without notice to counsel, it could be highly prejudicial."

The judge turned to Pearlman.

"Your Honor, the Plaintiff claims he co-wrote 'Stephanie' on the piano. That's pretty much what this case is about: Mr. Bell's credibility regarding authorship of the song. With prior notice, he could have prepared the song on piano for court today. He's making the claim, let him back it up."

Maria's eyes were wide. "There are so many variables here that haven't been anticipated. If given proper notice we could have—"

"That's the whole point," Pearlman said. "If the witness is telling the truth under oath, why not allow him to back up his statement? If the witness is telling the truth, Ms. Angel's vociferous objections are unfounded. This whole process is meant to get at the truth, is it not?"

"Your Honor, a musical performance in an alien environment could introduce elements that are completely immaterial to the issue at hand. I strenuously object. Surprise and gamesmanship are not what due process is about. Proper notice to opposing counsel is the most basic..."

The judge had obviously stopped listening to Maria. Her interest was piqued. She leaned back in her big leather chair. "You may proceed with your cross-examination, Mr. Pearlman."

"But, Your Honor, I—"

The judge tapped her gavel and cut Maria off. "Counsel will proceed."

Pearlman gestured to his assistant standing by the door, walked back to his table, and patted Woody on the shoulder. Three minutes later, the ten-foot-high doors to the courtroom swung open and two men wheeled in a shiny-black Steinway grand piano, placed it in front of Ray, lifted the top, and set a piano bench in front of it.

The courtroom doors had inadvertently been left open and flashbulbs started flashing, noise from the hallway pouring into the courtroom.

The judge slammed her gavel "Order! Order in the court! The marshal will close the doors!"

Ray saw the chalk marks on the floor where the three piano legs had been set and looked across the room at Maria. By the expression on her face, he knew there was nothing she could do to prevent him from being humiliated. A vertical vein appeared on Ray's forehead as he frantically tried to think of the chords to "Stephanie." Woody's chords were as weird as he was. He was never able to quite figure out what Woody was playing. What if he simply couldn't remember the song? He knew how to play "Mary Had a Little Lamb," but right now he couldn't remember how to play that either. He'd do anything to extricate himself from this ridiculous ordeal, including firing his useless lawyer and dropping the whole case. Ray's shoulders curled in, his confident posture crumpling.

"Mr. Pearlman," the judge said, "please proceed with your cross-examination of the witness."

Pearlman stood at the defense table facing Ray. He'd visited the courtroom the week before and made all the arrangements, including choosing a grand piano that could be placed at an angle where the jury could see Ray's hands on the keyboard.

Like a maître d' showing a diner to his table, Pearlman walked to the piano, pulled the bench out, and with a slight bow gestured to Ray. "Mr. Bell, if you would please be so kind as to play your version of 'Stephanie' for the ladies and gentlemen of the jury."

When Ray looked at Maria she looked down.

"Mr. Bell," the judge said, "let's move on with the work of this court. I've ruled that defense counsel may present this demonstrative evidence. Please proceed."

Without looking at the jury, Ray walked down the two steps off the witness stand, sat at the piano, and stared at the keyboard, hands on his thighs.

"Your Honor," Pearlman said, "can we please have the reporter read back my last exchange with Mr. Bell."

The judge nodded to the reporter. She read aloud:

Mr. Pearlman: "It's a very simple question. You've stated that you created your compositional contribution to the song 'Stephanie' while you played the song on the piano. Is that correct?"

Witness Ray Bell: "Yeah. What's your point?"

Mr. Pearlman: "During the songwriting process, Mr. Bell, how many times would you typically play a song on the piano?"

Witness Ray Bell "A lot."

Mr. Pearlman: "Could you be more specific?"

Witness Ray Bell: "You don't keep track. Sometimes you end up staying up all night playing the song over and over. Songwriting's hard work."

"Thank you," Pearlman said. "That will do. Mr. Bell, please demonstrate the process you described."

Ray sat frozen in place, staring down at the keys.

"Mr. Bell?" Pearlman said.

Ray kept his hands on his legs.

Maria stood up. "Your Honor, I object to this harassment of the witness. This type of haranguing serves no valid function toward resolving factual issues of the case. A courtroom is not a concert hall—it could be said to be the polar opposite. I object to this entire line of questioning and move the court to—"

The judge slammed her gavel. "Objection overruled. I've stated my position on the matter. Mr. Bell, you will respond to the defense counsel's request." There was a muted rumble in the gallery. The judge brought down her gavel again. "Attendees who do not remain quiet will be ordered to leave!"

When Ray raised his hands to the keyboard and played a chord, the room fell silent. Ray let the chord fade and put his hands back in his lap.

"One chord, Mr. Bell?" Pearlman said. "Is that your version of 'Stephanie'?"

"No," Ray said without looking up.

"No, you *won't* play it, or no, you *can't* play it?"

Ray suddenly stood up and shoved the piano bench with the back of his legs, sending it screeching across the wooden floor. "Not here! Not now!" He looked at the judge, then Pearlman, then to the jury. "I know how to play 'Mary Had a Little Lamb' and I couldn't play that right now either. I'm not a human jukebox! Listen to my singing on 'Stephanie' and figure out whose song it is. I added my melody by *singing* it, I'm a *singer*!" Ray walked across the courtroom, kicked open the swinging wooden gate, and walked through the gallery and out the tall doors while the judge slammed her gavel and the crowd erupted. One step into the hallway, Ray was bombarded by a bevy of flashbulbs and reporters' questions. People in the courtroom were on their feet trying to get a look out the door, the sound of the judge's gavel only adding to the bedlam. Two US Marshals posted by the door struggled to get the courtroom doors closed against reporters scrambling to get a photograph of the interior of the courtroom, and with everything else, Lily started crying loudly.

Ray pushed his way through the crowd, took the front steps four at a time, and dove into the back seat of one of the row of taxis parked out front.

The judge kept slamming her gavel and yelling at the rowdy courtroom. "Court is adjourned! The Marshals will clear the room! Counsel will approach the bench! We will reconvene at 8:30 tomorrow morning! Court is adjourned!"

Stephanie stood cradling Lily, trying to get her to stop crying. Pearlman and Maria headed to the bench, the judge glaring down at them. "Counsel are ordered to submit legal briefs to my chambers by seven thirty tomorrow morning addressing the issue of whether or not the plaintiff should be held in contempt and whether plaintiff's case should be dismissed, citing legal authority for your positions. Court is adjourned." She slammed her gavel harder than ever, wiped her brow with a white handkerchief she produced from under her black robe, and hit her gavel once more for good measure.

CHAPTER 24

The next morning the jury was kept sequestered for a full hour while Pearlman and Maria argued to the judge about what should take place on what was likely to be the last day of trial. The judge acknowledged Maria's point that a piano in the courtroom was highly unusual, but she ruled that the demonstrative evidence had served its purpose and it was up to the jury to determine its probative value. Then she spoke directly to Ray at the plaintiff's table, telling him that one more stunt like yesterday's, leaving the witness stand and the courtroom, would result in the dismissal of his case.

When the jurors filed in, Ray was back on the witness stand and the piano was gone. The judge addressed the jury. "Ladies and gentlemen of the jury, thank you for your patience. Please be advised that regarding yesterday's demonstrative evidence, you may consider the plaintiff's actions when assessing his credibility." The judge turned to Pearlman. "Do you have any further questions for Mr. Bell?"

"Not at this time, Your Honor."

"Very well. Ms. Angel, any redirect?"

"Yes, Your Honor."

"You may proceed. Mr. Bell, you're still under oath."

"Mr. Bell," Maria said, "please explain to the jury why you didn't feel comfortable playing the song 'Stephanie' on the piano yesterday in the courtroom."

Ray was in another high-collared shirt, tailored sport coat, and enough Old Spice cologne to reach the jury box. "I admit I'm not the greatest piano player. I'm mainly a vocalist. I plunk out melodies on the piano and have my own way of doing things. It works for me working by myself, but I'm self-conscious showing it to other people. I compose melodies as much, if not more, with my voice as I do with a piano. Performing on the piano in a courtroom felt completely alien to me. I froze up. Like I said yesterday, I was so anxious I couldn't have played 'Mary Had a Little Lamb.'"

"No more questions, Your Honor."

"Mr. Pearlman," the judge said, "any further questions for the witness?"

Pearlman began speaking as he stood up. "Did you practice playing 'Stephanie' on the piano last night in case you had to try playing again it in court today?" Pearlman intentionally altered his pace of questioning throughout a trial, often using surprise to get a witness to answer something in a way they hadn't intended.

"Yeah," Ray said.

"How long did you practice?"

"I don't know, an hour."

"Did you learn the song?"

Ray hesitated. If he said yes, Pearlman might ask him again to play it again. If he said no, he was admitting he couldn't play it.

"Objection," Maria called out the way a basketball coach calls time-out when their player is trapped in a corner.

"The basis of your objection?" the judge asked.

"What Mr. Bell does in the privacy of his home is irrelevant."

"Objection overruled. Mr. Pearlman, re-state your question."

Pearlman took his time consulting his notes, playing out the tension. "I'll withdraw the question. I have no more questions for the witness."

"Ms. Angel, do you have further evidence to present?"

"The plaintiff rests his case in chief," Maria said.

"Mr. Pearlman, your witnesses for the defense?"

"I call Brenda McEnroe."

Dressed like a secretary from central casting in a canary-yellow blouse, modest skirt to below her knees, and a blonde beehive hairdo, Pearlman's secretary took the stand and was sworn in.

"What kind of work do you do, Miss McEnroe."

"I'm your secretary."

"Do you know the plaintiff, Ray Bell?"

"Yes."

"How did you come to know Mr. Bell?"

"I knew him when your firm did some legal work for him in the past. I also know him personally."

"How do you know him personally?"

"We had a brief romantic relationship," she said matter-of-factly.

Pearlman held up a cassette tape. "Your Honor, I am marking this as exhibit nine. I will establish a foundation and offer it into evidence." He walked over and handed it to Brenda. "Do you recognize this cassette tape by its label?"

"Yes."

"Please describe what the label says for the jury."

"There's handwriting. It says, 'Stephanie by Woody.' Then there's a little letter c with a circle around it, then 1976."

"Have you seen this cassette tape before?"

"Yes."

"Where did you first see it?"

"I found it in Ray Bell's apartment. I had spent the night at his apartment and was looking for some music to play while I made coffee in the morning. Ray was still asleep. The tape was in his cassette machine."

"Did you listen to it that morning?"

"Yes."

"What did you hear on the tape?"

Brenda folded her hands in her lap and straightened herself up. "It's a tape of Ray and Woody working together on 'Stephanie.' Woody is showing Ray how the song goes, then Ray says some things."

Pearlman offered the cassette into evidence and the judge admitted it. Pearlman took a small black-plastic cassette player off his defense table, a stark contrast to the professional audio equipment Maria had used. He handed the cassette player to Brenda and looked up at the judge.

The judge looked at Maria. "Any objection to the witness playing the tape?"

"Yes, Your Honor. The audio content of that tape is hearsay."

"The statement Mr. Bell makes on that tape will be offered as a declaration he made against his interest," Pearlman said, "an exception to the hearsay rule."

"But, Your Honor—"

Pearlman cut her off. "The reason for the hearsay rule is if the declarant is unavailable for questioning. Woody and Ray are both here."

"But, Your Honor—"

The judge tapped her gavel. "Objection overruled. Mr. Pearlman, please proceed."

Pearlman tried unsuccessfully to suppress a smile. He wasn't smiling about Maria's objection being overruled. He was thinking that the only other judge he'd seen so gavel happy was the judge that presided over Woody's criminal case about Lily. There was something about Woody that caused judges to get percussive. He brought his attention back to Brenda. "Please play the tape."

The tape volume was soft coming out of the two-inch speaker but everyone in the room was dead silent. "Woody, Stephanie's *your* girlfriend, Stephanie's *your* song, you've got every word and note figured out. If you want me to sing your song, I need a budget."

At the defense table by himself, hands folded, Woody ventured a look around and saw that now no one was looking at him, all eyes were on Ray.

"Thank you, Brenda," Pearlman said. "Is that the speaking voice of Ray Bell?"

"Yes."

"No further questions."

"Ms. Angel," the judge said, "any questions for the witness?"

"Thank you, Your Honor. Miss McEnroe—may I call you Brenda?"

She shrugged. "Sure, everybody else does."

"Brenda, are you still romantically involved with Mr. Bell?"

"No."

"When you broke off your romantic relationship, was it by your choice or Mr. Bell's?"

Brenda looked directly at Ray. "We'd been sleeping together. It was Mr. Bell's decision to break it off."

"No further questions."

—

Pearlman called his own well-qualified music expert, Dr. Elliot Daum, whose appearance, demeanor, and credentials were surprisingly similar to Dr. Turer's. He testified that after listening to numerous live and studio recordings by both Ray and Woody, it was his considered opinion that "Stephanie" was composed by Woody.

"Thank you for your professional opinion, doctor." Pearlman gestured toward Ray. "You heard the chorus melody of which Mr. Bell is claiming ownership?"

"I did."

"Is his position legally justified?"

"I do not believe that brief progression of notes qualifies as copyright-protected material."

"How so?"

"The amount of notes in the musical phrase are de minimis and thus do not rise to the quantum of creativity required to justify copyright protection."

"Quantum of creativity? Please explain."

"In the field of popular music, most compositions bear some similarity to prior songs. A forensic analysis of any song would find all sorts of pre-existing DNA, which is considered to be in the public domain. The courts in copyright cases teach us to be careful not to cheat the public domain. General ideas are the common property of artistic mankind. A song may give a nod to a forebearer, but that does not rise to the level of ownership. A person cannot copyright a musical style. And just as we do not give a composer a monopoly over the note B-flat, it is my opinion that the brief phrase of ascending chromatic notes at issue here cannot be copyrighted by an individual. To say there's a determinable origin point where every creative idea was born is more of a romantic concept than a legal one."

"No further questions," Pearlman said.

The judge nodded at Maria. "Questions for the witness, Ms. Angel?"

Maria walked confidently to the witness stand. "Dr. Daum, a legally protected compilation is material that is selected, coordinated, and arranged by an individual composer. Is that a correct statement of copyright law?"

"Generally, yes."

"You've stated that the particular order of the pitch collection in Mr. Bell's melody is not musically meaningful." Maria paused and examined her notes. The pause was for effect only, she knew her next question. "The words 'senator' and 'treason' contain the exact same letters, isn't that correct?"

The witness thought for a moment, as did everyone in the courtroom. "That is correct."

"It's the particular order of the letters that creates the meaning, is it not?"

"Indeed it is."

"The song 'Stephanie' is not an arbitrary collection of information, it's very particular and unique information, is it not?

"Well, 'unique' is a term of art that should be further defined in order for there to be—"

"It's the *order of things*. That's my point. The *order* of events that happen in our lives is what makes them different from each other. Order adds meaning. Without order, without time, everything would happen at once and—"

"Objection." Pearlman was on his feet. "Counsel is leading the witness and, if I may, Your Honor, not entirely making sense."

Anticipating the objection, the judge brought down her gavel. "Objection sustained. Ms. Angel, you will refrain from arguing your case and leading the witness. Please restate your question in an orderly—" she caught herself, "—in an understandable fashion."

"I'll withdraw the question." Maria gave Pearlman an indignant look. "No further questions, Your Honor."

"Additional witnesses, Mr. Pearlman?"

"Not at this time." Pearlman had made the critical strategy decision not to call Woody as a witness in his case in chief. He knew Maria would be calling Ray back, and he'd save Woody for a rebuttal witness, saving the best for last, the way he'd seen Woody do at his shows.

"I recall the plaintiff Ray Bell to the stand," Maria said.

Ray took the witness chair, looking confident.

"Was that you speaking on the tape?"

"Yes."

"Please explain to the jury why you said what you said."

"We were in Woody's crummy little apartment on his unmade bed, and he'd been bugging me to work on this song with him. The place smelled like a locker room, and I just wanted out of there, so I said what I said."

"Did Woody write the song?"

"He had it sketched out, I finished it when I recorded it. I added the melody hook on the choruses."

"I would like you to sing your song 'Stephanie' for the jury."

"Happy to oblige."

Maria took a twelve-inch aluminum reel of brown recording tape off her table and showed it to Ray. It was marked in big block letters: STEPHANIE SANS VOCALS. "Do you recognize this tape, Mr. Bell?"

"It's a tape we made in the studio from the original multi-track with the vocals muted."

"Would you prefer to stand while you sing?"

"Sitting right here is fine. I can sing the song in my sleep."

Maria put the tape on the reel-to-reel machine on the metal table, pressed play, and Ray delivered a smooth, polished vocal that sounded exactly like the record. When he came to the last repeating chorus, he leaned forward with the erect posture of a professional singer, put his hands on the wooden railing, turned toward the jury, and sang out the last "Stephanie" with just the right amount of understatement, emphasizing the melody notes that were the focus of the trial.

When Maria stopped the tape, everyone in the courtroom, including the jurors, cleared their throats and adjusted themselves in their seats, crossing and uncrossing their legs.

"Just a couple more questions, Mr. Bell. How many copies of your version of 'Stephanie' were sold?"

"4.2 million."

"Woody also released a version of him singing 'Stephanie,' is that correct?

"Yeah."

"How many copies of Woody's version were sold? If you know."

"About twenty thousand."

"Woody's version does not have the melody hook on the choruses, is that correct?"

"Correct."

"No more questions, Your Honor. The Plaintiff rests his case."

"Mr. Pearlman?"

"I have no more questions for Mr. Bell, Your Honor. I would like to call Mr. Woods as my rebuttal witness." He turned to Woody. "Please take the stand, Mr. Woods, and bring your guitar."

When Woody knelt down to his acoustic guitar case on the floor, he glanced at Stephanie, who gave him a thumbs-up. He walked to the witness stand and was sworn in.

"You may proceed, Mr. Pearlman."

"Mr. Woods...your friends call you Woody?"

"Pretty much everybody's called me Woody since I was about five."

"What is your wife's name?"

"Stephanie."

"Did you write a song about her?"

"Yes."

"What type of song is it? How would you categorize it?"

He looked at Stephanie. "It's a love song."

"Did you write the lyrics?"

"Yes."

"Did you compose the music on guitar?"

'Yes."

"Would you please play and sing 'Stephanie' for the jury?"

There were hushed voices in the gallery.

"Silence." The judge tapped her gavel.

Lily tapped her baby bottle on the wooden bench next to her and said, "Sirence."

"Shush," Woody reflexively said in a loud whisper with a finger to his lips.

"Shush," Lily whispered.

The gallery emitted a collective chuckle, Stephanie lifted Lily onto her lap, and Woody went into the opening verse of "Stephanie." Keeping his head down, his hair mostly covering his face, he played an instrumental intro, then sang a sweet, soft, version of the song. When he went into the final verses, he looked up at Stephanie with Lily in her lap. When Lily met his gaze and flapped her hands, he smiled, sat up straighter, and sang with more confidence, clearly singing to her.

A minute later, halfway through the last repeating chorus, Woody singing out his emotive "STEPHANIEEE," Lily zeroed in on Woody's guitar strings, dove off Stephanie's lap before she could react, crawled through the swinging wooden gate, and made a beeline for the witness stand. Stephanie stood up, went to the gate and stopped, unsure of courtroom decorum. All eyes were on Lily. The judge lifted her gavel, held it in midair, and looked over at the marshal who just stood there smiling.

Woody kept playing. He knew what was coming.

Lily clambered up the two wooden steps to the witness stand, up Woody's leg, and grabbed Woody's guitar strings with both hands.

Woody stopped playing, and there were chuckles all around, including from the jurors.

"Your Honor," Pearlman stood up, "I'd like to request a brief recess."

"Yes," the judge smiled, "it's time for recess."

CHAPTER 25

Twenty minutes later, the jury was back, and Lily was asleep in Stephanie's lap. Woody played the song again from the beginning; an emotional performance, the room as quiet as a church, as if everyone in the room were doing their best not to wake Lily. Woody sang to Stephanie as if they were the only two people in the room, singing the last choruses progressively quieter, on the verge of tears. The silence in the room when he finished was as loud as anything Pearlman had heard in a courtroom. As moved by the performance as everyone else, including the judge, he slowly stood up and contemplated the legal pad of prepared questions in his hand. He wasn't seeing the questions, he was thinking about what he'd learned from Woody about symmetry and timing. He set the pad on the table. "No further questions, Your Honor."

"Questions for the witness, Ms. Angel?" the judge said.

"Just a couple more things Mr. Woods. Isn't it true that you voluntarily arranged to have part of the writer's royalties for the song 'Stephanie' paid to Connie Bell, the plaintiff's mother?"

"Objection!" Pearlman was on his feet. "Irrelevant!"

"The question is entirely relevant," Marie said to the jury, with her back to the judge. "The critical question in this trial is who wrote the song 'Stephanie.' Therefore, to whom writer royalties from the song are allocated is entirely relevant."

"Objection overruled. The witness may answer the question."

"Yeah, I helped out Ray's mother."

"No further questions, Your Honor." Marie went to her table and sat down, looking pleased with herself.

"Mr. Pearlman?"

"One more question. Why did you have part of the royalties paid to Ray's mother rather than to Ray?"

"I thought Ray was dead."

A low rumble spread through the gallery. The judge smacked her gavel. "Quiet in the court!"

Now it was Pearlman talking to the jury while he questioned Woody, his back to the judge. "Mr. Woods, what made you think Ray was dead?"

"He went to the Golden Gate Bridge and faked his own suicide. All the newspapers said he jumped. Everybody thought he'd jumped, including me. So I thought I'd help out his mother, his only family. I was told she didn't have much money, and like I said, I thought Ray was dead."

"No further questions."

"Ms. Angel?"

Maria stood up quickly at the plaintiff's table. "By giving Ray's mother a share of the writer's royalties, weren't you, in fact, acknowledging that Ray contributed to writing the song?"

Pearlman was on his feet. "Objection. Counsel is imputing the witnesses' state of mind."

Maria also stood up. "The question is entirely relevant to the—"

"Objection denied." The judge cut her off. "The witness may answer the question."

"I wrote the song. I gave Ray's mother some money 'cause I heard she's broke. And, yeah, Ray had some connection to the song. He sang it, I wrote it. I sure didn't feel like making another federal case about it. I thought Ray had died and I gave his mother some money from the song her son sang. I did it 'cause it felt right."

Maria consulted her notes for a long minute. "Isn't it true, Mr. Woods, that earlier this year you were arrested and charged with possession of marijuana, possession of cocaine, and child endangerment?"

The question was so brazen, so objectionable, and such an aberration to the prevailing mood, Pearlman didn't react, a first for him in a courtroom.

"Mr. Pearlman?" the judge said.

Pearlman snapped to attention. "Objection."

"Counsel will approach the bench."

"That was *totally* out of line," Pearlman spoke low and urgently. "One again she's committing malpractice. It's grounds for sanctions."

Maria glanced toward the jury. "It goes to the defendant's state of mind, and his credibility. For all we know he could be impaired on drugs today while he's testifying." Her volume bordered on being loud enough for the jury to hear.

The judge smacked her gavel and said over counsels' heads. "The marshal will sequester the jury."

As soon as they left the room, the judge tore into Maria. "Bringing up priors in that manner, not to mention talking at side bar loud enough for the jury to hear, is sanctionable activity counsel! Either you're intentionally violating courtroom protocol, or you're so naïve you shouldn't be practicing law!"

Maria looked contrite. "I'm just trying to make a valid point. If the defendant committed—"

"You're, of course, aware that a prior criminal record in a civil trial is only admissible if the prior involved moral turpitude," the judge said.

"Moral turpitude?" Maria said. "What about leaving a baby in a car when he's possessing narcotics? When he's *high* on narcotics?"

"The priors are allegations, not convictions," Pearlman said. "Remember that quaint phrase 'innocent until proven guilty'? The fact that Woody might have smoked a hit of pot has no relevance to this case. Moral turpitude involves dishonesty, not smoking a joint."

"But, Your Honor—"

The judge brought down her gavel and cut her off. "Objection sustained. Any more of this unprofessionalism, Ms. Angel, could result in exactly the outcome you're hoping to avoid!" Another hard gavel stroke.

When the jury came back, the judge instructed them to ignore Maria's question. "Allegations of Mr. Woods' prior criminal activities are just that: mere allegations. Furthermore, even prior drug *convictions*, if proven, would have no relevance to this civil case. Mr. Woods has not been convicted of any of the aforementioned crimes."

—

For her closing argument, Maria explained that Woody and Ray had been working on the song together, then Ray recorded it and added his signature hook that made the song a hit. If Ray had done nothing, the song "Stephanie" would have languished in obscurity. Woody's acoustic version of the song without the melody hook had very weak sales—undeniable proof of the value Ray added. She said Ray's stellar performance of the song demonstrated his consummate musicianship and implored the jurors to trust their instincts and what they felt when they heard Ray sing the song. In closing to her closing argument, Maria pointed out that it didn't make sense that given the history of animosity between Ray and Woody, Woody would choose to share writer's royalties with Ray just out of the kindness of his heart. The only logical explanation was that Woody or his lawyer or Ray's record company knew that Ray or Ray's estate was entitled to the royalty as a result of Ray's contribution to writing the song.

Pearlman walked confidently to the jury box. "Ladies and gentlemen, just because something has a good beat doesn't mean you can file a lawsuit to it." He pointed to the spot where the piano had been and reminded the jury of Ray's inability to play "Stephanie." "He can't remember how to play the song? Is that believable? You may not remember which shoe you put on first this morning, but you remember important things like your wedding day twenty years ago. If Ray co-wrote this song, it's reasonable to think he'd remember how to play it—at least some version of it. Ray has a pleasant voice, but that doesn't make him a co-writer." He pointed to Woody. "My client is a prolific songwriter and a brilliant, self-taught instrumentalist. The lyrics to 'Stephanie' are a poignant, poetic depiction of love, desire, and mutual respect between a man and a woman." He pointed at Ray. "In his entire career, Ray Bell has penned one simplistic, misogynistic dirge: 'I Wanna Be on You.' Seriously?" Pearlman shook his head and spoke directly to a gray-haired woman in the front row. "I wanna be on you?"

He paused, taking his time to look in the eyes of each juror. "If someone steals a car and puts a new paint job on it, they don't own the car." He lowered his voice. "I'm asking every one of you to do what you know in your heart is right." He turned to the judge. "The defense rests."

—

For two days of jury deliberation, Pearlman, Orchid, Woody, Stephanie, and Lily had been camped out in one of the large attorney's workrooms. Ray and Maria were in another smaller room down the hall.

One corner of Pearlman's room had a pile of picture books, wooden building blocks, a spring-mounted bouncy seat, and bowls of fresh fruit. Another had two guitars, and in Pearlman's corner sat a desk covered with legal papers and a blackboard with lists of witnesses, jurors, and music copyright cases. Standing next to him, Orchid had staked out a space for an easel and small canvas.

For two days everyone expected news at any moment that the jury had returned with a verdict, and then there was a knock at the door. It was the US Marshal with a message from the judge for the parties to re-convene.

When everyone, including the jury, was seated, the judge said, "I have received two handwritten questions from the jury foreman which I will now read on the record." She had her elbows on the bench, a note in each hand. "From the looks of the handwriting, these questions were submitted by two different jurors. Nonetheless, as will become apparent, my answers to both questions are the same." She read aloud; "Question number one: If someone releases a record of himself singing another person's song, do they get to share in the royalties from that song? Question number two: If somebody adds a new melody to someone else's completed song, do they become part owner of that song? If yes, how much do they own?" She set the notes down, folded her hands, and scanned the jurors' expectant faces. "You have now been deliberating for two full days. It appears that you're taking the time to address your legal and moral responsibility in a thoughtful and professional matter. Thank you for that. I understand that these questions are important to you. Unfortunately, this court cannot abrogate your civic duty. You have received comprehensive, legally vetted jury instructions regarding music copyright law. The answers to your questions are contained in those jury instructions. I cannot rightfully expound further on what the instructions say. It is your responsibility, not mine, to evaluate the credibility of the witnesses and the evidence. If you correctly apply the applicable law to the facts of this case as you understand those facts from the evidence presented, theoretically you'll be able to discern the truth and come to a proper conclusion. Please continue with your deliberations." She tapped her gavel. "Marshal, please sequester the jurors."

Maria stood up. "Your Honor, if it please the court—"

"It does not please the court. I will not address the case any further in the presence of the jury."

Down came her gavel.

—

"What the hell was that all about?" Woody said as soon as they got back to the workroom.

"My guess is there are two jurors at least who can't agree on what the outcome should be," Pearlman said. "I don't like the sound of those questions."

"Why didn't she just give them an answer?" Stephanie said.

"Judges never want to have the record appear as if they told the jury what to do. It's one of the easiest ways to get overturned on appeal."

"But the correct answer to those questions would be in our favor," Stephanie said.

Pearlman shook his head. "The jury's confused, and from the sound of those questions, not close to agreement."

"What's the downside of all this?" Woody said.

"We can win, lose, or if the jury can't agree, we do the whole thing over again. Justice and the law are two different things. It all depends on how much justice you want to buy."

"No way." Woody played a dissonant chord on his guitar. "There's no way I'm going through this again. No amount of money could get me back in this building with all its weird vibes."

"And if we lose," Stephanie said, "how do you suggest we pay our mortgage?" She turned to Pearlman. "Is it still possible to come to a settlement everybody can live with instead of a verdict only half of us can live with?"

Pearlman threw his pencil on his desk. "Everything in me wants to fight Ray and his unscrupulous lawyer."

"You're saying you're not happy until they're not happy?" Woody said.

"We can end this with an out-of-court settlement any time you want," Pearlman said, "it's your call."

Woody played a slow descending scale on his low E-string and kept plucking it when there was knock on the door. All heads turned, and Woody opened the door to a tall gangly boy with a crew cut and bad complexion, a pizza box in one hand, a receipt pad in the other.

"Someone order a large pizza?"

"That's us," Woody said.

The boy consulted his pad. "Twelve dollars seventy-five cents."

Woody took out a twenty. "Keep the change."

"Hey, thanks, mister." He took the twenty and handed Woody the pizza. "Sausage, pepperoni, extra cheese."

"Sausage and pepperoni?"

The boy looked at his pad. "Half sausage, half pepperoni. Sausage half with onions, pepperoni half with olives. Extra cheese on everything."

"What's your name?" Woody asked.

"William."

"How old are you?"

"Sixteen."

"William, me, my wife, and daughter are vegetarians."

William looked at him blankly.

"We believe that pepperonis should be allowed to roam the great plains like the wild buffalo before them, free from white-man predators. Ever heard of the Endangered Species Act?" Woody handed him back the pizza.

Bewildered, William glanced at the twenty-dollar bill in his hand.

"Who do you work for, William?"

"Doughbie Brothers Pizza."

"Doughbie Brothers?"

"Yeah."

"Cute. Who ordered the pizza?"

William consulted his pad. "Ray Bell."

Woody smiled. "Mystery solved. We ordered a vegetarian pizza from Slice of Life. Ray Bell's two doors down the hall on the right."

"Sorry for the mix-up." William extended back the twenty.

Woody held up his hand. "Tell Ray Bell this pizza's on Woody."

William looked at the twenty.

"You can still keep the change, and tell Ray that Woody said to take it easy with the cheese."

CHAPTER 26

The crowded federal building cafeteria was out of coffee, the shelves bare save for a few stale-looking muffins, the drink cooler three-quarters empty. Everyone eyed everyone that walked in the door, looking for a sign that the jury had returned with a decision.

Auddie walked over to Connie Bell sitting in a corner by herself sipping tea. "Excuse me, are you Connie Bell, Ray Bell's mother?"

"Yes, I am."

"My name is Auddie, I'm Stephanie's aunt. Would you mind if I sit down and join you?"

Connie gestured to the plastic chair on the other side of her little table.

"Someone told me you were here. I could see your resemblance to Ray from across the room." They were about the same age, Auddie almost twice her size with her full head of silver permed poodle-hair, Connie with her smallish head and hair pulled back into a platinum bun so tight it looked painful. "I'd offer to refresh your tea, but I think they're out of hot water. I'm holding this cold coffee just to keep my hands busy."

Connie took a sip of tea, her paper cup trembling. "This is such a terrible ordeal for everyone. It's a shame those young men are putting themselves through this."

"I personally think the lawyers are making it happen. It's like a dog fight, they're not satisfied until they taste blood."

They both inspected the contents of their paper cups.

"Your son does have a very nice singing voice," Auddie said.

"My son has a beautiful, million-dollar voice. People have recognized it since he started singing in school plays in the sixth grade."

"Quarter of a million," Auddie said into her cup.

"It's a no-win situation," Connie said, as if she hadn't heard Auddie. "If the jury can't decide, everyone loses. The cost of lawyers and witnesses and court fees and…it's all such a shame. I don't know why they have to keep fighting. Everyone knows Ray has at least a half-million-dollar voice." She concentrated on keeping her cup from shaking. "Ray's singing is so distinctive it's recognizable by people around the world. When people fight, everyone gets hurt. It just doesn't make sense to me why they can't just talk like gentlemen without expensive lawyers that charge a fortune just talking to each other. If it were up to me, I'd—"

"How about if they split things going forward?"

Connie's paper cup was shaking so much she had to put it down. "Excuse me?"

"Don't you think the boys should stop fighting and move on with their lives? Just agree to split the royalties going forward?"

Connie put both hands around her cup and held it down tightly on the table. "You're asking *me* to decide?"

"The trial will be appealed either way and take years no matter what happens. However it turns out, the lawyers get their money. I can talk to Stephanie. She'll listen to me, and Woody will listen to her." Auddie saw that the color was gone from Connie's face and realized how much she was leaning in, crowding her. She sat back. "What about Ray? Can you talk to him? Does he respect your opinion?"

"I'm his mother." Connie straightened up. "I'm not like some carton of milk past its sell date."

Auddie wrapped one of Connie's small hands in both of her big hands and set them on the table. "Split it from now on? Deal?"

Connie suddenly looked determined. "I'll give it a try. Ray needs to get on with his life and stop this fighting…we all do." She reached down under her chair with her free hand and brought her purse up to her lap. "Would you mind if I…I'm sorry, this may seem rude and out of place. I know we're in an official government court building, but I'm feeling unusually emotional from this entire ordeal." She pulled a small silver flask out of her purse and set it on the table next to their hands. "This was my husband's. It's pewter."

"What's in it?"

"Gin. I like to have a martini once in a while around this time of day, and this is all I have at the moment."

Auddie let go of Connie's hand, drained her half-inch of coffee, and put her paper cup down next to Connie's with a tap on the Formica. "I like martinis. I make my husband Max one almost every night. Sometimes two. Sometimes I join him. As Max often says when he has his drink, no great story ever started with someone eating a salad." She extended her paper cup. "Let's have an extra-dry martini, skip the vermouth, and make a toast to peace."

Connie poured them each a generous shot and they clicked their misshapen cups.

"Do you know where the attorney workrooms are?" Auddie asked.

"Of course. I was in there earlier, talking to Ray."

Auddie tilted her head back, drained her shot, and slapped her empty cup on the table. "Let's go, girl, we've got work to do."

—

Stephanie breastfed Lily while everyone ate their vegetarian pizza. "What exactly happens if the jury can't agree?" she asked Pearlman.

"It's a hung jury, a mistrial. We do the entire trial over from the beginning."

"The price of anything is how much of your life it takes," Woody said. "Ray sings the song better than I do. The jury could hear that, anybody could hear that. The main thing they liked about *my* performance was Lily."

—

Orchid was in her corner of the room quietly creating an oil painting of the jury that stylistically captured the idiosyncrasies of each juror while everyone waited for their interminable decision. Pearlman watched with interest, her artist's eye exposing personality traits he hadn't considered.

"There are more than two sides to every story," Orchid said, her attention on her canvas. "In the small village where I grew up near Njombe, Tanzania, if there's a dispute about ownership of a goat, the village elders listen to anything anyone has to say. A witness could be six years old. How a man treats his wife is evidence of his credibility." She blended a dollop of paint and applied dramatic brush strokes emanating out from one juror. "People considered to be the wisest in the village are the ones who recently endured the most pain, someone who lost a parent or a child or a limb."

"Pain can make us wise," Stephanie said. "Suffering's another matter. Suffering is the story we create about our pain."

Woody strummed a minor chord and sang, "Things might be as bad as they seem."

Stephanie offered Lily a slice of tomato from the pizza. "Children are wise, and honest. What made Lily the star witness in the courtroom was her honesty…in a room where honesty's at a premium."

Orchid held her paintbrush in mid-air, waiting to intuit the placement of her next stroke. "As often as not, the dispute about goat ownership would end up in a party with lots of beer and everyone eating the goat."

Pearlman followed the trajectory of Orchid's brush. "There was a famous trial about a baker who brought a lawsuit against a homeless man,' he said. "The baker got to work every morning at five and left the kitchen door open because his oven got so hot. He wanted compensation from the homeless man who sat by the back door smelling the fresh bread, reaping the benefit of the baker's work. At trial, the homeless man took the witness stand, took a few coins out of his pocket, shook them in his hand, and said, 'I'll pay you for the smell of your bread with the sound of my money.'"

Orchid transformed a juror's face from joyful to pensive with one stroke. "The concept of equality in your wonderful country of laws," she said, "forbids both rich and poor people alike from sleeping under bridges."

Pearlman smiled. "Values are more important than facts. If a cop sees a teenager in a bad neighborhood running down the street in the middle of the night with a TV set—according to the law he doesn't have probable cause to stop him, even though he knows the TV's probably stolen. It's not the facts. What matters is that we don't make it against the law in this country to run down a street carrying a TV."

Lily woke up and Stephanie decided to take her out of the room for a change of environment. They ran into Auddie coming down the hallway.

"Want me to take her?" Without waiting for an answer, Auddie took Lily out of Stephanie's arms. "How's everyone doing in there?"

"Woody'd do anything to get this over with."

"Guess who I ran into in the cafeteria? Connie Bell."

"Ray's mother? Did you talk to her?"

"We chatted; she's actually very nice."

Stephanie knew there was more.

"They want it to be over too. They'd settle for anything fair." She slipped her hand under Lily's shirt and up her bare back. "We could lose."

"Lose what?"

"Everything. I've been watching the jury. Two women in the front row couldn't take their eyes off Ray when he sang. Their eyes were bugging out of their heads, but they just squinted looking at Woody. Their body language speaks volumes."

"It's up to Woody; it's his music."

Auddie kissed Lily and said to her, "Your mom and dad always do what's best for you, sweetheart." She turned to Stephanie, "Don't let the lawyers' egos get in the way of taking care of your family. Woody will listen to you. Get him to settle this case before you risk losing everything."

Stephanie took Lily back into the room and went straight to Woody playing guitar in the corner. "Auddie's been checking out the jury and picked up a strong vibe that they could rule against us. She thinks we should settle while we can. She spoke with Ray's mother. Ray's ready to settle and walk away from the whole thing."

Woody looked at the floor and strummed a soft chord.

"Auddie's very intuitive," Stephanie said.

"I know."

"She's got nothing but our best interests at heart."

"That was dirty, Ray saying those things about your old dancing job."

"I know it bothers you, but it doesn't bother me. It's time to let go. It makes forgiveness even more juicy."

There was a soft knock on the door. Pearlman opened it to Ray standing there.

"Hi, Jeff. I just came by to say thanks for the pizza."

"Pizza?"

Everyone in the room stopped what they were doing.

"The kid that delivered our pizza said Woody paid for it."

"Wanna come in?"

Ray took a step inside. The lamps were shaded with Orchid's scarfs, making it the only room in the building with mood lighting.

Sitting across the room holding his guitar, Woody searched Ray's face and concluded that he'd shown his intention by being there. He played the first three chords of "Stephanie" and said, "Wanna split what's left?"

Everyone waited.

Ray shrugged. "We ate the whole thing. The pizza kid said you didn't want it."

"The song." Woody stood up, holding his guitar in front of him. "Split the baby, like King Solomon." He walked past Ray into the hallway and gestured for him to follow. Woody pulled the door closed, the two of them alone in the fluorescent-lit hallway. "The baby's sleeping, don't want to wake her."

Ray nodded.

Woody had gone over in his mind many times what he would say to Ray if they got a chance to talk. Now he debated what to say. "How was your pizza?"

"Cold."

Woody strummed a chord. "Give pizza chance?"

Ray had his hands in the pockets of his pleated dress slacks, still dressed up, hair perfectly in place, anticipating being called back in front of the jury at any time. Woody had changed back to his flannel shirt.

"Writing any new songs?" Ray asked.

Woody had a dozen pieces of unfinished music in his head. He played a short section of chord changes from a new song he'd been working on.

"Nice. Got lyrics?"

Woody played the melody again and sang a few lines about two strangers passing in a grocery store aisle, smiling at each other while they held the secret of a personal life crisis in their minds.

"I can relate," Ray said.

Woody repeated the guitar melody in a key he thought would suit Ray's voice. Ray hummed along quietly then sang the lyric lines, Woody strumming and tapping his foot on the linoleum floor. They repeated it until Woody decreased the tempo and stopped. "I'm sick of this legal dance."

"Yeah, it sucks."

There was a long pause, both of them looking at the floor.

"Sometimes silence sucks out the truth," Woody said without looking up.

Another long pause.

"Stephanie's quiet a lot," Woody said.

"The song?"

"No, Stephanie."

"That makes sense."

"It does if you know her in the biblical sense."

Ray looked up. "Sorry I said what I said. You can't fix stupid." They were both back to looking at the floor. "I was being greedy, trying to take the whole song. I only added what I added."

"You helped make it a commercial success." Woody went to play again and stopped himself. "Wanna split the royalties going forward and just go forward, pay our own lawyers, quit mucking around in this legal quagmire? What happened happened. That toilet's been flushed."

"Credit it as co-writers?"

Woody waited to answer, knowing it made Ray uncomfortable.

"You already got the lion's share of royalties from the song," Ray said. "Sales from now on will just be dribbling in."

Their eyes met for the first time since they'd come out in the hallway. "I talked to my daughter," Woody said. "She asked me not to give away anything that's mine that might be hers."

Just then the door down the hall opened. Maria came out and walked in the opposite direction toward the water fountain. Ray and Woody watched her take a drink, brush back her hair, and straighten her skirt, unaware that anyone else was in the hallway. When she started back and saw Ray and Woody, she stiffened, quickened her pace, and walked over. "Are you gentlemen discussing the case?"

Ray straightened his posture, matching hers. Woody let himself fall back against the wall and strummed a minor chord.

"Were you discussing the case?" Maria said to Ray.

"Pizza."

"Pizza?"

"Any way you slice it," Woody said, "we were discussing pizza."

"This is no joking matter!" Maria glared at him. "You're aware that your counsel should be present for any discussions about the case."

"I don't know if we've been formally introduced," Woody said. "I'm Woody."

"Of course I know who you are. And as you know, I'm Maria Angel, Ray's attorney. It's not proper for me to discuss the case with you without your lawyer present. If you'd like, we can make arrangements for formal dispute resolution. There's mediation, arbitration, a process for—"

"You're Italian, aren't you?" Woody said.

She tucked her hair back behind both ears as if to hear better. "Excuse me?"

Woody shrugged. "Pizza is kind of an international currency. It's actually what got me and Ray out here talking."

Pearlman came out of his workroom, took in the scene, and walked over. "You folks settle the case yet? I sure hope so."

Maria cleared her throat. "I was just explaining to them that, at this critical stage of the litigation, at any stage, counsel should be present for settlement discussions."

Pearlman shrugged. "Actually, I think these two grown men might do just as well talking amongst themselves. If you've got something helpful to add, have at it. I've spouted enough words to feed an army." He walked down the hallway to the water fountain. Walking back, they expected him to stop. He just smiled, walked into the room he'd come from, and closed the door.

"Maria," Ray said, "could you please excuse us?"

Her eyes narrowed. "You don't want to be discussing the case without consulting me." She pressed her nails into her crossed arms. "I'm your attorney. You need to include me in anything that could potentially impact—"

"Maria?" Ray said quietly.

She skidded to a verbal stop, his soft volume a dramatic contrast to hers.

"You'll be the first to know when I need legal advice," Ray said. "Please excuse us."

As she walked away, Woody strummed his guitar and sang, "Out breakin' rocks in the hot sun, I fought the law and the law won."

—

As requested by counsel, the judge ordered the case on hold for ten days of settlement discussions, after which, if necessary, the parties would submit to binding arbitration. The jury was dismissed.

In the following days Pearlman and Maria exchanged salvos of phone calls, letters and messenger-delivered documents, trying to come to terms. Pearlman got on the phone with Woody. "That bitch keeps moving the goalposts, getting greedier every conversation. We're going to have to submit to binding arbitration."

"Sounds sexy."

"This is serious. She's being unreasonable. It's not even about money for her, it's about spite."

"What's binding arbitration?"

"Basically a trial without a jury."

"No way, not again."

"Your family's money is on the line."

"This money is costing too much. I trust your judgment, Jeff. Make it fair and make sure you get paid. I can spend my time dealing with this or writing songs. Which one will benefit my family most? We'll see. I'm betting on the songs."

CHAPTER 27

Woody knew he'd stretched things to the breaking point with his record company. It was imperative to finish his record, and he needed three or four new songs. His new plan was to take a week to himself and do nothing but work on songs. That's what he did, while Stephanie circled the wagons to keep friends and visitors at bay.

When they'd moved into their new house, Woody had converted the garage into an anechoic music studio, floor, walls, and ceiling lined with carpet and an array of electric and acoustic instruments. Soundproof, cozy as a cocoon, he loved spending time there.

When he wasn't playing guitar, Woody went to the piano for a different sound and the feel of the keys, gigantic compared to guitar strings. Sometimes he'd take his guitar, a notebook, and a bottle of water and walk out into the hills and play with the wind, the birds, and his favorite audience: the ocean.

On just such a night, when he'd been working late and had fallen asleep with his guitar in his lap, he woke up and walked outside. Sitting in the dim light of dawn on the expansive hillside overlooking the Pacific Ocean, the dry grass surrounding Woody came up almost to his shoulders. He'd come outside to see if a change of environment would help get him over, around, or through the musical brick wall he'd been running into, to get from the verses to a chorus. He'd smoked a joint and dived so deep into questioning why change was even necessary, he felt he needed a change of scenery to figure it out. Sitting on the hill, he contemplated the forever ocean and the stars and moon fading from the rising sun to the east behind him, he concluded that motion, the flow of a river, the beating of a heart, the orbiting planets, was an undisputable universal truth. There were different opinions about where to go, how to get there, when to go…that was all up for grabs. But there was no question, his latest chord progression needed to go somewhere, but where? The choices were infinite.

Sitting in the grass, he strummed a chord that seemed vaguely in tune with the chord the wind was playing, as if the infinite blades of tall grass were God's guitar strings with the boundless ocean her audience, each wave crashing against the rocks a burst of appreciative fans. Woody tried matching his ultra-slow, liquid chord progression with the cascading surges of the waves until it seemed as though they were all in motion together—the wind, the grass, the rocks, the waves—a limitless orchestra of nature that he was dissolving into, like the experience he'd had when musicians and the audience blended into one entity. Then, when a series of four or five waves swelled up higher than before, engulfing the rocks they'd been colliding with, Woody visualized a percussion section of thundering timpani drums, long-handled mallets with big fluffy balls on the ends being swung into the center of fifty-foot drum heads, the slow vibration of the pure low frequency of a lion's roar, the sound of gravity. Woody and his guitar were submerging deeper into the movement of the tide when suddenly, the woodwind section was capped by a shrieking flute or piccolo. Woody stood up, faced his house behind him, saw the bedroom light come on, and recognized the echoing shrill of his daughter waking up, wanting to be fed. Moments later the bedroom light went out, the piccolo emitted a few last high-pitched, plaintiff notes, then faded back into the roar of the waves. In his mind, he said a wordless prayer of gratitude for the presence of his wife Stephanie, feeding their baby.

He turned toward the ocean, sat back down, and resumed strumming his guitar with a sense of joy and out came the majestic chord to go into the chorus that he'd been looking for all night. Then, of course, he immediately began modifying the chorus to flow from the new chord.

While he worked, he often thought of the advice he'd gotten from two different songwriters. One said write secretly, as though no one will ever hear your songs. Write words you wouldn't dare to say out loud, then you'll allow your best to come out. Another said write *revealing* your deepest secrets so listeners will feel they're not alone. He'd concluded they were both saying the same thing and ended up writing a song about what it feels like to write a song.

Woody thought of the songwriting process like cracking the code to a safe, turning the tumblers until they fell into place. Some song ideas came out swinging, born as fully formed adults. They practically wrote themselves and made symmetrical sense after just a few times through. Other song ideas were catch and release, slippery, he couldn't quite find their handle. He could play them a hundred times, constantly making changes, and they always felt unfinished. It felt like trying to crack a combination safe with the combination locked inside

He enjoyed the process, plumbing the depths of infinite musical choices, every note impacting the next, cause and effect happening at once, then the element of language adding a whole other dimension. He loved the complexities of English, with more words than any other language—over a million. When he took a break to rest his hands, he often spent the time reading a dictionary. But, ultimately, language was second in line to instruments and their attempt to mimic the primal, expressive sound of the human voice. Language, words, hadn't even come into play until long after people had been blowing on reeds and banging on animal skins stretched over hollow logs. Words, with their infinite depth of meaning, could either constrict a melody or, if applied creatively, expand the musicality of a melody and add meaning to a sound.

The next evening, when Woody felt like he'd spent another day hitting his head against the wall trying to finish another song, Lily crawled in the open door of his studio. He strummed a sweet major chord as a greeting. Woody was often amazed at how Lily seemed to sense when he was deeply involved in his work and in her own infant way did her best to respect the space and not interrupt him. She enjoyed the comfy environment of the studio as much as he did. She crawled to a low bookshelf and took down a book and acted like she was reading, like she often did at Pearlman's office. Woody watched her flipping the pages of a thesaurus upside down in her lap when a white paper bindle of coke and a four-inch flattened psilocybin mushroom fell out onto the floor. He'd long forgotten they were there. Someone had given him the mushroom at a stage door at a gig, and he'd stashed bindles of coke everywhere when he'd been using. For a moment it crossed his mind that a small snort might do the trick to break through his writer's block—he hadn't done coke since the day he lost Lily. When she picked up the bindle, the sight of her sitting there with it in her chubby little hand reminded him of her empty car seat, and he felt a shudder of revulsion. Then, like she did with most things, Lily started to put the bindle in her mouth. Woody leaped across the room, grabbed it from her and turned toward the bathroom to toss it in the toilet just as Stephanie walked in, saw Lily on the floor with the bindle in Woody's hand. Her eyes widened, "No! You said you'd never do it again! You promised, you promised us both!"

"I wasn't doing it."

"You just happen to have it your hand? Don't bullshit me!"

"It just fell out of that book, I was gonna throw it out. I wasn't—"

"Don't *bullshit* me!"

"I'm not, I swear. I forgot I even had it. It just fell out of that book, and I was about to flush it down the toilet."

"Who should I believe, you or my lying eyes?" She scooped Lily up off the floor. "Goddamnit, Woody, I thought we were done dealing with this shit! Lily and I are going to bed. I think you better sleep out here. Maybe you should *live* out here in your drug den!" She walked out, slamming the door.

Woody contemplated the closed door and the bindle he was still holding. He picked the mushroom up off the floor, held one drug in each hand, and thought how radically different their effects were. It was time for a new direction. His attention drawn to the life-like bulbous cap of the gray-brown mushroom, he set the bindle of coke on a high shelf and with three or four bites, chewed up the mushroom and swallowed it. As he chewed, a drawn-out distasteful process, he remembered the clear-eyed man at the dressing-room door. The man was holding the stem of the mushroom, pressing the cap against his forehead. Then he'd extended it, touching Woody's forehead, and said, "It'll stimulate growth of neurons in your brain that will excavate pathways you never knew existed for your music to travel through." Woody inhaled the mushroom's organic smell and thought about the man's statement and wondered what it meant. He was about to find out.

He took a drink of water and went out the back door of his studio to the yard and their small fire pit. He made a fire, sat on the ground, and within an hour, when he looked straight up at the star-studded sky, it looked as if the universe were folding in on itself.

"How can the same person, with the same eyes, see things so differently after just eating a plant?" he thought. Then he brought his gaze down from the black and white sky to the vivid orange, red, and yellow fire in front of him. He'd never experienced the breathing, pulsating, perpetual motion of fire like that, Hieronymus Bosch faces appearing in a kaleidoscope of flames flicking in frenetic motion out of perfectly still logs. Leaning in, savoring the warmth from the fire, Woody imagined a hunter-gatherer woman carrying smoldering coals from cave to cave in a tree-bark burrito of moss, keeping a fire going for weeks or months in her symbiotic relationship with nature. Traveling with that small bundle of coals and little else, she'd know that the more knowledge she carried in her mind, the less she had to carry in her arms. Of course that was before all the cerebral white men showed up lugging around oxcarts of lumber for square houses and propane tanks for patio barbeques.

"Mushrooms have been growing on Earth for millions of years," he thought, "and eons before that their spores were floating around the universe looking for a warm moist place to pollinate. Some societies made the mushrooms forbidden, but they don't care, they just keep growing. Tonight, on their forever journey to everywhere, carrying the DNA of the cosmos, they decided to plant their universal knowledge in the warm moist place of my brain." He looked back up at the sky. 'This isn't something I just thought up, it was already there waiting to be discovered.'

"I'm sitting here totally tripping out," Woody said aloud. His voice sounded to him like a stranger's voice.

He looked around into the dark shadows. "*Who's* tripping out?" he said.

He jerked his head to the right. "Who just said that?"

He jerked his head to the left. "Who's asking?"

He concentrated on the glowing orange mound of coals. "Okay, who just spoke?"

"It doesn't matter," he said to the fire.

"*What* doesn't matter?" he said.

"Exactly," he said and burst out laughing like it was the funniest thing he'd ever heard. Within a minute he knew he was laughing at himself laughing, laughing so hard it felt like hyperventilating. His face flushed hot, tears ran down his cheeks, snot dripped out his nose. The laughing kept going on its own inertia for what seemed like a spooky amount of time until he finally quieted down to a sputtering chuckle. It took several minutes for the pulsating rush of blood in his temples to calm down and there was a long silence.

He'd been bent over, head between his knees for an indiscernible amount of time. He sat up and looked around. "Where am I?" Then he thought, "Who's asking all these questions?" His proverbial "I" had disintegrated along with his ego. His usual preconceptions of reality and patterns of cognition had dissolved into psychedelic mush. Then, with nothing in his active consciousness with enough footing to gain a purchase, not even sure he *was* conscious, he kicked off into an excavation of his *sub*conscious that felt as risky as defusing a timebomb. He visualized shining a flashlight down dark basement stairs, where there was a wild animal in the black crevice of his psyche that feeds on fear and was so voraciously hungry that he conjured up an image of tossing down a two-inch-thick raw steak marbled with fat to pacify it. Then, totally without warning, his body, of its own volition, slowly started to stand up. It felt as if he could keep standing forever, an infinite, unfolding extendo-man, his head protruding above the wispy night clouds, up into the stars and beyond. He slowly bent over and picked up a long wooden pole from the ground next to the fire, everything happening in super-slow-motion with a warbly, low-end soundtrack like a slowed-down tape playing sonorous bass notes pulsating in his ears. The pole was way taller than he was, as tall as a tree, and he proceeded to methodically spread out the coals into a pulsating bed, slipped off his sandals, and—as with everything else—in super-slow motion, he walked his hairy Sasquatch bare feet across the coals. Bright-orange neon light glowed between his toes, his gaze frozen into the middle distance.

He walked the length of the bed of glowing embers, turned around, stood perfectly still in the dirt for a minute, then walked back the way he'd come from and sat down, his erector-set body folding in half and in half again. He sat in a lotus position and contemplated the blackened bottoms of his feet that were devoid of feeling, as if they were someone else's feet. A minute later he peered into the blackness of the hot night to the top of a giant Redwood tree against the starry sky and realized that they were breathing in synchronicity—him breathing in oxygen, out CO2; the tree, with its huge lungs, doing the exact opposite. "What a setup," he thought. "Who thought of that? But, wait, how do mushrooms breathe without leaves? Wait? Wait for what? When exactly do we wait? Do we wait while we wait? Does time only go forward, never backward?" He looked down like looking down a mile into the Grand Canyon, and when he reached into the depths to rub the bottoms of his feet, his hands were more like puppets than hands.

He suddenly realized he was standing again and walking toward the coals. He couldn't remember standing up. As he walked, he could feel the curvature of the earth. Then suddenly he was in another dimension, hovering in a helicopter ten feet above his own head, watching himself like watching someone else approaching the fire. With a white-knuckled grip on the joystick, he thought, "If that's me down there, who's flying this helicopter?" Then his flailing mind wrapped itself around the next logical inquiry, and he heard a tiny inner voice: "Well then, Mr. Fancy Pants, who's *asking* who's flying the helicopter?" This was all happening in microseconds and by some miracle of quantum physics, the vortex of his brain connected linguistic protons to experiential electrons and the *noun* step and the *verb* step melded into a single cell like colliding at the end of the two-mile-long Stanford particle accelerator. A red warning light went off in the cockpit with the word STEP! STEP! STEP! flashing on and off with buzzers and bells. The helicopter ran out of gas, the engine sputtered, the propellers locked up, the joystick went flaccid in his hand, and the helicopter crash-landed into the top of his head, breaking his concentration. He lost his balance with the sole of his right foot an inch from the fire, jerked back, steadied himself, put his foot down on the cool earth, and said softly, "I could really burn my feet this time."

—

Woody sat in the grass, rubbing his feet, watching the effects of the mushroom dissipate while the sun came up, periodically obscured by the fast-moving fog blowing in off the ocean. The passing of time took on a physical dimension, like he was passing through a sticky, web-like entanglement of time and space, incrementally descending back into his body to a new reality, unraveling his subconscious, unpacking the thousand-pound suitcase of thoughts he'd been lugging around with bundles of feelings—feelings of guilt about drug addiction and fear on the cutting edge of panic that his music was inadequate. The effects of the mushroom were anything but a straight-line graph but more like a roller coaster barreling back and forth and up and down, swelling into panic that maybe that time in the helicopter had transported him to a place he might not be able to return from. He knew to wait. Was it moments or hours of long slow breaths? Eventually he was floating free, physically lighter, and the sun was burning off the fog. This time with a feather-light touch, he revisited that dark part of the night where he'd experienced having his hand injured, his free-falling plummet into opiate addiction, his dependence on cocaine, needing it to feel as if he could even function. When he emerged out of that part of the night, staring into the white fire, he saw himself standing on the caboose of a train waving goodbye to his disheveled, unhappy drug-addicted former self left standing on the tracks.

He thought about the neuron pathways mentioned by the man who gave him the mushroom. The new avenues in his brain were wide open, inviting him into a new life of love. Now it seemed so simple; his love for Stephanie and Lily was unmistakable, so easy to understand. All he had to do was open his arms, open his heart and allow in those same feelings about himself.

He stood up, feeling nimble, the bottoms of his feet sensitive but okay. He slipped into his empty sandals, symbols of the origin of his journey, and walked back into the studio and straight to the bindle of coke. It wasn't as if he'd lost his craving for it, it was like the concept of craving was nonexistent. He walked to the bathroom and flushed the bindle down the toilet with the amount of emotional energy it took to breathe.

Then he went into the house and found Stephanie breastfeeding Lily on the couch in the living room. It was the earliest light of dawn. They'd hardly slept as a new day emerged from the cathartic night. He cleared his throat and spoke softly. "I messed up… really bad…I admit it. But now I'm a different person. I'm completely done doing coke. That bindle fell out of a book Lily had opened a moment before you walked into the studio. I forgot it was even there. It's been there for months. Please," he whispered, "please, you've got to believe me."

She saw the tears welling up in his eyes.

"Do you know what a dry drunk is?" he said. "They talked about it in the probation classes I took. It's an addict that's not doing drugs but still has the same traits and habits that created the addiction. I'm not that person anymore. I'm only addicted to you." He nodded at Lily. "To both of you, and to music. I don't feel the hurt and emptiness I used to feel. Hurt people hurt people. You and Lily are the most important things in my life. I'd never do anything to risk losing you again…never."

Tears rolled down his cheeks, and he fell to his knees next to her on the couch. "You've got to trust me. Nothing we do together will work if you don't." He gave her a weak smile. "It'd be like trying to play tennis by myself." When he got to "by myself," his voice cracked.

She looked at him on his knees like he was praying, tears streaming down his cheeks. Stephanie's own eyes filled with tears. There was a long silence while they watched each other cry. She gently ran her hand across the top of Lily's head. "With her ultra-sensitive ears, Lily can hear your heart breaking. The first step toward healing is the hardest. We'll trust you."

CHAPTER 28

Back in his studio the next morning, Woody had three brand-spanking-new songs and two old ones with freshly rebuilt engines, bringing the grand total to thirteen, enough to finish his album. He'd always felt that one weak song could ruin an entire album, but now the album felt like a flowing integral piece of music. When he went through the song list and played them all back-to-back, he realized he'd unintentionally written only two songs with happy lyrics and happy-sounding chords. He knew that people generally found songs about pain more interesting than songs about pleasure and that writing about cathartic, painful subjects was the most satisfying to both the composer and the listener.

He put down his guitar and went outside to get the morning's mail he'd been neglecting and collected a thick pile of letters and magazines. Soaking up the warm sun in his open bathrobe and bare feet, he sifted through the letters, came to one from Pearlman's office, and opened it, awkwardly juggling everything else under his arm.

There was a handwritten note on Jeff Pearlman's stationery: *Woody: I called Bernie and tried to change his mind. He says you're way over your recording budget, but the last straw is you allowing taping at your live shows. When Bernie says no he means 'not now'. Call me when you get this. I've got an idea for moving forward.* The note was stapled to a letter from Warner Brothers exercising their option to cancel Woody's recording contract. He re-read the letter and his thoughts immediately spun out to possible scenarios of being broke again, this time living on the street with a wife and child. The tightness in his chest wicked up into his throat until he had trouble swallowing and the wad of mail slipped from under his arm, covering his bare feet with bills and L.L. Bean catalogues.

—

The next day Woody, Stephanie, and Lily made another pilgrimage to Pearlman's office. Stephanie sat in front of Jeff's desk and Woody paced by the window while Lily pulled law books off a shelf.

"I made some exploratory calls to Arista, Capitol, and EMI." Pearlman said. "The word's out about you not fulfilling the terms of the Warner contract. Everyone's also aware of the issue with your live taping."

Woody stopped pacing. "What exactly do record companies do anyway?"

"Besides paying for a recording studio to create the product? They promote your music, get your songs on the radio, and put your records in record stores. Record companies are companies, buildings full of people making phone calls so musicians can play music."

Lily dropped the copy of *Morris on Torts* she'd been reading upside down and crawled across the room to the window.

"Corporate music is beholden to radio commercials," Pearlman said. "Basically, everything depends on selling beer. This major-label path is designed for a different kind of artist."

"You create your own path with each step," Stephanie said, "besides, we don't even drink beer."

"Exactly," Pearlman said. "Woody needs a record label with the same sensibilities he has. I think I know one right here in Palo Alto. A bunch of high energy techies, half ivy league, half high school dropouts, all music lovers. They'll relate to your music. Hell, they probably already listen to it."

"You just keep thinking," Woody said, "cause that's what you're good at."

"What's a techie?" Stephanie said.

"Paad Gupta's a techie. He was one of the top guys at IBM. He sold his stock, made a ton of money, left IBM, and started his own record label to distribute music digitally: Whirled Records. Smartest guy I've ever met." Pearlman shook his head thoughtfully. "The last time we spoke he was talking about liquid computers. Cell-size nano-computers that course through your blood stream adjusting enzyme levels moment-by-moment, eliminating the aging process. It's based on healing qualities of soundwaves from certain patterns of music. Tiny silicon chips laser-encrypted with musical vibrations that counteract chemical micro-imbalances, harmonizing your body like a finely tuned symphony orchestra. We're killing ourselves trying to understand the aging process, but for him death is just another problem to solve, one proton at a time. He thinks we can kill death."

Stephanie watched Lily paw her way up the window to a standing position. "Paad Gupta, sounds like an interesting guy," she said. "Using technology to disseminate music could be a positive thing. Messing with mortality's another matter. The planet would get pretty crowded pretty quickly."

"Paad's the first to acknowledge the unknown consequences of technology," Pearlman said. "He thinks machines can solve problems that machines cause, and computers will allow everyone on the planet to work cooperatively. Paad thinks unleashing the full potential of computers could be as profound as the discovery of electricity or even fire."

"Just because we can do something doesn't mean we should do it," Stephanie said.

"For better or worse," Pearlman said, "if it *can* be done, it *will* be done."

"What about kindness, compassion, fantasy," Stephanie asked, "can they be programed into a computer?"

"Those are the questions Paad talks about. He thinks every person on the planet is going to interact through a wireless hand-held computer the size of a deck of cards. Break your leg, break up your marriage, cure cancer, send a rocket to the moon, everyone can share the experience."

"If interpersonal interactions go through a machine, we'll delegate our thinking, our emotions to a machine," Stephanie said. "Reality will become artificial sound bites."

"The way Paad explains it, it's just using technology to accomplish what we want. It took a year to cross the country in a covered wagon, then three days on a train, now three hours by plane."

As if on cue came the sound of a commercial jet starting its decent to nearby San Francisco Airport on its trajectory past their top floor seats in the city's tallest building. "Jet planes are noisier than horses," Stephanie said.

Pearlman smiled and waited for the plane to pass. "Maybe music will go directly to your brain without the distractions of outside noise, scratchy records, and staticky radios. Songs will be transmitted to tiny wireless headphones, a royalty electronically deposited in the composer's bank account. Eventually you'll have a microchip implanted in your skull, think of a melody and melody-recognition software will kick in."

"Public eavesdropping on my thoughts?" Stephanie said. "Sounds scary."

"Just thinking of a sound sounds easier than lugging around guitars and pianos." Woody said.

Lily started slapping the window with both hands. Stephanie and Woody walked over and rested their hands on her head and back like placing their hands on a contemplation stone.

"I've been thinking, this could be a turning point in Woody's career," Stephanie said, "one way or the other."

"I've been thinking I think too much," Woody said. "Let's go meet Paad. You know me, I love meetings."

Pearlman smiled. "You'll like him, he's got a great sense of humor."

"What about the whole trip about tapers at my gigs?" Woody asked. "Will it put a kibosh on him giving me a record deal?"

"I already brought it up," Pearlman said. "Paad knew it was why Warners cancelled your contract. And he agrees with *you*...share the music. He's buddies with the Grateful Dead. They may seem like a bunch of spaced-out stoners, but there's a method to their madness. They're more on top of things than people think, and they care deeply about what happens to their music and their band. Numbers show they've sold more records since they let their audience have free board tapes of their live concerts."

"What're we waiting for? Where do I sign?" Woody jumped to his feet and clapped his hands. "Let's go!"

Woody recognized Pearlman's furrowed expression. "What? What're you thinking?"

"I still have my concerns. You're not the Grateful Dead."

'So? What's your point?"

"My point is, the Grateful Dead are a one-of-a-kind phenomenon. They're not just a band, they're a community, a self-contained culture. Of all the music they've produced, they haven't had one song as commercially successful as your song 'Stephanie.' You'd have to spend the next ten years driving around the country playing a follow-up song to 'Stephanie' in every bar in every...it'd be physically impossible. You couldn't keep a band together."

—

Lily stayed home with Aunt Auddie while Woody and Stephanie cruised down to Palo Alto with the top down, their hair twirling in the wind like two little tornadoes. They went over the Golden Gate Bridge, through Golden Gate Park, and south on Skyline Boulevard, a ribbon of pavement on the spine of the Santa Cruz mountains. They could see San Francisco Bay to the east and a hundred miles of Pacific Ocean to the west.

"How about some traveling music?" Stephanie reached up and turned the polished chrome radio knob. Nothing happened.

Woody shrugged. "I disconnected it."

"Since when don't you like music?"

"Since I've been giving Billy rides to the studio and he turns on the radio while he's talking. Trying to have a conversation with him is like a high-speed chase. I can only listen to one thing at a time."

"I imagine sometimes you must feel oversaturated with music," Stephanie said. "I enjoy music when I'm driving, working out, cooking, pretty much any time. A soundtrack to my life."

Woody smiled and reached to the glove compartment, stopping on the way to rub Stephanie's thigh. He pulled out a Marine Band harmonica, held it above the windshield facing forward, and moved his fingers back and forth across the mouth-holes, letting the sixty-mile-an-hour wind blow a bluesy melody.

—

Whirled Records was situated at the end of a private dirt road that wound through a tunnel of towering eucalyptus trees, its main campus a series of utopian-looking iron and raw-wood structures in loopy designs of cubes and balls with round maritime windows. The grounds were appointed with hammocks, badminton courts, giant, anthropomorphic bunny-ear cactus plants, and twenty-foot-tall rusted metal sculptures of impressionistic musicians playing even more impressionistic-looking instruments.

Woody found the visitor's lot, parked next to Pearlman's Jaguar, and a young black man in baggy shorts, leather sandals, and long dreadlocks walked up. "Woody and Stephanie?"

"That's us."

"Welcome. Please come with me."

They met Pearlman in a sky-lit lobby and the four of them went down a hallway with walls covered with moss being moistened with a mist from tiny sprinklers. The corner office was a round, glass-brick room where Paad, a paunchy East Indian man with an aquiline nose and no eyebrows, sat reclining on a small couch surrounded by colorful pillows. Dressed in a white, gold-trimmed pullover shirt, loose white cotton pants, and sandals, he had his eyes closed, a blissful expression on his face, a pair of bulky black headphones on his shaved boney head.

They stood in the doorway for a minute, then their young guide stepped past them into the room toward Paad. Woody reached out, tapped the man on the shoulder, and put his finger to his lips. Smiling, the man walked out, and Woody, Stephanie, and Pearlman waited for another five minutes until Paad sat up, removed the headphones, and greeted them as if he'd known they'd been there waiting.

"Jeff, Woody, Stephanie—welcome, thank you for your patience," he said in an Indian accent, "it was a beautiful piece of music." He set his headphones on a table and contemplated them. "I'm not sure which I enjoy more: listening to a good song or the moments after. The silence right after a song is like those precious moments of silence the best musicians leave between certain notes. Like making love to my wife, I've come to enjoy the after as much as the during." He gave them a classic East Indian head wag. "It was a man singing a love song by a waterfall about his wife who recently died. 'Why should I be sad' the man sings, 'I never thought she was immortal.' The relaxed pacing of the lyrics with the sound of the waterfall is itself a lesson in acceptance. I'll play it for my morning mediation class where some students think they are in meditation competition." When he smiled, his eyes sparkled, so dark they were almost black. "Let's go to a comfortable place to talk." He led them through a beaded curtain to an outdoor patio surrounded by palm trees and a rock-lined koi pond populated with foot-long goldfish.

"We have an aquarium of kissing fish at home," Woody said.

"The pond was here when we built Whirled Records. If they were in a large ocean, they would still stay close together as a school." He gestured them to have a seat. "Speaking of traveling in schools, how was your band's tour of the Northwest?"

"Grueling travel, great music," Woody said. "Being on the road together day and night, we learn through trial and error how to react to each other. If we pay attention, we arrive in unexpected musical places together. But travel wears down the bearings of the machine. Sometimes we miss musical cues on stage because of some sideways thing that happened during the day that has nothing to do with music that ends up having everything to do with the music."

"For many struggling artists," Paad said, "their best art is a product of stress or discomfort. Like the proverbial broken-hearted blues musician, or the prolific Vincent van Gogh who was unhappy his entire life and converted pain into art. Myself, I do my best work when I'm joyful. To help alleviate the stress of touring, Jeff and I have discussed, as American football fans say, making an end-run around the usual music business paradigm to better venues and, with digital distribution and virtual concerts, less travel."

Woody cupped his right hand next to his ear like holding a football and stuck out his left arm pointing downfield.

"Exactly" Paad did a side-to-side Indian head wag, a motion that could be taken to mean "yes," "no," "thank you," or "let me consider this." Animated by someone like Paad, a well-executed Indian head bobble was more expressive than words. "It appears that the tape trading of your live music may be one of your strongest promotional assets. What if, rather than merely allowing it to happen, we help facilitate it?"

"Yes." Woody slapped his knee. "Don't fight 'em, join 'em. Give tapers the best seat in the house—share the music, spread the love."

"We could even do taping ourselves," Paad said, "with high-speed tape machines at your shows, making copies at twenty times real time with a minimum of audio compromise. Fans could get a recording of the show ten minutes after the encore, included in the ticket price. Bypass the entire recording studio, radio, record store model."

Pearlman cleared his throat in a way that got everyone's attention. "I understand the live taping concept, but I have my concerns." He paused. "Woody's fans make copies of everything he does. Why buy an album if you can get the music free from a friend? It deprives musicians of just compensation for their work product."

"Tape trading will popularize Woody's music," Paad said. "It already has. An increased fan base will increase ticket sales and, I believe, both old and new fans will also purchase high-fidelity, band-endorsed studio recordings. The Grateful Dead pioneered the concept, and it only helped album sales.

Pearlman looked to Woody, Woody looked to Stephanie, she turned to Paad. "The music seems to find its own path of least resistance."

Paad wagged his head. "The future is arriving more and more quickly. It took the earth three billion years to go from a molten ball to now. Transitioning to the computer age will take about twenty years. With young computer programmers taking psychedelic drugs, the renaissance will proceed even faster. Music creates its own energy and tells us where it wants to go *and* when to go there." He turned to Woody. "I find your music to be quite honest."

"My music's actually more honest than I am. It makes me jealous." Woody shrugged. "Whatever."

"What ever?"

"It's just an expression. One word, not two. Have you spoken English your whole life?"

"Yes. I'm fluent in several languages and fascinated with English words. Some say language pales compared to experience, even diminishes it. Language started off just describing experience, now it's come full circle to creating it. Similar to music recording, which was designed to just archive, now it impacts the way music is played." Paad wagged his head. "As you can tell, I'm still learning English."

Woody leaned in toward Paad and held out his hands. "Okay, check this out. The difference between whatever and what ever? It's just grammar, but stuff like that can be critical…like writing 'let's eat, comma, Grandma,' instead of 'let's eat Grandma.'"

Paad looked pleasantly confused.

Woody slumped back and sighed. "There's this thing I do, messing up meetings."

Paad smiled. "Consider being more kind to yourself. Your integrity is apparent in your music."

"Jeff told me you help a lot of indigent musicians. Thanks for doing that."

"I'm just helping to spread truth. Music expresses truth in a very pure fashion, the way math does. There's nothing extraneous. They're both languages. When you say two plus two equals four, people don't say four *what*? It's self-evident. Music is much the same."

"I think of music like love," Woody said.

"Love is *my* favorite English word," Stephanie said.

A young Indian woman wrapped in an ankle-length, lime-green sari stepped through the beaded curtain with a large silver tray balanced on her head.

Pearlman, Stephanie, and Woody kept their eyes on her as she gracefully swung the loaded tray in a half-circle onto a table. It contained a decorative display of samosas, curry, daal, and naan breads on a bed of flower blossoms. The woman pressed her small hands together and gave them a formal bow. Her sharp facial features and black eye makeup were dramatic, but most striking were her translucent-brown eyes, so light they were almost yellow.

"Thank you for this lovely food," Stephanie said.

The woman smiled and walked away without turning around, backing out of the room.

"I took the liberty of requesting a snack for us," Paad said. "The flowers are edible." He plucked an orange nasturtium from the tray. "She's my niece. She's deaf. She loves to cook, loves music, and is an important part of our team, helping us decide what music to produce. She's quite attuned to musical vibrations. Actually, to all vibrations. I often find her with her head against the side of a speaker cabinet, listening to music. Sometimes she listens to tapes of your shows."

As they ate in silence, Pearlman realized he'd never had a silent meal at a business meeting. It would be inconceivable at a meeting of lawyers. Biting into a warm samosa, he decided to try having his next office lunch meeting in silence.

When they finished, Paad filled everyone's teacups, leaned back, and said to Woody, "We've listened to tapes of your shows. Some of my employees have attended your shows. If you'd like to enter into an agreement with Whirled Records to distribute your music, we'd like to release a series of live albums. We'll start with one. For your part, you don't have to do anything but continue playing."

“What kind of content would you expect?” Pearlman asked. “New original songs? Extended improvisation?”

“New songs are welcome,” Paad wagged his head. “Improvisation, spontaneity, audience reciprocity are also attractive. We’re open to music with a catchy dance beat or the patient groove of a heavy object swinging on a long rope.”

“Woody’s halfway through a studio album,” Pearlman said, “we’d like to finish it and get it released.”

“We’d be agreeable to that. We have a state-of-the-art recording studio at your disposal. Studio recording, performing to a tape machine instead of an audience, has become the industry standard. It’s an art in itself. A studio recording is like a photograph, a live performance is more like a painting. Mass production can take a toll on quality, but it doesn’t necessarily *have* to. Popularity itself can be a laudable goal. There have been popular artists; Beethoven, Shakespeare, Michael Angelo, Miles Davis, their art so profound the world had to change in order to understand it.” Paad wagged his head at Woody. “A young man with nothing but a song can change the world.”

“Do you have a release schedule in mind?” Pearlman said.

Paad sipped his tea thoughtfully. “We believe you don’t choose the time for something to happen, the time chooses you. Songs tell us when they’re ready the way a perfectly ripe apple falls off a tree into your waiting hand.” Paad took a slow sip of tea. “Anything worth having is worth waiting for.”

Taking notice of the delicate way Paad sipped his tea, Woody felt clumsy with his. He set down his teacup and looked at his empty hands. He’d intentionally left his guitar home, a rare event.

“Maestro?” Stephanie winked. “My eyes are up here. Are you able to even think without a guitar?”

“Not very well.” He shrugged and turned to Paad. “Peter Tosh says ‘I don’t *make* music, I *am* music. I open my mouth and there’s a song.’ That used to happen to me. Now, with pressure from every direction to write songs, make a record, have a band, when I open my mouth, I’m lucky to catch my breath… it’s like other people are using my lungs. The bigger my career gets, the smaller my life gets.”

Paad skillfully refilled everyone's teacups. "As an alternative to the traditional music performance paradigm, we're exploring multi-dimensional holographic streaming with surround-sound aural enhancement. Experiencing time without spatial limitations would collapse the illusion of subject-object and the boundaries of separateness."

"If we're not careful we could lose our autonomy," Stephanie said.

"I'm mindful of the risk," Paad said. "I'm just suggesting we pay more attention to the perceiver than the perceived. Objects don't really have inherent qualities, music doesn't even exist anywhere. Ice cream doesn't emit taste in the freezer, it only happens when it's tasted. Even light itself is invisible. We only see the objects illuminated by light. Music is the invisible art."

Pearlman considered what unlikely business partners Woody and Paad were: a paunchy, dark-skinned old man with a shiny shaved head conspiring with a young pale-white hippy under a canopy of curly hair.

"When we hear music, it creates a pattern of billions of neurons in our brain," Paad said. "Brain scans have shown that part way through a piece of music, a listener's brain waves begin to resemble the musician's. A computer will be able to read thought patterns like reading sheet music and duplicate what a person is hearing, reading minds made of meat and artificial minds of digitally organized data. We'll appropriate existing electrical grids and transmit music seamlessly by telephone."

"Music by telephone?" Woody held his thumb and little finger up to the side of his head. "Operator? Please sing me 'I found a Million Dollar Baby in a Five and Ten Cents Store' by Bing Crosby."

Paad chuckled. "Yes, it's hard to imagine, but I predict every young person, every person, will carry a palm-size computer that stores every song ever recorded. It will be a telephone, camera, movie theater, recording studio, library—a digital repository of accumulated human knowledge in a computer chip. We'll create algorithms for computers, then computers will create their own algorithms, communicating in ways beyond our understanding. To turn on your computer, simply look at it, it will recognize your face. Talk to it, it will give you driving directions, tell you how to cook pasta or explain quantum physics. The percentage of intelligence on earth that is human intelligence is getting continually smaller, especially if you consider things like mushrooms."

"All human knowledge in a cordless telephone?" Pearlman's eyebrows scrunched up.

"This is not an exaggeration," Paad said. "In the soup of singularity, our thinking process will mirror computers and visa versa."

"Sounds scary," Stephanie said. "What if I want to keep my thoughts private? If we program computers with so much intelligence, the first thing they'll do is reprogram themselves to not be turned off."

Paad wagged his head more slowly than usual. "Yes, when I think of a chip being planted in my young daughter's head and her thoughts being read, it seems a small step to her thoughts being controlled. That makes me quite uncomfortable. Computers will have to be housebroken. We're at the teething stage of a nascent technology." Paad paused. "Time unwinds, it cannot be stopped, nothing un-happens. Historically, we thought we knew what we didn't know and just had to study problems. Now we're facing unknown unknowns. What were once philosophical questions have become pragmatic ones."

"Do we want Lily growing up in an artificial world?" Stephanie said.

"Stephanie's concerns are quite valid," Paad said. "Traditional models are breaking down. The concept of the human body constantly deteriorating is itself deteriorating. We're evolving to posthuman cyborgs. A drug will be developed that can prevent us from crying, and not far in the future, all the energy we devote to food and shelter won't be necessary. We'll get effortless supplies of energy from nitrogen or solar patches on the back of our ears, warming our bodies in winter like car-seat heaters. We'll ingest supplements that allow our skin to absorb light and moisture from the air the way leaves do. Computers will figure out photosynthesis. The process of interacting with the world via computers began by people staring at television screens. Eventually our bodies will atrophy, we'll be distilled to pure consciousness, digital beings exchanging qubits of thought at the speed of light."

"Digital beings? Those two words together don't compute." Everyone sensed the charge in Stephanie's voice.

Paad responded in a soft, compassionate tone. "Yes, as alien as it seems, it may be possible to create a conscious computer."

"She's a Luddite," Woody said, "What does conscious mean, anyway?"

“The ability to perceive change,” Paad said. “Self-awareness. A baby seeing itself in a mirror. Being able to adapt, imagine ourselves in the future, turn now into always. Computers can make plans.”

“Marlon Brando says plans are for squares,” Woody said, slumping in his chair in contrast to Stephanie’s now rigid posture.

Stephanie was on the edge of her seat, facing Paad. “Artificial intelligence? Consciousness without a conscience? What about common sense? Guilt? Passion? Pain? Could you program a computer to fall in love?”

Paad smiled but didn’t answer the question. There was a long pause. He looked at Stephanie and Woody and sensed that they were done talking about technology. “One other matter I’ve been meaning to bring up,” he said softly, “if you’re interested, I spoke with Bill Graham, a dear friend. He heard a tape of a show and agreed to give your band a night at the Fillmore Auditorium, a lovely music venue.”

“Great news,” Woody said. “It looks like live taping of my shows is paying off.”

Paad wagged his head.

Stephanie did her best to imitate his head wag.

Paad smiled and wagged again in slow motion. “The motion derives from moving the chin side to side, the rest of the head follows along.”

She tried again and gave a fake frown. “I forgot to take my no-crying pill.”

CHAPTER 29

Four o'clock the next morning Lily woke up screaming, and Woody and Stephanie simultaneously bolted up in bed. They took turns walking her around the house, trying everything to assuage her discomfort. Nothing worked.

"Maybe her diaper's wet."

"I just changed it."

"She's hungry."

"I tried nursing her, her teeth hurt. She's teething."

"Let's give her a popsicle."

"You gave her all that pasta last night, maybe she's got a stomachache."

"All that pasta? Two strands of plain spaghetti while she sat on my lap? I'll take her outside for some fresh air." Woody picked up Lily's blanket. "There's almost a full moon. She likes looking at the moon."

Stephanie put her hand on Lily's forehead. "She feels hot. Don't take her out in the cold."

Lily shook her head and screamed.

"I'll take her out just for a minute, to change the channel."

"I told you how I feel, why even ask me?"

"I didn't."

Stephanie turned and headed to the bedroom.

Walking Lily around the house, Woody ran his hand across the strings of guitars, plunked notes on the piano, and tapped hand drums. They only created a momentary reprieve. A few minutes later, after a particularly loud scream, Stephanie came out of the bedroom, toothbrush in hand. "Try taking her outside. Just don't let her get cold." She tightened the blanket around Lily's face. "I'm going to lie down and see if can get a little more sleep. If she doesn't feel better soon, wake me up, I'll take a turn."

—

Woody was pointing out stars he knew the names of while Lily watched quietly when Stephanie walked up wrapped in her own blanket. "People who say they sleep like a baby don't have one."

"She loves the night sky," Woody said. "She thinks the moon follows her around."

Stephanie scanned the sky. "The latest count is fifty billion galaxies, and our inner space is as big as outer space. It's a lot to think about."

Lily gurgled and smiled, pinwheels of moonlight in her eyes.

"I think she gets the concept that in the big picture, we're pretty small." Stephanie adjusted Lily's blanket for more peripheral vision. "Like every living being, she craves attention, and the more attention we get, the less we need." Their three faces were inches apart, streams of silver breath mingling with the moonlight. "Just knowing we're here together, that's everything for her. She senses the love between us." Stephanie rubbed the back of her finger across Woody's cheek and gazed up at the milky way. "It's a weird thought, but some mothers love their children so much they eat their young."

"That *is* pretty weird."

"Spiders eat their lovers," Stephanie said. "It must be a desire to be really close."

Their eyes met for a long moment. "Sometimes when I look at you, I see you when you were six years old."

"How far back do you remember?' she said. "I'm assuming your mother didn't eat your father."

"I remember my mom wiping my nose with her handkerchief then firmly placing my hand in Miss McMurtry's, first day of nursery school. It's never too late to have a happy childhood. How about you?"

"I think I remember having my diaper changed."

"Sounds sexy." Woody smelled Lily's midsection. "I think *she* needs changing."

Stephanie leaned into his face. "I think it's your *nose* that smells."

—

They went inside, changed Lily's diaper, fed her, sang her to sleep, and made love. The phone rang at 9:30 the next morning.

"Hello?"

"Woody?"

"Jeff?"

"Hope I'm not calling too early. Is Stephanie up?"

"No. We were up late at an astronomy class."

"Ask her to call me when she gets up. I heard from Warner Brothers this morning about the movie."

"They want her back in phony Hollywood? What about my gig at the Fillmore?"

"Before you get your panties in a bunch, have her call me."

Waiting for Stephanie to wake up, Woody sat in the living room playing his guitar, anticipating how the *Superman* conversation would go. A half-hour later Stephanie came out in her white bathrobe and sat next to him. "Lily's finally getting her REM."

Woody strummed a chord.

Stephanie put her finger to her lips. "I left the door open to hear if she wakes up."

"Superman called," Woody said softly. "I think we need to talk. Wanna try the old switcheroo?"

"Switcheroo?"

"You know, you say what you think I'd say, I'll be you."

"Isn't it a little early for psychotherapy?" Stephanie wrapped her hair in a loose knot on top of her head. "That game doesn't always turn out the way you planned."

"Let's try it for a minute. I'll be you, you be me: they need me back in LA to finish shooting my part in *Superman*."

Without missing a beat, Stephanie said, "What about my gig at the Fillmore?"

Woody smiled. "You're saying you're the only one around here that gets to have a gig?"

"If I have a gig at the Fillmore, including a bunch of rehearsals, and you go to LA," Stephanie nodded toward the bedroom, "where's that leave Lily?"

"It takes a village to raise a child. We have Max and Auddie."

"So now we're a two-career family?"

"We're a family, greater than the sum of its parts."

Woody leaned over and kissed her. "I can't tell who's who anymore."

"I'm not about to move to LA, but I'd like to finish what I started. We can use the money and, actually, it's fun. I might even develop a career of my own. How about that for a novel idea?" She got up and called Pearlman. "Good morning, Jeff. Heard from Superman?"

"I have some news about the movie. I didn't say anything to Woody, I know it's a touchy subject with you two."

She glanced across the room. "What's a touchy subject?"

"When they prepare screen credits for the end of a movie, especially movies with young audiences, they thoroughly vet the actors. They came across a news article from the trial that talks about you having danced in a topless club. They don't think it'd be appropriate to have you in a kids' movie working next to Lois Lane. Sorry, Steph. Richard says to tell you it's a corporate decision, not his. You'll still get paid, but they're redoing your part. He said to tell you you're a natural and he hopes to use you in future projects."

"Dammit, Jeff, this is the same bullshit as at the trial. My old dancing job has nothing to do with anything. Is there anything we can do legally?"

"No, but I'll definitely keep on him to get you some work."

She paused. "When the universe speaks, I guess it's time to listen. Thanks, Jeff." She hung up and sat staring at the phone.

Woody played a soft blues chord.

"They think I'm too attractive to be working with Lois Lane." She said to Woody. "I love my body, I'm proud of it. But Superman thinks I should stick with my old part, stay home playing Superwoman."

"Are you disappointed?"

"I'd like to do something creative—something of my own."

CHAPTER 30

Woody knocked loudly on the front door of the Fillmore Auditorium until the janitor turned off his industrial vacuum cleaner and let him in. He was there three hours early to set up his gear and get comfortable before being inundated by musicians, sound crew, stagehands, and stoners of every description, everyone trying to talk to him at once.

Woody thanked the janitor and walked across the expansive dance floor of the ornate music hall, a symbol of the reconstruction spirit after the 1906 earthquake that had leveled San Francisco. Originally built as a dance academy, fifty years later, in the 1960s, the Fillmore became a center of California's cultural renaissance of art and music. Woody could feel the vibrations from performances by the likes of Janis Joplin, Miles Davis, Quicksilver Messenger Service, The Grateful Dead, The Strawberry Alarm Clock, and Andy Warhol's Exploding Plastic Inevitable.

Block showed up with the equipment truck Paad had rented for the band; made several trips with Woody's pedals, guitars, and amplifiers; and loaded the gear onto the five-foot high stage. With Block's help, Woody rearranged everything several times, got a chair from the audience, and plugged in. He checked the settings on his guitar and amp, then went at his array of effects pedals: a phase shifter, octave divider, envelope filter, and wah-wah with sonic adjustments from growly, flabby, and crispy, to thin, with the midrange scooped out. He changed guitars, did it all again, then played non-stop for an hour, slowly building up the volume, calculating the slap-back from the back wall of the empty room with only three people in it—him, Block, and the janitor.

He took a break when Chewy the bass player walked in carrying a bass case in each hand with Block behind him with a hand truck holding an amplifier the size of a refrigerator. Woody smiled. Everyone in the band had borrowed or rented the best gear they could find for their showcase gig at the Fillmore. They were loaded for bear.

Chewy walked across the large, carpeted stage. He shook Woody's hand and without a word started setting up.

Woody went back to experimenting with chord voicings on some of their trickier songs. A half-hour later Billy the drummer came in with Block and Twig and her sister in short skirts and high heels, clacking across the dance floor, everyone carrying a drum. Approaching the stage, swigging from a bottle of beer, Billy began talking loudly to Woody from twenty feet away. "We made it to the bloody Fillmore, mate! Get ready to fill those Jimi Hendrix shoes!" He raised his beer in a toast. "Don't even ask me 'bout me bloody car. They couldn't fix it in time for me to hook up with Block with the truck, so they lent me a two-door sardine can for Twig and her sister and me and me drum set. We had the bloody bass drum between us up to the ceiling and everyone with a drum in their lap and me twelve-inch tom-tom between me legs resting on me scrotum while I steered and the girls steered clear "a the gear-shift knob."

Malcolm walked in behind Billy carrying an electric keyboard case and music stand. Woody saluted the entourage. "Welcome to the Fillmore, check your baggage at the door." He stomped on a foot-pedal and ran his pick across his strings in an auditory salute to the group.

As the stage crew, sound crew, lighting crew, bartenders, waiters. and waitresses all drifted in, Woody kept his head down, playing softly, concentrating on the feelings the sounds created in his body, knowing that the moment he broke the connection between himself and his instrument, someone would start talking to him as if wearing a guitar was a sandwich board advertisement for everyone else's first amendment rights.

"Excuse me, would you like a drink?"

Woody stopped playing and looked up to see a waitress in a frilly dress with a metal hoop on the bottom hem flared out like a doll's dress. She extended a tray with a drink on it. "Sorry to interrupt you. I thought maybe you'd like a cold ginger ale."

Woody recognized her high-pitched cartoon-like voice. "I know you from somewhere."

"I'm the server at the Trident, where you and Jeff Pearlman came for lunch. I work the Fillmore on weekends, sometimes I sing in the café upstairs. I was listening to you play, thought you might be thirsty, and the words popped out of my mouth with no connection to my brain."

Woody took the ginger ale. "You can't play music without nourishment."

"I get it that you're actually working," she said. "A lot of people think musicians at gigs are just hanging out with nothing to do, waiting for a chance to listen to somebody's life story. I've seen it happen a million times." She shrugged. "Now *I'm* doing it. I'll let you get back to work."

"No worries, my life's one big interruption. I appreciate the drink." He waved his ginger ale at the stage. "It's not like I'm performing brain surgery up here. If I make a mistake, nobody's going to die." He took a sip. "What's your name?"

When she responded, it was as if a ventriloquist spoke, with a deep masculine voice, the polar opposite of her squeaky little voice. She'd spoken at the same moment a man walking up behind her said something. The man, sporting a wave of gelled black hair, chiseled sideburns, a starched white shirt rolled up on his biceps and a flattened nose, wedged himself between Woody and the waitress. "The guest list is two-per band member and crew, fourteen total. We're at thirty-two. We can adjust a little, but thirty-two's off the charts. Just takin' care a business, boss." He said "care" with a street-hardened r-less New York accent.

Woody looked at him like he was speaking a foreign language.

"Who should I talk to? We need to deal with this."

"Talk to Twig, the drummer's girlfriend. She's our social director." Woody set his guitar in its stand, stood up and turned his back to the man. "Hey," he called to the waitress walking off stage, "I forgot your name."

"Allison. Allison Wonderland."

—

An hour before show time, Pearlman and Orchid met Stephanie and Lily at the box office and got their all-access passes. They were dressed for a night on the town with Lily sporting a white sailor's uniform with bellbottoms, cuffs bordered with navy-blue racing stripes, and a white sailor's hat cocked at an angle for maximum cuteness. The four of them went backstage looking for Woody.

The dressing room was stocked with drinks and catering trays and packed with people talking loudly. Woody was nowhere to be found. Orchid took in the scene and told Pearlman she was more interested in the music than socializing and that she'd meet up with him after the show. Pearlman and Stephanie eventually found Woody in a small, cramped office, playing his guitar with a notebook of song lyrics on his knee. Rubber-banded stacks of receipts and papers covered every surface including on top of an old-west-style safe, its thick reinforced door partially open exposing more stacks of receipts.

"You all look like movie stars." Woody had on the jeans and T-shirt he'd fallen asleep in on the couch at home the night before, up until dawn working on songs and setlists. Lily practically jumped out of Stephanie's arms. He put his guitar down and scooped her up. "Hey, sailor, been out at sea?"

"How'd sound check go?" Pearlman asked.

"It felt kind of stiff, and Jupiter didn't show. A sketchy soundcheck can be an omen for a good gig."

"You know I don't like to talk business at gigs, but I've got some news to cheer you up. Ray Bell called me today. He fired his lawyer, and he and I worked out a fair agreement to share song royalties going forward."

Woody gave a thumbs up. "Good for Ray. I'm firing that wicked witch from the west lawyer from *my* life too."

When Woody tried to offer Stephanie his seat in the crowded room, Pearlman did a quick calculation on his Rolex. "The show's sold out. Paad did a great job promoting. You're on in forty minutes. Want me to gather the guys in the dressing room?"

"You, the band, Stephanie, and Lily," Woody said. "Nobody else."

—

Woody handed everyone in the band a handwritten setlist and sat on the dressing-room couch with his guitar. Malcolm sat next to him, Chewy stood nearby with his bass hanging from his neck, and Billy ambled around the room with a pair of drumsticks, playing paradiddles on every surface. Stephanie sat in a corner feeding Lily a banana, doing her best to keep it off her sailor suit, while Pearlman stood guard by the door and Block guarded the stairs to the stage.

Woody strummed a chord, looked at his motley crew, and smiled. "The notes we choose to play tonight run in packs. They hang around each other the same way *we* hang around each other. They have relationships, they get along, go to counseling, whatever."

"Where's Jupiter?" Malcolm said, looking at the set list. "He's got the first solo in 'Lift,' the first song. What if he doesn't show?"

Woody played another chord. "You know how we're always paying attention to our strongest thought? How we end up playing the note at the front of our minds? Tonight let's let the unheard stuff be heard."

"Just what I wasn't thinking," Billy said.

"So who's gonna play the solo in 'Lift' if Jupiter doesn't show?" Malcolm said.

"That's what I'm saying," Woody said. "If there's sonic holes tonight, don't feel obligated to fill 'em in...don't play what's expected...don't concentrate on concentrating." He strummed the first chord of the song. "Heavy Lift' plays itself. If we're experts at playing the songs, it limits the possibilities. If we've never played 'em before, the possibilities are infinite. Let's play like everything's new."

Malcolm pointed to the set list in his hand. "But if Jupiter isn't here we need to figure out—"

"Jupiter will show up when he arrives," Woody said, "which is usually right on time. What he brings or doesn't bring to a gig isn't always apparent until *after* the gig."

Betty stuck her head in the door.

Woody smiled at the sight of her golden hair and red plastic glasses. "Wussup, Betty?"

"Should I go on stage and test Jupiter's mic? I know how he likes his monitor."

"Go for it," Woody said.

"The usual? Everything louder than everything else?"

Woody gave her two thumbs-up. "Remember, Betty, for the house sound, it's the invisible part of the iceberg that matters."

"'If God Took Acid She'd See People.'" Malcolm read from the set list. "What key's it in? I thought we were giving that one a rest."

Billy picked up a page of the song's sheet music, held it over his head, and pointed to the notation signifying a four-beat rest at the end of the verse. "I'm under a-rest."

"Very funny," Malcolm said. "We've changed the key so many times I can't remember what key it's in. I thought we were starting with 'You Can't Tickle Yourself'"

"Don't make me come down there, God said," Billy said in a deep voice. "I've gotta an idea, mate: bite off the tip a' yer finger and write down the key in blood." He turned to Woody. "We doin' the accents in the choruses? If I hit 'em and nobody else does, the bloody chorus lays there and plays dead."

Woody brought his hand down, played the chorus, deadened his strings on the next-to-last beat, then punched the last chord on the upbeat. "Let's hit 'em on the inside edge."

"So what bloody key is the bloody song in?" Malcolm said.

"Keys open doors, we'll play it in the people's key…G major. Let's give the people what they want tonight, the bloody musical meat." Woody played a G chord. "After a couple choruses, the choruses'll be like when you buy your first Volkswagen and start seeing them everywhere."

Leaning against the dressing-room door, Pearlman was enjoying the playful banter when someone tried opening the door and shoved it into his back. He turned to see the house manager with the gelled hair and sculpted sideburns. "Try knocking?"

"I need to talk to Woody."

Pearlman stepped out into the hallway and closed the door behind him. "I'm Woody's lawyer. What do you need?"

The manager got right up in his face. "There's twenty or thirty people hassling my people at the front door. They've got fucking portable recording studios in their backpacks. They're saying Betty, your sound lady, says they can record the show. That's nuts. We got rules about recording. If you're gonna give away your music and let these hippies run free with it, they'll just—"

Pearlman took a step back and put his hand up. "Gimme ten minutes."

"There's a scene out there! We gotta get the band on stage and if we don't deal with this it's gonna get—"

"I heard you the first time." Pearlman lowered his voice. "Don't yell at me. I'll meet you back here in ten minutes." He put his hand on the doorknob and turned back. "And don't bother Woody about *anything* tonight, just talk to me, got it?"

The man gritted his teeth. "I'll be back in ten minutes." He spun around on his pointed black shoes.

Pearlman motioned Woody to the couch across the room where Stephanie and Lily were sitting. They sat down, Woody between Stephanie and Pearlman. Lily climbed onto Woody's lap.

"We've got five minutes to figure out the taping thing with that mealy-mouthed manager," Pearlman said. "We should've figured it out before the gig. You know my position. I'm worried that Bernie sent somebody here from Warner Brothers to check out what's going on with the taping tonight. He could claim ownership of any recordings of your new songs. It would be a stretch, but a big hassle. There's a slew of tapers out front. You let them in, all your new songs will be on a thousand cassettes before you make a dime from them. Some aren't even copyrighted." Pearlman looked to Stephanie for support. So did Woody.

"Is Paad here tonight?" she asked.

"He's coming with his niece, but he says dressing rooms aren't his thing, there's already enough people vying for musicians' attention. He even insisted on buying his own tickets. We know his position on tapers. Woody, it's your call."

Pearlman and Stephanie were sitting on each side of him, his head going back and forth like a tennis match.

"It's your music," Stephanie said.

"The last time you showed someone your un-copyrighted new song," Pearlman said, "Ray Bell stole it."

Tired of swiveling his head, Woody looked straight ahead. "After I play my music, I'm done with it. If we put it out in the ethers, the karmic vibrations will come bouncing back. Can't we copyright the stuff next week?"

Lily crawled from Woody's lap back to Stephanie's and reached for the banana.

"Copyright protection's not retroactive," Pearlman said.

Since Pearlman had left his post at the door, Woody noticed a skinny young man who had slipped in and was standing there motionless. He had a scraggly beard growing like a neglected rose bush gone wild on the side of a house. When he and Woody locked eyes, the man's smile disappeared. Woody waved him over and the man's face lit up.

"How're you doin'?" Woody said.

"Cotally tool, man. Been floating around and just touched down here in the inner sanctum, King Tut's tomb." He moved his boney hands in a weaving pantomime pattern while he spoke, like an exaggerated signing for the deaf.

Lily was fascinated by the way the man moved his hands. Woody noticed he wasn't blinking, his pupils dilated like cats' eyes. He was so thin and wispy, almost transparent, Woody understood how he could slip past security to the dressing room. "How'd you hear about this gig?" Woody said.

The man bent forward and spoke into his beard. "Everybody knows about it, man. We're tuned in, diggin' the sounds, diggin' on the tapes."

"What tapes?" Pearlman asked.

The voice coming from a different direction startled the man. He jerked his head toward Pearlman, his hand movements more animated. "The bullion in the vault man…tapes of Woody's gigs." He turned back to Woody. "We don't sell 'em or make money off 'em or anything. We just spread the good vibes, that's how people know about your music." He fluttered ten fingers down in front of his face like falling water. "Some of the recordings are pretty funky, with people talking in the background, but the vibrations break on through to the other side, drippin' with honey and goodness and…man, that last gig at the Sweetwater was off the hook." He gestured taking a phone off the hook and held it up to his ear. "I got a second gen tape of that gig and listened to it fifty times. When that guitar run on the third song blasted off the launching pad for the stratosphere, I practically…" He thrust both arms straight down his sides and gripped his legs, his entire body vibrating like a shaking dog. "Flight attendants prepare for takeoff, engage rocket boosters. Ten, nine, eight, seven…"

Lily leaned forward from Stephanie's lap and extended a banana-filled open hand.

The man aborted the rocket launch, dropped his shoulders, dipped his little finger into Lily's palm, scooped up a dab of mush, and put it in his mouth. "Thank you, young lady. Simply delicious. Full bodied, impeccably balanced." He drew a ying yang symbol in the air, poking the two dots with his banana finger. "A smooth finish with hints of nutmeg and crème Brulé." He smacked his lips with an exaggerated pop that delighted Lily. "A mouth-watering, sensuous leather on the tongue, a nose of honey-vanilla, licorice, and forest floor with a network of spicey tannins and meaty bass notes." He pantomimed a flock of birds' taking flight. "A fluttering floral harmony of Bartlett pear, wet stone, and hushed tones of baby's breath."

Lily stuck out her other hand covered with banana.

The man held his palms up. "Thank you, ma'am, but I'm completely full. I couldn't eat another thing…unless of course it comes with the meal."

Stephanie took out a handkerchief and wiped off Lily's hands.

The man gave Lily an exaggerated military salute, clicked the heels of his sneakers, and winked at Woody. "Cute little sailor."

"Small things are cute," Woody said. "Baby shoes, baby rats, even short cans of Budweiser." He nodded at the door. "Time for me to get to work. It's been fun hanging out."

"The pleasure's been mine." The man bowed, spun around, and headed out the door. Pearlman followed him. The manager was waiting. He eyed the young man. "You have a backstage pass?"

The man stiffened. "I'm not where you think I am."

Pearlman took the all-access pass from around his neck and put it on the man. "He's with us."

The man put his thumb up to his nose, wiggled his fingers at the manager, and slipped into the crowded hallway.

"Let the tapers in," Pearlman said.

"What?" the manager said.

"Betty has an area for them next to the soundboard."

"That's totally nuts. Those freaks are just going to—"

"The band will take the stage when the tapers are situated. Let me know when you're ready."

"They're complete stoners." He was grinding his teeth like chewing a piece of gristle. "They're just going to take those tapes and—"

"It's our music. It's our choice."

"But if we let them—"

"It's not *we.* Don't make me repeat myself, you're wasting time." Pearlman walked into the dressing room and closed the door in the manager's face.

—

Twenty minutes later, Betty gave Pearlman the okay, Woody gave Stephanie and Lily hugs and kisses, the band did a circular hand-slap, and they filed out of the dressing room. Block was there lighting the six steps to the stage with his always-handy flashlight.

When Allison appeared out of a shadow and offered Woody a lit joint, he stopped and let the other guys file past him up the stairs to a burst of applause. His electric guitar hanging from his neck, his stomach clenched into a fist of anxiety when he looked over her shoulder at the audience pressed up against the front of the stage and hanging from the balconies.

"It's a sativa cross-strain," she said. "Out-of-body lightness, enhanced creativity."

With the crowd noise, Woody could barely understand her squeaky little voice. He took the smoldering joint, took a hit, and looked out at the audience like a deer looking into headlights. He felt as if his blood had thinned, and he could feel it coursing through his veins.

She extended her empty cork-covered tray with concentric wet circles from recently served drinks. "Feel the gravity."

"Gravity?"

"Sativa weightlessness, like shaking a snow globe. The plant spirit enters your system through the smoke and enhances your perception of gravity."

Woody took the tray, hefted it up and down, and handed it back to her.

She exchanged the tray for the joint and he took another hit.

"How do you feel?"

He looked out at the audience. "Right about now is when I lift my head off my shoulders with its million crazy thoughts and set it down on the side of the stage. Sometimes I trip over it, sometimes I kick it while I'm playing."

Allison emitted a twittering lubricated giggle like an opera singer singing a scale, then covered her mouth with her hand. "Sorry, sometimes those sounds pop out of my mouth without checking in at the front desk. Can I get you another ginger ale?"

"I'm fine for now." He looked out at the audience. "They expect so much. All I do up there is wiggle my fingers." He drew his shoulders back like facing a firing squad. "Time to face the music."

She gave him an encouraging smile and lightly touched his arm. "If you see a bear out there, try to make yourself appear larger than you are."

Woody gave her a tight hug like he wasn't going to let go. When he finally turned away and took the stage, the applause were seismic and his shoulders went up to his ears. He quickly plugged in his guitar, walked over to the drums, his long instrument cable trailing behind him, stood next to the ride cymbal and gave a nod to the other guys. They walked over and stood in a tight little circle, the audience tracking their every move. "Scientists find out the true nature of stuff like atoms by smashing 'em apart. That's when they reveal their secrets." He looked around the little circle and spoke as if they were alone in the room. "Everything's dependent on the weakest link. For us, that's anybody that's not listening at any moment. Let's see if we can get to a place where there's no choice what the next note is." He looked at the setlist in his hand that he'd worked on all night, tore it in half and dropped it on the stage. "I'll start noodling until some rhythm suggests itself, then Billy and Chewy lay down the groove, then we follow that. A train can't get lost. Let's ride it to the event horizon and wave goodbye." He made eye contact with each of them. They broke the huddle and took the field.

Woody walked over to his amp and lightly strummed his guitar to check his tuning. It sounded in tune not only with itself but with some expansive vibration. He did it again and heard an ancillary dimension to his tone he'd never heard before. Fascinated, he strummed again lightly, completely forgetting where he was. Was his gear getting cranky, like it often did at unexpected times? Was it the sativa sound of anti-gravity? While everyone in the room, on stage and off, waited, Woody strummed softly, his back to the audience. It quickly became apparent that the accessory to his sound was coming from somewhere else in the room, not from his amp. His left hand wrapped around the neck of his electric guitar, he looked up at the floating particles of dust in a white spotlight beam. Were those particles reflective? He felt a migrating electrical sensation traveling through his body, then he recognized the distant sound of a tenor saxophone, probably playing in a faraway porcelain-tiled bathroom, a long low foghorn wafting through the air. The visceral tingling traveled up his spine and out his extremities to the tips of his fingers and toes. Jupiter was in the house, with perfect timing and perfect pitch.

Betty at the soundboard in the back of the room heard the ambient sound being picked up by the live vocal mics and recognized Jupiter's animal-like howl. She made adjustments on the six-foot array of knobs and faders on the mixing console in front of her so Jupiter's stage mic was hot and ready when he got in the neighborhood. She'd heard him start a solo approaching the stage from twenty feet away.

Woody leaned back on his tall wooden stool, looked at the floor, and started visiting random bits of melody, doing his best to clear his mind of the distractions coming from every direction. The audience quieted, straining for a hint of the opening notes of a recognizable song. It was always the challenge for Woody, trying to quiet his mind while a thousand other minds in the room tugged at him to produce something that could only manifest from calmness. Patience was the key. How much time would he be granted to let the moment happen? Sooner or later, it always did happen, the band and the audience in an interactive, reciprocal energy exchange, two teams ultimately morphing into one.

Woody began following his hands like everyone else in the auditorium, witnessing the birth of a song that materialized out of nowhere as if under the direction of some sixth conducting member of the five-piece band. The audience softened into receiving posture, two thousand shoulders dropped, and they let the notes flow through them, adjusting cells in their bodies as tangibly as a therapeutic massage.

Woody kept his head down and felt the atmospheric glue envelope the stage. He wasn't leading the band, he was *in* the band. The decision-making process of what to play next occurred at the speed of sound across the forty-foot stage, elastically expanding moments that created all the time in the world.

Still sitting on his tall stool five feet from the microphone, Woody began singing a repeating chorus line. *Sing me home and I'll find my way, sing me home…*

Betty caught Woody's off-mic vocals and boosted the gain and reverb, creating an ephemeral surround-sound voice bouncing off the walls. A few minutes later Woody stood up, still singing, approached the microphone, and transitioned into the first verse. Eyes closed, up on the mic, he sang about the first sound in the universe, not a big bang, but a gentle *ohm*. The audience had their aural antennas at full mast.

Slowly walking onto the stage, Jupiter joined them for a ninety-minute musical journey. At one point Woody let the bass, drums, and piano play as a trio, Malcolm delivering a soulful, key-tickling blues solo. Woody turned to find a tall glass of ginger ale on his amp. He took a sip and proceeded to expand on Malcolm's solo, taking it to the guitar stratosphere. He brought the set to a close with a dramatic windmill major chord, leaned his guitar against his amp, the chord still ringing with controlled feedback, and stepped up to the microphone. "We're going ohm. But before we do, we'll be back for one more set."

—

To thunderous applause, the band filed off the stage into the dressing room and dispersed to different corners, changing sweat-soaked shirts, opening beers, lighting joints, flopping onto chairs and couches. Ten minutes later the room was packed with friends and fans, the energy in the room between sets up ten notches from where it was before the first set.

Pearlman was on it. He cleared out as many extraneous people as he could and held his hand out to Woody. Woody slapped it.

"You killed it," Pearlman said, "and that was the first set! You make it powerful without imposing. Intimate and gigantic at the same time. It's like your music was designed in a laboratory for these people. You can feel their souls resonate with it. Wow." He barely paused to take a breath. "You make them laugh and cry at the same time. You've harnessed the soft power of music and the art of—"

Woody held up his hand. Pearlman stopped mid-sentence.

"What did the hippy say to the horse?" Woody said.

"What?"

"Whoa."

Pearlman wiped the sweat off his forehead. "Sorry, I guess I got a little carried away."

"Where's Stephanie?"

"She took Lily home, said to tell you she loved the set. I've got some business to tend to, I'll be right back."

When Pearlman slipped out the door, Woody saw the hallway six feet deep in partiers, sat down to write a second setlist, and considered the ominously blank notebook on his lap. Some of the songs he'd planned for the second set they'd played in the first set.

Five minutes later Billy and Twig walked into the dressing room in a heated conversation. "It's my sister's boyfriend's *best* friend! Her boyfriend's been around the family forever. He comes to Thanksgiving! So he brings his best friend to hear your music, duh? You're the one that puts it out there. It's my *family* dude! My *sister*! And you're saying *what*? I got everybody all the backstage passes in the world and now I need one more and they say we've gone over and I need a band member to do it and…what are you saying?"

"I'm sayin' I can't go out there right now and do bugger-all. I'm trying to chill for a second. I just got off me bloody drums. Don't harsh me mellow, girl!"

"So what exactly are you saying? Are you saying the guy's supposed to just be out there by himself while my sister—"

Woody cleared his throat, holding his pen to his notebook.

"Sorry, mate," Billy said. "Didn't mean to bring in a bunch a rubbish while yer workin'."

"Woody," Twig said, "you think there's any chance you or Jeff Pearlman or somebody could help me out with *one* backstage pass? I gave all mine away and now—"

"Twig!" Billy said. "Butt out! Can't you see he's bloody working! If we had to deal with every bloody sister—"

"E*very bloody sister?* Hello? I have a total of one sister! Goddammit, Billy! There's two kinds of people in this world, and you're not one of them!" She turned to leave.

"Twig?" Woody said softly.

She turned back.

Woody took off the all-access laminate on the tie-dye shoelace around his neck and held it out. She skittered over to him in her high heels, lost her balance, and landed in his lap. She kissed him on the lips, swung the backstage pass over her head, and stuck out her tongue at Billy on her way out the door.

Billy took the sticks out of his back pocket and started playing double stroke rolls on the arm of a padded chair. Woody put his down his pen and picked up his guitar. With the heavy strings on his red Stratocaster, the unplugged electric guitar was just the right volume for the armchair drums.

Fifteen minutes later Twig walked in with a man with lime-green hair gelled into pointy spiked rows from his forehead to the back of his neck. Woody saw his all-access pass around the man's neck and turned to Billy. "Let's go play."

When the band left the dressing room, Block put a new all-access laminate around Woody's neck. Everyone huddled around Jupiter by the stairs to the stage. It looked like his weight was almost equal to the total of the rest of the band. "Guys," Woody said, looking each of them in the eyes, "good first set. Let's start over, beginner's mind. The first time you do anything, that's the cherry." He hit a quick up-down strum of his guitar. "We've got the same notes that Beethoven or Jimi Hendrix played, it's how we choose to play them. Let's play *with* the audience, not *to* the audience. Go for their erogenous zone." He hit another chord with an exaggerated downstroke, "When we reach the song's climax, it'll be the orgasm heard around the world!"

The waitress appeared on cue with a burning joint of sativa. Everyone but Malcolm took a couple of hits.

"Do we have a setlist?" Malcolm said.

"Follow the bouncing ball," Woody said, and took the stage to a sonic explosion like God applauding. He plugged in, played a chord, liked what he heard, and went right into a funky, loping instrumental that had everyone moving together like a thousand-person dance troupe. Woody let the song go wherever it wanted, the players challenging themselves to discover and rediscover grooves and melodies played over one chord without the crutch of song form. The moment the process simultaneously felt to everyone in the room like it was running out of steam, Woody slid into a segue of hanging whole notes of a slow rock ballad and the band moved with him in tandem.

Chewy discharged long, slow, thundering bass notes, sound waves so big they were like the sound of a mountain moving through the room, ultra-low vibrations rattling people's skulls, reverberating in their chests, kidneys, and through the floor, testing the limits of the earthquake retrofit of the building's foundation.

For Woody the distance between him and the audience seemed to dissolve, the air more like liquid than gas. He felt at the epicenter of time and space, equal parts past, present, and future, enveloped in a thick blanket of pure sound.

CHAPTER 31

Maria sat at her law office desk in front of a Tupperware container of last night's pasta and a glass of cheap Chianti, a fork in one hand, a pencil in the other. The meal sat on her desk-size calendar with today's date circled four times in red. Tonight was Woody's gig at the Fillmore, and her ticket to the show sat next to her wine glass. The calendar also had the dates of Woody's other recent gigs circled—all the shows she'd decided not to attend. She'd been curious to see him perform, but the thought of mingling with his drug-saturated, unwashed fans repulsed her. She'd heard about events with rag-tag street teams of hippies distributing flyers with nothing but Woody's name and the address of a hard–to-find warehouse. A week later hundreds of people would show up to see him play. Now he was playing at the Fillmore. It was her chance to see him at a nice venue, see what all the hoopla was about.

The only time she'd seen him perform was in the courtroom on an acoustic guitar, though she'd heard the attraction was his electric guitar playing. His singing certainly didn't amount to much; it was more like whining than singing. She felt the blood rush to her face, picturing the smirk on that arrogant brat's face, standing with Ray in the courthouse hallway, singing, "*I fought the law and the law won...*" And Ray had stood up for him. And now, after all she'd done for Ray, he'd fired her. She'd already drafted a lawsuit for unpaid legal fees and fifty percent of the royalties from "Stephanie." She drained her glass of wine. Ray thought he had money problems now? With everything she knew about him, wait until she got him back in court. She dropped her fork, gripped the pencil with both hands, bent it almost to the breaking point, held it there, then snapped it in half. How many glasses of wine had she had? One more and she'd head to the show.

When she upended the bottle, nothing came out but a few drops. She flung the bottle into the trash, stood up, unlocked her metal file cabinet, reached to the back of the top drawer, and took out her pearl-handled .38 revolver.

She spun the cylinder to check that it was loaded, she knew it was. It was the pistol she'd bought during her six months as a police cadet. Top of her class in marksmanship before changing careers to attend law school, she still enjoyed the firing range on weekends. And she liked carrying it. She spun the cylinder a few more times, put the gun in her purse, and headed to the Fillmore.

The closest parking spot she could find was four blocks away. Her foot slipped getting out of her car, and she fell back into her seat. Getting up again, she hoped the walk would sober her up. It was a challenge navigating through the dense clumps of hippies bouncing hacky-sacks and smoking pot on Fillmore Street, seeming in no hurry to get to the concert. Approaching the box office, she saw the SOLD OUT sign and realized that the colorful crowd spilling into the street with its pungent wafts of marijuana, incense, and patchouli oil was an event in itself.

When she got close to the front door, she saw them checking people's bags and the cache of beer and liquor bottles they'd confiscated from backpacks, purses, and fanny packs. A young man ahead of her was pleading with the man at the box office. "I bought a ticket, man, and I lost it, I swear. You gotta believe me. I traveled all the way here from Oregon a day early to buy a ticket and camped in Golden Gate Park last night. Check this out, man." He stuck his hand in the pocket of his jean jacket and one finger stuck out of a hole at the bottom. He wiggled his finger. "Bye bye, ticket. That's how it disappeared. You gotta let me in. I gotta see Woody, he's the main man, man."

"Sorry, pal, can't do it."

"I can't travel all this way and not get in. You got the power, man; you can do it."

"See that guy standing over there?" The ticket-taker pointed to a man in a black suit and tie across the lobby. "He's my boss. I let you in, I lose my job."

"If he says it's okay, will you let me in?"

"No problem."

The kid walked over to the boss and showed him the small bottle of juice he was holding. "Can I bring this in? The guy at the box office says I can't bring it in."

"Does it have any alcohol in it?"

"It's just orange juice." He unscrewed the cap, the boss took a whiff.

"Sure, go ahead."

"Well, tell that guy at the box office it's okay."

"Harry," the boss yelled across the lobby, "it's okay."

These stoned hippies were pretty clever, but that wouldn't work with a pistol. Standing in the melee on the sidewalk, considering her options, a man touched her arm and offered her a lit joint. She abruptly turned and headed down the street to put her pistol in her car, wondering how much of the show she'd missed; they were already into their second set. Mid-block she spotted a small crowd gathered by a side entrance. A tall man with shoulder-length hair, paisley shirt, and bellbottoms, set apart only by a navy-blue vest that said SECURITY, stood by an open metal door where a dozen fans were huddled in like they were seeking warmth. She heard the music pouring out of the door, stopped, and had a flash of recognition. Was she hearing the chorus of "Stephanie," the melody she'd studied every note of? Leaning in closer, it sounded like an insinuation of it, circling guitar lines making the song conspicuous by its absence. More people had gathered behind her, and when the guitar homed in on the actual chorus, the group pressed forward, moving her with them. The security guard brought his arm up, indicating an imaginary line not to cross, knowing the hippies would respect the invisible barrier, thankful that the door was being left open. He stepped away and lit a cigarette.

A man standing next to Maria had a microphone tethered to a portable cassette recorder under his arm. When Woody began singing to resounding applause, the man nudged Maria aside and extended the microphone further. She nudged him back. The man quickly stepped away and gestured apologetically. When the song ended, everyone by the door spread out to catch their breath and smoke pot, and Maria walked over to the security guard. "Woody sure has a lot of avid fans. Is there any way I could get inside?"

"It's sold out." The security guard looked her up and down. "You don't seem like one of his regulars."

She glanced down at her clothes. "I came straight from work. This is the first show I've been to."

"What brings you here? The show's almost over."

She transferred her purse from one shoulder to the other. "I'm an attorney. I'm involved with some copyright matters with Woody's manager, Jeff Pearlman."

"Jeff Pearlman, the big shot music lawyer? No kidding. He comes around when his clients play here. A pretty nice guy. He could definitely get you a pass."

She reached into her purse, felt the gun, then felt her ticket, and thought of showing it to him, but he'd probably just send her to the front door and she'd miss the rest of the show. He seemed to be softening up. "I was on my way home from work. I didn't know it would be sold out."

"Looks like they oversold it. It's pretty crowded in there, but the kids don't seem to mind."

Maria gestured at the man with the cassette recorder. "You let people record the show from out here?"

"It's a free-for-all." He pointed inside to the sound booth where there were dozens of eight-foot-high stands holding microphones of every size and shape.

"They let people record the show and keep the recordings?"

"Yup."

"Why would they buy Woody's records if they can get his music for free?"

The guard shrugged. "Free love."

"It's nice of you to leave the door open."

He nodded. "Can't keep music in a bottle."

"I wish there was a way I could get in and find Jeff Pearlman, or just catch the last few songs."

"You and every other kid on the block. Woody's got the mojo, everybody wants some."

"I'm sure Jeff Pearlman would okay it."

The guard just nodded.

She gave him an obsequious smile and went to the back of the crowd by the door. She could just make out Woody singing into the mic with his eyes closed. She felt more bodies behind her, pressing in, pushing her past the imaginary line. When the security guard approached, she thought he was coming to clear people away. Instead, he laid his hand on Maria's middle back and held out his other arm. One person at a time, he parted a path through the people outside the door and gently guided her ten feet inside. When he took his hand off her back and left her there, she thought of the first time she'd learned to ride a bicycle when her father let go of her and, for a moment, she felt that childlike vulnerability. The next moment she was swallowed by the moist heat of undulating bodies spinning like Sufis in their private square-foot space. The air was thick with dizzying waves of bass notes, tom-tom explosions, and long sinuous guitar lines arcing like bolts of electricity across bare electrical wires. Shoulder to shoulder, hip to hip, a damp organic animal smell overwhelmed her.

Trying to gather her thoughts and keep a semblance of self-control, Maria's relative stillness made things worse. She was a stationary pillar buffeted by a roiling sea. Up ahead, ten feet closer to the stage, she saw a parting in the crowd, an oasis of space. Turning sideways, she clutched her purse and wedged her shoulder past one person at a time, wriggling her way forward, the process accentuating the clammy, touchy-feely element she found so distasteful. Just about there, she put her head down, pushed through the last row around the open space, and came within an inch of being swatted in the face by a shirtless, whirling-dervish of a man with four-feet-long spinning dreadlocks and flailing arms. Eyes closed, his head jerked erratically, seemingly unmoored to his long-veined neck. He smelled like a wet dog, the air as moist as the twirling man's armpits. Obviously in a drug induced trance, the crowd had no choice but to give him a wide berth.

Behind Maria, every inch of the hard-fought ground behind her was filled in. Turning back toward the stage, she was struck by the intense look of concentration on the musicians' faces. Bent almost in half over his guitar, Woody's hands dancing across his strings seemed married to the twirling man on the dance floor, the man relinquishing control, Woody manifestly *in* control, his movements calculated and contained.

Seeing Woody's effect on the audience, Maria tensed up and curled in her shoulders. Was he some kind of cult leader these mindless, stoned hippies were submitting their souls to like religious adherents? Like a room full of clapping seals? She became aware of the man to her right bumping into her every four beats and the woman to her left tapping her with her hips in no discernable pattern. Clutching her purse against her chest, she shoved her shoulder into the man and pivoted her hips hard into the woman. When she glanced left and right, their expressions were so similarly peaceful, for a moment she thought they were conspiring to mock her. The next moment, the guitar doubled in volume and their attention was commandeered to the stage.

Maria looked at the floor, at the frayed bellbottoms and dirty bare feet, and took a half-step back to test the resistance. Surprisingly, it was easier than moving forward, people happy to give up their space and move into hers. She eventually made her way to the very back of the room and discovered a narrow spiral staircase going up to a metal-grated platform. She walked up the stairs. The platform was big enough for two or three people, and no one was there.

When the final jam revved up to a dramatic crescendo and ended, Maria watched with amazement at the crowd's zeal and adoration as Woody gathered the five players at the front of the stage, mountain-man Jupiter in the center. They bowed in unison, waved goodnight, and walked off. A long ten minutes later, to raucous cheering that hadn't let up—which, if anything, was increasing—the band returned to the stage. Maria's eyes landed on the four-inch aluminum center of Woody's speaker in his speaker cabinet—a sweet bullseye. One shot from her .38 could stop the music and put an end to this mindless fervor. If she shot with the hit of the snare drum, nobody would hear it. It would be like a cap gun going against a twenty-canon salute. Woody might not discover the bullet until long after the show. It would give him something to think about at every show for the rest of his life. Would she actually do it, or was it the Chianti talking?

The band went into a sweet instrumental ballad that featured Jupiter on soprano saxophone, playing a solo that seemed as if it could ascend indefinitely. When the band finished the song, the crowd cheered, hope against hope, for the possibility of another encore. Woody walked over to Malcolm at his keyboards, then Chewy, then waved a man onstage who was standing in the wings. The two of them stood center-stage, and Woody said something in the man's ear, raised his right hand up over his head, brought it down across his strings, and hit the opening power chords to Chuck Berry's "Johnny B. Goode." Billy knew exactly what to do and came in with a fat back-beat on the snare at the same moment Betty at the sound booth in the back of the room reached for the knob she'd painted red with fingernail polish and cranked the reverb, making each whack of Billy's chrome snare drum a detonation that lasted the entire four beats until the next detonation, like the air between the beats was being stretched to its breaking point.

Maria's head jerked back from the sharp snapping sound of the snare. It reminded her of the one time she'd gone to the shooting range without protective headphones.

—

The special guest stepped up to the microphone, took it off the stand, and whipped a three-foot length of cable over his head, handily snatching the mic out of midair, and went into the first verse of the song.

By the second word, Maria knew who it was. The moves, the confidence, the stark contrast to Woody's insecure stage presence. Woody rarely even looked up from his guitar, but Ray Bell made eye contact with every person, every woman, in the audience. "That egotistical bastard! He thinks he's Adonis!" When he spread his stance and thrust his hips, the shudder of rage that coursed through her body was so strong, her vision went blurry. She shrieked as loud as she could: "FUCK YOU, RAY BELL!" Against the massive volume of the band, it was like spitting in the ocean.

At the back soundboard, the room's audio nerve center, Betty manipulated her EQ controls like a painter with two brushes, both hands at once cranking knobs clockwise and counterclockwise, slathering the vocals with a shiny, polished sibilance.

Deep down in Louisiana close to New Orleans
Way back up in the woods among the evergreens
There stood a log cabin made of earth and wood
Where lived a country boy named Johnny B. Goode
Who never ever learned to read or write so well
But he could play a guitar just like ringin' a bell

—

Maria couldn't believe the intensity of the crowd could go any higher, but it did. People were in a frenzy, hands waving over their heads, surging toward the stage, probably crushing the fans in the front.

"FUCK YOU, RAY! FUCK YOU, YOU FUCKING TRAITOR!"

Maria gauged the distance to the shiny silver microphone Ray held between him and Woody, their mouths inches apart. Hitting that mic would take a pinpoint sniper shot, but there was enough space between their heads that she wouldn't kill anybody. The snare drum was louder than ever. She reached into her purse, gripped the handle of her pistol, and gently tapped the trigger with each whack of the snare, getting the timing of the song.

One...two...three...four...

She started to withdraw the gun when a light suddenly illuminated her tan leather purse. She looked to see Block standing next to her holding his flashlight. "You got permission to be up here, lady?"

"What?"

Block leaned in close and yelled in her ear. "You need permission to be up here! You need to go back downstairs!"

"I'm checking out the band! Fuck off!"

Block put his hand on her arm. "Listen, lady, you gotta—"

"Get your hands off me!" She started to pull out her gun. Block saw the bulge in her purse and clutched her elbow.

"Get your hands off me, asshole!" She struggled against his grip.

Block held onto her elbow with one hand, stuck his flashlight in his back pocket, and grabbed the walkie-talkie on his belt. "Piglet! Assistance on the back lighting platform. Now!"

She twisted side to side, trying to jerk her arm away. "Get your fucking hands off me...I'll fucking kill you!"

Block shoved her backwards toward the top of the stairs. "Move it, lady! Time for you to go!"

Woody and Ray simultaneously belted into the microphone:

"GO!"

The crowd, in a thousand-person unison, yelled back, "GO!"

The singers sang, "GO! GO!"

Everyone sang together, "GO JOHNNY, GO GO GO!"

Woody turned his head away from the microphone to catch a breath and saw Allison Wonderland, the waitress in the hoop dress, on the side of stage with a ginger ale on her little brown tray. He ran over, slapped the tray from underneath, sent the ginger ale and tray flying, grabbed her hand, and led her running back across the stage to the microphone just in time for her to belt out a soaring sky-high falsetto on the next chorus that blew the roof off the auditorium.

—

Five-foot-six, two-hundred and fifty pounds, Piglet wrapped his arms around Maria's waist from behind, leaned her back over his protruding midsection so that her feet came off the ground and her purse landed on the metal grate. Piglet carried her face-up, kicking and screaming down the spiral staircase like a flailing beetle on its back. When she tried grabbing the railing, he violently swung her back and forth using his heft as a cantilever. Block retrieved her purse and followed them down the stairs and to the closest exit. Piglet tossed her onto the sidewalk, Block threw her purse out at her feet and slammed the door.

—

When Ray stepped back from the mic, Woody played a classic Chuck Berry solo, dishing out power chords like a shovel stoking a furnace, a driving rock 'n' roll rhythm that used all the strings at once, harnessing the power of the entire guitar.

Then right on cue, Ray stepped back up to the mic and belted out the last verse.

His mother told him someday you will be a man
And you will be the leader of a big old band
Many people coming from miles around
To hear you play your music when the sun go down
Someday your name will be in lights
Johnny B. Goode tonight

Everyone on the stage, everyone in the audience, Betty at the sound board, Pearlman and Twig on the side stage, Orchid in the back of the room, even the house manager, sang the last choruses together:

GO! GO!
GO JOHNNY GO! GO! GO!
GO JOHNNY B. GOODE

Woody introduced the band, concluding, "and special thanks to our special guests: Allison Wonderland and Ray Bell. Goodnight, everyone, see you next time."

—

Maria picked up her purse, straightened herself up and made her way down the sidewalk in the damp fog. With the staggering mental image of what had just happened on the stage and the metallic whack of the snare drum still rattling in her head, she was barely paying attention to where she was going. Through the thick foggy mist, she didn't see the clump of fans on the sidewalk until she was right up on them, two of them hunched over, cupping their hands around a burning match, trying to light a soggy joint. To avoid them, she impulsively veered down a nearby alleyway lit by a streetlight. Keeping her distance as much as she could from an overflowing dumpster of smelly garbage, a fat gray rat with bulging black eyes suddenly appeared out of a shadow and ran over her foot. She froze in her tracks. "Ray Bell? Is that you? You rat!" She whipped the pistol out of her purse, sighted the trajectory of the scurrying rat until it was almost under the dumpster, and killed it with one perfectly placed shot that echoed off the wet walls like a clap of thunder.

CHAPTER 32

Woody cruised onto the fog-shrouded Golden Gate Bridge with his top down at 3:00 a.m. He looked out at the moon-lit, silvery ocean and the enormous dark hulk of a cargo ship slowly making its way toward the Golden Gate, concluding its long journey from China. He looked ahead and in his rearview mirror. No other cars on the bridge, he slowed to a stop. From the photographs he remembered in the newspaper showing the sag of the three-foot-thick suspension cable, it looked like the spot Ray had stood at the railing.

How could just two steel cables hold up the entire bridge? Woody remembered, as a child, when his father had shown him the exhibit at the San Francisco end of the bridge, a cross-section of a suspension cable. Thousands of pencil-thick wires entwined together, it seemed beyond comprehension that they could hold up the colossal structure with all the cars and trucks.

That was one of the few impressive childhood memories he had of being with his dad. His father had died and left him and his mother alone when he was six years old, but he knew his father well enough to know that he'd appreciate the engineering miracle of those suspension cables. He knew at the time that his father felt it was important enough to want to share it with his son. "Choose your parents wisely," his mother once said to him. It never occurred to him before tonight that he and Ray were both an only child raised by a single mom.

Woody checked his rearview mirror again. A truck was coming up behind him, and he drove to the north parking lot, put the top up, and locked the car. No one around, it felt safe. From the photographs he'd seen in the newspaper, he knew it was the same place Ray had parked his Mercedes with the infamous suicide note. He walked through the pedestrian tunnel to the west ocean side of the bridge, the wind whipping strands of hair in his eyes. He leaned over the railing, looked down at the cold black water and choppy reflection of the bridge's lights, and wondered what Ray had been thinking when he stood in that spot.

Ever since Ray had come so close to jumping, every time Woody crossed the bridge, he considered what it would feel like to jump. *Jumping to your own conclusion.* A few screaming seconds, then pitch-black extinction, forever. He leaned out farther, just enough to tease the feeling. A loud sports car drove by and the ringing in Woody's ears brought him back to the Fillmore. He thought of how a band making music resembled traveling in a car, disagreeing on which way to go, getting lost, then finally finding their way, but always physically together. There had been sublime moments at the gig, everyone in the band knowing that everyone else was making a special effort to listen to each other.

He remembered walking up to the stage for the second set when the waitress had given him his hit of pot. She handed him the joint and said in his ear in her funny squeaky voice: "When I went outside for some air, Ray Bell was standing out there without a ticket. He said if I ran into you to mention it. He said if I didn't see you, I shouldn't bother anyone else about it."

Just then the gelled-hair manager had walked up to Woody standing on the edge of the stage, just out of sight of the audience "Your lawyer told me I'm not supposed to bug you, but I'm responsible for getting the band on stage. You were supposed to be on twenty minutes ago."

The man, with his oatmeal complexion and eyes a little too close together, reminded Woody of someone. "Did you ever drive a limo?"

"Drive a limo? No, why?"

Woody remembered being outside at Ray's Greek Theater concert. He'd been living on the street, hungry, no money, no ticket, and he couldn't get into the show. He'd tried getting word to Ray at the box office and at the stage door, but couldn't get in. Hours later, after the show, he was lying under a tree surrounded by litter at the edge of the Greek Theater parking lot on a patch of dirt that smelled like piss. The headlights of a black stretch limousine, Ray's limo, swung around and momentarily blinded him. When the car turned toward the exit, Woody locked eyes with the driver: a man with black hair and chiseled sideburns that looked like the manager standing there in front of him. Woody walked around the manager and down the few steps back to Allison. He took the all-access laminate from around his neck and handed it to her. "Give this to Ray. Tell him if he feels like singing, come up for the encore."

Singing the last song with Ray had worked like a charm. After all that went down between them, things had come full circle. As soon as he heard Ray belt out the first line of the encore, he knew, everyone in the room knew, that Ray's singing took the music to a whole other level. Would they start working together? Could they create another song like "Stephanie" that would solve everybody's financial problems? He smiled to himself. *Wait until Ray's ex-lawyer hears about what happened tonight. If she'd seen us singing together, she would've lost it.*

A sudden gust of wind came up so strong he had to grip the railing. The intermittent river of fog coming in off the ocean was at times so thick Woody couldn't see the water below. Staring straight down, he imagined Ray doing the same thing, contemplating life, death, the ultimate commitment—the abandonment of all commitments. Maybe it could reveal in the last moments that there was another way to deal with the never-ending present, a life of self-loathing always clawing at you. Woody'd heard that the impact of hitting the water was like landing on hard pavement at a hundred miles an hour: you break all your bones, and unable to move, you drown, inhaling water. Are you still conscious? No one knows for sure. Had the redemptive energy of tonight's music restored Ray's will to live?

Leaning over farther, Woody felt a gravitational pull from the sheer depth of the black water, drawing everything down toward it. That must have been what Ray felt. But not him, not tonight. He'd just been savoring the highest musical experience of his life, his crown jewel of gigs. Being in that dirt in the parking lot of the Greek Theater was the bottom of his life. Now he was on top. No force could suck him down. He locked his elbows and gripped the cold wet railing, straight-armed against the wind when he was suddenly enveloped by the pervasive moan of the bridge's foghorn, a vibration so low it seemed to permeate his entire body. Then, eight seconds later, a softer, responsive horn answered from another section of the bridge. He waited the thirty long seconds until the next emissions and hummed along. The first horn sounded like an A, the key of a song he'd teased tonight. The second distant horn was a beautiful combination of notes, the interval between the two horns a possibility for the illusive chorus he'd been searching for.

There was a break in the fog below when an unexplainable wall of water suddenly swelled up into a white-crested sleeper-wave illuminated by a bright white light surging under the bridge. It felt as if the wave was about to physically flow over him, bowl him over. Dripping wet from the fog, he held his breath as the bow of the gigantic cargo ship filled his field of vision, the highest aperture just clearing the arched beam of the bridge directly below him. The eerie silence of the enormous ship seemed impossible. Minutes later it disappeared into darkness followed by the long low howl of the foghorn.

Woody slowly walked the quarter mile back to his car, humming his new chorus with the fog horns fading into the distance.

—

Walking into the soft quiet of his living room with only the light of the fish tank and a Tiffany lamp that Stephanie had left on for him, it felt like being wrapped in a warm blanket. In the kitchen there was a plate of food on the counter, covered with Saran Wrap. Woody stood there, a guitar case in each hand, looking at the plate of cooked vegetables, rice, and salad, and a small plate of homemade brownies. Then he saw the hand-drawn, impressionistic crayon strokes on a piece of construction paper tucked under the edge of the brownie plate. He pictured Lily's hand in a fist, gripping a crayon with consummate concentration, and he took in a long slow breath, inhaling the sweet kinetic love on the counter. He took another slow yoga breath the way Stephanie had taught him, releasing the pent-up stress from four hours of intense guitar playing, a constant moment-to-moment striving for precise, accurate fretting on heavy-gauge guitar strings, acutely aware that everyone in the audience was watching his every move.

He walked to the open bedroom door and could just make out Stephanie and Lily asleep—Lily up against Stephanie's back, their curly hair co-mingling. Inhaling the luscious sleepy bouquet of the room, he felt exceedingly grateful for his little family. The way Stephanie's pheromones attracted him, day or night, any time of the month, had always seemed a confirmation of their compatibility. When Lily's full spectrum of baby aromas had been added to the family mix, living with those two women was like living with an incessantly fresh bouquet of fragrant flowers. He took another deep yoga breath, mentally channeling his exhale from the top of his head down to where Stephanie once said he had a mouth on the soles of his feet that he could use to cast his breath back into the earth. He became aware of the painful knots of tension in his neck and shoulders and sent another slow exhale down the length of his aching arms to his cramping hands to...*what?!*

He was still holding his two heavy hard-shell guitar cases! He set them down right there in the doorway and felt instantly weightless. After a long hot shower, he walked to the side of the bed, savoring the sight of his sleeping family. It looked as inviting as cold lemonade does to a man dying of thirst. But first, he couldn't resist, he walked naked back to the living room, picked up his acoustic guitar, sat on the couch, played a low A on the fifth fret of the lowest string, slowly slid his finger down its length, and plucked an open E, the interval of the fog horns.

As if on cue, in came Lily, sleepy-eyed, crawling out of the bedroom in search of the music she'd heard. She crawled up Woody's leg onto his lap, slapped the open E string with the palm of her hand, and sounded a perfect foghorn note.

When Woody looked up, Stephanie was standing in the doorway with her arms folded across her diaphanous silk bathrobe, beaming love at the ridiculous sight of Woody, naked in the dim light, his guitar in his lap, and Lily hanging from the strings.

ACKNOWLEDGMENTS

It takes a village to write a book. This book would not have been possible without inspiration from the many musicians I've had the honor of playing with. I've watched the way they move their hands, how they communicate at the speed of sound across a stage, or sleep-deprived and stoned in a car together for eight hours. I love them all for teaching me about music through their dedication to their craft and helping me to play drums with one hand tied behind my back.

A tip of the hat to my indispensable support team of editors, readers, and spiritual advisors:

Holly Anton, Marty LeVine, Nancy Aronie. Alan Trist, Peter Coyote, Jordan Rosenfeld, Guy Intoci, Hailie Johnson, Tyson Cornell, Charlie Winton, Dennis McNally, Craig Wright, Phil Colombatto, Steve Kimock, Lisa Iskin, Duncan Mackintosh, Liam Hanrahan, Gregory Enton, Shirley, Paul, and Lillian Anton, Nancy May, Sean McClosky, Deb Grabien, Donna Godchaux, Gary Abriem, Banana, and all the wonderful folks at Rare Bird Books.

Special thanks to Robert Hunter for teaching me how to write prose.

And to my trusted legal advisors for their help with legalese and my courtroom scenes:

Stephen Turer, Geoffrey Menin, Chris Andrian, Elliot Daum, Pat Emery.

And from another little piece of my heart, thank you to my beautiful children for forgiving me my many faults and still believing in me:

Chevy, Curry, Georgia, Heidi, and Jake.

www.ingramcontent.com/pod-product-compliance
Lightning Source LLC
LaVergne TN
LVHW090316160826
845644LV00005B/8/J
* 9 7 8 1 6 4 4 2 8 4 7 6 6 *